WRATHFUL SOULS

THE SONS OF TEMPLAR - NEW MEXICO
BOOK 3

ANNE MALCOM

Cover Design: TRC Designs
Editing: Kim BookJunkie
Proofreading: All Encompassing Books

For the women who feel broken. May you find someone to worship you. Who makes you feel whole and healed.

TRIGGER WARNINGS

This book is dark. For those of you who read *Wilting Violets*, you probably already suspected it would be.

There are some very triggering scenes featuring graphic violence, sexual assault, mentions of suicide.

Sariah's story is not an easy one, so I understand if this is where I leave you.

I promise, like always, she will get her HEA.

Anne

xxx

PROLOGUE

I TOLD myself I wouldn't scream.

Wouldn't beg.

Made promises to myself when it was clear what was happening. When it was clear who he was. *What* he was.

But although I excelled at keeping my word with my friends, I routinely broke every promise I ever made to myself.

Why should this be any different?

"Please," I begged, coughing a pitiful, wet sound. The single word was coppery, bitter, coated in the blood that filled my mouth.

His lips stretched out, exposing straight white teeth in a wretched smile.

"You wanted to think that you were different," he sneered, running the knife coated in my blood along my ruined, naked body. "That you weren't like the others." When he leaned in, I could smell the way my blood scented his body. My stomach roiled as I fought to keep from vomiting. Not that there was anything left inside me.

"But you're just like the rest," he whispered, the tip of his knife pressing against the soft flesh of my stomach. "Just another *whore*."

My scream echoed off the walls as he pressed the knife in. He didn't plunge it in. No. He did it with devastating slowness.

Patiently. So he could inflict the worst kind of agony. So I could feel the steel tearing through every layer of skin and flesh before puncturing my organs.

He wanted me to die slowly.

That I knew.

He wanted my last hours on this earth to be bloody, agonizing, horrific.

I'd seen the crime scene photos, hadn't I? Poured over them with a sick fascination, some kind of warped arrogance that I would be the one to find him.

And I guess I was.

But I wasn't going to be the one who exposed him. Wasn't going to be the girl who escaped. I wasn't special.

I was dying.

The cuffs around my wrists had rubbed the skin raw as I tried to slip my way out of them. I thought that my blood would make them slick, slippery, aid in my escape. But that shit only happened in the movies. When you were cuffed by a serial killer who also happened to be a cop, you didn't escape. You didn't outsmart them because you thought that's what you would do as the heroine of your story.

Every girl who came before me was the heroine of her own story, but that didn't change a fucking thing. Not when the villain, the real fucking villain, was in front of them, puncturing their skin with a sharpened knife.

"Whores giving their bodies to countless men," he continued as the blade cut through me. "So many, they don't even know who the father is when they get pregnant."

I let out a sob of agony when he ripped the knife out viciously. The pain was white hot. I didn't dare look down at my torso which must've been a shredded mess. I could practically feel the cold warehouse air kissing exposed organs as they slipped through the tears in my skin.

"You shouldn't be allowed to reproduce," he hissed, waving

the knife at me. My blood flew off the blade, small droplets hitting my face. "Shouldn't be able to grow life when you abuse your body. Trash it. When you don't keep your baby safe like you should."

When the hand not holding the knife reached down to cup me between my legs, bile mixed with blood in my mouth.

His eyes glowed at my revulsion, his face contorting into a shape that didn't seem human.

"No life will come out of you," he hissed. "And in death, you'll be mine."

The tip of the knife teased along the seam of my thighs, between my legs. For one horrendous moment, I thought he'd put it ... inside. I was already in agony, but being cut from the inside out? Maybe my body would protect me, maybe I'd finally pass out. Maybe I'd never wake up. That would be nice.

I tried to grit my teeth, narrow my eyes, rustle up my signature attitude. "Fuck you," I whispered, the words coming out weak and garbled.

He smirked at me, keeping the tip of the knife at my entrance.

"Oh, I will be fucking you, as you so eloquently put it. But not yet. I'll wait."

The knife hovered for a second longer before he stood up, staring at me with disgust before turning on his heel and walking out of the room.

I felt no relief as his footsteps receded. Because he'd come back. And I'd still be here.

They say history is written by the victors. Whoever the fuck 'they' are. But really, history is written to immortalize the villains into infamy.

This fucker would be famous. People had finally been catching on to the murders in the last month. Online sleuths were going crazy. Hell, I was the one with all of the fake social media accounts, spreading the word about the man who would eventually murder me. There was going to be a lot more publicity, especially with my death.

Yes, he would get more and more famous with every murder.

Eventually, there would be some kind of documentary, a made for TV movie. There would be books. Everyone would know his name.

But mine? No.

You know Ted Bundy, Jeffery Dahmer, but can you name one of their victims? Can you recall their hopes, dreams, the lives they lived before a sick piece of shit stole everything from them?

Yeah, history was not written for the victims. I'd be another nameless girl. Another body. People would speak about my injuries, my torture, on their podcasts in a grim tone but unable to cover the sick high they got from this stuff.

Girls just like me would watch the videos while doing their makeup, while drinking wine, while curled up in bed, covered in a veil of safety that was total bullshit.

I thought about my parents.

I hadn't spoken to them in years. Not since I screamed expletives at them while dragging my suitcase out the door of my childhood home. They'd called. Written letters. But I'd ignored them until the calls and letters dwindled.

They'd get the news their daughter died at the hands of a serial killer who targeted whores. Would they be surprised? They'd grieve. They'd pray. They'd bury me in the cemetery of a church I'd denounced.

But eventually, I'd be forgotten.

HANSEN

I'd seen a lot of shit.

Both while I was deployed and when I was wearing the Sons of Templar patch. Horrific shit. Shit that followed you. Gave you nightmares. Hardened you. Made you just a little jaded to the horrors of the world. And if you somehow didn't become jaded, living that horrific shit, it would eat you alive.

I'd turned some part of myself off. Had to. In order to survive. Many men who didn't find good women would never find that switch, the one that would bring your humanity back, ensure you didn't become ambivalent, cold and eventually turn into a monster.

I had a good woman.

Children.

I had a reason to keep my humanity.

But still, even then, I was hardened to the shit that would fuck up most people. Had to be. For my kids. My wife. Had to find a way to keep my distance so I didn't bring blood back into my home. My bed.

I had thought nothing could shock me anymore until we made it to the warehouse where Sariah was being held.

But seeing her cut through every fucking inch of distance I'd created to keep my humanity intact. It shook me in a way even the atrocities of war didn't.

Because this wasn't war.

This was a fucking twenty-year-old girl. Chained. Bleeding. In a state that I couldn't even comprehend for a handful of seconds.

Acid crawled up my throat, and it took everything I had to keep my lunch down.

Jagger paled beside me, the man who had seen worse shit than me, the man who literally let his family and the woman he loved think he was dead rather than let them see what war had turned him into.

One of the prospects turned and emptied his guts in the corner.

Hades, only fucking Hades, was the one not to stutter, to not fucking pause but step through, putting his boot in her blood—the fucking *pools* of her blood—and kneel down.

She scuttled away from him like a tortured animal. My stomach spasmed at the sight, swallowing bile once again.

I didn't hear what Hades was saying, but the man spoke softly, softer than I'd ever fucking heard the motherfucker speak while addressing Sariah, coaxing her back to reality.

I turned to Jagger, trying to get my head straight.

"Where's Colby?" I demanded.

Jagger kept his eyes on Sariah, blank and horrified for a beat before he visibly shook himself and focused on me, game face on.

But the motherfucker was shaken. You could see it in his eyes. I'd wager a guess you could see it in mine too.

"Five minutes out," Jagger replied. "Likely less."

"He can't see her like this," I sighed, staring at Hades as he inspected the cuff on her ankle.

"Too fuckin' late," a voice said from behind us.

We both turned to Colby who was standing right behind us, staring at Sariah with a vacant expression. Though he was a deadly fucker in his own right, he was jovial. Young. Easy to smile. He'd already done shit most men wouldn't in a lifetime. He'd seen blood. He'd drawn it. Yet somehow, it hadn't yet seeped into him. Somehow, I'd always thought of him as a kid.

But, Jesus, if he looked like he'd aged a decade in a manner of seconds.

A gunshot ricocheted through the large area, echoing off the concrete walls.

We were all accustomed to gunshots and weren't easily spooked, but each of us flinched at the sound.

I looked over my shoulder.

Hades had decided the best course of action was shooting the chain attached to the wall holding Sariah in place.

"You got her?" Colby spoke through gritted teeth.

His hands were fists at his sides. He was holding himself still. Rage sometimes made men try to split the world apart, made them spiral out of control. Those men were dangerous.

Others, it gave clarity. A brutal sense of purpose.

Those men were fucking deadly.

Colby was the latter.

I nodded once in answer to his question, realizing he was trusting her life with me.

"Good."

He didn't hesitate in turning and walking toward where we'd locked down the sheriff.

I sprung into action then, letting my training take over as I approached Sariah who was clinging to Hades.

It took up all of my attention, taking stock of her horrific fucking injuries and figuring out how to get her to a hospital before she bled out.

CHAPTER ONE

EIGHT MONTHS EARLIER

BEFORE THE SONS OF TEMPLAR burst into that warehouse and kept my heart beating, Violet Edwards saved my life.

She didn't know it, of course.

My best friend in the whole world didn't know who I truly was. Wasn't that fucking pathetic?

No one knew who I really was.

They thought they knew.

The girl with the designer clothes, the easy confidence, the sexual prowess, who always had a really good hookup for coke or Molly. Who knew where the best parties were and was always best dressed for a costume party.

Surface level shit.

I was well liked. Well respected. I was a party girl and was popular in various circles of our Ivy League campus.

It was nice. Cool. Especially considering where I came from. Who I used to be.

It was still a novelty, this version of myself. The one who wore clothes I'd stared at in magazines I'd hidden from my parents. Who fucked men and women without the Lord Almighty smiting me or the devil dragging me down to hell for my sins.

Yes, I was riding the wave of my newfound freedom, financial, sexual and otherwise. But I knew I would burn bright and fast. My past would catch up with me. Maybe I'd have a drug overdose. Maybe I'd get in the car with some drunk frat boy and die wrapped around a tree. These were all rather predictable outcomes of the lifestyle I was living. Yet it was only in hindsight that I saw what I was doing to myself.

And the worst did happen, didn't it?

I rejected some rich douchebag who was used to getting everything he wanted. And like any man who was rejected and entitled, he took what he wanted.

I tried my best not to think about that. Which was really hard when you had a house full of friends who cared about you and kept looking at you with worry and pity ... like you were the girl who was raped.

Because I *was* the girl who was raped.

And despite all my logic to the contrary, despite knowing it wasn't my fault at all, there was a little voice inside of me that told me it was punishment for my sins.

For being loud, loose, and for abandoning the chaste and good life given to me by the grace of God.

So I did the only thing I could do ... I partied my fucking ass off, drank too much, did too many drugs, and tried my best to bury all that pain inside. Oh, and lied to my best friend in the entire world.

If you didn't get it, I was already *mucho* fucked-up before I was abducted and tortured by a serial killer.

But I didn't know what horrors awaited me when I drove into the town of Garnett, New Mexico. I thought that I'd already gone through the worst of it. That I'd be okay.

What a stupid fucking bitch.

———

Colby Lee also saved my life. Literally and metaphorically.

Of course, the first time I met him I wasn't thinking that he'd change my life, save it and ruin it.

I wasn't thinking about anything other than my best friend in the world being pregnant by the much older outlaw biker she was in love with and was likely in crisis mode.

Violet had told me she was pregnant, so I'd dropped everything to get my ass across the country to be at her side and be there for her.

No, I had no plans on falling in love with an outlaw biker. I wanted to try to be there for my friend like she'd been there for me since I'd met her.

Now, I'm no saint—as my parents and their respective churches could attest to. So in the back of my mind, as I parked my car in the parking lot of the Sons of Templar compound in New Mexico, I was also kind of curious about this club of outlaw bikers.

I'd met two of them: Elden, who got my Violet knocked up, and her stepfather, Swiss. They were both patched members and hot as balls in completely different ways that appealed in equal doses. You know, if they weren't my best friend's baby daddy and stepfather respectively.

So yes, when I marched my Valentino clad heels into the Sons of Templar clubhouse and was faced with Colby, I was momentarily distracted.

Okay, more than a little momentarily distracted.

"Hey, darlin'," he drawled, smiling lazily in a way that I bet had been felt in many panties.

It was felt in mine too. For a millisecond.

"I'm not your darlin'," I mimicked his smooth voice and the endearment that would've pissed me off if said by any other man. At least I was good at pretending I was pissed off at least.

"If you'll excuse me…" I tried to walk around him, my eyes having scanned the large common area and zeroing in on a hallway, assuming it would lead me to Violet. I'd deduced that she

wouldn't be at her mom's house since Elden knew she was pregnant, and Elden was a protective motherfucker who wasn't about
to let his pregnant woman out of his sight.

I liked that for her.

Loved that for her.

He was the kind of man she deserved.

But a girl also needed her bestie.

She was still in college, and her mom didn't know she was with
Elden let alone pregnant. Her stepfather was protective as fuck
and would likely do something violent to Elden for impregnating
Violet.

My friend Violet would be trying to protect everyone from the
chaos. Everyone but herself.

So, I was making a beeline for her.

At least I was trying to.

The man stepped in my path in a way that told me he wasn't
going to let me go anywhere.

Which pissed me right off.

"Women, even women who look like you, cannot just go
waltzing through the clubhouse," the man said to me, looking me
up and down in a way that told me he was taking measure, and he
really liked what he saw.

Now, I was aware that I attracted the male gaze.

Especially considering I was head to toe in pink, complete with
leather pants and a bustier that showed off my ample assets and a
good amount of midriff.

I didn't dress for men. I dressed for myself, hard as that was for
the male population of this world to understand. They took the
way I dressed, the way I carried myself, as an invitation, as
consent.

I tasted acid at the memory of the man, no, the *boy*, who
thought he could take that from me.

I'd vowed I wouldn't let that incident change anything, change
me. I'd let myself fall apart, then I got my shit together. But I

hadn't dealt with it. Not really. Which was right on par for me since I was planning on becoming a therapist. And weren't all shrinks insane? That's how they got so good at dealing with everyone else's bullshit. Or maybe the reason I was becoming a shrink was so I could find comfort in knowing that everyone else was just as fucked-up as me.

"I can do and go wherever the fuck I want," I snarled to the man, pissed off. It was safe to say my already short temper with men had frayed even further since the ... incident, and I was really twitchy about them thinking they could tell me what to do.

No matter how hot they were.

And he was *hot*.

I put my hand on my hip, returning the assessing gaze he'd given me. Yes, he was hot. Tall. Taller than me, even though I was wearing sky-high platforms. He was wearing all black, including the leather vest that communicated he was part of the Sons of Templar MC.

He wasn't overly muscled like the other two members I'd met, but that didn't mean he didn't look strong and impressive. He really did. He was leaner, but his forearms were still sinewy, biceps still defined, shoulders broad.

He was of Asian descent, Korean if I'd had to guess. His inky hair brushed across his face in an effortless way. All of the angles of his face were sharp, defined. His dark eyes were playful and ... dangerous.

This man was trouble. And not because he had muscles and was likely armed.

I knew that because I'd done my research on the Sons of Templar MC. They were not some cute, little motorcycle club who wore leather, rode bikes and didn't so much as jaywalk.

No, these fuckers broke the law. They all had records. None recent, though. Which presumably meant they'd just gotten better at breaking the law. And not too long ago, the entire club was almost wiped out after a mass murder decimated practically the entire charter.

I was hip to the lingo.

Plus, I was a diehard *Sons of Anarchy* fan. Except for the last season. Why in the fuck Kurt Sutter thought he needed to go full *Hamlet* was anyone's business. We needed happily ever afters, goddamnit.

"You cannot go wherever the fuck you want, but I can direct you to my bedroom," he waggled his brows.

Though such a request from a man whose name I didn't know, who was leering at me so openly, should've sicked me out, it didn't. In fact, it tempted me. But just a little bit.

"In your dreams, buddy," I returned with a bite to my tone. "Now are you gonna step out of my fucking way, or am I gonna have to make you?"

In response to my threat, he smiled.

Asshole.

The grin was cheeky, cocky and, unfortunately, sexy.

"Though I'd enjoy seeing you try to make me, I'm gonna have to insist on you telling me who you are." His tone was still teasing but firm.

I wanted to scream. My threat was really kind of empty, though. I wasn't armed, and I logically knew that it wouldn't be a very even fight. Not that this guy would've fought me. I knew these men were badasses, but they weren't the type to get violent with women. Even sassy ones like me. Which was a shame because I was itching for a fight with someone.

"I don't have to give you my name," I told him instead.

"You're in my club. Think you do," he countered.

My eyes flickered to his cut. "I don't see a president patch," I spat back. "So you don't call the shots around here."

When he held out his hands to the empty room, I hated the way my eyes honed in on the flex of his biceps. "I'm the only one here, so yes, poppet, I am calling the shots."

"Poppet?" I repeated. "What are you, a nineteenth century Englishman?"

"You're gonna be fun," he snickered.

"And you're really getting on my fucking nerves," I retorted. "So, you need to tell me where I can find my friend, right now."

This man was obviously getting annoyed with me not fawning over his hotness because his smile faltered, and he stepped forward, close, too close, hands on his hips.

"I will ask for the fourth time," he murmured. "Who are you?"

Okay, now I was fuming. I blew an errant hair from my face before pushing my sunglasses to the top of my head. "I'm Sariah Cardoso. Who the fuck are you?"

The man's expression stayed blank for a few beats before his cheeky, sexy grin returned. "I'm the man you've been waiting for."

I arched my brow at him, making sure to look him up and down. "Honey, I don't wait for any man. I don't even pause for one. I'm here for my girl, who has gotten impregnated by one of you."

Movement behind him caught my eye. I spied Elden, looking delicious and wary first, then Violet.

"Her!" I yelled, pointing. "That's who I'm looking for. My bestie who got knocked up by him."

Target acquired. I gave one more spiteful look to the man who'd pissed me off—and somehow turned me on—before stomping over to my best friend and giving her all my attention.

Well, until my best friend's stepfather came in and got a little gung-ho with an actual gun and threatened to kill Elden for getting Violet pregnant.

But that story has already been told.

The main thing was, Colby and I started by bickering with an undercurrent of sexual tension, and it carried on like that for a long while... Me fighting my attraction for him, and him not even bothering to hide what he felt for me.

Unsurprisingly, it was a complete fucking disaster.

COLBY

It wasn't love at first sight. I didn't consider her 'mine' the second I laid eyes on her like some of my other brothers had with their Old Ladies.

First, all I saw was her face, tits and ass. In that order.

It wasn't every day a woman clad in all pink entered the club-house like she owned it and faced off with me.

She was fucking stunning. Unlike anyone I'd ever seen. She was wearing ridiculous pink shoes that gave her at least six inches, yet she was still petite. Her tits were glorious, encased in something that was hot pink and showed off the generous curves of her hips.

Though her body was the most impressive thing I'd ever seen, it was her face that captivated me. Her skin was porcelain, her lips making me think about a blowjob the second I laid eyes on them. Glossy, cherry red. Full.

Her eyes blazed with chocolate fire. Her nose was bigger than her delicate features, only making her more interesting.

Then there was the attitude. I'd told all of my brothers that if I ever did settle down, it would be with a quiet woman, to ensure I didn't go through the bullshit that they went through with theirs.

They'd all laughed themselves silly at that.

Watching that spitfire outdrinking my brothers, laughing, swearing and enchanting every single man—and woman—in the fucking room, I now understood why.

She'd arrived at the club without Violet—which made sense since Violet was pregnant, and Elden was unlikely to let her near a club party—again, walking in like she owned the fucking place. She didn't show an inch of self-consciousness at walking into a motorcycle club where she didn't know anyone.

I didn't know how she did it. But it was a fucking treat to watch.

Well, that was until my brothers started scrambling over each other in order to try their luck with her.

That's when my night started darkening. I'd planned on waiting it out, watching them fumble then taking her back to my room and fucking her senseless, finishing on those glorious tits of hers.

A good fuck. Nothing else.

Not very noble of me, but I didn't consider myself to be an overly noble guy.

Then I started to want to kill my brothers. I wasn't violent by nature. I got blood on my hands when the club required it, but I didn't relish in it.

Yet in that moment, it was very fucking satisfying, thinking of the crunch that would come with breaking Javier's nose.

No, I didn't know Sariah Cardoso was mine the first time I saw her.

But I knew the second time.

CHAPTER
TWO

I WAS on the roof of a biker clubhouse staring at the stars.

And I was drunk.

Prior to the last hour, I'd been a happy drunk. Playful. Flirty. I mean, who could've blamed me? I was partying in a biker clubhouse with a bunch of hot dudes with tats and airs of danger.

Totally unlike the college frat boys I'd been around the past few years.

The men of the Sons of Templar showed me what kind of boys I'd been interacting with.

As expected, they all hit on me. All of the single ones, at least. And it was tempting. Javier in particular was cocky, handsome and charming. But, although I could appreciate him in all of his masculine glory, he didn't do it for me.

None of them did.

Except for the man who had scowled at every single man who tried to pick me up. He himself didn't try to pick me up; he just glared at the men, then stared at me with some kind of self-satisfied grin that made me fear he could read my mind and knew that I wasn't interested in fucking anyone but him.

So of course, I flirted extra heavily with Javier and ignored Colby.

I wasn't sure when I stopped having fun. When the booze started dragging me down in melancholy, the room started feeling very small, and I started feeling very alone.

Hence me seeking out the roof. Being alone when nobody was around was much more tolerable than feeling alone in a crowd of people.

I'd been settled up here for a few minutes when the ladder to my left creaked. I knew that meant someone was ascending. There was a well utilized ashtray on a table beside the chairs I had forgone. It made sense that someone was coming up here to smoke and gaze at the stars.

I didn't move from where I was lying.

It was too late for escape, and I didn't run from shit anyway. Apart from my childhood.

A shape settled down beside me. I knew that it was Colby because it smelled like him. Leather and some kind of spicy, subtle cologne that was unexpectedly elegant for a biker.

I'd cataloged that smell from our first meeting a few days ago. Had bookmarked it as *him.*

Neither of us spoke for a long while. We just lay there, side by side, staring at the stars. The low thump of the music from inside the club was barely a whisper. Everything seemed quiet and peaceful. Like the whole world had stopped.

I'd never had a moment like that with anyone, especially not with a man. Especially a man who knew I was drunk and had been looking at me the way Colby had been looking at me since the first time we met.

A flash entered my mind.

I couldn't feel my limbs.

I was being dragged into a bedroom. There were hands up my dress and I groaned in protest, unable to articulate the word no. My arms flailed uselessly as I tried to fight.

"You killed him, didn't you?" I asked without looking at him. "The boy who raped me."

He didn't answer straight away. I didn't see Colby's expression in response to my flat tone, but his body did go solid beside mine.

"It's my fault," I whispered, staring at the ceiling.

Ollie, my roommate, was lying on the bed beside me. It was rare for her to come out of her room and get away from her computers. Then again, there were extenuating circumstances. I'd woken up this morning in an unfamiliar bed, without my panties, with a man who I did not consent to having sex with.

In fact, I had no memory of the night before. Except flashes of pain. Panic. Hands tearing off my clothes. Wanting to fight so terribly but my limbs not obeying.

"You're so fucking hot," a voice drawled in my ear.

His finger had been inside me then.

It hurt. A lot.

But it hurt more when he was fucking me, groaning on top of me. Tears had trailed down my face.

I'd had a lot to drink the night before.

But I'd never drank enough to black out.

Though it couldn't be called a black out when I still remembered the absolute worst of it.

The worst of it wasn't the rape. No.

It was waking up the next morning feel sick, used and dirty. It was crawling out of that bed before he woke up, pulling on my clothes—the fabric stained my already dirtied skin—and sneaking out of there.

I did not wake the man that raped me. I didn't rake my nails down his face, fight him, punish him like I should've done. No, I didn't do any of the things I thought that I'd be capable of doing to someone that hurt me. I ran home, even smiling and waggling eyes at people I passed who knew me, who assumed I was just doing another walk of shame.

"This is not your fucking fault," Ollie hissed.

She was furious. I'd never seen my friend so full of wrath. She'd tried to get me to go to the police. Then she'd tried to convince me to let her ruin his life virtually. She'd only relented when I broke down into a panic attack at the mere mention of such things.

"I go to parties," I whisper. "I have sex with men and women. I drink a lot. I'm easy. I make it so—"

"No," she interrupted sternly. "I hear where you're going and I'm not going to fucking let you poison your mind like that." Her hand slipped into mine. *"You have the right to live your life exactly how you want. Fuck whoever you want. Put whatever you want in your body. Nothing that you've done or even will do makes this your fault."*

Then I was back on the roof, waiting for Colby to tell me whether he was responsible for murder or not.

It was a question I'd been stewing over for the past few months. I hadn't exactly been in the calmest of headspaces when Violet had been arrested for fighting the guy who raped me. Actually, I'd been a hot mess. Not just because my friend had been in jail because of me, because I should've been the one in jail. I should've been the one who had to be pulled off the guy who violated me.

But it hadn't been me. It had been my small, peaceful best friend.

So yeah, there had been a bunch of guilt and shame attached to that.

I'd learned afterward that Elden had come from New Mexico to bail out Violet, with Colby in tow.

No one had said anything to me about either of those men committing murder.

But I could put two and two together. He supposedly died from a drug overdose the day after Elden and Colby arrived... Witnessing what I'd witnessed with these men, even in this short time, had only strengthened my hunch.

"Yeah, I did," Colby finally answered. He didn't speak loudly, but he didn't whisper either. Nor was there shame or guilt in his tone.

"Thank you," I said as my fingers twitched, brushing against his.

His pinky curled into mine.

"You're welcome," he murmured.

We didn't speak for the rest of the night. We just lay there, staring up at the sky.

And I didn't feel alone at all.

———

"Hold it in two hands," Javier instructed. "That one-handed shit is just for the movies."

He was standing close to me, his body brushing up against mine. I knew that he didn't technically need to stand that close. He was doing the thing that all men did when they were teaching women something, trying to get laid at the same time.

I understood that. And I didn't hate it. Javier wasn't being pushy, and he would stop if I was uncomfortable. He was just testing the waters. But my heart rate remained steady, and my panties remained dry.

"Hold it firm but not too tight," he added.

I found my grip.

"Good," he praised. "You need to line up your shot before you put your finger on the trigger—"

"What the *fuck* is going on?"

I whirled around to the source of the angry voice, the gun coming with me.

"Jesus fucking Christ," Colby cursed, striding forward and snatching the gun that I'd accidently pointed at him. "What the fuck?" he hissed, not at me but at Javier.

"Give me back the gun," I demanded. "And if you want to know what's going on, how about you ask me?"

Colby's furious gaze found mine. "I'm asking the fuck who decided to give you a gun."

"I asked for it, and I asked for the lessons," I shot back. "Since I'm a grown woman and not a toddler, and I'm assuming I'm still in an outlaw biker compound, I'm well within my rights to do so."

Colby just looked at me, his jaw twitching.

"Leave," he spoke to Javier, fury pulsating from that single word.

Javier, to his credit, didn't immediately back down. He almost looked like he was going to fight Colby, which was impressive as hell since Colby was scary as fuck right then.

Javier's eyes went to me. He shrugged once as if to say, 'what can you do?' then sauntered off.

"This is such bullshit," I snapped at Colby. "All I want to do is learn how to defend myself, especially considering my history and all the women dropping dead in this area. Yet I've got some over the top, cocky asshole snatching my gun off me."

Colby's nostrils flared, but I wasn't done.

"Or is that just another misogynist thing this club is doing?" I demanded. "If you're a woman, you can't patch in, you can't ride a bike, and delicate females can't handle the deadly weapon that the superior men shove down the front of their pants?"

"Fuck, you're a pain in my ass," Colby muttered.

"If I was still holding that gun, there would definitely be a pain in your ass," I retorted.

Colby's eyes twinkled. "And you're wondering why I took the deadly weapon out of your hands. You can't learn to shoot if the first thing you do is shoot someone who's pissing you off."

I tilted my head. "I disagree," I said sweetly.

Colby shook his head then lifted the gun, ejected and checked the clip before putting it back together.

"You should learn to shoot," he agreed. "Because of what happened to you, because of what's happenin' to women around here, and because men are fuckin' scumbags."

My mouth almost fell open in surprise.

"Because men are fuckin' scumbags, I'm gonna be the only one teaching you how to shoot," he continued.

I stared at him. "And you're not a scumbag?"

He grinned. "Not sayin' that. I'm saying Javier wants to fuck you."

"He's allowed to want to fuck me," I shrugged.

Colby's grin disappeared. "He is not. I'm gonna teach you or no one."

I cocked a hip. "So, you're saying you *don't* want to fuck me?"

"Didn't say that," he replied.

I tried to keep my expression even as my knees trembled.

"I'm gonna be teaching you or no one," he repeated.

This time it wasn't hard to keep the irritation on my face. "You're not the boss of me, nor is anyone in this club. I'm sure there are plenty of other, less fucking annoying, testosterone-fueled members who will teach me."

"No there ain't," he replied happily.

I hated his confidence. Hated the inkling I had that he was right. Javier had stood down in a heartbeat when Colby challenged him. Something nonverbal had happened there, something to do with some bullshit outlaw code. I didn't know everything about the Sons of Templar, but I was beginning to understand a lot.

I regarded Colby. He looked far too serious and far too sexy for his own good.

"What?" he asked, his tone teasing. "Afraid you're not gonna be able to control yourself?"

I gritted my teeth. "I can control myself," I lied. "This isn't gonna transition in to me getting into your bed."

"I know," Colby agreed quickly. "But your back will probably be grazed by that wall after I fuck you hard against it." He nodded to the concrete wall of the clubhouse.

My nipples pebbled, and my fingers curled. My pussy clenched as I imagined, vividly, Colby taking me here, in broad daylight. This little shooting range was out of sight from the road for obvious reasons, but the clubhouse itself wasn't far away. I could still hear the hum of various machines in the shop, the laughter of men.

Anyone could walk up here and see Colby fucking me.

Which made it all the hotter.

"In your dreams," I rasped. "Now, are you going to teach me, or bore me with basic sexual fantasies?"

Colby's mouth thinned at my tone, then he scowled at me, holding out the gun.

"First lesson, don't point a fucking loaded gun at someone unless you intend on shooting them."

I frowned, taking it off him, making sure to keep it pointed downward.

"Turn around," he ordered, voice cold.

My skin prickled hot at the command. Something about it sparked an unfamiliar desire, one that I didn't dare feed.

Yet I obeyed.

I turned, facing the long, narrow space that had been set aside for shooting practice.

"Grip the gun with two hands," he demanded, voice still cold.

I obeyed, my breathing shallow.

His heat hit my back as did his hard cock.

I sucked in a ragged breath, doing my best to ignore it.

"Got your target?" he murmured in my ear.

I nodded, unable to speak.

"When you're ready, take a deep breath, then pull the trigger gently as you exhale."

I held the gun steady for a few seconds, my eyes zeroing in on the target, trying to quiet my heart.

I took a deep breath in, then squeezed the trigger lightly as I exhaled.

There wasn't a loud boom since the gun was equipped with a silencer, but the power propelled me onto my back foot. Right into Colby's firm body and raging hard-on.

Power radiated through my arm, through my body.

I squinted at the target, seeing a small hole in the outer rim.

"Not bad," Colby said, his voice rough.

His hand reached around me for the gun.

"Next lesson tomorrow," he stated before he stepped back and left me standing there.

Which was a good thing since my blood was burning, my heart was thundering, and I'd been about to pounce on him and let him fuck me against the wall.

COLBY

I prowled through the clubhouse with the gun in my hand, an incessant buzzing in my ears.

"Bro, I didn't realize you were that serious about her—"

I placed my palm on Javier's chest and shoved. I'd never put hands on a brother before. But I'd never felt like this before. Like a fucking animal.

"You touch her, you're dead," I informed him then kept going.

Slamming the door closed behind me, I unloaded the gun then threw it on my bed. In the next moment, my hand was in my jeans, bracing myself on the closed door. It only took a handful of strokes to get myself off, thinking about the fury on Sariah's face, the defiance. Thinking about taking her, pressing her against that wall and fucking her brutally. Claiming her.

That fucking woman. She was driving me wild. Splintering all of the control I'd thought I had. I'd never wanted to dominate a woman before. Never wanted to redden a fucking ass.

But her?

Yeah, I was overwhelmed by the need to do it the more I got to know her. The more I heard her protests and saw her fighting her desire for me.

She wasn't going to give in easily, that I understood. No matter what she wanted, she'd made a decision, for whatever fucking reason. She was going to fight me every step of the way.

She was going to torture me.

And eventually, she'd pay for that.

SARIAH

During Violet's pregnancy, she was back-and-forth between Providence and Garnett which meant *I* was back-and-forth between Providence and Garnett.

I got a job at a coffee shop, not because I needed the money but because I enjoyed it. The coffee was amazing, and Julian—the owner—was a character, to say the least. It was a different kind of work than any I'd done since I left home, and I liked it. Everyone thought my parents were rich since I attended an Ivy League college, wore designer clothes, and prior to the coffee shop, didn't have a job to speak of. Everyone who didn't pay $200 a month to subscribe to my channel, that was.

The work was hard, my feet hurt, and some customers were assholes. I fucking loved it.

Unfortunately, word spreads in small towns, so it was quickly known that I worked there, resulting in Colby seeming to come in during every single one of my shifts.

He'd flirt mercilessly, and I'd shoot him down with the same lack of mercy.

He still gave me shooting lessons. I was getting really fucking good. At shooting and at not begging him to fuck me against the wall, in the dirt … any-fucking-where.

I'd never understood why people—men especially—were so fucking obsessed with guns. I'd always thought it was a compensation thing, like men with huge trucks and tiny dicks. I knew that Colby most certainly didn't have a tiny dick since it was pressed up against me during every lesson. I also knew that the power from firing a gun, accurately, knowing that you could control such a weapon, was akin to the high from a drug. And like a drug, it made me horny as fuck.

Once we were done, Colby would stalk off with a tight expression, leaving me standing there, breathing heavily, panties soaked.

I usually had to go straight to my apartment and use my vibrator until I felt like I was halfway satisfied.

But I never was. And Colby was relentless. I couldn't escape him in this fucking town.

I'd gotten good at masking my reaction to him sauntering into the coffee shop. He'd always hook his black Wayfarers into the front of his tee, hold open the door for slack-jawed women—and a good amount of men—who were coming or going. And his eyes were always, always on me from the second he walked in.

Even if my back was turned, I swore I could feel the hairs on the back of my neck prickle.

My skin would get hot, I'd feel my entire body tingling with his gaze, and my thighs would clench with need. It was really too much.

Colby would smirk as if he could read my mind, as if he knew that I was making a concerted effort to not seem interested.

I'd structured a vaguely irritated look on my face by the time he got to the front of the line.

"What do you want?" I demanded.

"Now, is that any way to talk to a customer?" he teased.

I scowled. "You don't like it, go somewhere else."

"There's nowhere else to go. This is the best coffee within a hundred miles."

"This is the best coffee in the fucking state," Julian disputed from the coffee machine.

Colby held his hands up in surrender. "That it is, my man." All of the Sons backed down whenever it looked like a confrontation with Julian was imminent. He was the one in control of the java, after all.

I rolled my eyes and sighed, all but tapping my foot in impatience.

As often as Colby came in here, he didn't have a regular order. Presumably because he liked prolonging our interactions as much as possible, torturing me as much as possible.

"You know, as much fun as our back-and-forth has been, you strike me as a girl who goes after what she wants," he drawled, leaning on the counter and getting way too close for my liking.

Regardless, I didn't move. That would've given him the impression I couldn't handle being close to him.

"*Woman*," I corrected. "And yes, I do go after what I want."

"Well, see, that's what's got me confused. Because I know that's the kind of woman you are, yet here we are." He waved his hands between us. "You're still fighting it."

I shook my head. "Or could it be that I just don't want you?" I asked sweetly.

"We both know you want me," he leaned even closer. "We both know it's me you think about when you make yourself come."

I gripped the counter tighter and swallowed. "Are you going to order something, or are you going to get yourself arrested for sexual harassment?"

He didn't lean back straight away, though the teasing glint in his eyes faded, and the pure hunger from that first shooting lesson made its appearance.

My knees shook, and my mouth moistened.

If he'd looked at me like that for much longer, I would've crawled over the counter and climbed him like a tree, audience be damned.

He leaned back after a handful of heavy breaths. The look was gone, the easy, playful expression back. He drummed his fingers against his chin, pretending to look up at the menu.

"Today I'll do a dirty chai," he announced. "Extra shot. And…" he looked into our full pastry cabinet. "A chocolate croissant."

I scowled at him. "Right away, *sir*," I said sarcastically.

"I like the sound of that," he said under his breath. "I'll like it more when it's just the two of us."

My step stuttered, but I managed to keep my expression even. This man was going to fucking destroy me.

CHAPTER
THREE

THINGS WITH VIOLET were going well. Really well. After her family's initial shock wore off over finding out her and Elden were not only a couple, but they were going to have a baby, everyone was supportive.

Except Swiss; he was still wary around Elden. Which made sense since I'd been there to witness the man literally pointing a gun in his face the very first time I'd been in the clubhouse.

Intense as fuck.

But I kind of got off on that. On the danger. The club itself. Practically everything about it attracted me.

Except Colby.

No.

Since Violet had made the decision to move back to Garnett and finish her degree online, I'd been going there as much as I could. Not just because I wanted to be there for my bestie, but because I liked it there. Something about the place spoke to me. The desert. The wild landscape.

And yes, the club. The women around it. It was so free. Without rules and judgment. It was the family I'd always wanted, so I was elbowing my way in even though I kind of had no right to.

Not that anyone made me feel anything but welcome.

I'd been careful not to be alone with Colby nor be drunk around him. That would likely end badly. The time on the roof didn't count. I tried not to think about that night. Tried not to think about how I was holding that time sacred.

There was also a serial killer in the area. Like a lot of young women from my generation, I was obsessed with true crime. For reasons unknown, we had a sick fascination with men who hurt women. Maybe we wanted to learn about it so we knew what to look for. So we were constantly reminded that we were never safe and that we needed to be on guard at all times.

I wasn't ready to delve into my reasons for this sick obsession. Instead, I was ready to catch a killer.

I'd recruited Ollie, our hacker roommate, to find out as much as she could. And she was really fucking good. There was a whole bunch of information that hadn't been released to the public and that social media somehow hadn't caught on to.

Women, all engaged in some kind of sex work—or woman who conventional misogynists would label as 'whores'—had been brutally tortured and murdered within fifty miles of Garnett. They were always dropped somewhere they'd be found. Carelessly. Like trash.

But there was always evidence that they'd been killed at another location. Though there were significant wounds, blood at the scene itself was minimal. The torture would take time and privacy. And there was evidence that this had been done by one perp. All of the women's wounds were inflicted with similar brutality and precision.

But the killer had dropped them all in different jurisdictions. As if they knew that the police stations would not communicate with each other. That the local news would put them as a footnote, if they wrote about them at all.

Most of the people investigating these murders would assume they were a result of the woman's lifestyle. 'Loose' women lived dangerous lives, after all. They gave their bodies to whomever could pay. And eventually, someone would harm them, or worse.

A story as old as time.

No one cared enough. No one would care enough until it was a pretty white girl from a good family.

And I had a hunch that this motherfucker was too smart for his own good. Meaning, he would continue choosing victims who wouldn't be so easily missed and wouldn't make the headlines.

The latest murder had just happened. This time, the girl was my age. In college. Paying her tuition by working at a strip club. She was pretty, from what some would call a 'low income' family. It seemed her parents had issues with booze and drugs, and she'd been in and out of foster care growing up.

But she had been trying to make something of herself. Taking charge of her own life.

Before she was brutally fucking tortured and discarded on the side of the road like she was nothing. Like she didn't matter.

This murder had hit close to home.

This girl could've fucking been me. Hadn't I come from a 'low income' family? Sure, my parents stayed away from drugs ... only to consume the Bible and its teachings in excess.

I was going to an Ivy League college, financing all of it by taking my clothes off for money. It made me mad. Fucking furious.

I had to do something beyond pouring over crime scene photos and musing with Ollie over potential unsubs.

Going to the police station had been my idea.

Arguably, I should not have taken my pregnant best friend with me, but in my defense, I didn't think taking her to a police station would be putting her in any danger. Plus, I didn't expect Violet to throw down with the sheriff.

I thought I was the one who was pissed off enough to go head-to-head with a sheriff who was doing nothing to protect women. But my bestie and her pregnancy hormones had me beat.

"I'm sure some of the nation's foremost news organizations

would love to hear about a jumped-up sheriff wanting to make a name for himself, not only ignoring a serial killer but then arresting two innocent, young women who simply want justice for a misunderstood group who have done nothing but good for this town," she spat at him, her face red, her eyes wild.

The sheriff had initially thought we were nothing but young girls, coming to disrupt his day. Once it became apparent that we were young women there to fuck up his life, his stare turned chilly. "I don't do well with threats."

"Good thing I'm not threatening you, I'm literally informing you of what I plan on doing if you don't leave the fucking Sons of Templar alone and start investigating these murders," Violet said evenly, not backing down.

I was so fucking proud; I was about to burst into applause.

"Violet," a masculine and very pissed off voice had barked.

And that was kind of the end of that.

I hadn't expected Elden and Colby to show up. Although I should've. I was coming to learn that the Sons of Templar ran this town. In addition to that, Elden was next level protective over Violet, so it shouldn't have been a shock that he was tracking her movements in some kind of way.

Colby was a … complication.

I didn't need to get wrapped up with an outlaw biker. Even one I was ridiculously and indescribably attracted to. One I'd fantasized about every night since I met him.

If he didn't wear a Sons of Templar cut, I would've already jumped into bed with him and gotten him out of my system.

But things were a little … messier now. I planned on being the coolest aunt ever, and I'd already fallen a little bit in love with Garnett, deciding to live there at least part-time after I graduated.

I couldn't shit where I ate.

From what I'd learned about the Sons of Templar, they had no problems bedding women and forgetting about them. Fuck, they had a whole stable of 'club women' who existed purely for the purpose of no-strings sex.

I thought that was kind of awesome for the women, who were all there by choice and who all got to ride some seriously yummy badasses.

But with me, it wouldn't be no-strings sex with Colby. He had an intense glint in his eye whenever he talked to me or looked at me, and I really didn't like what it promised. As much as I fucking loved the Old Ladies, I did *not* want to be one.

Also, I kind of had a boyfriend. Or had I broken up with him? Who could remember. All that mattered was that I'd been very sexually active after I met Colby, and I was pretty sure that would turn him off since 'their women' were meant to remain chaste and true to them from the moment they laid eyes on them.

Yuck.

Plus, there was the little nugget that I was taking my clothes off for men online for money. Yeah, he might change his mind about me when he found out about that.

And if he didn't, he certainly would be telling me to stop, which would not end well. I was just avoiding all of that drama.

Unfortunately, that meant I was also avoiding all of the orgasms.

You win some, you lose some.

Again, I had people back in Providence who could give me orgasms, and I possessed a great plethora of sex toys. I wasn't exactly missing out.

This, among other things, was what I was thinking about after Violet had gone gonzo on the sheriff before Elden and Colby arrived. Though I was pretty sure they'd caught the tail end of her speech.

Which rocked.

"Get on the bike, Violet," Elden ordered after we'd all had words about what we'd been doing in the police station.

A win for me, both Elden and Colby seemed to agree that there *was* a serial killer. They were not so hot on us getting involved in things, though. Correction, they weren't keen on a *pregnant Violet* getting involved which, in hindsight, made a whole bunch of sense.

Elden was appropriately pissed off. I felt a little guilty about that. Okay, a lot guilty. No more bringing the pregnant gal on my missions.

"It was fun while it lasted," Violet told me with a shrug.

I grinned at her. "I wish I'd recorded you dressing him down. Lost opportunity." It really was. She'd really given that asshole sheriff a piece of her mind.

"You're getting on the bike too," Colby demanded as both Violet and I were essentially perp-walked from the station by two outlaws. Which would've been funny if I wasn't quite so attracted to the one escorting me.

My gaze widened as it became clear he was serious. I folded my arms in front of me, legs spread in a battle stance. "You have ventured into a parallel universe, bless your soul," I cooed facetiously. "Oh, wait. Actually no, there is no universe where you can order me around." I glared at him. "There is no way in fuck I'm getting on that fucking bike."

Violet didn't serve well as backup since her man had practically dragged her to his own bike.

"*She's* getting on the bike." Colby jabbed his finger at Violet, who had indeed decided to hop on Elden's bike.

"She is pregnant with his baby, and although that doesn't give him the right to order her around, it makes a little more sense," I refuted. "Plus, I have a car here. One which, as a woman, I have a license to drive and everything. Since we've been allowed to drive and own property for the past few decades or so."

"Someone will come and get your car," he gritted out, obviously losing patience.

That made two of us.

I finger-waved to Violet as Elden's bike roared off before trying to walk to my car.

Not only was I unsuccessful, but I was yanked back into the warm body of a biker. Not where I wanted to be. If only my body would get the memo.

"You are getting on this fuckin' bike," Colby hissed, one hand holding me tight, the other delving into my purse.

He only managed that because I wasn't expecting even him to be brazen enough to go rooting around in a woman's purse. They were sacred.

When I tried to struggle, he only held me tighter, showing just how much stronger he was than me and how much my ovaries liked that.

I was a twenty-first century woman, yet it seemed my reproductive organs were not.

"You're essentially mugging me right outside a police station, asshole," I roared.

The jangle of my keyring sounded as Colby put it in his back pocket, releasing me.

"Don't think the sheriff is gonna be too motivated to come and save you from me, poppet."

My hands fisted at my sides, and I let out a little scream of frustration. Unfortunately, he might've been right. I didn't think we had made a friend in the sheriff.

"Fine," I huffed, gauging my options. "I'll walk."

I started off toward Main Street.

Again, Colby followed me. But he didn't grab me this time. No, *he lifted me bodily* and heaved me over his shoulder before walking to the bike in long strides.

"Put me down, you oaf!" I screamed, pounding his back with my fists. But regrettably, I had rather small, dainty hands, and he had a back of corded muscle that might as well have been concrete.

Colby plonked me onto the bike, my legs spreading for it on reflex, something he grinned at in satisfaction.

"Now, you can sit there of your own volition, or I can tie you to the fucking bike," he told me, sounding much too serious for my liking.

"You would not tie me to the bike," I scoffed, calling his bluff.

Colby reached into his saddlebag, unearthing rope that looked like it would indeed serve that purpose.

Outrage flared through me. "No fucking way," I hissed, not moving. "You tie me to the bike and we crash. I could fucking die."

Colby's eye twitched. "You're on the back of my bike, I'm not fucking crashing."

Now, it should've sounded ridiculous to have him declaring control over whether or not we crashed since there were a whole lot of other variables involved other than him, but it didn't. He truly sounded like he would not let harm come to me.

And worse, I believed him.

"Fine," I groaned. "But this doesn't mean anything you bikers think it means. I'm getting a ride on the back of your bike. I'm not 'on the back of your bike,'" I said, using air quotes at the ridiculous biker speak for going steady.

Colby just grinned lazily, taking me in as I sat on his bike. "Whatever you say, poppet."

And so help me God, my pussy pulsed a little.

———

"This isn't my place," I remarked, getting off the bike as soon as I could.

I tried not to make my voice sound breathy and turned on. But I really was. Though it was pretty much impossible to be completely outside of Colby's orbit when I was in Garnett, I had been doing my best not to get too close to him.

My tits pressed against his back, my arms wrapped around his waist, dangerously close to his belt buckle, was too fucking close.

Colby languidly got off the bike, not hiding his reaction to the ride.

My gaze panned down to his jeans.

Not hiding it at all.

I gulped.

"We're not going to your place," Colby said, his voice husky. "You're gonna march your beautiful ass in there, and we're gonna have a talk that's been a long time comin'."

Fuck.

He had the 'I mean business' tone. And he also had a 'we're gonna fuck' tone.

My pussy pulsed again.

I glanced to the gates that had closed behind us, gauging whether it would be in my best interest to try to scale them and run away from him.

"You can try, and I'd enjoy watching you do it, but I'd drag you back," Colby stated as if reading my mind.

I scowled, my head whipping back around to him. I was about to launch into a diatribe about how this was the twenty-first century, and men couldn't go about dragging women places against their will, but that wasn't exactly correct. Men in this century were still doing a bunch of shit to women against their will.

And Colby wouldn't *precisely* be doing it against my will. That was the problem.

"Fuck you," I spat instead, stomping toward the clubhouse.

My heart thundered as he fell into step beside me.

Men didn't make me nervous. Well, I'd taught myself not to let men make me nervous. When I'd first left home and found myself in a world utterly foreign from the one I grew up in, I was nervous during my first few encounters with men. Until I discovered the power I had over them.

Even after that fucking asshole date-raped me, I wasn't nervous or scared of men. Not exactly. I was more mindful, to be sure. Less reckless about who I drank around, though Violet wouldn't agree on that score since I'd launched into party-mode after I'd recovered.

I might have some other shortcomings, but I was pretty good at training myself not to let men intimidate me.

Except Colby.

He scared the shit out of me.

The prospect of this 'talk' scared me and excited me in equal measures, no matter how much I'd been fighting it.

I should've been relieved to walk into the clubhouse and hear music, and see a collection of men I'd come to know scattered around the bar drinking, obviously gearing up for a big night.

But I was not relieved.

I was disappointed.

"Fuck," Colby muttered from behind me when I stopped just inside the door.

His breath on my neck sent tingles down my spine and straight to my panties.

I didn't hesitate.

"Hey, boys!" I called out, pasting on a flirty grin. "Who's getting me a drink?" I asked as I sauntered toward the bar.

———

I was definitely drunk.

Not that I wouldn't be dancing on a table when I was sober … I'd totally do that. But being drunk made it a lot more fun.

And drinking with the Sons of Templar boys was also pretty fun. In addition to a lot of them being very attractive, they all liked to party. Not as hard as me, though. I even gave the youngest member, Javier, a run for his money.

Though Javier had kept a healthy distance from me since the incident with the gun.

Colby did not keep a healthy distance. He was within glowering distance, nursing the same beer the entire night. I did the best I could to ignore him. Then I did the best I could to get as drunk as I could when I couldn't ignore him.

Then, when I was tempted to not ignore him since I was so drunk, I thought the best course of action was to dance on the table.

Cheers sounded from around the packed room.

I smiled, moving my hips to the sound of the music, strutting along the bar as the men hastily moved their drinks out of the way.

The music ran through me as I dropped down into a squat, smirking at Javier as I snatched his beer, took a long pull and winked at him before straightening and continuing my performance.

My blood thrummed hot as the music vibrated through me. Though I'd always liked being the center of attention, it wasn't dancing on the bar in front of a bunch of outlaw bikers that got me turned on … it was dancing in front of Colby.

I was dancing *for* Colby, if I was honest.

To piss him off or turn him on, I wasn't sure. All I knew was that I was doing it for him, even though I wasn't even looking at him.

Although I was pretty drunk, I was waiting for him to do something. Because I understood Colby enough by then to know he would do something. It was childish. Petty. But I was doing it anyway.

And I was also right. Because I only made one more gyration of my hips before I was yanked off the bar, with him throwing me over his shoulder.

He grabbed me roughly but not enough that my head slammed into his back. He positioned it so I just kind of tumbled there gently.

Boos sounded from around the room.

I beamed at everyone as Colby stomped us out, not even trying to fight him. What was the point? Wasn't this what I had wanted all along?

The music receded as he took us down the hall and into a room that I knew was his the second we walked in because it smelled of him.

Colby placed me on unsteady feet then glared at me.

There was no playfulness in his expression.

"You got what you wanted," he said in a flat tone. "What are you gonna do now?"

"I have no idea what you're talking about," I jutted my chin upward. Suddenly, I was thinking that my plan maybe kind of sucked.

I hadn't expected Colby to be so pissed. Hadn't expected the room to be filled with so much tension, nor had I expected to feel so electrified by him.

"You know exactly what the fuck I'm talkin' about," he retorted. "You're playing games, Sariah. I don't like when women do that shit."

"Well, let me just make sure I act in accordance with what you like about women," I told him with a saccharine smile.

"I should fuck some sense into you," Colby murmured quietly, without even a hint of playfulness. Nor sultriness. No, this was pure deadly badass.

Fear speared through me at the evidence that this was not just a hot guy in a leather jacket; this was a bad motherfucker who was dangerous as fuck.

And I was turned on.

But fuck if I'd show him that.

I crossed my arms in defiance, meeting his eyes, careful to school my features. "A classic male," I tsked. "You think your cock is so important, so special it can change me into acting however you like." I crossed the distance between us then went up on my tiptoes, grasping the sides of his cut so his mouth was inches from mine.

A part of me, a very big part of me, wanted to abandon all of my plans of defiance and kiss him, let him fuck me against the wall.

But I was too stubborn for that.

"No man, certainly no cock, can make me act any kind of way," I told him in a whisper. "But..." I leaned in so our lips barely brushed. "I can promise you my pussy will change every single thing about you and make you fall at my feet."

Then I turned from him, going to join the club party, tagging a bottle of Jack on the way and not looking back.

CHAPTER
FOUR

I SIGHED when I looked at the caller ID of my ringing phone as I walked out of my class.

Normally, I would just screen him like I'd been doing for the past few weeks—since the party at the club—but I had an overeager male attached to my side.

Clarence was in a lot of my classes and just seemed to turn up wherever I went. It wasn't that he wasn't attractive... His features were pleasing, soft, and he even worked the thick rimmed glasses he wore.

But I didn't want a soft boy who followed me around like a puppy dog. I wanted a *man*.

Not the man calling me, of course. I had convinced myself of that.

I was answering only to get away from Clarence. No other reason.

"This is important," I informed him. "Gotta take it."

"Maybe we can catch up later?" he asked hopefully.

I sighed, vexed that all of my attempts to let him down gently had failed. Men very rarely accepted gentle rejections, yet when we did it firmly, they either called us bitches—in the best-case scenario—or resolved to raping or murdering us—worst case scenario.

"Let's not and say we did, Clarence," I told him without a smile. I held the phone up. "This is my outlaw biker boyfriend, and unfortunately, he'd beat the shit out of you if he knew you just weren't taking no for an answer."

"Hey, honey," I crooned as I answered the phone, staring at a pale and quickly retreating Clarence as I did so.

I was waiting for some cheeky shot at me for answering the phone that way, but I got nothing.

"Sariah, baby, need you to be calm when I tell you this. It's about Violet."

I stopped in my tracks, and it really felt like my heart stopped too. "Colby, I know you're experienced with women and are reasonably smart, so you know that telling a woman to be calm elicits the exact opposite reaction." I tried to keep my voice even but failed.

"Fuck, I know," he groaned. "I would've flown there and got you myself, but then you'd probably try to maim me for making you wait for the info."

"You're making me wait for the info now," I snapped.

There was a pregnant pause on the other side of the phone. One that made me want to empty my lunch all over my brand-new shoes.

"Gonna start this off by sayin' she's okay."

"Okay," my voice shook. "Now give me the rest."

"Just remember when I tell you the rest, that she's okay," Colby repeated in a calm voice.

"Give me the fucking rest, Colby!" I shrieked, so far from calm.

I knew there was only one reason Colby was calling, speaking like this.

Something had happened to her.

And although he was adamant that she was 'okay,' 'okay' was a pretty fucking broad definition. I was one to know.

"Violet was attacked at the club today," he began. "By the—"

"Serial killer," I finished for him in a horrified whisper.

The images from various crime scenes filtered through my mind. Gruesome. Brutal. Cruel.

"The b-baby?" I stuttered out.

"Baby is fine," Colby said.

I sagged in relief. The baby might have been unplanned, but it was already very loved. "I'll take the first flight—"

"Already got you sorted, poppet," he said, his words surprising me. "I'll text you all the details."

I'd been spending all these months focused on *not* letting Colby call the shots. Been careful not to submit to my desire to let him in, let him take care of me as it was obvious these men did.

But it was all that I could do to inhale and exhale right now.

"Okay," I wheezed.

"Breathe," he ordered. "It's all going to be okay."

For the first time, I held on to Colby, submitted to him. Because I had no other choice.

———

'Okay' was definitely a relative term.

Violet was okay in that she was breathing. That her baby still had a heartbeat. But she was lying in a hospital bed. And I didn't even need to look at *her* to see just how bad it was; all I needed to do was look into Elden's haunted eyes.

It knocked me for a six, seeing her lying there. Made my world tilt and confronted me with how important Violet was to me. What a gaping hole there would've been if things had ended differently.

I did my best to put on a brave face for her. The last thing the bitch needed was me falling apart and her having to comfort *me* after she'd faced off with a serial killer.

So I waited. Until I was out in the hall, down from her room.

Then I let the tears fall.

Unfortunately, I had an audience.

I should've known Colby would've been nearby. He was a Son and one of Violet's friends. The parking lot had been filled with motorcycles.

He'd picked me up from the airport. I'd fallen into his arms, given myself a moment to sink into his embrace, and then I'd stiffened. "Take me to her," I'd demanded.

For the life of me, I couldn't remember the drive there. All I could think about were the crime scene photos I'd poured over. All I could see were the countless stab wounds, the brutality. The excuse for a man who did that had hurt Violet.

So yeah, I'd been in somewhat of a fugue state with Colby earlier. Now I wasn't.

He didn't say a word, just yanked me into his arms and let me stain his cut with my tears.

We stayed like that for a while, me clutching him, quietly crying into his cut, reveling in how hard his chest was, how safe I felt in his arms.

Then after a while, I stopped crying, stopped feeling the pain and fear, and I started to feel pissed off. Really fucking pissed off.

"My best friend in the world was almost murdered by a serial killer, Colby," I hissed, my voice shaking. "My *pregnant* best friend."

A muscle in his jaw ticced, his posture tight like he was barely holding himself together. "I fuckin' know," he ground out. "I was there to see her covered in blood, a fucking knife in her."

My stomach roiled. Though his voice was flat and dead, I could feel the emotion radiating off him. He cared about Violet. And he considered himself the kind of man who would take care of those he cared about. He and the rest of the Sons were all blaming themselves for this happening.

Most especially Swiss and Elden.

"This happened in *our* club," he rasped out. "Where Violet was supposed to be safe. Where Jenna was supposed to be safe."

I bit my lip until I tasted blood. Though she was injured and likely traumatized for life, Violet was alive. The same could not be said for Jenna, one of the 'club girls' who had been brutally murdered. I'd seen her in passing. Spoken to her a little. She was nice. Sweet.

Now she was nothing.

It was one thing to become obsessed with these crimes, to grieve for a nameless woman whose smile I hadn't seen, whose laughter I hadn't heard. I'd been so fired up to get involved in this somehow, excited in a sick way. Yet now I felt cold and terrified.

"We're takin' care of this, Ri," Colby said, gentler this time. "No other woman is getting hurt because of this sick fuck."

"You're damn right," I agreed, straightening my spine and doing my best to fight back tears. "You fuckers better find him before I do."

I'd planned on using that as my exit line, but I barely got halfway around before a strong grip found my upper arm, and Colby yanked me to him.

Our bodies pressed together, my arm between us, our faces inches apart.

His breath was hot on my face, fury emanating off him as his eyes narrowed on me. "No way in fuck are you getting anywhere near this, Sariah," he seethed.

I will admit, I was somewhat perturbed at this rapid change in Colby, his unbridled fury and the way his hand was biting into my upper arm hard enough to hurt. Hard enough to bruise, actually.

Considering all that I'd gone through in the past handful of hours, I hoped I'd mustered up a decent poker face.

"No way in *fuck* are you telling me what to do," I snarled, leaning in so our faces were just inches apart.

Colby's eyes dilated, his grip tightening. I had to bite my lip so I didn't whimper in pain. I knew that if I did, Colby would've let me go immediately. But I didn't want him to let me go. I wanted him to hurt me more.

We were both breathing heavily. Both furious. Both terrified. Both out for the blood of the man who'd hurt our friend and was killing women without mercy or consequence.

I don't know who made the first move.

Later, I would convince myself it was him. Like it mattered. Because even if he had moved first, I didn't hesitate to respond. Enthusiastically.

Our lips crashed together with violence, with desperation.

His hand was in my hair, and he released the grip on my arm only so he could grasp my ass, lifting me one-handed.

I wrapped my legs around his hips, moaning into his mouth as I ground myself against him. He was already rock hard.

It did not occur to me that we were in a—luckily—abandoned hallway of a busy hospital. But it did occur to him, walking us into the nearest room which was somehow uninhabited.

The door slammed shut behind us. I barely noted that, grinding against Colby's jean clad cock with abandon, desperate for him. Desperate for release. I'd never felt this wild before. This over-whelmed with pure need. This frantic to feel alive.

Pain erupted in my scalp as Colby grasped a fistful of my hair, yanking so my mouth was no longer on his.

"Fuck, Sariah," he groaned, his voice guttural. "I've been waiting to taste you for fuckin' months."

I stared at him, heart thundering in my chest, pussy drenched. "Well, fucking taste me, then, Colby."

He let out a low growl from the back of his throat, knowing exactly what I meant. And he didn't hesitate. One second I was in his arms, the next I was thrown down on the thin mattress of a hospital bed.

There was no time for it to sink in that this was a hospital bed and the door he'd just slammed shut didn't have a lock.

No, there wasn't time for any of that because Colby had hitched my skirt up to my waist and torn my panties off.

I went up on my elbows to stare at him. I'd seen this man a lot over the past few months, thought I was familiar with him.

But this wasn't any Colby I knew. He seemed … frenzied. Out of control.

"Spread your legs, and show me that cunt," he ordered.

My body spasmed as I obeyed his order.

His eyes smoldered as he zeroed in on the apex of my thighs, staring at me, no, *devouring* me with his eyes.

I squirmed under his gaze, overwhelmed with need, conscious of the fact that someone could walk in at any moment—something that only served to turn me on further and make me more urgent.

"Colby," I pleaded.

"Give me a fuckin' moment, poppet," he murmured, still staring. "Been imagining what your pussy looks like for months." His eyes slid up to me. "And she does *not* disappoint."

I grasped the cheap sheets as he dove in right then, his tongue running along me with an accuracy that no other man I'd been with had possessed. Colby didn't need coaching or direction. He found the spot.

I let out a strangled moan, forcing myself not to scream as that would definitely alert someone somewhere, and no way could I have this end without an orgasm.

"You taste even better than I fuckin' imagined, too." Colby's voice vibrated against me.

My back arched as he went in again, mouth moving as one finger found its way inside me.

I knew my orgasm was going to rage over me in a matter of seconds. Never had a man made me come this quickly. It was usually a fifty-fifty chance that a man could even make me come. Not for lack of effort. It was just harder to get myself there with a man.

Colby got me there.

I cried out as the most intense orgasm of my life washed over me. Colby didn't stop, though. No, he kept going relentlessly as another climax peaked, as my back arched and my entire body trembled with the force of another orgasm. He continued assaulting me with his tongue and finger until I came again, barely recovered from the first two, half delirious, unsure if my body could even handle an orgasm that intense.

It could.

Barely.

Colby only stopped then, when my body quivered with aftershocks, my back finding its way back to the thin mattress, and I released my death grip on the sheets.

I blinked rapidly, coming back to reality as Colby thoughtfully —as if he weren't the man who'd just savagely went down on me in a hospital room—pulled my skirt back down.

On autopilot, I lifted my hips to help him, coming up on shaky elbows to regard him.

His eyes were frenetic, the veins in his neck pronounced. My eyes dropped down to his jeans, where it was really fucking obvious how turned on—and how well endowed—he was.

Even though my body was still recovering from what just happened, I found myself hungry for more. For him.

Colby rubbed his mouth with his hand, the movement somehow violent.

"I can't have you looking at my cock like that, Sariah," he grated out. "Not with the taste of your pussy on my tongue. Or I'll lose control and take you right here."

Cue pussy quiver.

"What's wrong with taking me right here?" I asked, forgetting all the vows I'd made to myself about staying away from Colby and definitely not sleeping with him.

What was another promise made to myself that I broke … really?

His eyes traveled to the door then back. "Because the first time I fuck you, I want to hear you scream my name." I shivered at the roughness in his voice. "And I don't want some fucking orderly or nurse coming in and getting an eyeful of you coming. That's for my eyes only."

Okay. All of these were good points. Except for the 'my eyes only' part. That was a little too possessive for my liking. But I was still riding high from my orgasms and was willing to let that slide. I swung my legs around so I could go up on my knees, grasping the sides of his cut and pulling him to me.

"If we can't fuck, then I have to do something about this," I murmured, reaching out to cup his hard cock through his jeans.

Colby let out a hiss.

I grinned in satisfaction at the power I already had over this man, not hesitating to kiss him quick and hard, tasting myself on his lips.

Then I jumped down off the bed on slightly unsteady legs and went down on my knees, working his belt.

To my surprise, I met resistance when Colby tried to drag me upward. I frowned up at him.

"Baby, the floors are hard, don't want you hurting your knees."

I blinked at the concern. Here was a man, hard as a rock, still overcome with ferocious need—every part of him was coiled tight—and he was worried about me hurting my knees while I sucked his cock?

Something warm settled in my stomach, but I quickly pushed that away.

"I can handle a little pain, outlaw," I murmured, pulling on his hands.

I sensed his hesitation, the warring of the gentlemanly side of him and the scoundrel.

Luckily for the both of us, the scoundrel won out.

The ground was indeed cold and hard on my knees, but my body was burning so hot that I barely noticed.

My hands trembled as I hastened to undo his belt and jeans.

I let out a sound of appreciation once I had him in my hand.

Long, hard, exquisite. There had not been a time in my life when I'd marveled at a man's cock. Not until then, at least.

I gripped him at the base firmly, leaning forward to lick him at his head.

Hands tangled in my hair. "Holy fuck, Sariah."

I trailed my tongue along his cock. This man was completely at my mercy. I'd always loved the power of this act. No matter that the woman was on her knees, she was the one who could bring her man down if she so wished.

But that was not the goal of today. So I wrapped my lips around him and went to work.

It had been established that I was not chaste or virginal. To put it crudely, I'd sucked a fair few dicks. And I was pretty good at it if I did say so myself. So I was used to various sounds of male appreciation.

But all of them paled in comparison to Colby. His guttural curses, the way his hands tangled in my hair, fisting it almost to the point of pain. It all served to rile me up even though I'd been more than thoroughly satisfied not minutes earlier.

"Sariah, baby, if you don't stop right now, I'm gonna fuckin' come in your mouth." I savored the way he grunted, sounding like he was battling for control.

I didn't stop. To the contrary, I continued with renewed vigor.

The hand tugging at my scalp pulled harder, and Colby let out a strangled growl as he released himself into me. I took him greedily, reveling in the new experience of letting a man do this. Not once had I let anyone finish in my mouth. It was something that felt too intimate and tawdry.

Not with Colby.

I took everything he could give, and when he finished, I ran my tongue around the head of his cock, cleaning him before I looked up at him.

His head was bent down to me, eyes meeting mine. The air seemed to crackle between us, and my skin thrummed with the weight of that gaze. It wasn't just sleepy and satisfied as I'd expected. It was somehow … fierce, too. Full of an ownership that unnerved me.

I tried my best to paint on a sultry smile, wiping the sides of my mouth demurely with my finger.

Colby's hands went under my arms, hauling me up his body, brushing against his half hard dick.

He used one of his hands to reach between us and put himself back in his jeans. But one of his hands stayed firmly on my upper arm, as if he sensed that I was ready to bolt.

My heartbeat began slowing. I wasn't trapped in a post-orgasmic fog anymore, realizing that the room contained more than just our bodies, our pleasure. There was a nifty little thing present called reality. And she was a bitch.

"This was about working out frustration and anger, nothing else," I rushed to tell him quickly before he could murmur anything that would mimic the expression on his face.

Colby didn't look surprised by my change of demeanor. No, he just smiled as if he'd been … expecting it.

"Whatever you say, poppet," he drawled cockily.

I yanked my skirt down farther, mindful that my shredded panties were nowhere to be found.

"I'm not your poppet," I grumbled.

Instead of arguing back, he shook his head, brushing my hair behind my ear and leaning in to kiss me.

I definitely should've pushed him away. Or at the very least, I shouldn't have stayed statue-like, and I definitely should not have kissed him back.

I didn't do any of those things.

I kissed him back. Eagerly.

When we pulled apart, I was breathing heavily once more and in a dreamlike state.

Until he spoke, that was.

Colby cupped my chin. "We're gonna go hunting. You're gonna

stay here with your girl, and when you're not here, you'll have a prospect on you wherever you go."

I gaped at him, all fond feelings quickly disappearing. "That sounded like a lot of orders which you are not at liberty to give."

Colby's grip on my chin tightened just a little, and his eyes narrowed. "Still got the taste of your pussy on my tongue, Sariah. Seems I'm at liberty to give orders that'll keep you alive."

I stared at him, waiting for him to let me know this was some kind of sick joke. He didn't.

I wrestled out of his grip, folding my arms and glaring at him. "Newsflash, buddy, whether or not you've tasted my pussy does not give you permission to order me around. And that right there," I pointed to him, "is why you'll never be tasting it again."

He chuckled. "I don't think so."

This time his cheeky, cocky grin did nothing for me. "*I* do think so. And I think I'll be making sure that *I'm* the one to catch the depraved serial killer who almost ended my friend," I added, surprising myself that I'd suddenly decided to catch a killer. It was a little much, even for me. But I didn't do takebacks, that would make me look weak. So I was committed.

"Do not get involved in this, Sariah," Colby barked, eyes dark and intent on me. They were filled with desire, but his tone was saturated in warning. "I'm fuckin' serious. This shit is dangerous."

I gritted my teeth against my own need mingling with irritation that he wasn't going to let this go.

I tilted my head, scrutinizing him. "Oh, you don't think I know that a serial killer with a body count in double digits is danger-ous?" My voice dripped with sarcasm. "Don't insult my intel-ligence."

Colby's jaw flexed.

"Careful. You may dislocate that jaw with all that clenching."

"I'm well aware of how intelligent you are," Colby bit out. "But I'm also well aware that you're reckless, you're loyal as fuck to your best friend, and you are angry. Angry enough to think you're invincible. To think that this shit can't touch you. But it can. And I'm not having this shit touch you."

Though I maintained my angry expression, his words hit me somewhere deep. Made me feel something. Like I was something.

"It is not up to you whether this shit touches me or not," I balked.

He stepped forward. "Yes, Sariah, it is. Because you're mine."

I jolted like he'd hit me square in the chest. Honestly, that would've been preferable to what he'd just said.

Moments rushed by as I was struck speechless, and his eyes burned into mine with a promise.

I swallowed glass, finding my words and my shields once more. "I'm not yours, Colby," I forced an icy tone. "And I never fucking will be."

This time when I turned and walked away, he didn't stop me.

CHAPTER
FIVE

I WAS BACK at the apartment I'd rented when I decided I wanted to be in Garnett at least part time. Although I loved staying with Swiss and Kate, and they had plenty of room, they were still firmly in the honeymoon stage, and I did not want to cramp their style.

Also, constantly witnessing how epic it looked being married to an outlaw biker was a little dangerous to me. Far too tempting.

Hence the apartment. There wasn't a whole bunch of stuff here yet, but what was here was badass.

An off-white sofa that looked and felt like a cloud. Black marble slab coffee table. A whole bunch of candles in the out of service fireplace.

The apartment itself was only a couple of rooms. The kitchen and dining area were open plan. Kitchen to the right when you walked in, large living area straight ahead with a small balcony that opened onto Main Street. There was a small but fancy tiled bathroom off the living room, showing my landlord had gone to a lot of effort and expense redoing this historic space while giving it a modern feel.

My bedroom was large too, another small balcony and an en suite with a large tub that sold me on the place. The realtor kept talking about the kitchen appliances, but the tub and the bedroom had already convinced me. The only appliance I needed was the fridge to store my booze.

My bedroom setup was most important, considering it was my moneymaker.

People–men–didn't think that they cared about the décor when a woman in lingerie was heeding their commands, but environment made a huge difference.

I didn't go with the cliché reds and passionate color scheme. Everything in my bedroom was shades of white and beige. Soft. Comfortable. Lamps casting a low glow. A safe place, not only for my clients but for me too when I turned the camera off.

I might've lived my life loud, wore a bunch of color, and pretty much seemed like the party girl who thrived on chaos, but I needed a little peace. A sanctuary.

And booze.

A lot of it.

Especially after what happened today.

I drained my drink. How fucked-up was it to almost have sex with a guy you've been lusting after in an empty hospital room? Especially when you were in that hospital because your pregnant best friend was almost murdered. By a serial killer. The one you've been low-key obsessed with for months.

The answer was very fucked-up.

"Because you're mine."

The words rang in my head, along with the certainty with which he said them. Colby had not said that shit to get into my pants. He'd said it *after* he'd gotten in my pants. Other women might've been turned on by a hot biker declaring them 'his,' but that shit could not snap my legs together faster.

And Colby knew it.

Because, despite all my efforts to the contrary, Colby knew *me*.

He said it even though he understood that those words would have me fighting him tenfold.

And though he might know a lot about me, more than I'd intended, he did not know everything. Because if he did, he'd never be declaring that I was 'his.'

I slammed my whisky glass onto the counter after I finished, taking a deep breath before painting a seductive smile on my face, adjusting my lingerie and turning on the camera. It was showtime, baby.

––––––––

"We need more info on this fuck," I said as I leaned in to do my mascara.

"I've got all the information the police have, maybe more, yet I don't have shit," Ollie replied, clearly as frustrated as me. Violet was dear to her too. And she really wasn't hot on a serial killer waltzing around, killing women at will and getting away with it.

"Do you think he's connected to the club?" I asked, biting my lip and frowning at my reflection.

That had been my fear since the details of what happened to Violet and Jenna had become clear. The killer had known how to get in and out of the club compound without being seen.

Ollie sighed, and I heard the sounds of keys clacking as she typed. "The killer obviously had at least a rudimentary knowledge of the clubhouse itself to be able to get past the security they have, which isn't anything to sneeze at."

I pinched the bridge of my nose. "It couldn't be anyone inside the club, could it?"

She laughed. "I ran background checks on every single patched member and prospect, which gives me a bunch of nothing since they've all got records of some kind and are all obviously violent," she continued typing. "But not a single one of them has a crime against a woman in their files. Again, not that that means anything. Whoever is doing this is smart. I'm saying that because I'm a fucking genius, and I don't even have a lead."

She was frustrated. As was I.

"We can't rule out a member," she continued. "But I personally think it's unlikely."

I agreed. The Sons themselves were not fucking stupid, and they vetted their members and then had a prospect period of at least one year.

"Okay, so time to try a new approach," I said, slipping into my dress.

It was simple, but it clung to my every curve. My hair was bouncy, shiny and untamed around my face. I'd done my makeup to look natural, but it literally took two times longer than some of my more dramatic looks.

"Do I even ask what that means?" Ollie asked.

I smiled into the mirror. "It means I'm going to seduce a sheriff."

———

It wasn't as hard as I'd expected it to be. When we'd had the showdown at the police station, the sheriff had seemed stiff, far too professional and like he would be a hard nut to crack.

But in reality, all I needed was hair, tits, ass and a great dress. Which I had all four of.

I'd been leaning against a squad car when he came out.

He frowned at me as he walked up.

Like I'd noticed the first time I saw him, he was a handsome guy. Square jaw, sandy hair, tall, with a purposeful walk. He also wore the shit out of his uniform. Not that I was really into guys in uniform. I kind of resented authority figures of all types.

I was more into men who wore uniforms in the form of leather cuts that announced their abhorrence for authority.

But I wasn't thinking about that right now.

I was on a mission.

"Not interested in another episode, Miss Cardoso," he said when he stopped in front of me.

I grinned at him. "It's Ms."

He didn't grin back, but I did see him do a quick sweep of me from head to toe. He tried to hide it, but I was an expert in men's reactions... He liked what he saw.

"And I promise, I'm not here to cause trouble," I added. "Well, unless you're into that." I fluttered my eyelashes.

He cleared his throat. "Ms. Cardoso, I'm a busy man."

"I'm aware, but even busy sheriffs have to eat."

His brow quirked, but he didn't reply.

"And even busy sheriffs get lonely," I murmured. "Especially in a town where the most eligible bachelorettes flock to the club you seem to despise."

As I'd expected, his lip curled at the mere mention of the Sons of Templar MC. He really hated them.

"I was under the impression that you are ... involved with the club," he replied, voice stern.

I shrugged. "My best friend's baby daddy and stepfather are patched members, and they throw really great parties."

Apparently, that did not make him happy, his mouth flattening into a thin line.

"But I'm not going to get in the middle of this particular feud." I stepped forward. "Really, I'm just after a good steak and company that knows their way around a wine list ... not a Harley," I purred, looking up at him.

It was a total lie. I'd been out with plenty of college boys who'd tried to impress me with their knowledge of wines by ordering $400 bottles. I was happy to drink the wine, but I'd come to understand that those were not the kind of men who made me hot.

The dials turned in his head—I practically watched it happen— and he'd stiffened when I'd gotten close to him.

This fucker was wound like a bowstring. But I did well with

tightly wound men. They wanted me because I was chaos, sexuality... I promised to feed the desires they buried.

"Dinner," he agreed.

I didn't let the surprise show on my face. Though I was confident, I'd had a moment of doubt when his hatred for the club showed. If he truly hated them that much, then his principles would tell him to stay away from anyone connected.

But men's principles were fickle when a woman was involved.

"Dinner," I agreed with what I hoped was a coy look.

"I'll pick you up. Seven." His words were clipped. Cold. They somehow prickled my spine.

"You know where I live?" I asked, coquettishly.

"Of course, I do."

Again, with the shiver. I ignored it. I went up on my tiptoes to lay my lips against his cheek. "See you then, sheriff," I winked before sauntering away.

———

Someone was pounding on my door.

And it was much too early.

Waking me up was a crime in and of itself. I'd slept poorly. As I often did. And when I dreamed, it was of the crime scene photos, of blood, violence.

So, when I shoved my silk robe on top of the camisole and panties I wore to sleep, I was pissed. Especially because the pounding did not stop.

Upon reflection, it wasn't a good idea to open the door to someone pounding while wearing nothing but silk and panties, but I was still half asleep and fully angry. In that state, I was deluded enough to think I could handle anyone.

"Tell me you're fuckin' kidding me," a feral voice growled at me the second I opened the door.

Yes, *growled.*

I squinted at Colby, trying to get my bearings.

I was not able to because Colby pushed through my door. In order to do that, he had to push me. Which he did. Forcefully.

It didn't hurt, but the way he manhandled me shocked me.

Shocked me enough so I let him do it until the door slammed behind him.

"What the fuck are you doing?" I demanded, trying to fight against him.

That was useless. He was stronger than me. And he was in some kind of rage. That much was clear. Exactly why, I couldn't pinpoint.

I slammed against the wall before I knew what was happening, Colby's palm on my chest, keeping me there. His fingertips almost brushed my nipples, which were already hard.

He was not turned on, though. Not in the slightest. Well, at least I couldn't see any desire in his fury-clouded gaze.

"I still taste your pussy on my tongue, and you go out on a fuckin' *date* with the man who is trying to bring down my club," he hissed.

Oh, there it was.

That made a little more sense.

Yet how he knew didn't make sense since the dinner only happened last night. And I'd been sure to go somewhere outside of Garnett because the chances of being seen by someone in the club or connected to the club were far too high otherwise.

"Who I have dinner with isn't any of your business." I was thankful that my voice didn't shake.

"Again, it was my mouth on your cunt two days ago, so yes, it is my goddamn business," he snapped.

"Your mouth could've been on my cunt five minutes before I went to dinner, and that still wouldn't be reason enough to come bursting into my apartment and physically assault me."

Flames practically flickered in his irises, his hand not moving. "If I put my hand down there right now, your pussy would be soaked," he said quietly. "We both know this isn't assault. And we both know you are my business. If you're gonna discount what we are, then I'm gonna focus on somethin' else. The sheriff is bad news. The fuck is ignoring the women being murdered in order to bring us down. He is ignoring your best fuckin' friend almost dyin' in order to bring down her family."

My cheeks flamed as he flung that information at me. All facts I knew, of course. But him hurling them at me with such naked fury made me feel shame that I shouldn't have been feeling.

"I'm aware of this," I gritted out.

"You're not aware since you had fuckin' dinner with him." He pressed harder against my chest. My heart thundered painfully underneath his palm.

"You need to be taught a lesson," he murmured.

His other hand split my robe then went straight between my legs, which spread on reflex.

Colby didn't take his eyes off me. "Yeah, soaking fucking wet," he licked his lips as his fingers slipped inside my panties.

My back arched the second his fingers found my clit.

Colby didn't wait to insert one finger inside, then another.

"You think you're in control here," he rasped out, fucking me with his fingers. "I realize you're used to that. But you've met your fucking match, poppet."

He bent to put his lips on my camisole, sucking on the hard peaks of my nipples.

Just as my body was about to break apart, his mouth was gone, his fingers were gone, and he was no longer pinning me to the wall.

I gasped as he raised his fingers to his mouth, tasting me.

"You go near him again, there will be fuckin' trouble."

And before I could even argue with him, he turned and walked out of my fucking apartment.

————

I was mad at Colby. Fucking furious.

Not just because of him depriving me of an orgasm. I'd finished myself off after he left, but despite the high caliber of my vibrator, my orgasm didn't measure up to what I knew I would've had with him.

Then there was the whole bursting into my apartment and acting furious about my date with the sheriff.

He had no right to do that.

The worst thing was, I could understand his anger. I knew I had betrayed the club I had become rather fond of just by sharing a meal with this guy, but I'd done it for a good cause. Despite my intentions, I hadn't gotten shit from him.

Instead, I got a steak, an angry biker, and half an orgasm.

I was frustrated and wondered if it was worth me continuing to act like I was interested in the sheriff on the off chance he let his guard down to tell me what he knew about the serial killer.

There was a slight chance it might work. If I committed enough to get in bed with him. Just the thought made me feel vaguely sick.

So back to the drawing board.

I didn't tell Violet about the date, or about Colby. She had only just recovered from her attack, was pregnant, and didn't need my bullshit.

Hence me being on my best behavior at the barbeque I attended before I left for college.

"Why do you fight it?" Violet asked, rubbing her stomach, eyes not on me.

They were on the huddle of men who were drinking beers and congregating around the grill.

`At first, I figured she was checking out Elden, considering she did that on a constant basis now that their secret was out of the bag, and her stepfather wasn't going to kill him.

But no, she was staring at Colby, who I had done my level best not to look at since he arrived. I'd also done my level best to avoid him. But the town was small, and there were many biker gatherings. Plus, I wasn't going to run from him. My willpower should've been stronger than that. Even though my entire body shivered as I ran my eyes over his cut, sinewy forearms, remembering the way his tongue had moved across my clit. What he tasted like. I had to stop myself from running into his arms right this second.

His gaze met mine, and I struggled not to flinch as if I'd been shocked. I quickly focused back on my best friend.

Who was smirking. The bitch.

"There's obviously something between you two." She nodded her head in Colby's direction. "He's hot. He's a good guy but also a really bad one in all the right ways… Just your type."

I sipped my beer. "I don't have a type," I lied.

Which before Garnett was kind of true. I wasn't picky about who I took to bed. Actually, I reveled in the freedom that came with being just a little slutty. I wore my sluthood as a badge of honor.

Sex had been drilled into me as something forbidden. Tawdry. So, I'd been drenched in shame in my teens while wrestling with hormones, unable to stop myself from putting my hands between my legs and bringing myself to orgasm every night.

I'd vowed when I left my parents' home that I'd never be ashamed of my body or my sexuality again. I'd celebrate it. And I'd done a pretty fucking great job these past few years.

But from the second that I laid my eyes on Colby, it was clear I had a type. And it was him. Not that I'd ever say that out loud. Or think it while sober.

Which I wasn't.

My bestie was preggers. I was drinking for two.

Violet gave me a knowing look at my protest. "You like him."

"Here I'd wanted a best friend who knew me better than I knew myself. Damn, that shit backfired," I muttered.

She smiled. "Too late now, bitch."

I sighed. "Where is your man?" I scanned the area, skimming

over Colby. "He's well overdue to come over here, ask if there's anything he can get you then throw you over his shoulder and have his way with you."

Violet giggled as her cheeks reddened.

The bitch was pregnant, and she was blushing. Because of Elden. Who was really hot. And gave her looks that melted all panties in the vicinity. He only had eyes for her.

"Stop trying to avoid the question, babe," Violet reached out to squeeze my hand. "Is it because of what happened?" She didn't wait for my response before plowing on. "I can understand why you'd be cautious, but Colby would never hurt you."

I resisted the urge to roll my eyes because my friend meant well. Even though I despised her gentle tone and the way her hand felt in mine.

"No," I replied firmly. "It has nothing to do with that." I pushed all thoughts of *that* away. "It has to do with Colby, and all of these men who love the whole 'woman is mine' routine." It was my turn to squeeze her hand. "I'm not gonna deny that it's really working for you, and that makes me happy beyond measure." Not a lie; I did love that for Violet. "Although I'd hoped we'd have been able to have a few wild months backpacking around Europe, partying our asses off before one of us got pregnant or hitched."

Though I knew that Violet was done the first time she spoke to me about Elden, I didn't think that she'd be a mother and a wife before she graduated college.

Not that I was resentful. At least I was pretty sure I wasn't resentful. My best friend had been through some shit, what with getting abused by her French boyfriend, getting pregnant by that same douche, having an abortion, then finding out her father had been beating up her mother for years, eventually almost killing her, then having her father kill himself, *then* getting pregnant to a man she loved, and almost getting murdered by a serial killer.

Yeah, she'd lived more than enough in a short time, and if

anyone in the world deserved to be treasured by an uber hot, older man, it was Violet.

"I would not be so good at being … owned," I chewed my lip.

Violet's gaze softened. "I get that the whole 'you're mine' thing is pretty archaic and at odds with everything we stand for as independent feminists, but it's different with them."

Her eyes went to the group of men once more, focusing on her husband then going dreamy.

Like a magnet, Elden's eyes went to hers, so full of expression and hunger, I felt like a voyeur looking in on a very private moment.

Violet turned her attention to me, though it looked like it took physical effort to wrench herself away from his gaze.

She sighed. "I don't know how to explain it, but it's not about him owning you… It's about you owning them."

I forced a wicked smile, not wanting to show how a part of me —a large part—desperately wanted that.

"Yes, well, as much as I love owning a man," I paused to drain my drink, "I'm gonna have to pass. Because as good as it looks on you, babe, I'm not planning on getting hitched or pregnant in the foreseeable future. And I'm guessing the cocky male in question wouldn't be on board with my plan on traveling around the world partying and fucking."

Violet bit back a smile. "I'm betting not." She looked between the two of us once more. "I have a feeling this is going to be interesting."

COLBY

I was still pissed at her.

Furious.

I'd stayed away because I'd surprised even myself by how rough I'd been with her in her apartment. But I couldn't fucking help myself. I'd been seeing red ever since church that morning.

Shit had been tense because of Violet's attack and Jenna's death. Even more so because it happened at the club and the fuck had gotten away with it.

We were all on edge.

But no one more than Elden. Swiss ran a close second.

Fuck, I was only her friend, and I could barely hold on to my goddamn shit when we rode up to the club to see a pregnant Violet covered in blood, a fucking knife sticking out of her shoulder.

Although we'd known about the killings prior to that, what happened to Violet and Jenna made shit fucking real.

"No one in a uniform is catching this sick fuck," Hansen had said from his place at the head of the table. "It'll be a man wearing a Sons of Templar cut sending this bastard to hell."

"It'll be Elden," Swiss cut in, speaking for the man who wasn't present because he refused to leave his wife's side.

Hansen nodded.

His eyes roamed to me before he spoke again. "We've gotta hope that the one silver lining in this is that these crimes happened within town limits which means the sheriff has no fucking choice in pulling his head outta our asses and doing some fucking real police work."

There were grunts around the table. Sure, we were keeping our less than legal dealings locked tight, but if the sheriff watched us close enough for long enough, he was bound to get something. At that point, we'd have to figure out a way to end the sheriff without it leading to us. It would be messy.

But that was for later.

"As it is, we've got somewhat of a problem with the sheriff," Hansen continued, his eyes finding mine again. "Or you will. And I'll urge you not to do anything to stir shit up with him."

I clenched my fists. "Why would I do anything?"

"Because it seems he went out for dinner with Sariah last night."

There was flat silence at the table.

Though I had not outwardly declared that Sariah was mine, my brothers had caught on to what had been left unsaid.

"She *what*?" I seethed.

"Wire has him on surveillance," Hansen explained. "As well as all the women connected with the club. For safety purposes. Her cellphone pinged at the same restaurant, so he did some digging, found out he picked her up from her apartment and dropped her off there later."

Red tinged my vision.

"Right," I pushed up from my chair.

"Don't do anything stupid," Hansen called after me.

As much as I was tempted to put my fist through that sheriff's face, I wasn't that far gone. Plus, it wasn't the sheriff who was playing games here.

It was fucking Sariah.

And I knew what she was fucking doing. She was trying to use her considerable sex appeal to wring information from the fucker. She was still prying into this killer even though I fucking told her not to.

Hadn't I expected that, though? Sariah was not one to do what she was told, and now that Violet had been hurt, apparently, she was not one to consider her own safety.

I wasn't sure if it would've been worse if she'd gone out with him because she'd wanted to fuck him. All I was sure of was that I wasn't myself when I barged into her apartment that morning.

I didn't like how out of control I was. And though Sariah'd had some words to say, she fucking liked it too. I'd jacked myself off constantly to the memory of the fire in her eyes, those hard nipples and how fucking wet she'd been when I'd fucked her with my fingers.

Yeah, that made it all the more complicated.

Though I wanted her, ached to put her over my fucking knee, I'd stayed away from her since then. She wasn't going to stop looking for the killer, meaning she wasn't going to stop putting herself in danger, so we had to find him first.

The problem was, we didn't have shit. We had Wire, one of the best fucking hackers in the country, and a club full of men with all sorts of skills, yet none of us could track down a murderer. Even though almost everyone wearing a patch was also one.

But this twisted asshole was different. The club killed when we needed to. When we were threatened. To protect our own.

Some members might've even found joy in those kills, like Swiss or Hades. But that joy didn't come from ending innocent lives. It came from punishing those who deserved it. Those who had signed up for their death when they'd committed an irreparable wrong.

None of us could fathom the kind of monster who killed women like this.

I'd assumed my fury toward Sariah would peter out given time. That I'd be able to face her, claim her without that hungry animal inside of me taking over.

But seeing her at the barbeque, the day before she was due to leave, the memory of her pussy juice had my mouth watering.

She was wearing a dress, floral and tight over every curve, brushing her calves. She wore cowboy boots underneath it, and her hair was obscured by a straw hat. Every time I saw her, she was a different version of herself. I never knew which kind of Sariah I was going to get. And I fucking loved that. Loved every version she'd presented.

Which made it all the more difficult to stay away from her the entire barbeque.

I'd given up by the time night fell, and it was clear she was drunk.

I followed her inside as she stumbled unsteadily to the kitchen for another drink.

"Say your goodbyes," I ordered, grasping her upper arm.

Her eyes widened in surprise when I grabbed her, then both

irritation and arousal flashed in those hazel pools. Both of those things got me hard.

"What?" she asked breathlessly.

"Say your goodbyes." I jerked my head to the party outside which was winding down. Most of the members had small children, and the ones who didn't had already left to continue the festivities back at the club.

"I'm takin' you home," I told her.

Until this moment, Sariah hadn't protested my hold on her arm. She'd flushed the second my skin made contact, proving she felt the same I did whenever I touched her.

Pure fucking need.

Now, though, she fought.

"You're not taking me anywhere," she shook her arm.

I held fast. "You're drunk. You're not driving."

"Someone else will take me."

"I'll take you," I snapped, thinking of doing just that. Of what her ass would look like presented to me as I fucked her hard from behind.

Sariah's breath hitched as if she could read my mind. I could practically see the naughty fucking fantasies running through her mind.

"I thought you were mad at me," she jutted her chin upward.

My hold on her tightened, and my dick got harder at her defiance. "I'm fucking furious with you," I agreed.

Sariah's tongue ran along her lips, reminding me of the way it had moved across the head of my dick.

My cock threatened to burst out of my jeans, struggling not to take her to the nearest bathroom and fuck her there.

"Say your goodbyes," I repeated, planting my feet.

Sariah searched my face. I could see she was debating whether to argue with me further. But I also saw that she liked this. That she wanted me. The last time I'd seen her, I'd left when she was on the brink of an orgasm.

Now, if she was anything like me, she would've tried to get herself off as soon as possible. And it wouldn't have been anything compared to what we'd shared together.

"Fine," she whined, looking at me through her lashes.

My body relaxed. But I knew the fight was far from over.

———

I'd wanted her on the back of my bike.

But the night was chilly, she wasn't wearing enough clothes, and she was drunk. So I drove her car, trying to keep my focus on the road and not on the skirt of her dress that I knew she'd purposefully hiked up.

Her legs were spread wide, showing the flawless, creamy skin of her thighs.

I was sure I was going to rip her steering wheel off from the force I was clutching it. I'd had to prevent myself from stopping on the side of the road every second of the ten-minute drive back to her apartment.

Sariah knew this, and she'd teased me the whole fucking time.

Neither of us had said a word. We didn't need to. The fucking tension between us was crackling.

She'd strutted out of the car, swaying that luscious ass of hers up the stairs and down the hall to her apartment.

I should've gotten a medal for my fucking restraint. Which I possessed only because I'd been drinking soda the entire fucking night. If I'd had a drop of booze in me, we'd be fucking on the hall floor.

Or more accurately, we would've been fucking in the desert.

My cock twitched at just the thought. I had so many needs, so many ways I wanted to take her. This back-and-forth needed to stop so I could fucking claim her.

"Well, you got me home," she said after we got inside and she'd whined about me doing a walk-through. She was in the living room, and I was keeping my distance in the kitchen. "Now what are you going to do with me?"

My entire body screamed to tear off her clothes and take her on her living room floor.

I stayed rooted in place.

"Get you water and painkillers." I stared at her for a beat longer before shaking myself and going to the fridge.

The fucking thing was empty except for a giant tub of edible cookie dough, various bottles of champagne and a bottle of ketchup.

Shaking my head, I found a glass and filled it with water from the fridge dispenser. I opened the cabinet above the fridge and located a bottle of painkillers amongst a bunch of vitamins and inexplicably, a pair of shoes.

I'd been planning on trying to get some food into her too, but she didn't have anything that would soak up the booze.

Sariah was naked when I turned around.

I prided myself on not dropping the glass on the floor or shattering it with my hand as my fist clamped around it.

Her body was as perfect as I'd dreamed it would be. Her nipples were hard, dark against the white of her full breasts. Her hips curved perfectly, the V between them showing a sexy patch of hair. Her legs were sculpted and long.

I wanted to worship every inch of her. Punish every inch of her.

My cock threatened to bust out of my fucking jeans.

"Are you going to stare at me, or fuck me, outlaw?" she purred.

I almost did it. Fuck, I even took a step forward before I caught myself.

She frowned when I stopped walking toward her.

"I'm not fucking you while you're drunk," I forced the words out, battling against my need, willing myself to go against my morals.

Her mouth opened in an 'O' of shock. I saw a flash of hurt cross her face before she quickly disguised it with fury.

That hurt look speared me in the fucking chest.

"Well, then get the fuck out of my apartment," she told me calmly, not moving to pick up her clothes. She was obviously comfortable with her body. As she fucking should've been.

"This isn't rejection, Sariah," I told her. "I'll fuck you drunk plenty. I just want the first time to be sober."

"No," her brows narrowed. "You don't dictate the terms of when I have sex."

"I'm trying to do the fuckin' honorable thing," I threw up my hands.

"Well, I want to be fucked by a dishonorable man, and you've just lost the chance at ever being inside me."

I knew Sariah. I'd tried to learn her every expression, every cadence. And hearing her tone, seeing the ire in her eyes, I knew she was making a vow.

Though I ached to fight her, it was not the time.

I placed the water and the pills on the counter.

"This isn't over," I promised her.

"Yes, it is."

CHAPTER
SIX

SARIAH

COLBY and I didn't speak until Violet's wedding.

He was obviously seriously pissed off, and the feeling was mutual.

I was busy planning the wedding anyway, trying to keep everything from the blushing—*literally*, that bitch was always blushing when Elden was around—bride and trying to keep up with school work. In addition to working my cameras. I'd been averaging about three hours of sleep a night, supplemented heavily with Adderall and caffeine.

Still, I was exhausted.

But the wedding was worth it.

To see Violet, walking down the aisle in the place that their future home would stand, seeing all of her family around her, and most importantly, seeing Elden's expression of pure adoration and worship… Yeah, it made it all worth it.

I might have even shed a few tears.

Then I consumed a lot of drinks.

Unhealthy coping mechanism, I was aware. Maybe I was

drinking in order to make it easier to break a promise. The one I'd made to myself and to Colby.

That we were over.

Even though we weren't even anything to begin with.

It had hurt. Burned like a thousand sons of bitches when I'd stood there naked and he'd shot me down. Yes, I was drunk at the time, yet I refused to find anything admirable about his rejection. All I knew was that it made me feel hurt and somewhat like a whore and I didn't like it.

Upon waking—with a headache thanks to being too stubborn to drink the water Colby left—I realized that he had actually done the right thing. I was more than consenting the night before, and I wouldn't have woken up feeling taken advantage of, despite my past. But I would've woken up and blamed the entire thing on the booze and would've pushed Colby away. Whether or not he knew that, was the question. I was scared of the answer.

Therefore, I didn't think about it.

I was really good at compartmentalizing.

I packed up my bags, called Violet for a quick goodbye then got the fuck out of Garnett, knowing I'd have to be back for the wedding I was planning and the birth of my bestie's baby.

By then, hopefully the situation with Colby would be controlled.

As it happened, I didn't have the Colby situation under control. I'd spent the entire ceremony hot and uncomfortable, sure I could feel his gaze on me the entire time.

I supposed it could've just been because I looked good. Which I did. You weren't supposed to outshine the bride on her wedding day, and I didn't because that was impossible. Violet wore a dress that made her look like a goddess and was glowing with happiness and love. There was not a creature on this earth more beautiful than her.

I *maybe* came in a distant second. But even that was debatable with all of the club women dressed to the nines and their respective husbands all but drooling over them. This fucking town attracted gorgeous people.

At least I looked as if I were part of the club. My hair was tousled with braids and soft curls, wildflowers woven through the dark strands. My makeup was soft, sultry, the same tones of the burnt beige of my silk dress. My brown eyes looked wider, and my cheekbones looked more sculpted than normal. I'd learned to contour my larger than normal nose since it was going to be on my face my entire life, and going under the knife scared the shit out of me.

The dress I wore draped over every one of my curves, left my shoulders exposed and dipped way down in the back.

So yeah, that could've been part of the reason why Colby kept staring at me throughout the entire ceremony and reception.

But it was more likely because of what had been left unfinished between us, despite the finality of my drunken words.

A prickle of knowing sent ice down my spine —that maybe we'd never be finished.

Hence me drinking even more than I normally would, which was already a lot. Despite the sheer volume of booze that I consumed, I found myself disturbingly sober as the night progressed.

Though there was still a lot of dancing to be had, great music and a seemingly unlimited bar, I found myself venturing away from the action—something unheard of for me. I ventured away because I no longer felt the heat in my body from the weight of his stare. No longer felt hyperaware of his presence. I even went so far as to scour the entire area for Colby's distinctive figure, but I could not see him.

What I could see was a shape outside of the various lights and lanterns illuminating the space we'd created for the wedding.

Through process of elimination, I deduced that it was him. The married bikers weren't apt to go and sit on their own in the dark because they were attached at the hip to their wives. And the single ones definitely weren't about to do that since they were on the hunt for someone to spend the night with.

Plus, Colby's bike was still there. His was sleek, mostly black with a harsh red streak running the length of the bike. An intricate dragon.

I'd marveled at it many times when I didn't think anyone was looking, infinitely curious about the origins of that dragon, the meaning.

I'd spent a lot more time than I wanted to admit wondering about Colby, his life before the club, what led him here.

It must've been the booze, the weird energy that weddings created or the desert air that made me take leave of my senses and wander over to the dark spot where Colby had situated himself.

I was somehow present enough to snatch some pillows from a nearby chair and a blanket. The night was crisping up, and silk provided no barrier between my body and the wind.

The ground crunched underneath the heels that I'd stubbornly refused to take off even though my feet were killing me, and they weren't appropriate for the terrain. But I liked the pain of heels, liked that the sharp sensation from every step kept me in the moment.

Colby didn't say anything when I approached though his body stiffened. I held my breath as I sat beside him, putting the pillow down first—the desert ground would wreak havoc on this custom silk number.

"I can't do this shit with you right now," Colby said, voice foreign.

It was cold and also ... tired. Weary? He sounded much, much older than he was.

I bristled at the clue his tone gave me. A hint at some kind of trauma, something in his past that aged him that way, that sent him on the road to seek out an outlaw biker club.

Now, I've never considered myself a nurturing person—I fucking hated babysitting and didn't find children overly charming—but I found myself desperate to take care of Colby in some way. To take away his pain.

"Okay," I replied instead of biting back with some smart remark that was second nature to me.

I didn't know whether that surprised Colby or not since it was hard to see his reflection in the inky night, lit up only enough to show his shape.

We were silent for a while, the sounds of the music and the raucous partygoers filtering through the stillness of the desert.

"I liked Violet the second I saw her," Colby said. "Not in the way everyone probably expected me to." He shook his head. "Swiss saw that, luckily. Which was why I didn't get any shit from him when we hung out so much. Elden likely saw it too, which was why he didn't kill me." He chuckled without humor. "I liked her because of what she brought to the club. Some kind of fuckin' … normalcy, I guess?" He ran his hand through his hair. "I'm not in an environment where I encounter many people the same age as me. Sure, there are some other younger members, prospects, but they're in the life. They're not going to college, frat parties. It was … nice, I guess, to have her as a friend. I thought of her more like a … sister."

He stopped abruptly, clearing his throat.

I heard the pain in his words. Felt his deep-seated agony. But for the life of me, I couldn't think up what might be causing it, I couldn't say anything that might coax it out of him. Damn me for drowning myself in fucking champagne and then deciding to do those shots with Javier.

If I were sober, I might've had a better shot of navigating this conversation.

As it was, I didn't know what to say. So, I didn't say anything. I just laid my head on his shoulder.

Colby's body tensed for a split second before he relaxed, lifting his arm so I could tuck myself comfortably into his side.

He was warm. He smelled of him. I felt encased. Safe. For the first time in my life, I felt like I was in the exact right place at the exact right time.

"I have always pretended I belong in places," I whispered drowsily. "I'm really good at pretending." I sighed. "But I've never felt more like I belonged until I found this club." My eyes were heavy. Colby was warm, and the booze was taking over. "I've never felt like I belonged until I found you."

I didn't even know I'd gone to sleep until I woke up, covered in a blanket, lying almost entirely on Colby, his arms tight around me, the sun rising.

That was the first time I slept with Colby.

And little did I know, it was the last time I'd feel safe and at peace.

TWO WEEKS LATER

Never go to a second location.

That's like, True Crime 101. Everyone with even a scrap of common sense knew that your chances of survival went down drastically if you let your assailant take you to a second location.

You make a scene. You fight, scream. Especially if it's in the daylight, if there are other people nearby. Killers are unlikely to want to be part of a scene, risk getting caught. Your chances of them hurting you are much lower, and even if you are injured, that's preferable to whatever hideous bullshit they have planned at the second location. And once they got you to that location, your odds of making it out alive were slim to none.

I knew all of this. And maybe all of the victims who were ultimately killed knew this. But when the situation arose, I doubt anyone thought logically about things.

Plus, in my situation, the killer in question was a cop.

The sheriff, to be exact.

But I didn't know that at first.

None of my spidey senses tingled when I pulled my car to the side of the road, the lights of his patrol car flashing behind me.

My mind was on other things. Namely, how I'd crept off at dawn and left Colby sleeping in the middle of the desert two weeks ago. A dick move. But what else was I supposed to do? I woke up hungover, confused and scared of what I'd shared.

Hence me running, avoiding him and trying to figure out what the fuck my plan was.

"You know, if you wanted another date with me, you could've just called," I told the sheriff when he made it to my window. I smiled, pushing my sunglasses to the top of my head.

I was feigning interest, obviously. The date had been painful. The sheriff, though objectively attractive, was a total snooze. And way too much of a professional to let me get him drunk enough to pump him for info.

Nor was he interested in my many expert attempts to seduce him. Though he was strong, older, and in a position of authority, he'd seemed almost … awkward on the date, stiffening and moving away from me whenever I got too close.

It had been a couple of months since the date, though, so I'd thought he'd be over it by now.

But bad dates tended to stick with you.

So not only did I have a bad date, but I had a guy who was obviously pissed about the bad date with the ability to give me traffic tickets.

The sheriff didn't smile back at me, studying me coldly through his aviators. He looked handsome in them; he was a handsome dude. But now that I'd gotten to know his personality, he bored me.

"Do you know how fast you were going?" he asked in a flat tone.

I sighed. "No, but nowhere near fast enough if you could catch me." I gave him a flirty, sexy wink.

"Speeding is not something to be so flippant about," his lips were a grim line. "Someone could've been killed."

I leaned slightly out of my car window to survey the desolate road we were on. Garnett wasn't exactly a bustling metropolis, and we were outside of town proper. I'd been on a mission to find Violet the best baby gift. I was, after all, going to be the best aunt to the little sucker, spoiling him or her with expensive and totally inappropriate gifts.

"I think we're good," I told him as I slowly trailed a pink nail along my chest.

Apparently, he was not amused. "Can you get out of the car, please?"

I gaped at him. "Seriously, dude? I was going a *smidge* over the limit. Don't you think you've got better things to do? Like catch a serial killer?"

Ollie and I still had no leads, which was pissing me off.

"I think if you don't get out of the car right now then I'll have to make you," he said with his hand on the butt of his gun.

I restrained an eye roll because he looked a little too trigger happy for my liking. It was clear that he was blaming me for the bad date, and he was using this as some kind of power trip.

I sighed as I got out of the car.

Men.

He probably just wanted to show that he had the ability to get me out of the car, make me do a field sobriety test, make himself feel like a man, then send me on my way.

What a douche.

Then there was the whole thing where he'd stormed the club and arrested Elden for trying to protect Violet.

Yeah, mega douche.

"You happy?" I asked, slamming my door shut a little harder than necessary.

"Get in the car." He nodded to where his cruiser was parked behind mine.

"That's a little much," I frowned. "This has been fun and all, but I think we both internally agreed that we weren't gonna do the second date. Give me the ticket and let me get out of here."

The grim line was now gone. Same with the blank look. His face … transformed underneath the glasses.

My chest tightened. Something about this situation was wrong. Something about *him* was wrong.

"You can walk to the car, or I can cuff you and drag you there," he offered.

I hesitated, looking into my car where both my phone and purse were sitting.

Before I could argue further or try to jump back in my car and drive away, charges be damned, he grabbed my upper arm tightly, much too tightly, then dragged me toward his car.

"Hey!" I cried. "This is police brutality."

"You were resisting." His hand locked harder around my bicep against my struggles.

"Oh, so you want to lock me up so you feel strong?" I hissed, trying to plant my feet, hoping that this was the time Colby or one of his brothers decided to go on a midday ride.

"You're really going to be sorry about that," I continued. "The Sons of Templar kind of like me and everyone kind of hates you."

He stopped abruptly, turning to face me with that warped, chilly expression on his face once more.

"Everyone likes you because you sell yourself, like a *whore*," he spat.

My breath caught at the unexpected venom he'd spouted. Plenty of rejected men had called me a whore before. But this came from an angrier place. A violent place.

Understanding flashed right about the time everything went to shit.

COLBY

The second I rolled up to her car, I knew it was bad. My whole fucking body went ice cold as the gravel crunched underneath my boot, and I inspected the inside of her car.

The driver's door was still open. Keys were still in the ignition. Her goddamn purse was sitting in the passenger seat along with her phone and wallet. Sariah never went anywhere without her phone, and she spent a fuckload of money on those purses.

"Nothing wrong with the car," Jagger said, closing the hood after a quick inspection.

"There wouldn't be," I replied. "He has her."

Jagger's face was calm, casual. "We don't know that, brother."

I struggled to keep my shit together, pushing past the icy dread that had overcome me from the second I saw her car. It wouldn't do shit right now for me to lose it.

"We fuckin' do," I countered. "He's taken time since his last kill. He didn't get Violet, and he's pissed. He'll be channeling that anger at the club. We know that. And he's been lookin' for an opportunity to take someone else connected to the club."

Wire had worked up a full profile on the motherfucker. He'd looked at the time between each kill and had scoured the country, looking for what would've been his first kill in order to give us a clue to his identity.

The problem was, there were a lot of sick fucks in this country. A disgusting amount of savage crimes against women that remained unsolved. Even with Wire's resources, his talent, and his ability to replace sleep with energy drinks, it had been taking way too much time to get this guy.

And we'd just run out of it.

"You're right about all of that," Jagger agreed. "But I can't see this guy venturing away from his typical victim. Violet was only targeted because she stumbled upon him. He's more likely to go after club girls or someone like Freya or Macy."

Though Freya, Hades's Old Lady, didn't do it anymore, she'd stripped at the local club for years and had been pretty popular.

She was retired now, but that didn't mean that she was out of his crosshairs. Which meant Hades was even more over the top protective of his wife, which was saying something.

Macy had also been a club girl, before my time, before she was married to Hansen. Though he was slightly more levelheaded than Hades, I knew my president made sure Macy never went anywhere alone.

"He's got her," I repeated, averting my eyes from the car, unable to look at it anymore. I feared I was going to lose my lunch.

Jagger just looked at me. This fuck was smart. He'd been through shit. He had the same sense I had. He was just doing the job of a good VP and trying to keep a possible liability—me—calm.

"Yeah," he agreed after a beat. "He's got her." He clapped me on the shoulder. "But we'll find her."

I nodded. Of that, I was fucking certain.

But the sick feeling in my stomach did not go away.

We'd find her. But something dark and twisted inside of me knew we wouldn't find the Sariah who'd laid her head on my shoulder. Who danced with abandon. Who smiled easily and threw attitude even easier.

Something horrible told me the Sariah we'd find would be someone else entirely.

SARIAH

I woke up chained.

On a cement floor.

In what looked like a warehouse.

I had a killer fucking headache.

The asshole must've brained me with the butt of his gun or something hard enough to knock me out.

Apparently, he wasn't just a cop.

He was something else.

Something else that did not mean good things for me.

The warehouse I was in looked broken down and abandoned. Crying out for help was my first instinct, but my gut told me the sheriff was smart enough to take me somewhere no one would hear me scream. In addition to that, I didn't want to alert him to the fact that I was awake if he was nearby.

The chain on my ankle jingled as I struggled to get up off the floor. It was quite a struggle since my hands were cuffed behind my back. My center of gravity was off thanks to my pounding head and general terror.

My stomach lurched at the various shaped, large stains on the cement floor. They weren't bright red. They were dark maroon.

Dried blood.

Panic constricted my throat as I frantically yanked my ankle, looking for a give in the chain, searching around the sparse area for something to use to pick a lock.

Nothing.

Not a single thing nearby I could use for a weapon or some kind of wrench.

And, upon closer inspection, the chain at my ankle didn't have a lock. It looked like it had been … welded on?

But that couldn't be right. Getting hit in the head might've knocked me out for a few minutes, tops, but no way would it have left me unconscious for the time it took for him to get me here and chained up like this. That shit only happened in the movies. I'd done enough research into true crime to know that knockouts didn't give the killer countless minutes or hours to do what they needed to. They had five minutes, max.

My tongue was thick in my mouth, and I felt discombobulated.

The fucker must've drugged me.

I struggled to think of the police files I'd read on his previous victims, how long he kept them alive, how long they'd had. But it was never said. Not only because most of the investigations were half-assed but because he purposefully took women who had fluctuating schedules. Sex workers.

His last victim had been Jenna at the club. He'd killed her quickly and brutally, not taking the time to torture her like he had the others. He hadn't killed anyone since then. That meant whatever depraved need inside of him was hungry for torture.

I was in deep shit.

As horrible as it sounded, it was good he brought me to his obvious torture location, telling me he planned to spend some time on me.

My mouth went dry at the very thought.

"Get it together, Sariah," I scolded myself.

Since I obviously couldn't escape, I would have to do my best to either outsmart him into unlocking me or delay him from doing whatever he was going to do in order to give the club time to find me.

And hopefully, they'd be looking for me.

I wasn't known to stick to any kind of schedule, but I also wasn't known for leaving my car, or my purse—a brand new YSL, thank you very much—on the side of the road.

Someone would find my car, the club would know something was up, and they'd start looking into me.

Then they'd likely find out the truth about how I made my money, where I came from. Whether or not the sheriff knew about my cam business remained to be seen. But the Sons had a hacker, so they would be digging into every corner of my life, trying to find me. I hadn't gone to a bunch of effort to cover my tracks digitally. If someone wanted to find out about me, they would.

Colby would.

That wasn't good.

Him saving me wouldn't really help with the narrative I was trying to create between us. The narrative being that there *was* no us.

But getting killed by a serial killer was kind of worse. I'd deal with the consequences of my deception after I got myself out of this situation ... safely.

———

A metal clanging sounded, a door opening and shutting. Much too soon. Since only a handful of minutes had passed, I had not yet figured out how to get out of the situation safely. All I'd done was open some pretty nasty wounds on my wrists, trying to wrench my hands from the cuffs.

I watched Elijah saunter across the cavernous warehouse space. He walked unhurriedly, confidently. Why wouldn't he be confident? He had me chained up in a warehouse that I was presuming was in the middle of nowhere, and he had a perfect success rate.

"I've got to say, I'm surprised," I said when he made it to me. I forced myself to sound comfortable, cocky even. In reality, I was fucking terrified. The way he was staring at me was ... inhuman. It made me feel cold all over, fighting to stop my teeth from chattering.

"You know the bad thriller, where you guess who the killer is in like ... the first five pages?" I asked. "Well ... you, sir, have worked up a good twist."

Though in hindsight, it did kind of make sense. The weird, eerie feeling I had on our 'date.' His knowledge of the security and layout of the club—he'd just stormed in, arresting Elden a few months before. Yes, the small details added up now that I'd been kidnapped by him. I wondered how long it would take the club and their hackers to connect the dots.

Elijah didn't say anything, just knelt down, his knees cracking as he did so. I hadn't noticed he was holding a large piece of fabric that unrolled to...

"Oh, a big package of torture implements," I jeered, swallowing past the knot in my throat. "Is that meant to scare me?"

There were knives. A lot of them. They weren't stained with

blood or rusty. No, they were gleaming, spotless, well-tended to. That was almost worse than the cliché, bloody torture implements.

"Yes," Elijah replied, fingering the weapons lovingly. When his eyes found mine, I stifled the urge to recoil. "It should scare you because you know exactly how I intend on using them." He tilted his head, assessing me. "You know how I use them because you're infatuated with the morbid. You're impressed by me."

I rolled my eyes, sickened by how close he was to the truth. I'd never been impressed by him, but I was infatuated with his crimes.

"How about disgusted, you cowardly piece of shit," I snarled. "You really think you're anything to be impressed by? You're misusing power and strength against vulnerable, young women to trap them, then you murder them while they're chained up and defenseless. There is nothing impressive about that. How about you unchain me, and then we'll see how you fare when your victims can fight back?"

My bravado was entirely unfounded, but I believed that I at least stood a chance against him if I could get out of these handcuffs. And if not, I would make sure to get a lot of his skin under my fingernails. There was no way he was getting away with this. Whatever happened here, I was going to be the last woman who wore these chains.

"You're here because you deserve to be here," he replied, squatting down so he was at eye level with me, so I could see cruelty and madness dancing in his gaze. "Loose women deserve to be punished."

His passion was horrible. He was utterly unhinged from reality, madness leeching off him like sweat. I didn't understand how he'd managed to keep the veneer of sanity on for so long without anyone noticing.

It scared the shit out of me. But I wouldn't let it show. Couldn't.

"Oh, let me guess… Your girlfriend cheated on you?" I decided my best bet was to get him talking, try to figure him out. "Or you fell in love with a sex worker who drained you dry?"

His cheeks flushed in fury. "I would never stoop so low as to be with a *whore*," he yelled, spittle flying from his mouth.

"Okay, so no girlfriends," I mused, settling my back against the cement wall, my chain clanking as I did so. I was getting to him. "No girlfriends ... so maybe your mom?"

I may not have graduated yet, but I'd taken enough psych classes to understand that he had some deep-seated issues with women.

And more often than not, when men had issues like Elijah obviously did, it started with the woman who birthed them.

His eyes blew wide when I said that, his posture changing. "Shut the fuck up." His tone was calm now. Measured. Which somehow was even more terrifying.

"Mommy issues." I shook my head. "How predictable," I scoffed.

Pain exploded in my cheek as he backhanded me.

I'd never been hit before. Sure, I'd been raped, but he'd at least drugged me first. A proper gentleman dirtbag. Being hit in the face *hurt*. My brain rattled in my skull, the pain serving as a stark reminder of how serious this situation was.

This wasn't a game. This wasn't some fucking true crime documentary I was watching with a bottle of cheap wine. I was living this.

I spat out blood and glared at him. "Not even man enough to punch me? Figures."

I waited for him to explode, for what reason, I didn't know. Maybe so he'd go into a frenzy and kill me quickly? Was I that ready for death? No. I was just more terrified of the alternative.

For a second, he looked like he might just end it all here. His face was pink with rage, his fists clenched at his sides, and his mouth was curved into a gruesome scowl.

But then it all just ... went away.

In a blink, his hands relaxed at his sides, his shoulders slackened, and his expression turned blank. Cold.

My heart was in my throat, and my skin began to crawl from his eyes on me. He looked like a reptile. Heartless. Soulless.

"No," he answered calmly, reaching over to his unrolled set of torture implements. He picked up a knife that glinted in the light. "We're going to do this right."

CHAPTER
SEVEN

COLBY

I WAS COMING out of my skin.

But I was doing a real good job of hiding it.

I was aware of every second that went by. Every second we didn't have her was a second he had her. And we'd seen the crime scene photos, we'd seen what he did to women.

"We've got Wire on the line," Hansen said as we sat down at the table.

We'd already gone to the fucking sheriff. Although we each hated the fuck, we needed as many eyes out looking for Sariah as possible. But the fuck was nowhere to be found. Luckily, the deputies were loyal to us and were already scouring the town for her.

They probably wouldn't find her.

Wire, our hacker, was our best chance.

"Okay, so no leads on who took her, but I know why he took her," Wire's voice came through the speaker, talking rapidly as was characteristic to him. "Sariah Cardoso is also known as Daisy Sunderland online," he continued. "She's actually quite famous in the cam world. Has tens of thousands of monthly subscribers."

My stomach bottomed out. I knew every person in the room was looking at me, but I kept my gaze on the phone.

Even though I knew nothing about fashion, I paid very close detail to everything she wore. I understood that she wore expensive shit. Understood that she had diamonds dangling off her ears. She drove a nice fucking car. Went to an Ivy League school and carried herself in a way that I'd connected with people who came from money.

"But her parents…" I trailed off. Both Violet and I had assumed her parents were rich, Sariah had mentioned it a couple of times. Why would we believe anything else?

"Her parents live in Utah," Wire said. "Still paying off their thirty-year mortgage. Her dad owns a furniture store that barely breaks even. Mom is a teacher. They barely make enough month to month to stay afloat."

I clenched my fists on top of the table. Sariah's life was unraveling before my fucking eyes. These were details she should've told me. Details I should've coaxed out of her, preferably while she was naked.

"Okay, so she fits his victim profile," Hansen grumbled, eyeing me.

"Yeah, she does," Wire agreed. "She's also been digging into this guy. Her hacker friend has found shit on him that not many people have. Impressive, really."

"So have you got any fucking idea where she is?" I demanded, not needing to hear about Wire's technological hard-on for another hacker.

"Negative," Wire responded. "But I'll find her."

Hansen ended the call.

The room was thick with silence.

Yes, we'd find her.

But everyone in the room knew that time was running out to find her breathing.

———

Violet was in labor. I'd known about it for some time, yet she'd fucking made me promise to keep my mouth shut. That went against everything inside me. Everything that cared for Violet and respected her husband.

But I was barely able to think straight, and she'd tugged on my need to find Sariah.

So, I'd kept my mouth shut as long as I could.

Until it became really fucking obvious what was going on.

She was now refusing to go to a hospital.

Elden was like a caged fucking animal. Swiss was pacing. The woman, unsurprisingly, remained calm.

We were at church once again, with fucking nothing. No word from the sheriff. No leads on Sariah. Fucking nothing.

It had been hours.

Hours.

The chances of us finding her alive were slim. And the chances of finding her unharmed were none.

None.

I hadn't memorized every inch of her skin as I should've. Hadn't learned it. Hadn't tasted enough of her. My memories of her smooth, perfect body would remain that … memories.

"There's still a chance," Lucas said as the door closed. "We can still find her, she's gonna be fine."

I stared at my friend, my brother. "Jenna was stabbed fifty-two times," I reminded him. "Fifty-two."

His shoulders visibly sagged.

"The last victim before her was tortured for *hours*," I continued, my voice shaking. "He tore off strips of her skin while she was alive. Her ovaries were outside of her body. Her hands were almost amputated by the cuffs he used; she was that desperate to escape."

"One of the victims nearly tore her hands off trying to get away from him while he was *vivisecting her alive*!" I roared.

I could feel it, fury crawling up my throat. My vision had black spots dancing in it.

The sound of a phone ringing echoed in the silent room. I waited for someone to answer. No one did. Because it was my phone.

I scrambled to answer it, hoping to hear Sariah's tired voice, her tales about how she'd escaped unharmed.

"Am I on speaker?" an unfamiliar woman asked.

"Who the fuck is this?"

"Put me on fucking speaker now," she demanded.

Unable to say why, I did as she asked.

"The killer is Elijah Burrows, otherwise known as Beau Granger," the woman on the phone said.

Everyone in the room went still.

"How do you know this?" was Hansen's measured answer.

"I know it because I've spent every spare hour I've had looking for him since Sariah got me involved in this," she replied. "And I've been breaking laws that would have me locked up without a key in order to find him in time ever since I heard Sariah was taken."

I straightened in realization. "You're Ollie."

"The one and only." All business, she pressed on. "Beau was born to what I understand you refer to as 'club girls,' she spoke quickly, not unlike Wire. "From what I can tell, it was rough. She was eventually murdered by the club."

"Makes sense why he hates us," Hansen muttered.

"I don't give a fuck about his history. I want to know his location," I slammed my hand not holding the cell against the table.

"Get in line, buddy, and hold on to your shit. You can unleash it when you get him." I could hear Ollie typing in the background as she spoke. "He's smart enough not to have his cell on him or take the squad car to his location, but I'm digging into his and all known alias's purchase records for a vehicle that I'm really fucking hoping isn't some ancient Ford I can't track."

Though I wasn't really a praying type of guy, I found myself pleading with the unknown.

The sound of keys tapping was the only sound we heard for what felt like ages before Ollie spoke again.

"Bingo," she whispered.

My hand was starting to cramp from holding my cell so tightly.

"Okay, he's got a Pathfinder, and it's equipped with a GPS tracking system," she murmured, sounding distracted. "Hacking into that system now…"

It only took a few seconds, but they were the longest of my fucking life.

"Got it," she said. "Warehouse. Looks like thirty minutes away."

"Send the details to my phone," I barked, hoping that Sariah had thirty minutes.

SARIAH

What happened with the knives was about as worse as anyone could imagine.

No, it was much worse than anyone could imagine. I'd thought I understood what was done to his previous victims because I'd seen the crime scene photos, read about the injuries.

But I knew jack shit.

I didn't know what it felt like for cold metal to tear through skin, muscle and organs. I didn't know pain existed where your very bone marrow seemed to scream for mercy. And scream I did.

Pleaded. Cried.

I did all the things that many people probably thought they wouldn't do. And he did many things that weren't in the police reports. Horrible things. Evil things that made me look forward to death.

I didn't remember a whole lot about the rescue. In my defense, I was in a pretty bad way.

Elijah—or whoever he was—had done a number on me by that point. Death was close. I knew that. Could feel it. Was looking forward to it. I'd never tasted anything sweeter on my tongue than the oncoming mercy of death.

Death meant no more pain. No more torture.

I'd thought I was a fighter. Fuck, that was part of this whole identity I had going on. It was pitiful how quickly that part of me was lost. How all of me was lost in this cold warehouse.

That's when the rescue came.

Elijah had gone somewhere, maybe it had been for an hour, maybe a moment. Time was hazy.

All that I knew was I was alone with my pain and filth, and then there were people. Saving me.

Except I was already gone.

I was expecting Colby to be the one bursting in, getting to me first. But it was Hades.

And I was glad for it. Or at least I thought I was.

Glad... A good feeling. It couldn't have been that.

He'd said things, Hades. Things that made my heartbeat steady somewhat. He was almost … gentle. Which was funny considering he was the scariest biker of them all, covered in tattoos and emanating a general air of death that had nothing to do with his name.

It was nice, though. Having death unchain me. I didn't feel quite as dirty and ruined as I would've if Colby saw me like this.

Chained up like a dog.

COLBY

They'd already incapacitated Elijah. Or Beau. Whatever the fuck. He was bloody, unarmed and chained up.

Like Sariah had been chained up. Bleeding on the concrete.

I couldn't think of her like that.

My eyes raked over him. The man we'd all overlooked. The one we'd underestimated. Yeah, we thought he was going to bring problems for the club, and we'd been planning on taking care of him one way or another.

But we'd fucked around. Because we were focusing on finding the fuck who was hurting women, and that was priority.

We'd found him now. But it was too late.

He had blood on his hands.

A lot of it.

It was hers.

He was coated in her blood. It even stained his mouth.

I no longer felt cold, empty or determined. I'd been determined to find Sariah alive, had turned off all emotions in order to do that. And now I'd found her alive … barely. Fuck, I wasn't even the one who found her. One of her friends did, half a country away. I'd done nothing. I didn't find her. Didn't protect her.

My fists were crunching against his flesh in the blink of an eye, hot rage taking over me. I had only one need right now: to kill the man who'd hurt my woman.

I'd killed before, but not for pleasure. Out of necessity. For the club. It never made me feel good. Fuck, it made me sick for a week after.

But the only thing I felt while watching him bleed, watching his face cave in, was pure satisfaction.

Until someone fucking pulled me off him.

In the end, it took multiple someones.

I fought them like a fucking animal because that's what I was. I was a rabid beast with only one purpose.

Hansen took hold of my neck while Jagger had my hands behind my back. "Lock it down," my president told me through his teeth.

I struggled to get out of Jagger's hold as Elijah/Beau groaned behind Hansen, proving that I was not. Done. Yet.

"Colby," Hansen said, louder this time. "The time for him will come. But you only have one chance to be there for your woman right now. You make the choice to prioritize revenge over her and you'll regret it forever."

His words filtered in slowly, fighting against all of my instincts to kill.

He was right. Choosing to kill Elijah now would be a path I could never come back from.

"Let me go," I demanded, trying again to jerk my arms from Jagger's hold.

Hansen searched my face, as if he were gauging something.

"Let me the fuck go," I repeated, sucking in a breath, forcing a steady exhale. "That choice is mine to make."

Hansen nodded to Jagger who released my arms.

Then I made my choice.

SARIAH

He finally appeared.

I'd been expecting it. Dreading it.

Hours ago, I'd been hoping for it. Praying for it. For him.

But that time had come and gone.

Hades had held me in his arms while Hansen had gone over my many wounds with a pale face, bandaging the worst of them, saying I needed to get out of there stat.

I was guessing that even field surgery wasn't an option at this point. That was a relief.

Maybe I'd die on the way to the hospital.

It was a comforting thought.

The air was chilly when we walked out of the warehouse, an icy bite against all the holes in my body.

There were a bunch of bikes everywhere along with the club van.

I tried my best to avert my eyes from the men milling around. I didn't need to see their faces. The pity, the fury, the worry, the disgust.

Hades was the only person who hadn't looked at me differently. Who didn't make me want to crawl into a hole and die.

So I burrowed closer into his cut with what little strength I had.

We stopped walking.

Or more accurately, someone stopped us.

"I got her."

I froze at Colby's voice. It was thick with emotion. Intense. Sounding deeper and older than it had been before.

It hit me like a Mack truck, and I didn't move. Couldn't.

"You got it locked down?" Hades asked. His voice was even, the same tenor I'd heard from him the few times I'd been around him socially. That made me feel ... better, if that was possible. At least the state of me hadn't rattled this man. He'd seen worse. I wasn't the worst. I tried to hold on to that.

"Give me my fucking woman," Colby replied in a tone that made my teeth hurt.

It brooked no argument, it communicated that he was ready to take me by any means necessary.

I had no say in this. Maybe I could've tried to protest, but what was the point? I didn't want to hear my voice right then, didn't want to speak with the same mouth that had pleaded for mercy just moments—minutes? Hours?—ago.

Wordlessly, I was transferred from one biker to another.

I kept my eyes squeezed shut and my body limp as that happened. No matter how careful they were, the movement sent agonizing pain searing through my body. I sank my teeth into my lip, drawing blood so I didn't whimper out loud.

Not that making a whimper would've made any difference, since it was pretty clear I was in a bad way. But I didn't need any more masculine concern. It was practically choking me already.

The tender way that Colby brushed my blood-matted hair paralyzed me.

"Baby," he said in barely a whisper before laying a kiss on my forehead.

I squeezed my eyes shut tighter as I pressed my face into Colby's cut, unable to look him in the eye.

The feel of his chest, his smell mixed with leather and blood, was almost enough to make me want to tear myself apart.

I didn't move, didn't dare breathe, because if I did, then I'd be fighting with everything I had to get out of his arms. And I didn't have much fight left in me. Especially since I knew that Colby wasn't about to let me win. His arms were locked around me while he simultaneously cradled me like a wounded animal.

It did help that I was weaving in and out of consciousness, the journey to the van filled with agony and blank spaces in time.

Conversations happened around me, I was aware of that. Colby didn't contribute much, just stroking my hair and murmuring things to me.

I was hoping to fall into the abyss at some point, but destiny was not that kind.

My nails dug into the flesh of my palms as the van went over bumps in the dirt road, driving us away from the warehouse.

"We need to get Sariah to a hospital," Hansen said cautiously, his poker face on. All the men did. But they were pale. They were holding it together because they were badasses who'd seen a lot of shit, but I guessed my condition was in the upper levels of their experience with fucked-up shit.

Figures, since I barely felt alive.

Yeah, I'd wished for death pretty consistently for an extended period of time. I'd also wished for rescue, but that time had come and gone. Even with my heroes here, death still seemed tempting, especially considering the way they looked at me.

Especially the way Colby looked at me.

His hands were covered in blood. It could've been mine. I was covered in a lot of blood.

Mustn't think about that.

His arms around me, whether they were covered in my blood or someone else's, was a torture in itself. My skin crawled from the hands embracing me like I was broken.

But I didn't say anything.

"Hospital?" I rasped out the word. I recoiled at the sound of my meager, pathetic voice. The thought of the bright lights, the sterile smells, the foreign hands … it terrified me. Even though a small, rational part of my brain told me I would die if I didn't go to a hospital, everything else inside me protested at the idea.

A whimper slipped past my lips when Colby jostled me to put his phone to his ear. "We got her," he said into the phone, arm still around me. "We're en route to the hospital. I'm guessing Violet's already there."

My depleted strength perked up. "Violet?" I croaked. "Why would she be at the hospital?"

Colby's eyes had been on me the entire time, and his eyebrows raised at my question, still listening to whomever was on the phone.

That pissed me off. *I* was the one bleeding and gravely injured. I was pretty sure he should've been giving me his attention, regardless of if it was the President of the fucking United States on the phone.

"Got it," he said. "We'll keep you updated."

"What is wrong with Violet?" I demanded, gripping his hand with my blood-stained fingers. My nails were broken, some of them torn off completely. By pliers or from raking them against the concrete? Both, maybe.

Colby didn't answer right away. He seemed to be weighing his words.

"She's in labor," he told me after looking at Hansen then back to me. "She refused to go to the hospital until we found you."

I almost wanted to laugh. I probably would have if I still retained that ability. My stubborn best friend. My selfless best friend.

"Where is she?"

"The club, but—"

"Then we go to the club," I cut him off.

A muscle pulsed in Colby's cheek. "Sariah, you're bleeding from multiple injuries."

"I'm well aware of that, since I'm the one who was there when aforementioned injuries were inflicted," I snapped at him.

Colby flinched. Actually flinched. I didn't feel any victory in that. I was trying my best to disconnect from him. His hands on me, his tortured expression... I could not survive thinking about what I looked like in his eyes right now.

"Ri." My name escaped him in no more than a whisper. "You're covered in blood... I know you don't want Violet to see you like this."

I blew out a heavy breath. No, I didn't want Violet to see me like this. I didn't want anyone to see me like this. But I'd already had an entire motorcycle club witness my state.

Mustn't think about what they found.

"Then we will get me some clothes," I declared through the pain. It was constant now. Part of me.

Colby stared at me, as if he were measuring my resolve.

I didn't think I looked very strong in that moment, but if anyone tried to stop me from being there for Violet, I'd fight with everything I had. Unfortunately, I didn't have much left of me right now.

———

"I don't like this," Colby grumbled as we walked into the club.

Well, we weren't really doing much walking. I was moving my feet, and he was making it look like he wasn't half dragging, half carrying me. Which he was.

"I don't care what you like or don't like," I lied.

His molars crashed together, his eyes shimmering with fury and concern. And something else.

Terror, maybe.

Whatever it was, I knew this was tearing him apart. Seeing me like this, knowing he'd been too late to save me and now he wasn't even taking me somewhere where they could save my life. I wondered if he could feel that I was slowly dying. Surely not. He would've dragged me to the hospital kicking and screaming if that were the case.

I must try to hide the fact that I'm dying.

Hurting him like this wasn't fair. But then again, life wasn't fair.

We'd hastily covered me in clothes. I hated the weight of them on my skin. I couldn't even remember how they got on my body, couldn't for the life of me remember where they got them from. I suppose that didn't really matter.

But I felt bad for the person whose clothes they were. I had stained them with my blood. Luckily, they were black, so you wouldn't be able to see it from a distance OR more importantly, if you were in the midst of labor and had other things to concentrate on.

"We're not hangin' around," Colby whispered as we walked down the hall toward the source of the screaming. "She gets a glimpse of you, then we're goin' to the fuckin' hospital."

"You don't call the shots here, buddy," I replied weakly. "It's the women in charge here, since one of them is bringing life into this world and the other is on her way out."

Bad joke, but not entirely untrue.

Colby's firm but gentle grip on me tightened, and he grabbed my head to turn it toward his face.

"You are not fuckin' dying, you hear me, Sariah Cardoso?" he growled. "You are stubborn, you are infuriating, and you don't do anything unless you want to do it, even fuckin' dying. And you're *not* doin' that."

I did my best to maintain a stoic expression. "You really think I'm the one who decides whether I live or die?"

"Yes, Sariah, I do," he hissed, his hands unyielding clamps.

We stayed like that for a while, probably too long considering the situation. I felt a moment of peace then, a moment of hope that everything would somehow be okay.

"I cannot do this!" Violet screamed from Elden's room.

Our moment was lost. A good thing too. Ruined people like me didn't get moments. Ruined people like me didn't get anything.

I fought my way out of Colby's arms then made a beeline for Violet, fueled by a sudden burst of energy.

Colby cursed as he rushed to catch up with me. Just in time too, since my surge of strength petered out when I made it to the door.

"Bitch, you better fucking do this," I ordered, looking into the room. Violet was there with a very intense looking Elden along with Kate and a lady who I hoped was a doctor since she was all up in Violet's vajayjay.

Violet herself looked sweaty, pale, exhausted and in agony.

"If I just escaped that sick fuck, then you can give birth to a tiny baby," I added, trying to make my voice sound normal, upbeat. To my ears, it sounded like I was playing a part. I was pulling the strings of a corpse that looked and sounded a lot like me.

Violet's eyes had been squeezed closed, yet they opened when I spoke.

"You're here," she exclaimed, sounding utterly exhausted.

I stretched my mouth into what I hoped was a smile. "It takes a lot more than a deranged serial killer to get me down," I joked weakly.

The world tilted, so I grabbed on to Colby's arm. He held me upright.

I kept my focus on Violet. "Now, please don't embarrass the cause by bitching out at this moment. Let's have this baby."

There it was. My pep talk, such as it was.

And it might've been the last thing I uttered in this world.

Which was fine.

It might've been poetic and all, Violet bringing pure, innocent life into this world and me leaving it, stained and ruined.

The sound of a baby screaming had me sagging against Colby in relief.

Then I felt really fucking cold.

Then I didn't feel much at all. Which was great.

CHAPTER EIGHT

COLBY

SARIAH WOULDN'T WAKE UP.

She was there, shouting at Violet one minute, then she was just gone. I literally felt the life drain out of her.

She went cold, limp, and her skin turned gray.

I gathered her into my arms, and we were speeding to the hospital in record time. Time she didn't have.

"Hold on, poppet," I murmured, clutching her close and kissing her head. She didn't respond. Her chest was moving, but barely. What little breath she had was coming out in horrid, wet, rough croaks.

The death rattle.

I'd heard it before.

Knew that it meant the reaper was coming for what was due.

"You can't have her," I rasped as the van screeched into the parking lot of the hospital. "You can't have her," I repeated, holding a dead woman in my arms. The woman I loved.

It wasn't the first time I'd been in a situation like this. I knew the weight of it. That awful weight. I understood the smell, the feel, everything.

"No!" I roared. "No!"

"Brother," Hansen called from somewhere.

I shook my head to clear the cobwebs from my brain.

Nurses and doctors were staring at me in terror. Or more accurately, at the arm not holding Sariah. It was holding my piece. Pointed at them.

"You need to hand her over," Hansen said calmly.

Then Hades was there. Had he been in the van the entire time? His hands were prying mine from Sariah, letting the doctors and nurses transfer her to a gurney.

My world was swaying, fragmenting. I was living half here and half in the past. In another lifetime.

"Give me the gun, you go to your girl," Hades said.

He was in focus again. Hansen was gone. As was the gurney Sariah had been on just moments ago. Had I fucking blacked out?

"Gun," Hades repeated.

I all but tossed him the gun, sprinting to catch the doctors who were trying to save Sariah's life.

But I'd felt it leave her already.

She was gone.

SARIAH

I remembered Violet screaming.

And a baby being born.

Then the rest rushed in.

Knives. Agony. Blood. His creepy smile as his hands had touched my insides. My screams echoing off the cold, concrete walls.

I tried my best to push all of that aside, to instead focus on the knowledge that my best friend was now a mother.

But the pain, the blood, the rattle of the chains all rushed forward, demanding to be acknowledged.

Though I was on drugs—a lot of them, my mouth dry and full, my body seemed much lighter than it was, and there was no physical pain—I wasn't given the numbness of mind. I wasn't blessed with the initial confusion I saw on the movies when patients woke up ... the whole, "where am I?", "what happened?" kind of thing.

I knew exactly what happened. I'd been very aware that I'd been dying. And I'd been doing it quietly. Not because I wanted to die exactly, but because I didn't want Willow's birth to be further tarnished by the monster who did this.

So I gritted my teeth through it.

And then, when I heard a baby screaming its lungs out, I kind of collapsed.

The rest of the details were fuzzy.

There were a lot of urgent yells from Colby. There were doctors. Beeping.

Then there was nothing at all.

Until waking in the hospital bed.

My vision was foggy, and my throat felt swollen. A hazy memory of waking some time before with something in my throat came to me.

Intubated.

So yeah, it must have been bad.

Though it took great effort, I continued blinking the grit out of my eyes, if only so I could stop seeing the nightmares working behind my lids.

Except they weren't nightmares.

They were memories.

My extremities were numb, but there was a constant pressure on my left hand.

He was blurry at first, but I knew who he was before I'd even regained my sight.

Colby.

Sitting at my bedside, clasping my hand, head bent downward.

He was holding himself rigid. Like if I tapped him with my finger, he'd shatter. I could practically *see* the tension rolling off his body.

"I'm guessing this isn't heaven, the thread count of the sheets would be better," I joked with a rasp.

Colby's head snapped up as I spoke, his hand squeezing mine even harder. I suspected the massive hands might've hurt if not for the drugs. As it was, the look in his eyes speared through me worse than any kind of physical pain.

"Ri," he exhaled, the single syllable drenched in pain.

"In the flesh," I said, continuing to try for the flippant attitude. I couldn't handle the naked emotion on his face. I glanced down at my torso, covered by a gown and a sheet, but I knew what was underneath. "Mostly," I added.

Colby's brows narrowed. "I almost lost you." He laid his lips to my hand.

The tender kiss made my insides twist painfully.

I tried to pull my hand back, but Colby held fast. As I'd expected him to.

His eyes blazed with unshed tears and unsaid vows.

"The bitterest tears shed over graves are for words left unsaid and deeds left undone."

The quote was from Harriet Beecher Stowe. I didn't even know my mind had held on to it. But it was apt. Because that's what Colby was doing. He was a man sitting by a hospital bed that may as well have been a grave.

"Don't," I whispered as he opened his mouth. "I know it might be customary for people, men in particular, to give big romantic speeches at the bedside of the woman who almost died, but we're not going to do that."

Colby's lips pressed into a severe line. He looked like he might push me on it. Which is what these guys were known to do.

I wanted to hold up my palm to stop him, but he still held one of them in his hands, and the other wasn't strong enough to lift from the bed. I knew that because I tried. The best I could get was a wiggle of my fingers.

My weakness scared me. It reminded me of just how powerless I'd been against ... *him*.

I bit back tears. No fucking way would I be crying about this. I couldn't. If I did, I wouldn't be able to stop.

So, I sucked in an unsteady breath and narrowed my eyes on Colby. "I also know you guys are all about claiming women, especially when they're in some kind of danger. It's like an aphrodisiac to you fuckers."

"No, having a horrible fucking glimpse of what the world would be like without the woman I *know* is mine makes it so I'm not so goddamn patient anymore," he gripped my hand tighter. "And it makes it my life mission not to have harm come to you again."

"There is the speech, despite my efforts," I sighed. "It must be physically impossible for you not to make deathbed vows."

"First of all, you're not on your fuckin' deathbed," Colby snapped. "Second of all, you need to stop joking about this shit. I watched your heartbeat stop. *Stop*, Ri. I saw the doctors giving you CPR." Colby's voice shook.

My chest burned. I was an exposed nerve right now, aching to lean into this. To tell Colby that he was the person I was thinking of during my whole ordeal. To let the story play out ... the one where I let myself admit I was his, get out of the hospital, get together, live happily ever after.

Oh, I wanted that with a desperation I didn't know I was capable of possessing. Before, I'd been fighting him off for some valid reasons, but mostly because I enjoyed it. Because I kind of liked the chase, liked playing games.

I cursed myself for being so immature.

Because now I'd never have my happily ever after. Not with Colby. Not now. Not after what happened to me. I was broken in a way I couldn't even comprehend. All I knew for certain was there was no way I could stand to be loved, treasured, cherished.

There was no way I could say all of that out loud, though.

Never. Because Colby would just take all of that as his eternal calling of proving to me that I was worthy and that we were meant to be together.

The simple thought of all the energy it would take to fight against him made me want to sink into the mattress never to return.

"I don't ... I can't do this right now," I told Colby honestly, my voice sounding pitiful. "I don't have the strength to go into this, so I'm asking you to stop."

Colby stared at me for a long time. I wanted to look away. I hated seeing the way he looked at me. Hated what that made me.

Colby's posture relaxed a smidge.

"Okay, baby," he murmured softly.

I didn't relax. Not even a little.

But thankfully, I did lose consciousness.

––––––––

The next day, I slept more than I was awake. Colby was by my side every time I woke up. He hadn't changed his clothes or seemingly moved from the spot.

As much as I didn't want him to see me, couldn't stand the weight of his eyes on me, the prospect of being alone in the sterile room was much worse.

Every time I woke, I didn't gently rise to consciousness. No, I jerked awake, sweating, terrified, convinced I could feel the weight of a chain on my ankle.

Each time that happened, Colby was there, quietly reminding me that I was okay, that I was safe.

The words didn't help much. I was not okay, nor was I safe. I wasn't even out of that warehouse. Not really. Something grave told me I'd never fully escape from that warehouse.

Doctors came and went, telling me things I already knew. That I had almost died. That there had been massive blood loss. That it was a small miracle I'd survived. That I'd be scarred for the rest of my life.

I hadn't wanted to look underneath all of the bandages on my torso, which was where the worst of my injuries were, but I did it anyway. There was nothing to be afraid of anymore. I'd seen pure evil, survived the worst of the worst, all the fear had been sucked out of my marrow. And I couldn't fear my own body. I had to live in it for the rest of my life. I had to make myself familiar with the new wounds.

And they weren't pretty.

There were a lot of punctures, some small and shallow, others ragged and much, much deeper. They were red and angry and promised to make my favorite midriff baring outfits a thing of the past.

Unfortunately, as I was growing stronger, I was awake for longer periods of time. Therefore, I was subject to Colby continuing to do the whole 'you are mine' routine. That routine consisted of him giving me intense looks, his jaw flexing whenever my injuries were brought up or I winced in any kind of way, and him trying to control my life.

"You need to tell Violet you're here," he said. "And you need to fuckin' eat."

I scowled at him, then at the tray of hospital food. "This isn't food."

"I'll go and get you whatever you want," he offered immediately.

I rolled my eyes, tempted to send him off on an errand but terrified to be alone in this room.

"If you didn't notice, I'm on a bunch of painkillers right now and recovering from near death. Although you might expect me to be craving a cheeseburger, a couple of bites of this is about the best I'm gonna keep down for the foreseeable future."

Colby dragged a palm over his scruffy chin shadow.

"You can buy me some chili cheese fries when I get out of

here," I added for reasons unknown. When I got out of there, I needed to get as far away from Colby and his orders, his proclamations, and his jaw ticcing as humanly possible.

"I'm gonna hold you to that," Colby said as if he were reading my mind.

Yeah, I was gonna have to deal with that … soon. But not now. We had other fish to fry.

"You are not telling Violet shit," I told him with narrowed eyes. "If a single biker ruins her first week of motherhood with this bullshit, I'll be making you all eunuchs."

"You almost dying in the goddamn hospital is not *bullshit*," Colby seethed.

"I'm alive, aren't I?" I sighed. "And you need to lighten the fuck up. If anyone gets to be moody and pissy, it really should be *me*."

Colby looked properly chastised, and I almost felt a little guilty for milking my condition. But if a girl couldn't milk it when she was almost killed by a serial killer, when could she?

"Okay, we won't call Violet," Colby conceded.

I sucked in a breath, picking up a cracker on the tray of food and nibbling at it.

"See?" I told him between bites. "You lose some, you win some."

"I nearly fuckin' lost everything."

Again, with the brooding.

"If we're not calling Violet, we're calling your parents," he informed me. "They're not your emergency contact, Violet is. So I need their number."

I shook my head to make sure I wasn't having some kind of episode. But Colby remained there, clad in black, looking way too good for a guy who hadn't changed clothes or slept properly in days.

"You won't be getting their number." I tried to act calm. I was pretty well practiced at expertly diverting all conversation away from my parents. Hell, I'd even done that with Violet, my closest friend.

My closest friend who I was keeping a bunch of secrets from. Secrets that were no doubt common knowledge now.

Can't think about that. One thing at a time.

Colby glanced over to the chair where my purse was sitting. Luckily, they'd retrieved it when they found my car on the side of the road. It felt like a relic from another life.

"I'll just get their number from your phone," he shrugged, making to get up.

"You can't call my parents," I shrieked, trying to get off the bed but unfortunately not having enough energy to do so. Even my voice was thin and weak.

Nonetheless, Colby paused. "Sariah," he said gently, and fuck, did I hate the gentleness. "You almost died, baby. Your parents need to know. They need to see you."

"They do *not* need to know, and they especially don't need to see me," I argued, my already withered heart shriveling some more.

I held up my hand when Colby opened his mouth, presumably to argue.

"If you call them, they would come." Tired already, it took effort to speak, my voice scratchy. "Because their only child is in the hospital, and they would want to be by her side because that's the godly thing to do." I kept my eyes on Colby, though I ached to look away. "Then they'd walk into this hospital and see a bunch of outlaw bikers, and the guards you probably have at my door even though the threat is over."

Colby didn't say anything to this, I assumed because he knew I was right.

"This would just disturb them," I continued. "They'd avert their eyes and try their best to ignore them, but then they'd come in here... And you'll be here."

Again, Colby didn't argue this because, again, I was right.

"And then they wouldn't be able to ignore you, but they'd try," I sighed. "Because they'd be presented with this." I weakly waved my hand down my body. "And it would definitely shock and upset them because despite all of their flaws, they do love me." Inexplicably, tears stung the backs of my eyes. That made me angry. I'd told myself that I'd shed enough tears over them.

"But, eventually, the shock and concern would recede, and they'd find a way to subtly let me know that this wouldn't have happened if I hadn't abandoned them and God," I plucked at the sheet beneath me, forcing my voice to stay even.

Colby stared at me for a long time. I guessed that everything about my past had been dug up when I was taken. I hadn't dwelled too much on that, since there was a whole lot more for me to dwell on. I'd have to face up to it all eventually, though.

This was the first time I'd spoken about my parents to anyone. Even Violet.

I expected Colby to push it on my parents. Doing so was part of his nature, after all. He'd been intent on knowing me before all of this happened. Now he had a captive audience.

But he just nodded succinctly. "Okay, poppet."

Then I let out a long breath.

One battle won. About a million more to come.

———

Colby had put my phone and some other belongings at my bedside, my toiletries in the bathroom. I was wearing my own pajamas. I'd put them on only because it was sweet of him to go to the effort, but the reality was that the silk against my skin felt like razor blades. I was no longer the person who bought pajamas like these. It felt wrong. Sickening. Pretty things against my ruined body reminded me of every cut, every incision, every plea I'd made.

But I was white-knuckling my way through it. I had a feeling a lot more of that was ahead of me. A lot of white-knuckling.

Colby was out in the hall, talking to the doctor. He did that a lot. I guessed he was trying to figure out when they were going to discharge me. That didn't interest me. Actually, the thought of leaving terrified me. Discharge meant reality.

But I couldn't stay in the hospital forever. Violet had already been blowing up my phone, asking where I was, if I was okay, when she could come over.

I'd managed to hold her back by telling her I was fine and just wanted to recover a little more before seeing the baby.

I knew she wasn't convinced because she was continually calling me. And I continually ignored the calls, texting her saying that I was 'sleeping' or whatever the fuck.

The Old Ladies were all blowing up my phone too. It obviously was not a secret, what happened to me. But it seemed so far, the bikers were keeping their mouths shut about my stay in the hospital. Which surprised me since Violet said they gossiped like schoolgirls. Maybe they were that afraid of me. Or of my fragile mental state.

I had managed to fend off all of the women's texts and calls thus far, but Ollie was not one to give up.

If you don't answer the fucking phone right now, I'm flying down there.

My fingers went numb. Ollie was not one for empty threats. Ollie was also petrified of flying.

Though I really didn't want to, I answered when my phone buzzed a few seconds later.

"Holy fuck, bitch," Ollie snapped.

"Hello to you too," I muttered.

"You are lucky that I can hack into hospital databases, so I knew you were going to survive," she said in a surprisingly thick voice.

Ollie was rattled. I could hear it. I'd become somewhat immune to the way Colby had been looking at me and speaking to me. But hearing one of my best friends sounding rattled, hearing *Ollie* sound so rattled, it sent rocks to the pit of my stomach.

This was reality. This was a taste of what I was going to get when I got out of this hospital and had to face everyone in my life.

Before all of this, I'd been proud of the family I'd found since mine disowned me. Now I wished that not a person in the world cared about me. Somehow, I had decided that that would be easier than seeing the pain, grief and pity on people's faces.

"I'm like a cockroach. I was always going to survive," I joked.

"It was pretty fucking touch and go," she replied.

I swallowed hard. "But I'm here."

"I'm so sorry," she whispered, her voice broken. "I should've found out who the fuck was earlier."

"You stop that right now," I demanded. "No one fucking knew. I had dinner with the fuck and didn't know. The Sons had their best hacker on this too."

"Their best hacker is a man and not fucking *me*," she rebuked. "He should not have slipped past me. If I had—"

"If ifs and buts were candy and nuts, we'd all have a merry Christmas," I interrupted her. "You are a fucking badass. You are the best hacker in the land. Shit happens."

"Yes, shit happens," she agreed. "Your hairstylist fucks up your hair. You have a fender bender. You text the person you were talking shit to someone else about. *Getting kidnapped by a serial killer is not 'shit happens'.*"

Ollie was spiraling. Likely because of the situation, but I knew her well enough to understand she had probably been up for far too long and had far too many energy drinks, punishing herself for not obtaining the information sooner.

"Ollie," I stated firmly. "This is not on you. This is not on anyone but him. And I know you would never let that fucker win by letting him blame you."

She huffed over the phone.

I almost wanted to smile.

I hadn't done that yet.

"You coming back to school?" she asked.

Nausea swam through my stomach at just the thought of it. School. Assignments. Classes. It seemed so fucking arbitrary now. Plus, if I wanted to become a psychiatrist, I'd have years more in school. Years.

I struggled to hold down my meager breakfast.

"Of course," I lied smoothly.

"Okay, well, keep in touch, or I'll track your phone."

"You already track my phone."

"Touché," she muttered. There was a pause, a long one. "Love you, Ri."

My lip trembled. "Love you too," I croaked.

My hand was shaking, barely strong enough to put the phone back down. That was just a taste of what I was going to get once I got out of here, and I was already exhausted.

There was no way I could handle more of that.

But I didn't have any other choice.

———

I woke up to a dark shape at my bedside. That wasn't outside the norm. Actually, this was the norm. I wouldn't have known what to do with myself if I woke up alone in this hospital room. I'd been trying to tell myself, and him, that he didn't need to be here. But he didn't listen to me, and I was secretly thankful for that.

But it wasn't Colby sitting at my bedside.

It was Hades.

My body tensed as I locked eyes with him, and I was hurled back into the moment he'd found me in the warehouse.

He was a scary dude. Not just because of his tattoos, including the ones on his face which were badass but intimidating. His whole look, his whole demeanor, made you realize you were in the presence of someone who had done dark shit. Seen dark shit. This was a whole other breed of person, rare and fucking deadly.

But that wasn't what he was for me in that warehouse.

He was my dark fucking knight. He was the only man capable of wading into that dark, horrendous place I was residing in to drag me out.

"Hi," I croaked, feeling uncomfortable.

He didn't reply right away, his eyes skating over my body. "He's gonna die slowly," he told me in a way that was meant to reassure me. Like it was a gift.

I supposed for a man like Hades, it was a gift. Torturing my almost murderer was his version of a fruit basket.

"Thank you," I wheezed. "For being there."

He nodded once. "This is gonna fuck you up," he said. "Gonna take you to a place not many people come back from. Doesn't matter how strong you are, how many people you have around you." He paused, his eyes darting around the room. "And you are strong. The fact that you were still breathing when we found you shows me that. Most people give up in that kinda situation. Before the body gives up, the mind lets go. Lesser people would've been gone by the time I arrived. You weren't."

He let that sink in while my heart thundered, struggling to wrench myself out of that terrible memory.

"I feel like I am gone," I admitted without planning to.

He nodded curtly. Not with sympathy. With understanding. "A part of you is. And you're gonna have to decide whether you're gonna go lookin' for who you were before or turn into someone else. There's no right way or wrong choice. You've got people whatever path you choose. It's likely you'll either forget or resent that for a while, but you got people. And you got me. When you feel those demons scratching at your door and you've got no way out, you call me." He motioned to the phone on my bedside table. "Number's already in there."

I bit my lip until I tasted blood so I wouldn't let the tears fall. Crying would've felt like a failure in front of someone like Hades.

Because I couldn't speak, I just nodded rapidly.

He didn't say anything else, just got up from the chair and walked from the room.

Hades and Colby met at the door. They did the weird, man chin-lift thing before Hades left.

Apparently, I wouldn't get a reprieve.

Colby's eyes slid over me, assessing. Concerned.

"What was he doing here?" Colby asked, holding two coffees and a paper bag with grease at the bottom.

"Telling me his beauty routine," I replied, gratefully taking the coffee. "He has flawless skin."

"Sariah," he warned.

I rolled my eyes. "I am not required to tell you about every conversation I have with someone."

"My brother was talking to my woman, and you've got tears in your eyes. I need to know something."

The need I had to escape was overwhelming. I wanted to run.

"Can you stop with the 'you're mine' bullshit?" I groaned. I wanted to yell, scream, but my body wasn't strong enough. "We are not fated. There is no other-worldly connection here." I waved my hands between us, gasping at the agony that came from the simple gesture. "You were interested in me at first because of my tits, ass and face."

"Not in that order," Colby smirked. Or at least he was trying to. His smile looked nothing like it had before. It tore up my insides.

"You were interested in me because of my physical attributes," I scowled. "There was attraction. If we'd given in to that, if I was easy, had let you fuck me the first day you met me, then all of your interest would've been gone. But I didn't. I said no to you, and that made me infinitely more interesting. You only decided I was 'yours' because I wouldn't give myself to you. So please, let's stop pretending it's anything more than that."

Colby was no longer smirking. The lines bracketing his mouth were hard, eyes filled with fury.

"You were mine the second you strutted into my club wearing head to toe pink and an expression like you were ready to fight me or fuck me," he growled. "You were mine when you showed how you were willing to drop everything for your friend. You were mine when you didn't even blink when my brother pulled a gun. When you fought for women who most people dismiss.

"Jesus Christ, Sariah." Colby angrily ran his hand through his hair. "Don't know how to make it clearer to you. Livin' this kind of life takes a particular kind of man. And that man needs a particular kind of woman. Sure, it's nice if she's got a fuckin' gorgeous face, amazin' tits and an ass that gets you hard just by looking at it."

Though he was really mad, and I hadn't thought I was awake … down there, I felt a flutter below my waistline.

But Colby wasn't done.

"Sure, you have all those things, babe," he continued. "But that's not what makes you mine. It's because you're not afraid to throw attitude, because you're loyal to those you love, to a fucking fault. Because you can handle anything this life throws at you. It's not just that you're the perfect Old Lady, which you fucking are. It's that you're perfect for *me*."

The speech was good.

Like, take your breath away type good.

Like put it in *Gray's Anatomy* or any romantic movie type good.

It almost got me.

Almost.

But then he had to use the 'P' word.

Colby was breathing heavily, staring at me, invitation in his eyes. He looked ready to cross the distance between us and claim me. Properly.

And fuck, did a large part of me want that.

But even that part of me was tarnished, battered, ruined.

"I'm not perfect for you, Colby," I whispered. "I'm not perfect for anyone."

He opened his mouth to argue, and for once, destiny decided to cut me a break. The doctor came in with news of my discharge and a lot of aftercare instructions, prescriptions and information to quell any conversations about our relationship or lack thereof.

I wasn't off the hook, though. I wouldn't be until I figured out a way to push Colby away—for good—or run from him.

CHAPTER
NINE

"SHE'S the most beautiful thing I've ever seen," I whispered, staring down at the scrunched-up face of the newborn baby.

"She is, isn't she?" Violet's smile was tired yet dazzling.

My best friend had given birth—without any drugs and at the club—less than a week ago, and she still looked absolutely gorgeous.

There were slight shadows under her eyes, but other than that, she had the whole new mother glow-thing going on.

Then again, she had a husband who was constantly hovering in the background—just in case he needed to jump in front of a bullet for his two girls—and a mom who was in the kitchen, washing dishes from all the gourmet food she had made.

Macy had just left after dropping off a giant care package. Freya had done a few loads of laundry, folding and putting it all away before she left.

Caroline was on a coffee run.

The whole 'it takes a village' thing was really in play here.

You could feel it, smell it, *taste* the love in this room. It was sour on my tongue.

I was tarnishing it with all of my ... wrongness. I couldn't escape feeling it. Because of the way people looked at me. With concern, with pain. With the knowledge of what I'd been through. Maybe only rudimentary knowledge, to be fair, because if they really knew what had happened, I wouldn't be able to stand anyone looking at me.

Even holding this angelic, innocent baby seemed wrong. I shouldn't have been touching her, corrupting her with what I was. But I couldn't let that show. Couldn't let anyone catch a glimpse of just how badly I was really doing. Then, out of love, they'd want to be there, want to help me recover. I couldn't have them knowing there was no recovery for me.

"Your Aunty Sariah has the cutest Gucci booties for you," I cooed, yet my voice sounded strange, hollow, superficial.

"*Gucci* booties, Sariah?" Violet repeated. "She's gonna grow out of them in like a second."

I smiled up at my best friend. The gesture was painful, like my cheeks were splitting open. "Then you and hubby better get started on baby number two."

Violet blushed, as if she hadn't just given birth. "As much as Willow is absolutely the center of my universe, I'm not anywhere near ready to push another human out of me. Especially when I've got a degree to finish and our house to design."

Her eyes trekked over to Elden who was watching the scene from the barstools in the kitchen, Colby beside him. The two of them were meant to be talking amongst themselves, but they were both just staring at us in that intense, possessive way of theirs.

I leaned in to sniff Willow's head, inhaling that perfect baby smell. I hated that it was corrupted with the scent of dried blood and my own vomit. For a second, I wasn't in Violet and Elden's little cottage that smelled like chicken and rosemary.

For a second, a long second, I was chained by the ankle in a warehouse, my blood chilling my skin as it left my body.

"Sariah?" Violet's probing question jerked me out of my flashback.

Once again, I was with my friend, holding her newborn baby.

I struggled to paste on a smile, feeling revulsion at myself for thinking such despicable things while holding a baby.

As if on cue, Willow wriggled and let out a cry.

Babies could sense things. Like when they were in the presence of evil. And I was stained with it.

Elden practically launched off the barstool and was across the room before Violet could even lean forward.

"Got her," he said, reaching down with his big hands, expertly taking the baby from my arms and cradling her against his chest.

Elden was a pretty grim motherfucker. Smoking hot with the rough beard liberally dotted with gray, intense blue eyes and huge muscles. But, except for when he was around Violet, I'd never seen the fucker gentle. That was when he turned into a completely different person. He … melted.

And he did the same for his daughter.

It was also a pretty sight to see the big bad biker cradling his baby daughter.

Violet was ogling her husband unabashedly.

A genuine smile split my lips then, seeing the love between the three of them. The family that they'd become.

And I was an intruder, caught in a moment she didn't belong in.

Suddenly, I felt like my skin was two sizes too small for my body.

I tried to push off the sofa and bolt, but I was still healing and moving a little slower these days.

Colby did a really good rendition of Elden's earlier move, leaping off the barstool and crossing the space between us in the blink of an eye.

I would've yelled at him for being overprotective except I kind of stumbled into his arms from the head rush I got from getting up too quickly.

"Easy," he murmured, steadying my hips then brushing my hair from my face. "You okay?" His tone was soft. Concerned. Any woman would've likely swooned at a biker being so tender with her.

But I fucking hated where the tenderness was coming from. He was waiting for me to fall apart. He was treating me like I was this broken, weak thing he needed to preserve. To save, somehow. Yet the time for saving had come and gone. If only he could understand that. I wasn't the victim anymore. I feared I'd turned into a monster of my own.

"I'm good, cowboy, chill," I told him, stepping from his arms. Or at least trying to.

He tightened his grasp on my hip, communicating his disagreement.

"I can stand on my own, Colby," I said through my teeth.

He didn't let me go, he just stared at me like there weren't a whole bunch of people in the room. Like he *could* stare at me like that. Like I was worth staring at.

Panic clawed at my throat, and my stomach curdled even though all I'd had to eat was copious amounts of coffee and a few bites of the muffins Kate had made earlier.

I needed to escape. Fuck, in that moment, being back in that warehouse would've been preferable. I could handle a crazy killer torturing me. A hot outlaw being tender with me? Nope.

"I need to talk to Sariah," Violet blurted.

I glanced at her in relief, wondering if my best friend saw my panic or if it was just a happy accident. Either way, I capitalized on the opportunity.

"Why don't you go and do ... whatever it is you do," I told Colby. "I'm going to talk to my best friend, and I can walk on my own two feet as I do." I resisted the urge to poke my tongue out at him as I stomped out of the room.

Luckily, Violet followed me quickly after and grabbed my arm in order for me to lean on her. Which was good because I was pretty close to collapsing, and that would've really ruined my storm out.

"You literally just gave birth. It should be *me* helping *you* walk down the hall," I whined, hating how vulnerable I was. Hating how every step was a reminder of what had happened to me. I was desperate to be strong, self-sufficient, but that went out the window when I couldn't walk unassisted down a fucking hallway.

"Babe, you are recovering from being attacked by a serial killer," she countered. "Birth is a completely natural thing for the body to go through ... *that* is not." Her voice trembled slightly as if she might burst into tears again. She'd already done that once when Colby and I had arrived. She'd all but collapsed into my arms and sobbed for what seemed like five straight minutes. My eyes had stayed dry. My mouth had filled with blood from my teeth tearing into the flesh of my cheek, trying to survive my friend's arms around my body.

I frowned. "Still, it's also natural for the mother to be able to rest and be spoiled by everyone around her after carrying the baby for nine months, then pushing her out."

Though I'd gone through some seriously gruesome shit, I still shuddered at the thought of Violet pushing a human being out of her vagina a few days ago.

Violet smiled as we sat down in the armchairs in her bedroom, the French doors opened to give us a great view of the garden and the desert beyond.

"Have you seen this place?" she waved her hand around. "I am barely able to lift a glass of water without someone offering to help."

That was true. "As it should be," I shrugged. "You deserve this."

"Babe, you deserve it too." Violet reached over to hold my hand. "You deserve to rest. To heal. You deserve to be taken care of. You don't have to always be strong."

My world rocked at my bestie's thoughtful words. She saw me. Even in the midst of one of the biggest changes a woman went through in her life, she was watching me. Because that's the kind of person that Violet was.

I battled against tears, determined not to be the victim.

"Girl, I have to be strong," I told her in a choked voice. "The only other option is letting him win."

It was the most I'd spoken about … him since they found me. Colby had tried to coax information out of me, vibrating with rage and concern as he did.

"You saw my injuries," I told him from where I lay in the hospital bed. "Use your imagination."

"I am using my imagination," he growled, nostrils flaring. "That's the goddamn problem."

Fortunately, a nurse chose that moment to come in, and he was forced to shelve the conversation. I'd shut him down whenever he tried to bring it up. Colby wanted to press me, I saw that. But he held himself back because he was treating me with care.

And although my actions seemed to the contrary, I was treating him with care too. There was no way I could tell him that even his worst imaginings paled in comparison to the horror I'd been through.

"He lost, Sariah," Violet said softly. "He lost because you fought him and survived. And he's … gone."

Neither of us really knew if he was technically gone or not since no one had seen hide nor hair of him. Both of us had been kind of busy.

But we knew he wasn't in police custody. No way would any of the Sons let that happen. And apparently, the local cops were back on the Sons of Templar's payroll since no one had come to interview me.

I also knew that Colby had very bruised and bloody knuckles that were only just now healing.

The sheriff was either dead or wishing he was. That should've mattered to me a lot more than it did. I should've been demanding to know where they were keeping him, if he was alive. I should've been vying for a piece of him, to watch him die, maybe even kill him myself.

But that wouldn't change what he'd done to me.

And even worse, I didn't think I was strong enough to face him. I wanted to be the badass bitch who strode in there with her head held high and a Glock held steady. I wanted to impress the outlaws with the vengeance I could dish out. But I knew for a fact that if I even tried such a thing, I'd vomit or pass out or do something that would yet again cement Colby's assertions that I needed to be taken care of.

"I don't want to talk about him," I said, my voice quivering.

Violet's forehead crumpled with concern. I could see her battling whether to push me a little more or give me space. I knew that look because it was on Colby's face whenever we were together.

"Okay," she conceded. "But we are going to talk about *something*."

I sighed. I'd been waiting for this. Violet knew—just like everybody in the club knew—why I'd been targeted as a victim. Ollie had called to give me the rundown on what the Sons knew, still spitting tacks of fury about the whole situation.

I appreciated her anger. It was a lot easier to swallow than the pity.

Though I was recovering from a whole lot, it was always in the back of my mind that the entire club and everyone connected to it knew that I had been earning all my money from taking my clothes off on camera.

Not that I thought they were talking about me or judging me. That wasn't their style. Freya, Hades's wife, had been a stripper. Macy, Hansen's wife, used to be a 'club girl.' Everyone was about alternative lifestyles and never cast judgment on anyone else.

But Violet was different.

"Why didn't you tell me?" she asked, not with accusation, with a delicate kind of hurt.

Which, in my opinion, was worse than any kind of anger. Violet and I didn't have secrets, at least that's what she'd thought. She'd pretty much spilled everything about her life to me the first day I met her.

And I'd returned the favor by lying to her, by refusing to talk about my background or my family. Not because I didn't trust her.

I trusted her with my life.

That was the problem. My life was a very careful house of cards I'd created. Too much truth and it would all come crumbling down.

But hadn't it all tumbled already?

I nibbled on my lip, trying to find the words.

"Is it because you thought I'd judge you?" she asked, her eyes welling up. "Because I'd never—"

I reached out to grasp her hand, the first time I'd initiated touch with someone since before the warehouse. "Babe, I knew for a fact that you wouldn't judge me," I told her honestly. "I just…" I sighed. "I liked that you knew me as Sariah who was confident, who had no cares, perhaps rich parents and not the unwanted black sheep in the family who could only take her clothes off in order to keep her in designer duds."

"I know you as the Sariah that you *are*." Violet's eyes continued to shimmer. "In here." She pointed to my heart. "I understand why you wanted to keep it to yourself, craft your own identity, but you don't have to hide anything from me. It won't change how I feel about you."

I smiled, forcing my tears back. "Thanks, babe."

"Are you … still going to do it?" she probed gingerly.

I tugged at a loose thread on my pants. She again asked the question without judgment, only curiosity, maybe a little concern.

I'd been thinking about it, trying to think about what happened now. What my life looked like now.

"No," I replied. "I always knew that wasn't something I'd do forever. Apart from purchasing an excellent wardrobe, I am somewhat savvy with the stock market and crypto currency." I grinned. "So I can officially retire from the business. It served its purpose … a little too well," I joked.

Violet didn't smile.

"Do you want to talk about it?" she asked. "What happened while he … had you?"

"No," I answered without hesitation, the room suddenly freezing.

Violet blanched at my tone, maybe my expression. I'd tried to school it. "I can't even begin to understand what you went through, but I know that keeping it inside isn't going to help you heal. You can talk about it."

My nails bit into my palms.

The knife tore into my stomach as vomit and bile stained the side of my mouth. He smiled when I let out a cry.

"No, I can't," I shook my head.

"Sweetie—"

"I can't, Violet," I bit out, harsher than I'd intended.

Violet's eyes widened, looking surprised but not hurt. For a second, she looked like she was going to push it further, causing me to strike out like a cornered animal. And I really didn't want to hurt my best friend. Really, really. But I feared I wouldn't have a choice if she pushed.

"Okay," Violet relented quietly. "Okay. But you can talk to me. Whenever you're ready."

I nodded, relieved. "I know."

"Promise?" she asked, raising a brow.

"Promise," I lied.

I wouldn't be talking about what happened to me to another living soul.

———

"Knock knock."

I looked up from the TV. I was on the fourth season of Real Housewives and was slowly losing touch with reality … just how I liked it.

Kate walked through my front door with a large basket. Declan was nowhere to be found, which didn't surprise me. His father was absolutely in love with him and barely let him—or Kate, for that matter—out of his sight.

"I brought pastries!" Kate announced, holding up the basket. "And coffee." She set the basket down on my kitchen counter then went about finding plates. Kate had been here often enough that she knew her way around. She'd helped me move in and shop for furniture.

I gathered myself up from my spot on the sofa, feeling somewhat embarrassed that it was the middle of the day, and I was wearing the same clothes I'd slept in and was watching trash TV.

Kate didn't act as if I had anything to be embarrassed about. She hummed softly as she moved around the kitchen.

I didn't know Kate before she was married to Swiss. From what Violet told me, she wasn't always like this. She used to wear neatly pressed designer clothes, always had perfect hair, and acted like a "Stepford robot" when her husband was around.

It was hard to connect the woman Violet told me her mother used to be with the woman who was practically dancing around my kitchen. Kate wore faded jeans, spike-heeled, bright pink shoes and a light pink tank. Her hair was styled in messy curls, and she had 'biker babe' makeup on.

Sometimes she dressed up in designer gear, but most of the time she wore this kind of stuff. And she drank, smiled easily, and bickered with her husband who was completely infatuated with her.

In short, Kate was kind of my idol.

She had gone through a terrible eighteen years being married to a man who abused her. Though I couldn't fathom what that would be like, I figured that it would scoop out the insides of a person, leave them empty.

But Kate was anything but empty. She acted like she'd never had a moment of pain in her life.

I supposed she gave me a little bit of hope.

Maybe I wouldn't always be this empty.

"I kind of went overboard," she smiled as she arranged a plethora of baked goods on a large serving tray I didn't even know I had. One of the women had likely brought it then put it away. I was never in my kitchen, but it had been well utilized by the women of the Sons of Templar MC in the weeks since the attack. I'd barely left the apartment, knowing the media and murder tourists had descended on our small town. Thanks to Kate and the others, I was never without food, booze or company.

"You didn't have to do that," I said as I perched myself on a barstool. I knew better than to offer to help her with anything. No one had let me lift a finger in my own apartment, even though I was finally gaining some of my strength back. Physically, at least.

Kate stopped arranging a stack of pastries to look at me. "Yes, I did," she replied. "I'm sure Freya's been by with all sorts of vegan goodness ... tasty and healthy." Her nose screwed up.

Freya had indeed been around with a bunch of stuff that looked appetizing and might've tasted it too if I'd had the guts to taste it.

"But sometimes you need tasty and decidedly unhealthy." Kate waggled her brows then pushed the plate and coffee toward me.

I took the coffee first, thankful for it. My caffeine consumption prior to this had already been on the high side. Now I was probably in danger from having some kind of cardiac episode from overstimulation. Not that I noticed. I still felt exhausted every moment of the day.

When Kate settled on the other side of the counter, I could tell by her energy what was coming.

Kate and I had become close the moment we met. Before I got

the apartment, I'd stay at her and Swiss's place, even if Violet wasn't there. She'd accepted me not just as Violet's friend but as a member of the family. As had Swiss.

Both of them had been around since I was discharged, both treading softly.

The entire club had shown their support in one way or another. Cautiously.

Which I hated.

Hades's visit to the hospital was the only interaction that didn't make me feel ruined and ... wrong.

Kate's soft and loving gaze was almost too much to bear.

Where was a shot of tequila and a ketamine chaser when you needed it?

"I know what you're going to say," I tried to head her off at the pass. "I'm fine."

Her eyes shimmered as she rounded the counter to sit on the stool next to me. I hated her closeness. She smelled clean, of expensive perfume, of a life I'd never have.

"No, you're not fine," she stated simply.

I clutched my coffee cup, surprised it didn't explode.

"Something terrible happened to you, honey," Kate murmured softly. "And you didn't have your mom there when you came out of it."

"It's better that she wasn't," I sniffed, shocked that she was even mentioning my mom. But it was painfully obvious that no one outside the town of Garnett had come to my aid. That I had no one. No family. I might've felt more shame over that if I wasn't already overwhelmed by things to be ashamed of.

"Maybe." Kate stroked my face. It felt like knives opening up the skin of my jaw. "But I want to tell you, from the second I met you, I've considered you part of my family. And I've got some experience in the deadbeat mom department, although I'm not about to comment on whether your mom is one or not because I don't know anything about her."

I nibbled on a pastry, leaning away from her touch. For all the things that my mother was, she was never a deadbeat. She took care of me when I was sick. She cooked my favorite food when I was in a bad mood. She'd told me she loved me. She brushed my hair. Bandaged skinned knees.

My chest ached inexplicably.

"You're like a daughter to me," Kate continued. "And it's my job to be here for you as much as I can be for as long as you need me."

I tasted old pennies as I ruined my lips with my teeth. My own blood in my mouth was the only thing that calmed me enough when people were being caring. Nice.

"I appreciate that," I told her, voice cracking.

I thought I might just bite my own lip off if she stared at me any longer.

But Kate was a mom, so she had the mom sense, and she stepped back, returning to the kitchen to clean things, rearrange my fridge.

"Colby isn't going to go away, you know, honey," she told me from the fridge.

I tore apart a croissant so it would look like I had consumed some. "I know," I sighed.

She closed the door and focused on me. "You'll feel good things again, honey," she said with conviction. "You're worthy of them."

My teeth locked as I tried to keep my expression even. I couldn't even speak, couldn't even utter a lie.

Luckily, Kate didn't continue, returning to her tasks and keeping the subjects light.

But her words had settled inside me like a boulder.

———

If there was ever a time to fall apart, it was after you survived getting tortured by a serial killer.

There was literally no one in the world who would argue with a girl who decided to take to her bed for like a week after surviving that. Even if it were for a month.

There would be no one in the world, and especially no one in Garnett, New Mexico, no one involved with the Sons of Templar MC, who would argue with me for doing such a thing.

To the contrary, almost every single person in the club and connected to it would likely encourage such an action. They'd do it with understanding words, soft, pitying gazes. They'd surround me with the love and warmth and family they'd created, allowing me to heal amongst them.

As one of them.

If circumstances were different, the old Sariah would've jumped at such an invitation. I'd yearned to be part of a family for years. Pretty much since I'd left my own behind—or when they kicked me to the curb—and set out to find people who wouldn't judge me. Would accept me. Wouldn't make me feel like trash.

The Sons of Templar ticked all those boxes and more.

The men were hot as balls, dangerous and muscled yet somehow respectful. They knew how to have a good time, weren't afraid to cause a little chaos and lived for sex, booze and their patch.

And the women... In my opinion, the women were more badass than the guys with their motorcycles, guns, muscles and tatts. The women were their backbone. They had killer fucking style, they partied hard, and each of them had conquered their own demons before coming here. Each of them served as a pillar that held this whole place up. And they had all welcomed me with open arms.

The problem was, I wasn't the old Sariah anymore.

I didn't even think of myself as a person.

I didn't feel like one. I felt like an object. Something carved up, ruined, beyond redemption. An artifact of a horrific crime.

I wasn't anything.

And I certainly wasn't Colby's, like he kept saying.

As history went with the Sons of Templar, when a member decided a woman was 'his,' it was only a matter of time before the woman in question accepted that with glee. If a time even existed when a woman had fought it.

But I was going to fight.

For my life.

What was left of it, at least.

———

"What the fuck are you doing out here in the middle of the night?" Colby rumbled from behind me.

I'd figured he'd find me sooner or later. Maybe he was tracking my phone. I wouldn't put it past him to have bribed some doctor to implant a tracking chip under my skin. I'd been impressed with myself for managing to get out of the apartment in the middle of the night without him noticing.

I didn't look at him, though I did hold my breath as his warmth pressed against my arm. I had to do my best not to inhale his scent, not to let him too close. Colby had noticed that I had somewhat of an ... aversion to him being near, and he'd made adjustments accordingly. Unless he was in protective alpha mode.

Which he definitely was right now.

"I'm ... tying up some loose ends," I replied.

Colby was likely frowning at me right now, but I had other things to do.

I tossed the can I'd been holding in front of us.

"You may wanna step back," I told Colby, reaching into my pocket.

"Sariah—"

"Seriously, dude, if you want to save your eyebrows and not maim that pretty face of yours, you should step the fuck back."

I moved backward, causing Colby to move with me.

I flicked the lighter on, staring at the dark shape in front of us.

There were no words, no ceremony. This wasn't something that needed to be ritualized. I didn't need to be here for a moment longer than necessary.

The lighter went flying in the direction of the empty gas can I'd tossed, illuminating the thin trail of gasoline leading from the entrance of the warehouse and reflecting off the puddles of it I'd spilled around the space, mingling with the dried blood. Mine and many other women's.

"Holy fuck," Colby muttered, his shocked face alight as the warehouse quickly went up in flames.

The heat was indescribable, forcing us both to take a couple more measured steps back. In the movies, they always stood watching calmly as if their eyebrows weren't getting scorched off, so I hadn't bargained for just how intense the wall of heat would be.

Colby pulled me to his side and slightly behind him.

I know he felt me stiffen at the contact, but he didn't let me go.

We both watched the warehouse burn for a while. The crackling and spitting of the angry blaze taking over the night. If only my memories could go up in flames so easily.

Colby turned me to him, grasping my hips lightly.

Him touching me in such close proximity to the place that had changed my life forever was almost too much to bear.

"Why didn't you tell me you were doing this?" he asked, still watching the flames. "Actually, why didn't you ask me to do this for you? You didn't need to come back here."

I rolled my eyes and jerked myself away from him. Finally, a viable reason to get out of his arms that had nothing to do with my trauma and everything to do with my temper.

"Why didn't I ask *you* to do it for me?" I huffed, putting my hands on my hips and my back to the flames.

"Yeah," Colby clipped out, clearly not noting the warning in my tone.

"Because it's not your fucking job to burn down warehouses for me."

"Yeah, Sariah, it's my fucking job," he blew out a heavy breath. "It's my job to make sure that you don't come to the place that will bring back trauma for you."

"You have no idea what does and doesn't bring back trauma," I yelled as a crash sounded, presumably from the roof caving in. "And you need to stop with this." I waved my hand. "Trying to get in the way of me finding my way. I did this because I needed to do this. Having a man do it for me isn't going to do anything but make me feel more powerless. Make me weaker." I pinched the bridge of my nose in frustration. "Jesus, Colby. Don't you understand that the more you try to protect me, the more you're fucking me up?"

I was screaming now, and tears were rolling down my cheeks. Because of the smoke. It had to be because of the smoke.

Colby stared at me for a beat. I hoped he might continue to yell at me, pretend that it was indeed the smoke. But he didn't. He did something much worse instead. He stepped forward and hauled me into his arms.

"It's okay, baby," he murmured.

"It's not!" I cried against his chest, pounding my fists against it, trying to fight my way out of his arms. Colby held me firm, taking my blows, taking my wrath.

Eventually, the fight left me. Everything left me.

Then Colby held me as I stained his cut with my tears and watched the warehouse burn.

CHAPTER
TEN

I HAD BEEN DRINKING, though I wasn't drunk. I was careful of that. If I was drunk, he would notice because he noticed everything about me. Whenever he was around, his eyes were on me, cataloging every inch of me, concern and anger simmering right underneath the surface.

I hated him looking at me. Hated being around him.

But I knew asking him to leave would be futile, so I ignored his presence during my recovery and tried my best not to engage with him.

That was hard considering he'd been by my side since I woke up in the hospital.

He slept in my apartment, in my bed. He seemed to understand my aversion to being touched because when we slept in bed together, he didn't hold me. He just lay there and held my hand as the TV played whatever show I was trying to drown out my inner noises with. He didn't let my hand go. All night.

And then there was the night at the warehouse. Neither of us had spoken about it, thankfully.

So technically, I wasn't doing really fucking well at avoiding him.

I wanted to tell him to leave. That was on my list of things to do after tonight. But the truth was, I was terrified of being alone with my thoughts. Whatever scant seconds I was alone, I had to dig my nails into the inside of my palms to stop from screaming.

There were multiple, half-moon shaped scabs in varying degrees of healing to prove this.

I'd needed Colby during my recovery. It was, unfortunately, that simple.

But I was mostly recovered. I'd had my final checkup with the doctor today. My stitches were out, my scars were angry, shades of red and pink, and my body was as healed as it was ever going to be.

My mind was another story.

Colby didn't need to help me up and down stairs anymore, didn't have to follow me around, waiting to catch me if I stumbled. After tonight, I wouldn't need him.

Hence the plan.

But in order to commence with my plan for the night, I needed liquid courage. Again, to propel me to do this, not to actually get me wasted like I wanted to be.

I'd had a drink or two to take the edge off every single night, but I was never alone. Violet, Macy, Freya, Kate or Caroline were with me when Colby wasn't. None of these women were against a strong drink, and not a single person judged me for treating my wounds with alcohol. But if I drowned myself in it like I was craving to do, I'd have no shield. The women or Colby—whomever I was with—would break through, and I'd break down. That was not an option.

Once I was gone, I'd stop at a dive bar somewhere and get absolutely blind drunk. It was a comforting thought.

But for now, the two tequila shots I'd slammed as I heard the telltale rumble of Colby's bike had to be enough.

He'd only left me alone because there was a prospect sitting on his bike across the street, watching my apartment. I was always being watched. Which I found darkly funny since I wasn't in any kind of danger. The man who had hurt me was long dead. At least that's what I assumed.

Maybe it was just habit for these men, becoming used to their women being under threat of something horrible happening to them, not accustomed to how to act after the horrible thing already happened. These were men of action; they needed to feel as if they were fulfilling a purpose. Hence the constant presence of someone riding a Harley, wearing a cut, and packing a piece.

It might've been considered cute...

If it wasn't infuriating and didn't make me feel suffocated and trapped, that is. Oh, and wasn't a constant reminder of what I was: a victim.

At least the world didn't have that label for me.

The online community of true crime junkies had finally found out about the New Mexico serial killer. Luckily, no one had made up some stupid nickname for him.

Unfortunately, as I'd predicted, the media had focused on the villain instead of the victims.

Elijah's—birth name Beau Granger—face was splashed on every news channel, on every social media site, resulting in reporters and wannabe true crime podcasters and YouTubers descending on Garnett and surrounding areas in full force.

The powers of the Sons of Templar might've been many, but even the club couldn't stop society from being morbidly fascinated with serial killers.

What they and Caroline—former kickass journalist—were able to do was make sure that my name didn't appear in any police reports, so no one knew that I was the surviving victim. The only surviving victim.

And now that the local police were back on the Sons' payroll, they were able to fudge a lot of the documents about what really happened to Beau, saying he was killed while police were trying to apprehend him, and someone fucked-up by having him cremated too soon.

This was no mean feat since there were a lot of different eyes on our little town, not the least of which was the FBI. The California chapter of the Sons had a pretty impressive hacker who did their magic, and I knew that Ollie also had broken a few federal laws to keep my name and the Sons of Templar outside of the spotlight.

Still, there were individuals and news crews trying to interview the residents of Garnett. Although that didn't last long since the locals straight up refused to speak to anyone. Julian wouldn't even let them in his café.

There were still hanger-ons, but since I didn't get out much, I barely saw them.

That would all change tomorrow.

My fingers thrummed against the kitchen counter as I waited for Colby. The roar of his engine had petered out. Depending on his mood, he might've been saying something to the prospect, dismissing him, shooting the shit. But he knew I was up here alone, so even if he was in the mood to chat, he'd likely be rushing up to make sure I hadn't slit my wrists or anything.

I didn't miss the way everyone was watching me, practically holding their breath, waiting to see which way I'd go.

It made sense. They didn't even know what I'd been through, not in detail. But the men had seen the state I was in, and it was likely they'd shared some of that with their wives. So understandably, they were waiting to see if I'd try to check out.

The idea was tempting.

I'd thought it over half a dozen times. How it would be easier on everyone to no longer have to stare at the relic of such a horrific crime, how Colby could abandon whatever sense of duty he felt toward me and find a woman who wasn't scarred and soured. It would be easier for me too. Waking up every day, walking, talking, *breathing* was a fucking effort. Everything was so hard. So painful. Death offered a sweet respite.

But I couldn't. Couldn't do it to myself. To Violet. To my friends who cared about me.

Most of all, I couldn't let *him* win. Because that's what he'd wanted, after all. Me dead. If that was the end result of all of this, then he got what he wanted. And though the peace that death offered was mighty tempting, I would never let a man win.

My ears perked up at the low thump of Colby's motorcycle boots against the hardwood hallway.

My hands started shaking as I stopped thrumming my fingers on the counter.

Unable to sit still, I jumped from my stool, smoothing down the dress I was wearing self-consciously.

I was never self-conscious about my fashion sense. That kind of stuff always came naturally to me. Not that I was ever allowed to wear any of the things I wanted to while growing up. And when I was old enough to get a part-time job and buy the clothes I wanted, there were daily yelling matches between my parents and I about my 'attire.'

When I earned money, the big money—from taking off my clothes behind the camera—I started buying the clothes I really wanted.

Since I was found, I'd been wearing sweats and Colby's tees.

On the rare occasion I did go out, I wore jeans and one of Colby's tees.

The designer clothes, the silks, the lace, were spoils of a job that almost got me killed.

Yet another reason why I'd needed the liquid courage ... not only for what I was planning on doing but to be able to don the clothes I was wearing while I did it.

I'd decided on simple. A black dress. Silk. Calvin Klein. It used to skim over my considerable curves, clinging in all the right places. My appetite had all but gone since my attack, though everyone around me was not so subtly presenting me with all kinds of delicious food.

I humored them as much as I could, acting like the food was delicious and not turning to ash in my mouth.

Because of this, the simple slip dress hung loosely on me, though luckily, my cleavage was still ample enough to fill out the top.

I'd curled my hair in beachy waves, put on my sultry makeup look—smokey eyes, blush high on the cheeks and a subtle pink lip gloss.

I'd left my feet bare because what was the point?

Underneath the dress was my nicest La Perla set. A black corset, tiny panties and matching garters.

I'd vomited while putting it on, after seeing myself in the mirror. But at least it covered up my scars. My mouth tasted like mint and tequila now.

The door opened, and Colby stopped in his tracks when he saw me standing there.

His eyes slid up and down my body. There was definitely hunger in his gaze, but it was gone so quickly, I could almost convince myself I'd imagined it.

Colby closed the door, acting as if I was wearing sweats and no makeup.

"What do you want tonight? Mexican? Or we could go to *Violet's*?" he asked casually. Or what looked to be casual. The last offer, to go to Kate's restaurant, was meant to sound offhand but was really part of a larger plan to: a) get me out of the apartment and doing normal things, and b) start the process of gently wooing me.

The biker, the one not six months prior, who had promised he'd do me against the wall to 'fuck some sense into me' was now suggesting a fucking date at a tasteful restaurant. Like we were thirty-year-old accountants or some shit.

"I need you to fuck me," I said.

Jumping right in was the best I could do. I knew I'd probably lose my nerve otherwise.

All tenderness fled from his face as his expression turned carefully blank. "Sariah..." His tone was a warning.

I sighed heavily, knowing this was coming, knowing he wasn't going to hop to it like he would've before this happened.

Before you were ruined. Sullied.

I stole myself against that cold and evil whisper, against the pain of that truth.

"Before you try to be the good guy," I pushed a loose hair behind my ear, "remember, you're a biker. You're wearing that patch in order to make sure you don't have to be the good guy."

"You have no fuckin' idea why I wear this patch," he snarled, the previously blank expression replaced with palpable anger.

Fury.

Instead of shrinking away from it, I grinned. He'd been so fucking careful with me, it was nauseating. I needed this. Needed him to stop treating me like I was broken. Reminding me I was in tatters.

"Whatever." I waved my hand in dismissal. "We're not talking about your reasons for patching in. In fact, I don't want to talk at all … unless I'm saying harder, deeper or don't stop."

Colby's eyes blazed with naked desire before he shut them.

At least he was still interested.

"If you refuse me, like I see you're about to," I continued, "if you tell me it's too soon, I need to heal or whatever the fuck, I'll leave." I pointed to the door. "I will drive my ass to the clubhouse and find the first man willing to fuck me." The air in the room felt heavy with the danger radiating off of him, and I relished in that.

"You are not leaving this fuckin' apartment," Colby seethed. "And no way in fuck is any other man touching you if he wants to keep his hands."

He leaned as if he were about to surge forward, as if he were about to grab a hold of me tight enough to leave bruises.

I tensed in anticipation, but he held back at the last minute.

He was holding on to his control. Tenuously, mind you, but still holding.

"I won't leave this apartment," I agreed. "Unless you refuse to fuck me." I took a quick breath. "I understand that I don't look the same as I did before. That I—"

I was willing to list the things that had changed about me, both on the outside and the inside.

But it seemed that Colby was done. He surged forward, clutching the back of my neck with his hand, staring into my eyes with the force of a thousand suns. "You stop right there," he hissed. "You say or even think that there is anything on this world that can make you less fuckin' beautiful, that will make me stop wantin' you, you're goddamn mistaken."

I fought against the burn behind my eyes as tears threatened. No fucking way I'd let them fall. It would throw this whole plan off.

Colby searched my eyes. "But, baby, I can't have our first time being … this."

I wanted to scream. "We're not fucking virgins, Colby. And the absolute last thing I need you to be doing is turning me into some fucking Madonna or putting me on a pedestal, hyping our first time to be something special like we're teenagers on goddamn prom night."

Colby ran his hand through his hair. "Jesus Christ, Sariah. I'm not doing this. You've got some other motive here."

Fuck him for knowing me too damn well.

"Stop trying to be the good guy."

His forehead wrinkled. "I'm not the fuckin' good guy, Sariah."

"Yeah, despite the cut, the club and the bike, you are. I won't tell your secret," I rolled my eyes. "But you are. You came in and saved the day. You sat by my hospital bed. You've been here every night. And now, when you've got the chance to get what you've wanted from me for months, you're saying no. Because you think you're taking advantage of me. All good guy traits."

His eyes bore into me as his nostrils flared.

"When we found out where you were, when we got to the location *he* was holding you in," his words were sharp, saturated in fury, "I didn't go to you first. I went to *him*. My first thought was vengeance, not your well-being. That's not a good guy trait." His words dripped with disgust. In himself. He'd been holding on to this. Letting it rot inside of him. Blaming himself.

He was trying to turn me off with that little story. I didn't know if it would've worked with another woman or not. It didn't matter. I wasn't any other woman.

I was done with this argument. And words weren't working, so it was time for me to use my wiles.

I slipped the dress off my shoulders, shimmying out of it so it pooled at my feet.

Colby let out a harsh breath as his eyes ran over me. This time, the hunger in his gaze wasn't fleeting. No, it stayed.

My nipples pebbled as my body battled between natural desire and manufactured shame and fear.

Between whom I had been—a sexual person. One who gave into my desires without shame and at will.

And who *he* turned me into. Someone uncomfortable in her own skin. Unable to look at herself in the mirror, to shower without underwear.

"Don't you see?" I whispered. "I need you inside of me. I need my mind occupied by memories of something other than … him. I can't have the last time a man touched me be like that. Can't let my body be a graveyard."

Colby jerked then. Jerked like I'd struck him.

I hadn't meant to play dirty. Fuck, I hadn't even meant to say that, but I was getting desperate, and really fucking vulnerable, standing in my underwear.

Colby relented then, tagging the back of my neck with his hand and forcing our mouths together.

The kiss wasn't gentle, and I was glad about that.

I violently kissed him back, with need, not hesitating to jump up and wrap my legs around his waist.

Colby palmed my ass, pressing our bodies closer together and showing me just how into me and my lingerie he was.

I let out a groan of pleasure as the scant fabric of my panties rubbed against the hard denim.

We both moved quickly. Hungrily. Desperate for one another.

This had been a long time coming, after all.

Plus, fast was good, very good. No time to think about things.

He didn't stop kissing me while walking to my bedroom, and I didn't stop grinding myself against him. My skin was on fire, my mind desperate to clutch on to my desire, to focus on the feel of Colby's hands, mouth and cock … nothing else.

Colby kept kissing me as he laid me down on the mattress.

I mewed in protest as he stood up, looking down at me with piercing whisky eyes.

"Take your clothes off," I ordered.

A vein in his neck pulsed. "Your wish is my command."

He whipped off his tee then made quick work of his jeans and motorcycle boots. I wanted to revel in the defined abs, the sculpted muscles, the tattoos covering his body. But reveling took time. Time I didn't have.

So, I lifted my hips and hooked the edges of my panties, pulling them down quickly and efficiently before tossing them across the room.

I leaned up this time to snag the back of his neck and force him down on top of me. At least I tried to.

I frowned when Colby resisted.

"Not so fast," Colby murmured. "Need to get you ready." His fingers trailed along the top of my corset, down to where my nipples were rock hard underneath the lace. "Need to see you."

His words were cold water washing over me, the oxygen leaving my lungs and my heart constricting uncomfortably.

"You don't need to do any of that," I bit out, narrowing my eyes at him. "And you are not the one in charge here." I put more pressure on the back of his neck. "I want your cock inside of me. Now."

Colby stiffened, his eyes dark. I knew him well enough to understand that he was hungry for me, fucking starving—plus, he was hard as a rock—but he was holding on to that bullshit duty he felt to take care of me.

"Colby," I murmured, my body ready to break out in trembles if we lingered in this standstill too long. "Please."

Colby stared at me for a moment. "Fuck," he blew out a heavy sigh.

For a second, I worried that meant he'd changed his mind.

But it was a short second.

Colby's mouth crashed into mine once more, and we fell back on the bed, him on top of me, bracing himself so I didn't take his full weight.

The kiss was nice. Better than nice. Colby and I might've had our problems, but we never had an issue with our chemistry.

He was a good kisser. A fucking great kisser.

But even he wasn't great enough to chase away memories.

His putrid mouth was against mine. I wasn't even strong enough to bite his tongue like I did last time. He'd punished me for that. I tasted copper. My own blood. His lips were gone, but his hands were there, forcing my mouth open as he poured something down my throat. I gagged as I swallowed, my stomach spasming.

"Sariah," Colby's voice was firm, strong. An anchor to the current moment, something I could use to pull myself out of the past.

But it wasn't enough to hide my reaction. My skin was ice cold, my breaths were short and shallow, and my fingernails were gripping him so tight I'd drawn blood.

His face was painted with concern, jaw strained. He was cupping my chin, stroking my cheekbone with his thumb.

"Sariah," he said again.

Shit. I'd fucked it up now. He was going to stop this, going to treat me like I was damaged, too broken to do anything as simple as fuck without having a nervous breakdown.

We moved in a blur, but he did not separate himself from me. No, he flipped us so that I was on top of him, straddling him, his hands on my hips.

"You're in control, Sariah," he said, eyes glued to mine. "You have the power here."

I blinked rapidly as I struggled to understand. He wasn't stopping this for my own good like I'd thought he might. No, instead, he was … submitting to me.

My body was no longer ice cold. My mind was no longer in that warehouse. I was here. With Colby.

My hands found his chest, my heartbeat quickened, and my desire returned. Tenfold.

I lowered myself, brushing my entrance against his hard cock, coating him with my wetness.

We both let out sounds of pleasure as I moved back and forth, teasing the both of us, readying myself.

Not that it took much; I was already soaking and primed for him. I'd been the one intent on making this fast, leaving no time for thinking, no time for flashbacks, but now I was the one dragging it along.

My eyes were locked on Colby's as I ran myself along his hard length, my sensitive body already crying out for release. The cords in Colby's neck were defined with evidence that he was right on the edge too. His hands were locked on my hips, to the point of pain. I liked that. Enjoyed that he was too far gone to be worried about me. That's what I'd wanted all along.

Unable to control myself anymore, I sank down, filling myself with him. I cried out in pleasure as my orgasm rushed forward, quicker than ever before.

My eyes were squeezed shut as I rode him, desperate to lose myself in our connection, in the pleasure.

It didn't feel the same. Sex. Being there with Colby, I didn't feel the same as I had during sex in the past. Every sensation was more intense, all of my senses were heightened, and I could tell I was teetering on the edge of an abyss.

I chased it, desperate for a release, for a second of escape.

Colby's hands at my hips tightened past the point of pain. He was restraining me.

My eyes opened, and I glared at Colby. Or at least tried to. My eyes found his, then ran over the taut ridges of his body, the beautiful ink covering his torso, to where we were connected.

"Sariah," he growled.

I found his gaze once more.

"You don't close your eyes the first time you ride my cock," he ordered. "You don't close your eyes *whenever* you ride my cock."

I tilted my head, trying to fight letting out a cry of pleasure as his cock twitched inside of me.

"You cannot make me do anything," I sassily informed him.

He grinned wickedly. His hands grasped my hips tighter, then he surged upward, at the perfect angle.

My body cried out in pleasure, and dark spots danced in my vision as my orgasm hurtled forward.

But Colby didn't continue his motion, and his hold on my hips meant I couldn't even create what I needed.

"You look at me while you ride my cock, or you don't come on it," he said.

I wanted to yell at him, I really did. Wanted to fight him on it. And if his aforementioned cock wasn't inside me at that very moment, I might've argued. But it was. And it felt wonderful. I felt wonderful. For the first time in recent memory.

So I didn't fight him.

I kept my eyes open as his hips thrust up once more. My body stiffened, teetering on the edge, and my fingertips went numb. Colby was staring at me. Into me. His striking face was carved with pleasure. Reverence.

Which was why I'd wanted to close my eyes in the first place.

I wasn't anything to revere.

I was nothing.

Before I could tumble down that rabbit hole, Colby began moving again. I cried out as my walls spasmed around him.

"There you go," he murmured, the hoarseness of his voice galvanizing me.

I took control of our movements, my body moving in tandem with the waves of pleasure crashing through me, greedy for more, for them to last longer.

"There she is," Colby grunted, hooded eyes glued to mine. "End it, Sariah. Take me there."

Though I really wasn't hip on following Colby's orders outside of the bedroom, it turned out I was super into it when I was riding him.

So, I took him there.

———

"You gonna let me take this off?" Colby asked, fingertips brushing along my corset then down my midsection.

I shivered at his touch which wasn't entirely unpleasant. It was pleasure mixed with ... something else. Something wrong. Even though there was fabric in between us, he was touching the raised and puckered skin. He was feeling where I'd been torn open. The spots where vital parts of me had spilled out from.

Every muscle in my body went stiff.

Colby leaned up on his elbow and studied me with a frown. "Not gonna push you to take it off," he said quietly. "I just want you to know that we're gonna work up to it."

His palm settled on my stomach, as if in challenge, to see if I'd admit how uncomfortable it made me feel.

But in order for me to admit I felt uncomfortable, I would have to bring the warehouse into the bedroom. I would have to bring *him* into the bedroom. And he already took up enough space where he sat now, in the corner, watching.

I knew it wasn't a ghost or anything—even though I totally believed in all of that—this shape was a figment of my own mind. I knew enough about psychology to know that.

"I don't want to work up to anything but my next orgasm," I purred, clutching his wrist and moving it downward.

Colby didn't fight me as I positioned his hand where I wanted it, nor did he hesitate to find the spot.

My eyes rolled to the back of my head as he worked my clit, still sensitive from the orgasms he'd given me.

Colby's lips grazed my neck.

"Gonna fuck you now," he murmured.

"You better," I moaned, arching my back in pleasure.

"You gonna handle me bein' on top this time?" he asked, still working his finger.

I locked eyes with his before tracing the contours of his face, his jaw, his dark eyes, the high cheekbones. This was the Colby I'd known for over a year. The one who infuriated me, consumed me and made me feel safe.

"Yeah," I whispered.

Colby didn't hesitate to climb on top of me, nor did he hesitate to enter me.

I threw my head back in pleasure as he filled me completely.

"You better hold on tight, poppet," he grunted. "I'm plannin' on making up for a lot of lost time tonight." He plunged in harder. "And tomorrow morning." Another thrust. "And the next day." He clutched my neck as he filled me to the hilt, bringing me to the edge. "And the next."

My body writhed in pleasure as his movements brought on another world-bending orgasm.

Colby was a man of his word.

He did a whole lot of making up for lost time.

And I figured if I'd waited for him to wake up the next morning, he would've continued to.

But I didn't stay.

I crept out of bed, dressed quietly, then retrieved the bag I'd packed and stowed in the hall closet the night before.

I doubt it would've been so easy to do that without waking him if he hadn't worked so hard at pleasing me.

Because he'd worked so hard at claiming me.

He owned me.

But he'd never know that.

Eventually, he'd forget about me.

CHAPTER
ELEVEN

ALMOST TWO YEARS LATER

"YOU'RE A HARD WOMAN TO FIND," a smooth voice said as a large form occupied the barstool next to me.

My body stiffened the second he spoke. The second that familiar cadence ran along my skin. My soul.

I did my best not to look like his voice or his presence affected me. It was hard. Exceptionally so. The fact that I was pretty close to being wasted helped.

I stared at my glass for one more second, internally cursing that it was half empty. It was always half empty with me. I sighed and drained it before I turned in my stool.

"Not hard enough," I replied to Colby, meeting his eyes, thinking the shroud of booze hovering around me would serve as protection.

It did not.

His gaze, hard and soft, angry and worried, familiar and strange… It did what it always did to me.

Unraveled me from the inside out.

Not that I wasn't in pieces already.

His hair was longer. He had it fastened in a messy bun at the nape of his neck, strands of unruly black hair escaping to frame his face. The angles were the same, his cheekbones sharp and high, his brows dark, eyes breathtaking. Though he seemed to have gained some weight, beefed up.

Colby raised a brow. The gesture itself was casual, teasing almost, but his posture was stiff. He had a strange energy that punctured my drunken haze. He seemed more intense. More dangerous.

"One of the best hackers on the continent wears a Sons of Templar patch, baby," he reminded me. "And he had a fuck of a lot of trouble locating you."

I tapped the rim of my drink, signaling to the bartender for another. He smiled at me, and I attempted a flirty wink.

I wasn't sure if it worked, but he did take my glass away and put another one in front of me in record time. He ignored Colby. Which I found interesting.

"I've got a friend who is not only a great hacker but a woman. We always do it better than you," I replied, trying to match his playful tone. It felt like we were back at the club bar, trading jabs good-naturedly in between all of the sexual tension.

Like it was almost two years ago before everything else happened.

But we'd never be back there. We'd never be back again.

I took a long sip of my whisky in order to distract myself from the ache of that truth.

Colby watched me drink with an intense stare, and I waited for the order. The alpha request that seemed to be the norm for these fuckers ... trying to control their women under the guise of taking care of them.

But the alpha request I was expecting did not materialize. He just kept staring at me in a way that made me struggle not to squirm in my seat.

The last time we were together, and awake, he was inside me, and I was crying out his name.

My body responded to the memory, especially given the lack of male attention I'd had in the past year.

"I'm not going back," I stated, trying to hide my desire.

His eyes danced with something that told even my wasted mind that he had caught a glimpse of my sexual hunger. "Back where?"

I suppressed an eye roll. "To Garnett. I assume that's why you're here, to come in, guns blazing." I glanced at his cut, at the holster he was wearing underneath it. "Literally." I looked up to meet his eyes. "Here to save the day."

I held my breath as he leaned forward, a scowl tilting his plump lips. It was bad enough, him sitting close. It was bad enough smelling him. It was bad enough laying my eyes on this man and wanting to hate him, wanting to make him hate me.

I didn't know what I was expecting from Colby, what I was dreading and longing for at the same time. His fingers brushed mine as he took the glass from me.

My body recoiled at the simple touch.

Colby didn't miss that, but despite a quick flash in his eyes, he didn't react. He brought my glass to his own lips and sipped my drink.

"Not here to save the day," he told me. "Here to have your back."

The words sobered me somewhat. "Excuse me?"

Colby placed my glass down. "I'm here to have your back while you're doing what you're doin'. Make sure you're not alone."

I pursed my lips and clutched my fists.

"But I am alone," I shrugged. "Even if you're sitting right here, I'm still alone."

Colby flinched, presumably at my tone and the words. I'd expected that. I'd structured the words to wound, hadn't I? I was drunk, and it had been a long while since I'd been in the presence of someone I cared about. My isolation had sharpened me. Made me cruel.

Colby's features darkened. "Then you'll sit here alone, with me. You'll do whatever you're doing. Alone. With me."

The words cut through my alcohol fueled haze. He was serious. Very serious. And he'd been looking for me for over a year by the sound of it. My hope that he'd forgotten about me dashed. Then again, hadn't I kind of been expecting this? Expecting him to chase me?

"You're supposed to yell at me," I whispered.

Colby frowned in confusion. He had obviously been expecting more back and forth, more of the bitchy Sariah. Unfortunately, she had abandoned me. "Say what?"

"You were supposed to yell at me," I repeated. "Come in here, all alpha protective mode and tell me I'm being stupid, putting myself in danger, then try to strong-arm me back to the safety of your presence."

"Not gonna yell at you, Ri," he sighed.

The benevolent tone almost wrecked me, but I held fast. "Why not?" It didn't sound like a question. It sounded like a plea.

"'Cause I can't do that." He reached out to stroke the back of his hand against my cheek.

I didn't flinch at this contact. Instead, I did the unthinkable…. I leaned into it.

"Yeah, you pissed me off, confused me, and hurt Violet by disappearing with nothing but a note, but that doesn't mean I'm gonna stop caring about you. Doesn't mean anyone is gonna stop caring about you."

That time, flinching was unavoidable as his words hit home. I'd done my best not to think about what I'd created by running away. I had told myself it was for the best, but I knew my best friend well enough to know that I'd hurt her by leaving.

That's why I was always on the move, always drinking… Anything to distract me from thinking about what I'd left behind. My friend. Her new baby. My new friends. My degree. Oh, and the person I used to be. Although I didn't leave her behind. She died in a cold warehouse.

"You wanna leave now?" Colby asked as I finished my drink.

I did not want to leave. Because I *wanted* to leave. The bar, like most I'd been patronizing over the past year, was dark, shabby and mildly depressing. Exactly how I liked them.

Now Colby was here, looking at me, making me see what he saw: a drunk, sloppily dressed in the middle of the day.

Not cute.

If we walked out together, the harsh sunlight would illuminate the dark shadows under my eyes, the way my hair was dull, stringy, washed with cheap motel soap. Not to mention the ripped jeans, Walmart sneakers, oversized flannel and the stained white tank I had on.

I didn't want him seeing me like this. I didn't want *anyone* seeing me like this. Which was the whole point of me running around the country, drinking in dive bars, wearing polyester.

But what other option did I have? Drink more until I fell off my stool and Colby carried me out unconscious.

"Yeah, I guess we can go," I sighed.

I was looking down when I spoke, unable to meet Colby's eyes, growing painfully sober painfully quick.

Colby grasped my chin, tilting it upward so our eyes met.

"Stop thinkin' it," he ordered.

I pulled back, his hand dropping. "Thinking what?"

"Whatever bullshit you're tellin' yourself right now."

"Unless I've missed something, you do not have the ability to read minds," I snapped.

"Can't read your mind, I just know you. Understand you. So, I know you're thinking all sorts of shit right now because of that." He motioned to the empty glass. "Because of the pain you're trying to dull. I'm not judging you for how you're dealing. Not a fuckin' bit. But I'm asking you not to be so fucking hard on yourself. And I'm also telling you that nothing is going to change how I see you."

My eyes welled up with tears. All of the words were delivered with a firm sincerity as well as a kind of tenderness I wasn't equipped to deal with.

Instead of saying anything back, or worse, bursting into tears, I hopped off the stool and snatched my purse.

"Let's go, then."

I turned and stomped toward the exit, angrily swiping my eyes, knowing that Colby was following me.

Knowing Colby would always follow me.

————

We rode back to my motel on the back of his bike.

I'd walked to the bar from my motel, knowing that I was never sober enough to drive by the time I came out. Colby wasn't about to let me walk or get an Uber.

There wasn't much point in fighting him on it. I was tired. Beaten. And fuck, if a girl just didn't want to wrap her arms around a hot biker and ride off into the sunset with him.

So I let it happen.

Well, not the ride off into the sunset part since we were driving to my shitty motel in Eureka Springs, Arkansas. The town itself wasn't shitty. Actually, it was pretty kick ass. Old Victorian houses were perched on cliff faces, lovingly restored. The whole place had a feeling of magic about it.

There were plenty of nicer places I could've stayed in town. Hell, there was a nice hotel that was supposedly haunted that the old me would've jumped at. But I was haunted enough these days.

So, a motel with peeling wallpaper and scratchy sheets was what I got.

To his credit, Colby didn't say a word about my accommodations.

My nerve endings were still singing from the vibration of the bike, from having my arms around Colby's warm, strong body. I felt alive for the first time in over a year. It was uncomfortable.

"I'd offer you something to eat," I muttered once I'd unlocked the door, "but this is all I've got." I waved to the bottle of whisky that was sitting on the bedside table.

My scant amount of clothes were folded neatly in a duffel bag.

"I'm kind of living Sam and Dean style," I explained as he glanced around the room, which I'd thankfully kept clean. "You know, cheap motels, bad takeout … no hunting demons, though," I added, trying for a joke.

It didn't land since it was a little too close to the truth. My demons did hunt me. Hence the running.

Colby didn't speak, he just leaned against the closed door, staring at me.

It was infuriating. I'd always expected him to find me. And I'd known it was only a matter of time before I went back to Garnett if he didn't. I'd been a shitty friend and worse godmother. And I wasn't far gone enough to *completely* destroy all of my friendships.

I'd spent my free time—of which I'd had a lot—thinking about what it would look like when Colby saw me again. I figured he'd be pissed. I'd snuck out right after we'd had sex, after all. I assumed he'd have a whole bunch of questions and commands.

Back at the bar, he'd surprised me. Caught me off guard. And he was continuing to do that with his quiet staring.

It didn't help that the past almost two years had been good to him. Great to him, to be honest. He had a shadow of stubble over his angular jaw, making him look older and more rugged.

I was into that.

And something simpler… I'd missed him.

"I had plans, you know," I blurted. "I was on a mission. I was going to lure in men who hurt women. Punish them. Ollie was helping."

She wasn't exactly supportive, considering the danger involved in such things, but she also didn't try to stop me or rat me out. She was a good friend. And she had the ability to constantly track me and my phone, telling me she'd send the Calvary in if she didn't hear from me regularly.

"I know you had plans," Colby said calmly. "I know you."

I laughed without humor. "Well, that makes one of us."

Colby scowled at my words. He wasn't into my self-deprecation, obviously.

"Since I've been running around the country all this time, do you know how many men I've punished?" I asked him. "None," I said without waiting for him to reply. "My plans of being a badass bitch, avenging angel went out the window when faced with the reality of it all." I looked at my feet. "I have discovered that I'm all talk and no action. I'm weak."

Colby was done at this point, communicating that by pushing off the door, crossing the distance between us and grasping on to my neck harder than he ever had before. "I'm not listening to this shit."

I glared at him, my heart thundering in my chest. "What are you gonna do? Try and talk me out of this?"

"No," he stared at my lips. "Gonna fuck you out of it."

I barely had time to digest this because Colby pulled on my neck, and our mouths crashed together.

I planned on fighting him, I really did. This was way too complicated, and I had way too many demons battling for my attention.

But Colby's lips probed mine open. Not softly. With none of the tenderness from earlier.

No, he was mad. Furious.

And so was I. So I kissed him back with all of my fury. His hand tangled in my hair while another found my ass, forcing our bodies together.

My hands found their way between us, desperate to find the skin of his abs underneath his tee.

He growled into my mouth as I raked my nails down the hard

muscle and then down farther, working at his belt with desperation.

We were both animals, wild and desperate to touch each other, mark each other.

Colby let out a rough gasp when I fastened my hands around his bulging, rock hard cock. I smiled against his mouth, satisfied with the power I was holding in my hand but also desperate to have him inside me.

Colby didn't let me have the upper hand for long. My hand lost purchase on his cock as he tore my flannel off.

I froze when his fingers tried to pull the bottom of my tank upward.

Colby sensed the abrupt change in my demeanor and stopped.

My eyes met his. "It stays on," I said quietly. Fuck, I wanted to sound more authoritative. It was *my* body, this was consensual sex, and I had the right to demand to have whatever parts I wanted of myself covered.

Except it wasn't my body anymore. Not even an inch of it.

Colby was going to stop now. This was his reminder of what happened, what I had become. How complicated. Broken. Hungry as he was for me, he wasn't going to push me when I was obviously hanging on by a thread already.

Colby's hands stayed at the edge of my tank for a second longer before they let it go.

Instead of stepping back like I'd expected him to, he went to work on my jeans.

I was too surprised to do anything but let him pull them down, stepping out of them, leaving me in the tank and panties.

"Fuck, Sariah," Colby's eyes raked over me. Then he grasped the back of my neck and was kissing me again.

The mattress wasn't soft against my back when I fell on it. It was so shitty, the landing kind of hurt. But I liked that.

Satisfaction filled me when my nails scraped the skin on Colby's back, drawing blood and a hiss of pain from him.

"Naughty girl." He nipped my neck with his teeth before moving his lips downward.

My hands tangled in his hair as he suckled my nipples through my tank. I writhed underneath him, need growing stronger with every passing second.

"Can I see them?" his head tilted up as he cupped my breast in his hand. "I won't pull it down any farther."

I held my breath, his fingers toying with the top of my tank. I desperately wanted his lips on my skin there, I wanted to please him like that. Wanted him to please me like that. But that required trust. Trust that he wouldn't get lost in the moment and tear my shirt away. That he wouldn't venture to parts of my skin I couldn't have him seeing.

"Okay," I whispered, my voice shaking.

Colby grasped one of my hands that had been clutching the sheet and turned it over to kiss the scars on the inside of my palm.

My body had begun to relax yet tensed again as he pulled down my tank to expose my breasts.

"I've been fuckin' *dreaming* about these," he licked his lips, riveted by my breasts.

My heartbeat slammed in my ears and my pussy pulsed at the hunger in his gaze.

I cried out when his mouth found my bare nipple, teeth grazing against the sensitive flesh.

Colby took his time working on each one of my breasts, driving me crazy as he alternated between tenderness and a rough desperation that showed the wild, more dangerous side of him.

I lapped up both versions, on the cusp of climax from just that. I'd always thought that was utter bullshit. I'd always needed clitoral stimulation plus penetration to really get there. But if Colby kept up much longer, I was going to lose it.

Colby must've sensed this as I'd been writhing underneath him, rubbing against him, desperate for any kind of friction.

He gave my nipple one last nip before moving. Downward.

I held my breath as he hovered over my stomach, careful not to linger near my abdomen, thoughtfully pulling my tank town when it rode a little high.

My legs opened for him as he inspected the wetness of my white cotton panties. Gone were the silks and laces of La Perla.

From the look in Colby's eyes, you'd think I was wearing the most exquisite lingerie money could buy.

His finger trailed over the top of my panties to where I was wet. It was torture. "You're almost there, aren't you?" he rasped, the hoarseness in his voice somehow adding to how turned on I was.

My head moved rapidly, shaking then nodding. I didn't quite know what to do with myself.

Colby smirked wickedly. "I gotta make you come in my mouth, then you'll do it around my cock."

The way he looked at me, touched me, his tone … it created a hunger in me that begged to be sated.

"Yes," I hissed.

Colby didn't make me wait any longer. He pulled my panties to the side and dove right in. I cried out in ecstasy as I tugged at his hair, my body already wracked by an orgasm.

I hadn't brought myself there the entire time I'd been on the road. I'd deprived myself of that. I didn't know whether it was punishment or something else. My last orgasm had been with Colby, and I didn't want to sully that.

Having been so long, I lost all sense of control, of comprehension, of reality when his mouth worked against my clit. It was fucking glorious. One wave washed over me only to have another building. Colby was relentless devouring me, pushing a finger inside as I clenched around it.

When I didn't think I was going to survive another wave, his mouth was gone, he was gone, and his hands were under my hips, hauling me to the edge of the bed.

His belt rattled.

My vision sharpened just in time for me to see him free his cock, position it at my entrance and thrust inside.

I clutched the sheets and muffled my scream.

"Yeah," Colby groaned, holding on to me, staring at me, fucking me ruthlessly.

My body was sensitive, only just starting to recover from the life-shattering orgasms from moments ago.

Colby's torso was glistening with sweat, his muscles carved from the exertion. My delirious gaze roved over him, desperate to catalog every inch of his skin. The tattoos I hadn't inspected before. The most distinct of them was a red dragon starting from his shoulder and finishing just above his cock.

"Sariah," Colby growled in between thrusts. "What the fuck did I tell you about your eyes?"

My gaze snapped back up to his face immediately. Our eyes locked, and my body jerked with another orgasm.

"That's better," he grunted, fucking me harder. "Don't you take those eyes off me. Let me watch you while you come, and then you watch me while I fucking empty myself inside you."

"Yes, Colby." I was barely able to get the words out as I spiraled out of control.

Though my orgasm was the most intense I'd had in recorded history, I never let go of Colby's gaze.

CHAPTER
TWELVE

"I WAS PLANNING on resisting a whole lot more," I admitted against Colby's chest. He was completely naked.

I still had on my tank and nothing else.

"I know," he replied, his deep voice vibrating against my cheek.

"Of course, you know," I muttered. "Because you know everything." There might have been a bite to my voice. I couldn't explain the resentment I felt towards Colby for his familiarity to me.

Maybe because it felt like he was familiar with a ghost. That he knew the dead parts of me as well as pieces of this new, warped and wrong version.

Colby moved us so I was no longer splayed on his chest, hovering above me, not giving me all of his weight.

"I'm far and away from knowin' everything," he replied. "But I know that this … thing between us, whether we like it or not, is impossible to resist. I've struggled secondhand, knowing what you've gone through, what you've had to do to survive." He brushed the hair from my face. The gesture was tender, but it felt like he was forcing it. I could hear the tightness in his voice, the thinly veiled rage.

The trauma.

"Been tryin' to put myself in your shoes," he continued. "Scared the shit outta me, doing that. Because I don't know everything you went through. No one does. You won't tell us because you're protecting us. You don't want anyone to know what you went through because if we did, then you fear we'd be doing whatever we could to keep our eyes on you."

The words were tender. True.

Which only pissed me off.

I wriggled out from underneath him, giving him a hard shove before launching myself off the bed.

It was only then that I realized my tank had ridden up, the thin sliver of daylight peeking out from the cheap curtains enough to illuminate every scar on my body.

Panicked, I tugged the tank down then snatched the closest thing, which just happened to be Colby's tee.

The fabric was soft, worn and washed so many times the print on the front was too faded to even decipher.

It smelled like him.

I hated that.

Colby frowned at me as he sat up, resting his back on the headboard and not bothering to cover his naked body with a sheet.

That made it hard to maintain my anger.

But not impossible.

"Did you think I was going to put a gun in my mouth?" I asked coldly.

"Yes," he replied.

His simple and quick response made me go back on my heels.

"On my worst day, yeah," Colby murmured. "Not because I didn't think you're fucking strong, but because I know how vulnerable the strongest of people are under the wrong circumstances."

The ground felt like it was shaking underneath me. I felt too vulnerable. Too naked. "You don't know *anything*." Rage blurred my vision. And shame. Shame that the man I wanted to see me as strong, desirable, and anything but broken, had seriously thought that I might take my own life.

"Really?" he asked with a cocked brow. "I know what my little sister's brains looked like against the wall of her bedroom."

The air left me in a whoosh as his words echoed in my brain.

"The first gunshot I ever heard was that of my sister taking her own life," he continued. "And that gunshot was the first inkling I had that there was anything wrong with her. She was strong. Smart. Feisty. She was so fucking strong that she hid all of her pain away, buried all of her sorrow so deep even people living in the same house as her couldn't see it."

Tears rolled down my face. The first I'd shed since … since I was sobbing in that warehouse, begging for my life.

I'd been successful in fighting them for almost two years. I'd been able to chase away my own sorrow, but Colby's took up this entire room. It was impossible for me to not grieve the pain that I hadn't seen so close to the surface.

I wanted to apologize. I wanted to touch him. Comfort him. But I had no fucking clue how to do that.

My legs were unsteady as they took me over to the bed, sitting gingerly. Colby didn't move to grab me, and I didn't nestle up against him as I ached to do.

"I've never asked about you or your family," I realized in a whisper.

"Well, since you spent the majority of the time we knew each other fighting me and fighting us, it would've been counterproductive to get to know me," he said dryly.

I didn't smile.

"What was her name?" I asked, tugging at the comforter.

"Alyssa."

I forced my eyes to meet his. There was pain there, that much was plain to see. And how much he'd loved his sister. But there was something else that was hard to explain. A … distance. He'd removed himself from this loss in order to survive. I understood that. Had been living that.

"Is what happened to her the reason..." I trailed off.

"The reason I patched in?" he deduced.

I nodded. It was the question I'd been wondering since the first time I saw him.

"Yeah, to put it simply," he shrugged. "Our parents were first generation Americans. My grandparents came from Korea in pursuit of the American Dream." He shook his head, gathering his hair at the nape of his neck then fastening it with one of my many hair ties cluttering the bedside table.

"They had barely anything to their name and worked their asses off to send their kids to school," he continued, "on both sides. My Dad is a doctor, he has a small family practice. My mom worked there with him once we were in school."

He said all of this without warmth or emotion. I didn't recognize this version of Colby, but I related to him.

"They wanted the best for us because they wanted us to have great lives," he explained. "They pushed us but showed us love too. We respected them. Wanted to make them proud. Alyssa worked hard. She was smart. Funny. Kind. Everyone knew that she was destined for great things. No one knew that she was planning her death instead of her future."

My body shook, and for the first time in almost two years, I was entrenched in someone else's horror instead of my own. Colby's. And I would've gone through what I went through a thousand times so he didn't have to recount the story of his sister's death in that resigned tone.

"It tore us apart," he recounted coldly. "My parents were devastated, of course. Broken. But they also grieved in a way I couldn't understand. From my perspective, it seemed like they didn't care. It seemed like a disservice to her memory to bury all of their feelings inside and act like everything was okay—the exact thing that killed their daughter." He shrugged. "I was an angry, selfish teenager. I didn't know shit about life, just knew that I much preferred being angry to lettin' the sadness in."

He reached over to snag the bottle of whisky I'd left on the bedside table, taking a long pull then wincing. It was warm and cheap, but it did the job.

"My grades suffered," he said after he swallowed for the second time. "I quit every sports team I was in. Drank a lot. Fucked a lot. My parents didn't know what to do. The longer I stayed in that house, the angrier I became. It got to the point where I knew it wasn't safe. *I* wasn't safe. So I left. And like a fuck of a lot of my brothers, I found the Sons of Templar MC instead of a jail cell or an early grave. Pure luck. Or something bigger, if you believe in that shit."

Something in me wanted to laugh. Not because any of this was funny.

"My parents believe in 'that shit'," I informed him. "And they would think you finding yourself in an outlaw motorcycle club after leaving your family home was an act of the devil."

Colby pulled in a knee, blinking at me. Then he burst out laughing.

It unnerved me, seeing him laughing like that, having that ability so soon after venturing into the darkest part of his past. I admired that about him. Admired him.

"Maybe," he agreed when he finished laughing. "But I think he's done more for me than his estranged daddy."

I shook my head, smiling although I hadn't thought it was possible just moments ago. In this life.

I crawled up to him, unable to stand the distance between us anymore. He immediately put his arms around me, and I felt safe. Whole.

"I'm so sorry about Alyssa," I whispered.

He stroked my hair. "She would've liked you."

I tilted my head upward to look at him. "Even though I've been torturing you for years?" I was only half teasing.

"Especially because you've been torturing me for years," he smiled. "She always thought I needed a challenge with girls."

I grinned back. "I bet I would've liked her too." I nestled into his chest.

Though I'd thought I'd never feel close to another human being again, that I'd always be alone, whoever I was with, I had never felt closer to Colby.

———

It was dark, nearing midnight. Or after. I didn't know which. I'd dozed off against Colby's chest after he'd told me about Alyssa, both to sleep off the booze I'd consumed and because I was exhausted in general.

But my sleep had been thin. I'd been conscious of Colby's arms around me, and I knew that he was watching me close enough to see that I wasn't completely out.

"I'm hungry," I'd muttered at some point.

Colby had immediately jumped into action. Which meant I jumped into action since we were tangled up in each other. He had informed me that he wasn't letting me out of his sight. I'd moaned about it while I dressed, but I'd secretly been glad I wasn't going to be in this room alone.

We'd picked up cheeseburgers we'd eaten in bed. It felt gluttonous and glorious.

The TV was playing reruns of *Shark Tank,* and I was once again splayed on Colby, still wearing his shirt.

He was wearing nothing but his underwear. I'd been lazily trailing a pattern over each of his tattoos. Some of them were what you'd expect from a biker... skulls, flames, that kind of thing. Most of them were connected with his heritage, I guessed. There was script in Korean, a roaring lion, then the dragon. The only splash of color was the streaks of red in the ornate design. Just like his bike.

I wanted to ask about it. Know more.

"You're not going back to Garnett now, are you?" I asked instead of the question I was really curious about.

"Nope," he answered immediately.

"That's what I feared," I muttered. Which, unbeknownst to Colby, was a complete lie. My real fear was the exact opposite. That he'd come here on some kind of mission, out of some warped sense of responsibility to make sure I wasn't *completely* self-destructing—which I was optimistic enough to say I wasn't—and then he got to fuck me again as a bonus before he left, after fulfilling his duty.

That was undervaluing who he was as a person. But I liked to live in the worst possible scenario now, rather than have any hope or faith. If you believed that the best would come to you, when life showed you how bad it could get, it hurt that much more.

I used to be all about affirmations and the Law of Attraction, and look what happened to me.

"You knew I was going to find you," he murmured. "And you knew I wasn't going to let you go."

I traced a dagger on his chest with my finger. Yeah, I had known that. In the back of my mind. Wasn't that why I was running?

"I can't go back there, not yet," I admitted. It was a shameful thing to say out loud. I'd been gone for so long already, put my entire life on pause to roam around the country and accomplish nothing more than damaging my liver.

"I know," Colby said without judgment.

He was being so understanding. Kind. Tender. It was infuriating and gave me no foothold to start an argument with him. Especially since he'd shared about his sister. It was inescapable to me now, knowing that my own badass biker was broken in his own way. And despite the state I was in, I didn't want to make that worse.

"You want us to be together," I said.

"We are together," he rumbled against my hair.

I rolled my eyes. "You know what I mean."

"I do know what you mean," he sighed. "And I stand by what I said. We are together now. And as far as I'm concerned, we've been together for a long fuckin' time."

There it was. A foothold for me to get pissed off.

I pushed off it and pulled myself from his arms, scrambling off the bed for the second time that day. A little dramatic and erratic, but I wasn't exactly in my right mind.

"That's not fair, nor is it true," I huffed.

He dragged a hand down his face. "You knew we were meant for each other the second we had it out in the clubhouse the very first day."

I scowled at him. "I knew you were hot, and if things weren't more complicated, we would've fucked, nothing else," I lied. "And beyond that, I did fuck other people after we met. I wasn't chaste. Didn't save myself for you."

Colby's glare could've singed me. "When I put my lips on you, when I tasted you, did you let any other man in there after that?"

Fuck.

"Yes."

It was obviously not the answer he was expecting because his nostrils flared, and his body went stiff.

As much as I wanted to continue that, to push him away, make him mad at me, make him want to leave, I couldn't do that to him. Not entirely.

"I gave myself to *thousands* of men," I continued. "I took off my clothes for them, let them see things that even you haven't. I sold every inch of myself." I tried my best not to let my voice shake. Before everything happened, I'd been proud of how I'd been able to make so much money by owning my sexuality.

Now it felt shameful.

Colby's posture relaxed some. "You didn't sell your body."

"Yes, I did."

"You know what I mean," he said through gritted teeth.

"So, what would you do then, if I told you that I *had* done that?" I demanded. "If I'd let a man fuck me five ways from Sunday for a paycheck? That I let *many* men do that."

Colby stared at me for a long moment, but his expression didn't change. "Wouldn't do anything different," he said. "Doesn't change shit."

I bugged my eyes out. "That's a fucking lie."

Colby surged forward and grabbed on to me, drawing our bodies close together. "Don't fucking tell me I'm lying when you're so tangled up in your own lies that you can't even see the truth." I fought not to shiver as his warm breath tickled my cheek. "I'm holding back, Sariah. Because I can see you're a raw fucking nerve. Because not an inch of you has healed, and I'm not gonna be the cause of any more cuts." He gripped me harder. "But don't fucking push me."

So help me, the warning in his tone made me hot.

"What are you going to do if I keep pushing you?" I purred.

His eyes shone first in shock then in hunger.

"I'll fucking punish you."

Heat blazed between my legs. "Then punish me."

There was a long pause before Colby responded, a warning blaring in his tone when he finally did. "Sariah…"

"Don't," I hissed. "Don't you dare act like I'm breakable. Ruined. Not here. Not wanting this. I want you to break me, Colby. I want you to … dominate me."

He didn't pause this time. In the blink of an eye, I was turned, Colby brutally manhandling me.

My back arched as his palm raked over the skin of my ass and the other pushed me down on the bed so I rested on my elbows.

Colby leaned forward to cup my soaked panties. He let out a moan when he felt how turned on I already was.

I rocked against him, already desperate for the friction of his fingers.

His hand moved to grip my hip, holding me steady.

When I complied with his nonverbal command, he hooked his thumbs into the corners of my panties and pulled them down to my ankles.

My knees shook as his hand found my ass again, slipping forward and lubricating himself with my arousal, teasing me for a second before his hand was gone.

I held my breath as I felt his hand move upward, my body tensing.

Pain exploded on my skin as his palm came down on my cheek.

My body spasmed in pleasure.

"That's for running away from me," Colby bit out.

He didn't hesitate to hit me again, right in the same spot, not holding back. My teeth sank into my lip as I moaned.

"That's for thinking I wouldn't want you."

Another slap.

"That's because I fuckin' wanted to."

My skin was stinging with pain, and my pussy was pulsing with need. I wouldn't be able to take much more. The pain I could take, it was the need that I couldn't handle. My body was taut with desperation, ready to explode.

Colby's lips soothed the stinging skin as he softly kissed me. His hand cupped me between my legs but didn't give me the friction I needed.

"Knees on the bed for a second, baby," he commanded, voice low and rough.

I obeyed, weak as he removed my panties from my ankles before he set my feet back down and slowly pushed my legs wider.

He kept his hand there, firm, restraining me.

My hips pushed up, restless, needful, trying to present myself to him as much as I could.

When his cock pressed against my entrance, I let out a sound of need, of pleasure.

"What do you want, Sariah?" he asked in a sexy rasp.

"I want you."

His hand bit into my hip. "You want my cock, or you want me?"

"Both," I answered without thinking. "Please."

"You begging me to fuck you, to make you mine?"

"Yes." I was half mad with need. Nothing else mattered.

"That's my good girl," he grunted, and then he was inside me.

Not gently.

Brutally.

I came the second his cock filled me up.

He spent the rest of the evening fucking me so hard, I barely remembered my own name. The only thing I did remember was that I was his.

COLBY

She fell asleep quickly.

Which made sense.

One glimpse at her, even drunk in a dingy bar, I could see exhaustion etched into her features. I could see what had been drained out of her. Everything. Everything I knew about her. Everything I loved about her.

Even with all of that, she still lit up that fucking place. She still burned bright, even if the flame was lower. It was my job to stoke the fire, protect it and try my best to make her burn like she did before.

I'd known that was going to be hard from the second we found her in that warehouse. I knew that it would be my life's fucking mission the second I saw her curled up, chained up, covered in blood. Knew it every time I looked into her eyes after that. It scared the shit out of me. The emptiness there.

I saw Alyssa in her in many ways. Both were strong, smart and intent on not letting anyone know how much she was struggling. Wanted to protect people from their pain.

And that fucking terrified me.

Every moment of looking for her, I half expected to find her body. Not because she wasn't strong. Fuck, she was the strongest person I'd ever met. But strength had nothing to do with it. There was only so much a person could take. Even the strongest person in the world.

She clung to me in her sleep tighter than she ever had while she was awake. I could see her trying to create distance between us, trying to push me away. Fuck, I understood it. I would give her anything she wanted, anything she needed … except distance from me.

I didn't want to sleep because I didn't want to lose a moment with her in my arms. I didn't know what the future was going to bring, but I knew her sleeping in my arms wasn't in it. Sariah was going to continue to fight this, try to push me away.

She'd already given me the best fucks I'd had in my goddamn life. Having her bent over the bed, watching her ass redden underneath my palm, feeling her fucking soaking for me … Jesus. My cock twitched just thinking of it.

But the physical stuff was never our problem. That was beyond our control. Whatever chemicals or pheromones drew people to each other, we had them tenfold. But as much as I wanted to, I couldn't use sex to bring her back.

Moving slowly so I wouldn't wake her—even though she was deeply asleep—I got my phone from the nightstand, dialing.

It was late there, but I knew she was waiting for my call.

"Colby," Violet spoke urgently. "You found her."

I stroked Sariah's hair. "I found her."

"And she's okay?"

"Baby?" I heard from the background.

"Shhh," Violet scolded Elden. "I'm talking to Colby, he found her. Is she okay?" she asked me.

My eyes ran over the frown Sariah wore, even in her sleep. I felt how strained her body was, muscles tensed as if she were ready to run, or ready for a blow.

"She's gonna be okay," I told her.

"You're going to bring her home." It wasn't a question.

Violet and I had kept in contact whenever I was on the road following Sariah's trail. We both had the goal of getting her back to Garnett, back to the people who loved her, cared about her.

I'd been prepared to drag her there if need be. As time went on, I'd gotten more desperate, my mind too focused on getting her back to where I could keep her safe. But after finding her, I was beginning to understand that dragging her back to Garnett might be the quickest way to lose her.

She'd been chained, literally, by a man who altered the course of her life. I wasn't going to do that to her.

"I don't think she's ready for that," I answered Violet honestly.

There was a long pause. Violet loved Sariah. And Sariah loved her back. I knew that her absence was only because of some kind of warped perception she had that she was saving Violet the grief of watching her unravel. I knew Violet understood that too.

"Will you take care of her?" Violet whispered.

"Of course," I promised. "Not gonna let her outta my sight."

"Okay," she sighed. "Bring her home when you can."

"I intend to."

I ended the call then continued staring down at Sariah, trying to figure out how I was going to protect her from something that had already destroyed her.

SARIAH

Colby took me out for breakfast after the best sleep I'd had in years.

I'd been to a bunch of places all over the country throughout the past almost two years. Objectively beautiful places with quaint main streets and impressive restaurants. Before all of this, I would've gone to every one of them, anxious to try every kind of delight available to me, desperate to taste every inch life had to offer.

But the only thing I gave importance to lately was coffee.

I ate only when I had to, and when I did eat, I deliberately went to run-down chain restaurants. It didn't much matter what I ate, it all tasted the same anyway. Plus, eating food made with preservatives and chemicals, without love or zeal for life, that was somehow easier to swallow.

But Colby had chosen the place, and I'd gone along with it. He had made me agreeable with multiple orgasms this morning.

The café was cute, to say the least. It was decorated in light colors, a lot of the spring sunshine streaming through the many windows. It smelled of high-quality coffee and baked goods, the plates of food coming out of the kitchen impressive.

My mouth watered, surprised by how hungry I was.

I was suddenly aware of all of the light in the place. It was doing great things for Colby. His hair was messy in a way that made it look like he'd spent time on it. I knew he hadn't; I'd watched him shower then slip on a wrinkled tee, black jeans, his cut and boots.

His hair had dried during the ride from here to the café.

His sunglasses were hooked on the front of his tee. His lips were pink, full, maybe from all the work he'd done with them this morning.

He looked like a fucking model.

And I was wearing torn jeans, a black bodysuit and one of Colby's zip up hoodies that I'd stolen from his duffel.

I'd put my hair into a quick braid, knowing we'd be on the bike. I swiped on my usual makeup, smudged liner and a lip gloss I didn't know the age of.

Suddenly, I was self-conscious of how I looked in this harsh light, amongst all the soft colors and pretty pastries. Especially compared to Colby. He was a biker Adonis, and I looked like the cheap escort he'd paid for the night before.

Colby seemed unaware of the way my posture had tightened as he tagged the back of my neck so he could kiss me quickly on the lips. "First thing, I need some strong coffee and food I like." His eyes slunk up and down my body, somehow in appreciation. "Then I need to witness you eat a meal. Maybe even two. Love your body, however it is, but I also want to see you nourished."

Nourished.

Such a simple word.

As if a meal and a coffee would heal everything that was wrong with me.

Arguing with him was futile. Communicating my fucked-up and complex emotions was impossible.

"They better have pancakes," I grumbled.

Colby's lips tipped up in victory.

———

The café did have pancakes. Delicious pancakes with fresh berries and fancy sauces since they were too hip for regular maple syrup.

But I ate the entire plate and enjoyed them. Colby watched me while digging into his French toast. We didn't speak much, but it felt comfortable.

It felt … surreal.

Not twenty-four hours ago, I'd been hungover—since blackout drunk was the only way a girl could get at least a few hours of sleep without nightmares. I'd been looking at a black hole of a day, dreading how I'd have to fill in time before I could plant myself in another dive bar. I'd been drenched in guilt at the numerous calls and texts from Violet, Kate and everyone back in Garnett.

Self-hatred had coated me like oil, despite how red my skin would be after a scalding hot shower, scrubbing at it.

Yet here I was in a funky café with Colby like it was normal. Like *we* were normal.

Suddenly, the sweet and tart taste of pancakes disappeared.

"How have you even had time to do this?" I asked, pushing my plate aside. "Isn't being a Son kind of like a full-time job? I know Hansen is cool and everything, but I don't see how he'd be okay with you going MIA."

I didn't think that Colby had been trailing me the entire time, but I got the impression that he'd been on the road for a long time.

"Getting to you has been my full-time job," Colby answered. "Hansen knows it. Understands it. Whole club gets it. This is where I need to be."

Instead of getting warm and melty at his tone and the look in his eyes, I pressed the heel of my hand to my forehead. "Ugggh, that's so embarrassing."

"Embarrassing?" Colby's eyes turned stormy.

"Yeah," I said. "The whole club of badasses knows that you've been running around, chasing me because I can't handle my shit."

"That's stopping right now." Colby twisted to grab the back of my neck. He was able to do this because he was a 'same side of the booth' guy. "Every man in that club saw you that day."

I grimaced at the thought of it.

Colby's gaze didn't falter, gripping me harder. "When I tell you men in our club have been through shit, I mean it. We don't shock or scare easily. When I'm telling you that every single man in that club is changed from seein' you, I'm not lying. And before you act like that's a bad thing, you let me finish."

My insides cramped and my mouth went dry. I was desperate to argue with him, to run. But I didn't. I let him hold me like that, waiting for him to continue.

"It changed us, seeing you," he murmured. "The aftereffects. We were all spared the fucking horror of having to endure what you did. And still, it fucked-up even the most hardened of brothers. Yet you're here. Breathing. Joking. Teasing. You're here, changed, but you're still fucking you. That's not something to be embarrassed about. That's something to be fucking proud of."

I struggled to fight the tears that were trying to force their way forward. Even if I was going to let myself cry, it certainly couldn't happen in some hip café full of girls taking photos of their food.

"You need to go easy on me," my voice shook. "There are only so many intense things you can say in a short period of time. Unless you haven't noticed, I'm kind of jumpy. I don't want to run again, but if this keeps going…"

I trailed off, hearing the words coming out of my mouth.

"That sounds a lot like a threat," I cleared my throat, brave enough to meet his espresso eyes. "It's not, I promise. I don't want to run, but…"

I trailed off again, not ready to cut myself open, especially here where the bright lights would illuminate my tarnished insides.

"I know," Colby said faintly as he stroked my jaw. "We'll pause on the intense talks for now. How about a little fun?"

I searched his face. "Fun?"

His eyes twinkled. "Yeah, I think we're both overdue for a bit of that."

————

"You plannin' on staying on the road forever?" Colby asked conversationally as we tucked into our dinner.

We'd spent the day as tourists, wandering around the charming main street, going into kitschy stores, not bringing up anything serious. I knew it was simmering under the surface, though.

"I don't really have plans," I picked at my fries.

I'd dropped out of school, given up my room in Providence, canceled all plans. Though I had kept paying for my apartment in Garnett. My bank account remained healthy thanks to a few smart investments and because my expenses had been slashed by ninety percent since I no longer indulged in designer clothes, shoes, purses or any of my costly beauty maintenance routines.

Colby nodded, taking a bite out of his burger.

There were no follow-up questions, no pressure to get me to do anything, say anything.

"I miss them," I blurted.

Colby looked up at me.

"Violet and Willow." I closed my eyes for a beat. "I've been the worst godmother and best friend."

"You have not," Colby pointed a french fry at me. "You're not gonna pile guilt on top of all the shit you're feeling."

I laughed without humor. "Of course, I am. It's threaded into all of it."

I abandoned my fries and emptied my beer, lifting it to the waitress, signaling for another. What I really wanted was three shots of tequila, but Colby had already been subject to my hard drinking ways. That had been embarrassing enough.

He didn't seem to cast judgment over my rapid consumption of beer. He continued lazily eating his burger, waiting to see what came out of my mouth next.

"I love horror movies," I sighed. "At least I used to." I chewed on the inside of my cheek, thinking of how I'd talked myself into watching one a few months ago, deciding I'd let fear rule my life way too long. I'd managed less than thirty minutes before I turned it off, curled into a ball, clutching a bottle of whisky the rest of the night.

"Fuck, I don't even know if the love for them was organic or born because my parents forbade them, letting me know they were a direct invitation to let the devil into your home." I used to roll my eyes at that, but now I couldn't dismiss it quite so easily.

Not that I thought the devil existed in the sense they did. There was no singular man in the bowels of hell, waiting to punish all the sinners. No, there were thousands, millions of men with the devil inside them, waiting for the perfect woman to unleash hell on.

"Anyway," I waved my hand. "Loved them. But I hated how they always ended with the final girl, bloodstained and tired, walking down a deserted road or finally defeating the killer ... end shot. I wanted to know what happened afterward. How her life went on. Was fascinated to see what kind of woman she grew into after surviving all of that."

I smiled in thanks as the waitress set down my fresh beer, waiting for her to leave before I continued.

"Now I know why they don't make movies about the final girl."

His eye twitched, and I knew he was fighting from going into alpha protective mode. We were in a crowded pub, after all. Not that that had ever stopped him.

"They don't make movies about the survivor because people aren't strong enough to see what it takes to be that final girl." He put down his burger. "Because they're scared to see that. A woman who survives monsters, one who can walk through the darkest night of her soul, one who still shines after that—that scares the shit out of patriarchal society." He paused to sip his beer. "They don't make movies about women like you because they're fucking terrified."

I digested his words, hoping that chasing them down with beer would help get them down easier. It didn't help.

"Did you just reference patriarchal society?" I asked, teasing.

He smiled. "I've learned some things since meeting you."

And catching me by surprise, I did something I never thought I'd do again.

I laughed.

CHAPTER
THIRTEEN

I WAS nervous when we finally made it back to the shitty motel room. Not just because I was seeing it with new eyes. Which I was. The space had been okay for me to stew in my own self-pity and trauma, but now that Colby was here, it was … dirty, wrong. Just like me.

The walls were too thin. The bathroom was stained, and the shower barely dribbled lukewarm water. I found myself longing for Egyptian cotton sheets, a huge tub with bubbles, and room service in a five-star hotel.

A piece of the old Sariah coming in, perhaps? Certainly not.

My nerves weren't just coming from our less-than-ideal environment. It was because the day was good. Could even have been considered as great. I had not had a great day in two years. I hadn't even had a *good* day in two years.

I didn't trust it.

Something was coming. I could smell it. Like a summer storm, when the air gets thick and everything is a little too still.

Colby didn't seem keyed up like me. Sure, he had his moments where the fury, worry and male intensity seeped through, but his overall demeanor remained casual.

This only made me more anxious as I flitted around the room, straightening up the half empty bottles of whisky, fluffing the shitty pillows.

"Ri."

I turned, and Colby was standing close to me. Too close. My body tingled with need and terror. I'd been alternating between these two states all day. Right after I was found, Colby saw and respected my problems with space and touching. Now, even if he sensed me stiffen when he held my hand or pressed his body against mine, he didn't back down. He was going for immersion therapy, I guessed. I wasn't sure if it was working.

Then again, we'd pretty much started this whole thing with us tearing each other's clothes off and fucking, so I'd kind of screwed myself over in that department.

"Like the clothes, babe." His eyes ran over me, highlighting his appreciation.

My skin sizzled from the not-so-subtle gaze.

"But," he lifted his eyes to regard me. "They are not you."

The attraction I was feeling fizzled out quickly. My emotions were giving *me* whiplash.

I put my hands on my hips. "And who, pray tell, do you think I am?" Without giving him time to answer, I continued speaking. "You had a glimpse of a girl in flashy shit who called you on your crap and said no, making her more interesting to you." I held up a hand as he opened his mouth to speak. "Nuh-uh," I tutted. "You saw only a speck of who I was, yet you think you can tell me what I'm not." I shook my head violently. "No way, cowboy."

He stared at me, face impassive. But I swear, I saw his mouth twitch as if he were suppressing a grin, the asshole.

"You done?" he asked after a handful of seconds.

The casual tone in which he asked this made me want to rake my nails through the skin of that pretty face of his. Or scream in his face. But interestingly, my rage had struck me silent and sedentary.

"You're done," Colby decided, his head bobbing as he reached into the large duffel I'd been dutifully ignoring.

I lifted my chin in defiance, pretending I was not at all interested in what he was retrieving from it when really it was fucking killing me, not knowing.

"Knew your fancy shit was expensive because it looks it," Colby muttered. "But fuck, did I get some sticker shock with these bad boys."

Out of my peripheral vision, I saw him place something on the bed. Still, I didn't look.

Colby let out a sound that was dangerously close to a chuckle. "But then I remembered the first time I saw you. And fuck, do I still remember every single thing you had on your body, and I remember vowing I'd see all of that shit on my floor once I got you naked. So it's worth every penny."

Holy *shit*.

Cue the skin sizzling. The desire piquing.

He grasped my chin so I was forced to look in his direction.

Or I would've if I didn't squeeze my eyes shut in defiance like a fucking toddler.

The grip on my chin tightened. "Open your eyes, Ri," Colby requested, voice featherlight.

Now, I was stubborn as fuck. And I had already decided I would not open my eyes. I would keep them squeezed shut, same with my mouth, and wait this fucker out.

But my eyes opened of their own accord.

Colby was staring at me, his eyes blazing with reverence, tenderness. So much of it, it almost knocked me off my feet. Too much of it. Much more than I could handle.

But I was still rooted to the spot, unable to move, even though I wanted to run. Even though I *needed* to run.

"Actually, the thought of those fancy ass clothes on the floor were the first thing that entered my mind because you're fucking gorgeous, and I was thinking with my dick," he continued. "But

not long after that, I thought about those fancy ass clothes hangin'
in a closet I built for you." .

My breath left me in a rush.

But he wasn't done.

"I couldn't have known it then, but you haven't had people
give you things. Build you things." He moved his hand up to
stroke the tiny scar on my cheek. It was miniscule compared to the
rest. Created with the sharpest edge of a knife, just because he
could.

*"You think you're so perfect" he whispered, his breath hot and foul on
my face. "But you'll be ugly, ruined when I'm done."*

Though Colby's touch was impossibly tender, pain exploded
beneath his fingertips. Pain that was even more intense than what
created that scar.

I covered my face with my hands.

"Life has only taken from you," he whispered, pulling my
hands from my face. "And I don't want to do that, Ri. Want to give
you things. Everything. Starting with this." He nodded his head to
the bed.

Again, outside of my control, my gaze went there. To the box.

The tan shoebox with white script.

I looked at it, trying to process what I was seeing. While I did
this, Colby let go of me, only to take the lid off the box to expose
what was inside.

Boots.

Christian Louboutin boots, to be exact.

Not just Christian Louboutin boots but Kate boots. One of their
most iconic fits with buttery leather and a spiked heel that looked
needle thin and sharp enough to cut a bitch.

I glanced from Colby to the boots then back.

"You picked these?" I asked him, my voice weak with shock.

He shrugged. "With a little help from Violet. I didn't know who
the fuck was who in the designer world. She introduced me to
Christian, and I chose those."

"No one has ever given me a gift like this," I whispered.

He smiled sadly. "I know."

My hands shook as I touched the leather. I'd shunned all the decadent things I'd surrounded myself in, clothed myself in. I'd told myself it was for a good reason. And maybe it was. Maybe it was the only way I could survive ... then.

But what was my long-term plan? Bounce around shitty motels and become a barely functioning alcoholic for the rest of my life?

"This isn't a message that I'm expecting you to be the woman you were before," Colby said as I ruminated, pulling my gaze from the boots to him.

"I've got no expectations about who you are now," Colby continued. "You're gonna be different, and I'll fucking treasure every new part of you because it was born from your need to survive." His hand fastened on my hip, the other clutching my neck. "You can be whomever the fuck you need to be, and I'll still want you. And I'm willing to bet that this new person will still need to kick ass wearing ridiculously expensive, ridiculously sexy boots."

My chest felt too full. It had been hollow for so long, the beating of my heart splintered my ribs.

"I-I don't know what to say," I confessed, smiling, surprised that my face could still do that.

"Don't need to say anything," he murmured. His cheeky grin was gone, replaced by something somber and soft. Almost ... reverent, tilting the earth beneath me.

No one had ever looked at me like that.

"Your body is not a graveyard, Ri," he referenced what I'd said almost two years ago, cradling my face. "It's a garden. And it's blooming now."

For the first time in years, a tear trailed down my cheek, a tear for me. And fuck if it didn't feel like it was watering something, nourishing something.

Colby wiped the tear away with his thumb. "Now," he rasped.

"Take off your clothes and put on the boots so I can fuck you in them."

My blood sang at his request.

Which I didn't hesitate to obey.

———

It was safe to say my new boots were the foundation for the construction of the new me. Not that they fixed everything. Even Christian Louboutin couldn't fix me completely. But it was a start.

Even though we didn't explicitly say anything about leaving, I started packing once we were dressed again.

I still hadn't graduated to taking my shirt off during sex, and I was grateful Colby didn't push me. I wasn't ready for that yet. But I was ready to get out of this motel.

Colby didn't say anything as I stuffed my scant belongings in the duffel, deciding to trash the beauty products that consisted of a cheap bar of soap, cheaper eyeliner and lipstick.

"We're gonna need to stop at a Sephora," I told him when I returned from the bathroom.

He nodded, the smart man that he was.

"Before we go back, I need to, um … I think I need to go to Utah," I stated, not looking at Colby. "I think that's what I've been lying to myself about this entire time. Driving around the fucking country looking for something, thinking it was vengeance when really, I'm just a kid who wants her parents' approval."

Saying it out loud was all the more confronting. I'd been lying to myself for a while now. I hadn't wanted to admit that I needed anything from my parents. I didn't want to need anything from anyone.

"Okay, got a condition, though," Colby said without hesitation.

I braced for the condition. For him to demand I recount every second of what happened in that warehouse. My fingertips went numb, and my knees started trembling.

"I'm not getting your name tatted on my ass," I teased, trying to hide the terror that had just coldcocked me.

Colby looked at me with a blank expression for a handful of seconds before he burst out laughing.

I watched him as he got a hold of himself, petering down to chuckles. It occurred to me then that I hadn't seen Colby laugh like that in ... years. *Years.*

Just because I hadn't seen it didn't mean it hadn't happened. We'd spent a good amount of time apart these past years. But I got a feeling that he hadn't laughed like that in years.

"Isn't that what you bikers do?" I stomped with false irritation, unable to keep the grin off my face. "Don't you brand your women like cattle?"

This renewed a second round of chuckling that made me feel warm.

"We don't do *anything* to our women without their express condition," he replied seriously. "Though I wouldn't mind getting your name on my ass."

I rolled my eyes.

"If the lady would be willing though, I'd prefer it on my chest," he amended.

I narrowed my eyes on him. "You better still be joking."

"Do I look like I'm joking?" his eyes were twinkling, but he still looked far too serious for me.

Colby was not joking. About getting my name tattooed on his chest.

"I can't handle that right now," I told him honestly.

"Okay," he replied easily, still alternating between his laidback casualness and the intensity that had come with the presentation of the boots.

"What's the condition?" I braced myself.

"We get someone to take care of your car, get it back to Garnett, and we do the trip on my bike."

I gaped at him. I didn't doubt the club's ability to arrange that. "On the bike?"

He nodded. "Might take us a little longer, but it's a good time of year for it. And I'm selfish. It's been almost two years without you. Riding across the country with you on the back of my bike is as close to heaven as I can dream up."

My body tingled and warmed at his words. I couldn't even rustle up any kind of sarcastic comment to deflect from the real feelings he was communicating.

"It's not going to be good," I warned Colby, pushing away that warm feeling. "The meeting with my parents," I clarified. "It's going to be ugly."

Colby cupped my face. "I can deal with ugly, babe."

He was right. He dealt with me. He'd been at the warehouse that day. And somehow, he was still here.

This won't last. You'll corrupt him with the evil inside you.

The cold, ugly, taunting voice wasn't unfamiliar. It had whispered to me since I died in that warehouse.

But for once, I didn't listen to it.

———

I let myself enjoy the road trip.

As much as I *could* enjoy it, at least.

The nightmares were still there. But so was Colby when I jolted awake, covered in sweat. He didn't pry about them. He held me tight, kissed my head and didn't protest when I climbed on top of him, desperate to feel alive, to feel warm and full again.

Food was still difficult. But not as difficult since I found out that Colby was an avid foodie, and he scouted out top-notch restaurants, diners and cafes in every small town we stopped in.

Ditto with the towns and our accommodations.

He'd not only mapped out the entire trip, but he'd structured it so that every town we stayed in was charming and beautiful. Gone were the cheap and dirty motels I'd called home. In their place were boutique hotels, inns and standalone cottages. All of them were tasteful, luxurious and reminded me of the things I used to like.

Colby didn't let me pay for a single thing. I argued, of course. We argued a lot. The trip wasn't sunshine, flowers and rainbows. Though I might not have been operating at full power, I still had some sass left in me. And though Colby was treating me with care, I still pissed him off plenty.

The difference now was … make-up sex. With plenty of spanking.

I didn't look too closely at my need for him to dominate me during sex. To hurt me. I was sure I'd dissect that with a therapist in many years. Colby didn't shy away from doing it either, especially since he saw how much I got off on it.

We were both feeding something that had been born that day at the warehouse, for better or for worse.

It took us over two weeks to cross the country. They were the best two weeks I'd had in years. Even before the warehouse.

Colby and I had never spent that kind of time together. I learned intimate things about him. Like how he had to run first thing in the morning. Or—something I discovered on the second day—have vigorous morning sex. Despite how he'd teased me at the café for ordering all sorts of different coffee drinks, he only drank double shot espressos. He took quick showers.

He read every night before bed. And wore reading glasses. Him, with his shirt off, his dragon tattoo, his muscles, his hair pulled into a bun and fucking reading glasses… You could've put that shit on a calendar.

After I jumped him the first night I saw him like that, the next day I led us to a bookstore. Even though I'd been overloaded with shit to read for classes when I was at school, I'd still liked to read for pleasure.

Violet liked steamy books about fairies, and I enjoyed them too, but my lane veered more toward the Stephen King vibe.

Again, with most of the things I'd loved, it was born out of rebellion. Stephen King wrote about monsters, demons and magic. I hadn't even been allowed to read fucking Harry Potter. My parents were all about censorship. So I, of course, had made a hobby of reading banned books.

Though I ached to escape into different worlds these past years, every time I'd picked up a book, the words on the page had merged together to form a big black hole.

When I tried it in the bathtub of our hotel, with bubbles surrounding me, a candle burning, a glass of whisky beside me, knowing Colby was in the next room, I managed a bunch of chapters until the bathwater turned cold.

I'd called that a win.

Sure, I had some losses too. I still couldn't be fully naked in front of Colby. I froze when he even accidentally brushed my midsection. I was still leaning on booze too much. There were many parts of the day where my skin felt filthy, my body felt like a corpse.

Ollie kept in regular touch. As did Violet, and there were many photos of Willow which burned my throat, fertilizing the guilt that was growing inside of me.

The closer we got to Utah, the tenser I got.

Though I would say, it was hard to be too tense when I spent a large portion of the day pressed against Colby's back, speeding down the highways, watching the burnt amber landscape pass by. Having put all my energy into hating the environment in which I grew up, I'd been blinded to just how lovely it was.

My fingers curled tighter around Colby's midsection as we drove through the town I grew up in.

One of his hands released to cover mine, squeezing it in reassurance.

It was then, right then, every ounce of oxygen in my body froze. My lungs seized.

It felt like I was having a stroke.

Instead, I was realizing with that simple hand squeeze—and a fuck of a lot of shit that came before it that wasn't simple at all— that I loved Colby. That I was *in love* with Colby.

And I was certain, if there was a way for me to launch myself off this bike and run into the desert, I would've done it. Except I didn't quite have that option. There was absolutely no escape. Worse, we were heading to the one place in the world I thought I'd truly escaped from.

But like that warehouse, I was never really going to escape Silverhead, Utah.

My nerves were shot as the bike parked outside my childhood home. It looked more or less the same as it had when I left it. Small but well maintained. The shutters had been freshly painted a dark blue. The flowers in the window boxes were blooming. The grass was green and freshly clipped.

My mother's dependable Toyota was in the driveway as was my father's pickup. Both were routinely serviced, and the tanks were always full. Though there was never a lot of money around in my household, my parents worked tirelessly to keep what they had sparkling and in good condition. Which made me feel all the more uncomfortable throughout my childhood. I was always spilling, smudging, dirtying their pristine, little life.

And here I was about to do it all over again in a spectacular way.

"You'd think having survived a serial killer, I would be able to face up to my parents without fear," I joked weakly, standing at the front gate.

Colby's hand slipped into mine. My heart grew to an uncomfortable size. Like the fucking Grinch. I wasn't built to feel this. Well, maybe I had been, before I'd been disfigured so completely.

"I still haven't been able to go home," he admitted. "So I think you're impressive as fuck."

I looked at him with a smile, warmth blooming inside of me.

"I'll come with you," I promised. "When or if you decide to go home. I'll be at your side."

It was a reckless and dangerous promise to make. Hadn't I already made plans to detonate this relationship once we got back to Garnett? Surely, I had. It was clear to me we couldn't last. That I would only bring him more pain. Yet there I was, making promises. I was leaving carnage wherever I walked.

Colby pulled me to him, and our lips crashed together in a kiss that was not appropriate on a small-town street in a conservative town, especially not in front of my childhood home.

I kissed him back anyway.

"Gonna hold you to that promise, poppet."

Fuck. I'd gone and done it now.

But on the plus side, some of my anxiety shifted from the present to the future. So, I barely noticed that Colby had walked us to the gate and toward the front door. It sank in about halfway there. I was going to be seeing my parents for the first time in years. Experience told me that this would not be a happy reunion. Not because I was turning up with a biker in an MC cut—though that wouldn't help—but because of all the reasons I left. I didn't doubt my parents had wanted me to come home for some time. But they wanted me to come as the daughter they'd always wanted. They wanted me to come home scarred from the world and all of its sins, ready to accept their lifestyle and ready to accept my place in their world.

I *was* scarred from the world and all of its sins. Just not in the way they would expect.

I might've ran if it weren't for Colby at my side. No, I *definitely* would've ran if Colby hadn't been at my side. I never would have made it to the state, let alone inside town limits.

As it was, I still considered running and dragging him along with me. My upper body strength was shit, and I hadn't exactly been hitting the gym these past two years. And it was too late. We didn't even get to knock—or run—because the door opened.

My mother was likely drawn by the sound of the motorcycle and then saw two strange looking people walking up her walkway.

Her face was pinched, ready to get rid of us, stressed about what the neighbors were thinking. She probably had the cordless in her hand, fingers poised to dial 911.

My mother cared a lot about what people thought.

Evidenced by her outfit on a Saturday afternoon. She wasn't going anywhere. My parents didn't go out on the weekends—except for church. Saturday was for cleaning the house, top to bottom. I could still smell the lemon and vinegar that fragranced my weekends.

Her cleaning was obviously done since she was wearing a long skirt, a sensible blouse, and her hair was pulled back into a tight bun.

She wasn't wearing makeup. My mother never wore makeup. She'd never needed to. She'd always been stunning. Her dark hair was shiny, full. Her eyes were hazel and arresting. Her features were delicate, like the rest of her. She was trim, short. My mother kept in shape.

Her hair was streaked with gray now. Her face had more lines. She was still lovely.

It took her a moment to recognize me since she was focused on Colby for a few moments, clutching the door as if preparing to slam it in his face.

My mother excelled at judging a book by its cover. I was honestly surprised she didn't call the police then and there.

"Hi, Mom," I said, my voice weak and small.

Her entire body jerked as she looked at me. Really looked at me, blinking rapidly as she took me in.

I'd been intentional with my outfit. I didn't make an effort to conform to what would make my parents more comfortable. They had to see me for … me, such as I was. Though it was a toned-down version of the 'me' I was before the attack. Plus, I had limited space in Colby's saddlebag. I was wearing black leather pants and the boots that Colby had bought me. My black tee was skintight and would've been cropped in another life. But the one I wore was long, tucked into my pants to ensure no scarred skin was on display.

My hair was down in wild curls, and my makeup was dark and over the top, complete with red lipstick. I'd felt the need to wear armor. Fuck, I'd been half tempted to stitch a scarlet 'A' to the breast of my tee but decided that was pushing it a little far.

I held my breath, waiting for it. Waiting for my mother to take stock of me and for me to come up lacking. But when her eyes met mine, they were glassy.

"Praise God," she murmured. "Praise God," she repeated louder.

"John!" she shouted, her voice hoarse. "John! Come here, our girl is finally home."

Then to my utter shock, my mother snatched me from Colby and pulled me into an embrace.

I was so shocked, I even hugged her back.

CHAPTER
FOURTEEN

IT WAS safe to say I was on unsteady ground. I'd arrived prepared for battle. Prepared for the disappointment, the hurt. I'd truly come for closure. So I could shut these people out of my life. So I would no longer wonder. So I could put them firmly in their box then reassure myself that I hadn't done anything wrong by cutting them out of my life.

But I'd be lying if I said I didn't nurture a small hope, deep down, that something else would happen. That my parents would hug me, love me, make me feel worth … something.

The reality was, that love was harder to weather than their disappointment.

My father had indeed come running to the front door, though he'd had a slightly more reserved response than my mother originally had. But he did hold me in his arms for a long time, his tears wetting my hair.

My father looked older too. His hair was still dark, full, with liberal streaks of gray. He was clean-shaven as always. His silvery gray eyes were surrounded by lines. He was wearing a wrinkle-free blue shirt and beige slacks. He wasn't quite as large as I'd perceived him to be as a kid, but he was tall, stocky. He had always taken care of his body, but he still enjoyed eating and didn't exercise a whole bunch.

When he let me go, awkward introductions were made to Colby. My mother had shaken his hand enthusiastically saying, "Thank you, thank you for bringing my daughter home."

"She brought herself," he returned. "I just gave her the ride."

The front door was still open at that point. When my mother's gaze landed on the motorcycle at the curb, I swear, she didn't even blink.

"Come inside, you must be starving," she urged. She didn't even ask Colby to move his bike somewhere down the street or hide it in the garage. Hell must've frozen over while I wasn't looking.

Things had been somewhat of a blur since then. My mother and father stumbling over each other to feed us, make us comfortable. Both of them kept staring at me, not in judgment, but almost as if they expected me to disappear.

Dinner was how I remembered them to be. Everything made from scratch, including the bread. My mother didn't believe in anything processed. We were served water or fresh juice. Neither of my parents drank. I was aching for a cocktail.

We ate in the formal dining room, a lace runner in the middle of the table, candlesticks and white china salt and pepper shakers arranged neatly.

My father said grace.

I briefly considered protesting this as I had many times before. My parents were tensed as if they were waiting for me to do that. It occurred to me how predictable I was in this house. I'd prided myself on being chaotic, an individual, an anarchist against an oppressive environment. But there, my actions could've been tracked like clockwork. It was interesting.

It also occurred to me that I'd gone there for a fight. I'd gone there to reinforce all the negative ideas I had about these people.

So instead of playing the part that everyone at the table was so used to, I took my mother's hand and remained silent as my father said grace.

I couldn't say if they were surprised or not.

The food tasted different than it had before. Better than it had before. I ate two servings. Which made Colby smile in satisfaction.

The conversation was stilted and awkward. I could tell my parents were desperately curious about what my life had looked like over the past years. I also sensed that they didn't want to make a wrong move and end the dinner with me screaming at them and storming off.

I had a history of doing that.

And they had a history of coaxing me into doing that.

"So, Colby, what is it you do?" my mother asked midway through the meal.

I pursed my lips, inexplicably wanting to smile at the seemingly innocuous question. I did internally applaud my mother for asking the question rather placidly and without any kind of judgmental undertone.

Again, the teenager in me wanted to shout, "He's in a motorcycle club, embodies every single thing that you fear, and we're *fucking*." But I kept my mouth shut.

"I'm a mechanic," he replied with a smile. Colby had been relaxed, friendly and at ease since the second we walked in. He was also subtly but openly affectionate with me. He always had his hands on me.

Right then, his hand was on my thigh under the table.

Though it wasn't at all appropriate, my body responded to that hand on my thigh with an ever-growing need. I'd discovered that my sexual desires had not dissipated in recent years. Hadn't even dulled a little. Like the booze, I used it in excess to drown out my screams coming from that warehouse.

"That's a good solid job," my father said.

My mother nodded in approval. "Very respectable."

I almost choked on my juice.

Colby shot me a look.

"And, uh, Sariah … school is still going well?" my father asked hesitantly.

He was venturing into territory laden with emotional land-mines. My parents had not wanted me to go to college so far away. They had not been able to afford to send me to an Ivy League. And even if they could have, they would've done everything in their power to stop my mind from getting corrupted by such 'dangerous ideas.'

They had wanted me to go to some kind of religious based college. They weren't overly concerned with which religion—since they were Mormon and Jewish respectively—as long as it was somewhere that instilled a healthy fear of sin and promoted a 'godly life' … whatever the fuck that meant.

The news of me going to Brown wasn't met with conventional parental happiness. The news of me dropping out would likely be met with conventional parental disappointment and maybe some sort of 'I told you so.'

"School is going well," I replied, not lying. As far as I knew, the college was still in business, still squirting out graduates. I just wasn't one of them.

"That's great," my mother exclaimed, an octave higher than normal.

My father cleared his throat. There was no more food to focus on.

"Um, we're kind of tired," I said. "Long drive."

"Of course," my mother quickly stood up. "I've got fresh sheets on your bed and kept your room just as it was."

This surprised me. I was sure she would've ripped down all my posters the second I left and disposed of all contraband. Maybe the weed I hid in my underwear drawer still remained.

"Colby, I've made up the guest room for you," my mother added.

"No need, I'm sleeping with Sariah."

I could not hide my gape as those words came out of Colby's mouth. My eyes went to my father, holding my breath and waiting for him to argue.

My mother didn't even make a peep.

They just stared blankly between the two of us, silent for a few awkward moments.

My father then did the unthinkable... He nodded, clapping his hands together. "Right, then that's sorted."

"Right," I repeated, unable to look at Colby.

"Well, um, goodnight, then," I spluttered.

"Let us know if you need anything, honey," my mom smiled at me.

Honey. When was the last time she'd called me that? Often, I realized, scouring my memories. I'd just shut it out. Focused on the fights, the rules, the stifling feeling of the role I was supposed to play.

"Yeah, I will," I responded awkwardly. "Goodnight."

"It's so good to have you home, Sariah." Mom clutched her hands in front of her, her tone telling me she meant it.

"It's, uh, good to be home," I replied. And I realized I meant it too.

"I cannot believe I'm here in my childhood bedroom, sleeping with a *boy,* and my parents are aware of his presence," I said, slipping Colby's tee over my head.

I was trying something... Getting changed in front of him. I still did it quickly, so he only saw a flash of my scars. But he saw them. Because he watched me intently whenever we were in a room together. His jaw didn't lock, his face didn't change into a mask of fury. Or worse, revulsion. If anything, hunger sparked in those dark irises of his.

That gave me some increased confidence and niggled at my need to give that last part of myself to him. Trust that with him.

Maybe.

"You didn't even have to sneak in the window or anything," I teased, pushing those thoughts away for the moment. We'd already done enough hard things today.

Colby chuckled. "Do I want to know how many boys snuck in that window?"

I glanced at the window, contemplating lying. "No," I admitted. "You are the only man to see all of this."

I gestured around the room that was cluttered with books, my Harry Potter box set front and center since that had offended my mother so greatly.

Movie posters from *The Lost Boys* and *Pulp Fiction* were pinned up, old Cosmos sat in piles. It was pretty much every piece of pop culture I could get my hands on to outrage my parents at the time.

Looking around, it made me feel nostalgic, embarrassed and confused. I'd spent so much time crafting myself into a person who was the exact opposite of them that I didn't truly know who I was.

"So, I'm popping your cherry, then?" Colby's taunt jerked me out of my thoughts.

I looked over at him. He was sitting propped up in my double bed, shirtless and sinful.

"My cherry is long gone. Unfortunately, I wasn't *that* good of a girl."

"You gonna be my good girl and get into bed with me?" he asked.

My toes curled.

"You're not gonna fuck me in my childhood bedroom with my obsessively religious parents under the roof." I folded my arms underneath my boobs. "I think this house repels sex."

"I am gonna fuck you in the room that no one else has, yeah."

My thighs pressed together. "I had you pegged as a guy who was too respectful for that."

"I'm respectful enough," he snickered. "Me not fucking my woman every single chance I get is disrespectful to both of us."

I bristled at the 'my woman' thing and was about to nip that in the bud, but Colby got sick of waiting, and he knifed up, crawled to the end of the bed, grabbed me by the arm and pulled.

I tumbled down, laying on top of him for a split second before he flipped us, and his tee was no longer covering my body. He'd ripped it up and over my head, twisting it so both my arms were still restrained in the fabric.

My nipples pebbled, and my breathing shallowed. I was already soaking fucking wet.

I barely even thought about the fact that my entire midsection was exposed to him for the first time. I was exposed and vulnerable.

"You gonna be able to be quiet, or do I have to gag you?" he rasped out, mouth inches from mine.

My blood heated at the question. I was never into being gagged. Not even before. Enough people tried to silence me. But suddenly the prospect was ... inviting.

Colby's eyes smoldered. "Yeah, see you want that." His hand tweaked my nipple.

I let out a restrained moan.

"I'll gag you." He kissed my neck. "Tie you to the bed and fuck you so hard that you'll come until you forget everything but me."

A low moan crept from my throat as I squirmed against his mock restraints. The restraints might've taken me back to that warehouse, where I had no control, where a sadistic man was hovering over me, telling me what he was going to do to me.

They might've if the man was anyone but Colby.

As it was, he was redefining what being restrained meant, he was rewriting history, and he was doing it in my childhood bedroom.

His mouth traveled from my neck, down to my nipple. Again, I let out a strangled cry as his lips fastened around it.

I was so wrapped up in need, in pleasure, I didn't notice his lips had moved down to my abdomen until they were there, grazing my scars.

My body battled against the icy cold feeling that washed over me and the fire that came when Colby's hand found my pussy, rubbing my clit atop my panties.

He didn't put pressure on my skin, his lips were barely there, but every time he made contact, agony mingled with ecstasy. I struggled against his tee. If I'd wanted to, I could've gotten out. If I told him to stop, he would have. Immediately.

I almost did. My mouth opened to tell him I couldn't do this, that I wasn't ready for this. Then his finger rubbed my clit, and his head tilted up so his eyes met mine.

There was no revulsion there. No pity. Only need.

"You're fucking gorgeous, Sariah."

And before I could respond, before I could argue, his mouth was no longer on my midsection, it was right where his fingers were. Except there was no longer a barrier of cotton between us.

Surprising even myself, I came the second his mouth touched my sensitive skin.

But Colby didn't stop. My hands were still above my head, tangled in his tee.

Colby's mouth stayed there for all my aftershocks, sending me over the edge, multiple orgasms melding into each other.

I quivered with exhaustion when he slid up my body, laying a gentle kiss on the worst of my scars. I flinched at the contact, not entirely from pain but from a new sensation. His mouth was coated with my pleasure, covering the space of my greatest shame.

I didn't have enough presence of mind to completely process that, which was probably good.

Colby's mouth brushed against mine, kissing me deeply. I tasted myself on him, and I loved it.

His naked torso brushed against mine, my nerve endings singing and screaming in unison.

One of Colby's hands locked around my still bound wrists, the other bracing him on the mattress to hover over me.

Then he was inside.

His mouth on mine stifled my moans of pleasure, my body struggling with the sensation of being so full while still so sensitive.

I loved it. Every time Colby was inside of me, I felt complete. Whole. Alive.

I was so far gone, I might've said something I regretted. If his mouth wasn't covering mine, I might've told him I loved him.

Luckily, he didn't stop kissing me. And my final orgasm crashed over me so intensely, I lost the ability to speak.

A close call.

Too fucking close.

———

After having what was possibly the most intense sex of my life—in my childhood bedroom with my parents down the hall, no less—I was exhausted. Every one of my limbs felt like lead, my breathing slowly returning to normal.

I was curled up against Colby, my leg thrown over his hip, my head resting on his chest. His arm was around me, underneath his tee—I'd put it back on. We'd made progress, but not *that* much progress—drawing patterns against my bare skin.

"It's hard," I whispered against his chest. "Seeing them. I've turned them into villains my entire life, blaming them for so much when really, they were just doing the best with what they had." I drew lines on his pec. "It's all too confronting, realizing that if I want to blame my parents for anything, it's blaming them for loving me the only way they knew how."

He stroked my hair. "I think that's what fucks us up the most, our parents fucking us up even though they love us."

My fingers trailed across the dragon on his chest. "Where does this come from?"

He looked down at his chest as if he were seeing the ink for the first time.

"Alyssa was a talented artist," he smiled. "She loved to draw." There was more warmth in his tone than when he'd described her in that shitty motel room. "She wanted to go to art school, make a career out of it, but she knew our parents wouldn't approve of that. So, she focused on her studies like the dutiful daughter she was. I've spent a lot of time wondering if she'd been allowed to pursue her passion, commit to it, if things might've been different. I imagine my parents thought about that a lot too."

He played with a strand of my hair.

"Maybe it might've changed things … for a time," he sighed. "But I don't think it would've fixed things. It isn't that simple." His eyes searched mine. "Nothing ever is."

He looked back down at his chest.

"I got it after she died, right before I left home."

My fingers traced the intricate lines, the dragon all the more meaningful now.

Though I was a rebellious teen and a wild college student, I had yet to put ink on my body. I wanted it. But I didn't know myself well enough in order to understand what I would want on my body permanently.

For a second, a split second, I toyed with the idea of one. One that made me think of Colby. A reminder.

But I shoved that away.

I already had enough marks on me that I couldn't take off. Enough reminders.

"Out of suffering have emerged the strongest of souls; the most massive characters are seared with scars," Colby's deep voice filtered through my mind.

When I peered up, I saw that he was no longer being introspective, he was focused wholly on me.

"Kahlil Gibran," Colby murmured.

I vaguely remembered the name from a philosophy class, though I did not recognize the quote. It struck me, nonetheless.

"I appreciate the gift you gave me," Colby continued, fingers traveling closer to my midsection.

I stiffened, but he didn't go all the way to my scars.

"I've been with women," I informed him, changing the subject because I really wasn't ready to talk about this right now.

"I know," he said.

I focused on my breathing, waiting for him to elaborate.

"We did surveillance on Violet, on you," he cleared his throat. "I know you've been with women."

I sucked my teeth. Of course. Now that the Sons' hacker had delved into every area of my life, there was nothing Colby didn't know about me. "Okay, so if we do this—"

"We're doing this," Colby interrupted.

I sighed in exasperation. "*If* we do this, are you going to request a threesome with another woman?"

His gaze went stormy. "No fuckin' way. No one else touches what's mine except me."

"Okay, so no threesomes." I wanted to grin or roll my eyes at the way he went from zero to over-the-top protective caveman in milliseconds. "But other guys have thought, at the beginning at least, it was hot that I am attracted to both men and women. But eventually, it becomes a problem."

Men loved the idea of women together when it was a performance for them. But when it was clear that women did it for their own pleasure and not for them, they became far too threatened. Too suspicious of every friend. Jealous of everyone.

"I'm not other guys," Colby grumbled. "And I don't have a

problem with who you used to be attracted to. As long as you're mine."

I groaned. "We'll talk about the whole 'you are mine' thing later."

"Talk about it all you want, it's not gonna change it," he replied stubbornly.

I scowled at him. "I'm too tired to argue with you."

His lips spread into an infuriatingly dazzling smile. "Well, go to sleep, then."

"Your cock isn't inside me, so you don't get to give me orders," I fired back.

He flipped us seconds after I'd got the last word out. My panties were gone, his cock freed and poised at my entrance after only a few seconds more. I blinked at him, trying to get my bearings, my body way ahead of me, pussy primed and ready for him.

"Again?" I breathed.

He showed his teeth in a wicked smirk. "I'm a young man, poppet, and I'm a man who has you in your bed. I'd have to be dead not to be ready to fuck you."

My skin tingled in anticipation.

Colby didn't wait for me to say anything else, he just slammed into me, covering my mouth with his hand to muffle my cry from the unexpected pleasure.

"You. Are. Mine." He growled with every thrust.

My body submitted to him, my eyes holding steady with his. I didn't argue, mostly because of the hand on my mouth but also because I couldn't argue. He was claiming every inch of me. The truth was, he'd claimed every inch of me the second our mouths had touched in that hospital a million years ago.

"Say it," he rasped, eyes wide and wild.

I moaned from beneath his hands, my orgasm hurtling forward.

"Say it," he repeated, removing his hand.

Though I was almost entirely mad with pleasure, I managed

one harsh look and kept my lips sealed shut. Until he rammed into me so forcefully, it teetered on the cusp of pain. I fucking loved it.

"I'm yours," I exclaimed, right before my orgasm washed over me.

Colby was still asleep when I woke up. It was early. Really early. Though he wasn't the kind of guy to sleep in, we hadn't established much of a routine these past weeks. I think it was as much of a vacation from reality for him as it was for me.

For once in two years, he wasn't chasing me, wondering what I was doing with myself. I hadn't considered how much of a toll that would've taken on him, how it might've exhausted him.

Not until I woke that morning, in my childhood bedroom, with the dim morning light filtering through the lace curtains.

He was lying half on top of me, as he did every night. I couldn't move in the night without him feeling it, without him waking from my nightmare with me. But I hadn't had a nightmare last night, hadn't broken his sleep. He looked younger when he was asleep. More his age. He was only a year older than me, but I'd never considered him as a peer, not in that way. He'd always seemed older, wiser. Which made sense since trauma aged us. I was lucky it only happened on the inside, otherwise I would've looked two hundred years old.

There was no crease between his dark brows. His forehead was smooth.

I wished that he could be the man that his sleeping form gave him the potential to be. The man whose sister had survived. Who hadn't gotten tangled up with a wrecked woman who was apt to destroy his life, injecting it full of more tragedy and pain.

As much as I wanted to be one when I was a teenager, I wasn't a witch. I didn't have the power to raise the dead or change the past.

So, I carefully extracted myself from his embrace instead, dressing quietly.

It was a testament to how exhausted he must've been that he didn't notice me putting on a tank and some sweats, using the facilities and then slipping out of the room.

It was before seven, and the house was filled with light and activity, the sounds of cupboards opening and shutting in the kitchen filtering down the hall. I remembered screaming at my mother from my bedroom, telling her off for waking me up so early.

"Good morning," I greeted her, lingering uncertainly by the entrance to the kitchen.

My mother was at the stove, and she either hadn't expected me to get up this early or had forgotten I was even here.

She jumped, turning with a spatula in her hand, the other on her chest. Her eyes flew over me in surprise, and again, I wondered if it was because I was awake or there at all.

Then they warmed.

"Sariah, you're awake. I was just making you and your, uh, you and Colby some breakfast. Does he eat eggs and pancakes? He looks like the kind of fellow who follows a specific kind of diet."

I smiled because Colby's muscled and sculpted body did hint that he tracked his macros. "Yeah, he eats everything."

"There's coffee, fresh." Mom nodded to the drip espresso that indeed was fresh. My mother drank it, though my father abstained because the church forbade it. I, of course, started drinking coffee when I was twelve for that very reason.

I was grateful for something to do, rather than stand awkwardly, unsure of where to put myself.

It was funny, being back in that kitchen where nothing much had changed. The countertops were the same, the cabinets maybe had a fresh coat of sage green paint. The dining table in the middle of the room was set for breakfast, this time with four plates, bowls and cutlery.

I was so distracted by the strange familiarity of the room that upon reaching into the third cabinet for a mug, I didn't even notice that my tank had ridden up. My mother's strangled gasp told me just how high it had risen.

Her horrified gaze was focused on the ugly, raised, jagged scar that was about two inches long. Just above my hip bone. It was surrounded by smaller ones, less red and angry but still ugly.

I quickly snatched a mug, tugging my tank down with the other hand.

But the damage had been done.

Mom's hand was shaking as she took the eggs off the stove and walked toward me.

My entire body turned to stone. She must've noticed that since she stopped before she was close enough to touch me.

"W-what happened?" she whispered. "Who did that to you? Who hurt you?" The last two questions weren't quite a whisper. They were louder, darker, angrier, and more venomous than I'd ever heard my mother's voice sound.

I clutched the handle of the mug, walking to the coffee pot and pouring so I had something to do.

I gripped the counter, bracing myself as I contemplated how to respond. A lie. A lie would suffice. I could say I was mugged. That I was in a car accident. That I'd been involved with a cult that believed in mutilating your own body.

Any and all of those would've been preferable to the truth.

"I was taken." My voice was hoarse. "By a man who hurt women." I grasped the counter harder. "A man who killed women," I corrected. I placed the mug on the counter so I could hug my stomach. "But not before he hurt them first."

My mother's ragged breaths filled up the room, yet I couldn't look at her.

"He took me, he hurt me because of the … lifestyle I lived," I choked out, unable to get any more specific. "He punished me for my sins, just like you said I would be."

I finally looked at her then, not sure what I was expecting to find. Disgust, maybe.

My mother's face was a mask of pain and sorrow, her eyes glassy with unshed tears. "Oh, honey," she whispered. "You have done nothing that you deserve to be punished for. Nothing you could ever do would make you deserve ... *that*," her voice cracked as she looked down to my stomach. "I used religion like a weapon because I thought I could protect you from the evils of this world with it." She wiped angrily at a tear rolling down her face. "I couldn't fathom that you could be hurt that way and blame yourself because of what I instilled in you. My baby."

She crossed the distance between us, her arms wrapping around me.

"My baby," she repeated.

And though I hated the embrace of people who loved me, who wanted to comfort me, I found myself melting into my mother's. Collapsing into her. And although she was a small woman, who I'd never considered strong, she took all of my weight. All of my sorrow.

COLBY

When I woke up, Sariah wasn't beside me.

So, I woke up pissed.

First off, I woke up terrified. Sariah's warm body was not underneath mine. Her hair wasn't strewn across my skin. The rise and fall of her chest wasn't the first thing I saw when I woke up. Her scent wasn't the first thing I smelled. Her skin wasn't the first thing I tasted.

And for a fucking horrendous moment, I was sure I'd dreamed it all. That I was still staying in cheap hotel rooms, chasing her, not knowing if this was the day she ran out of strength.

Luckily, it was only a moment, but that moment was more than enough to ruin my fucking morning.

I threw on clothes and opened the door, intent on finding Sariah, informing her that I'd punish her later. My cock twitched at the very thought. And at the low tenor of her voice coming from the direction of the kitchen. Same with the smell of coffee.

"You're a mechanic, right?" a voice asked from behind me.

I was so jumpy I almost pulled my piece. Which I wasn't carrying. I figured it wouldn't have been a good idea to come into an already unpredictable situation armed.

Sariah's father stood behind me, wearing a plaid shirt that looked like it had been ironed, same with the crisp blue jeans. Though it was early, he looked like he'd been up for hours.

I cleared my throat, nodding as I recovered from his greeting.

"Good." He jerked his head, presumably indicating for me to follow him as he walked to the end of the hall and out a back door.

I hesitated for a second, glimpsing back toward the kitchen. Sariah was safe here, in her childhood home. But it wasn't just for her sake that I wanted to lay eyes on her. It was for mine too. Though this was important. I could tell by the look in her father's eyes.

I followed him out the door.

The hood of his truck was up, tools laid neatly on a rag on the engine.

"Givin' you trouble?" I asked, squinting at the engine.

"Ah, a little. She's old but dependable, needs me to give her some quality time every once in a while." He glanced up at me. "Like a woman that way."

I chuckled. "You're not wrong."

He was looking at me with the eyes of a wary, tired, worried father. But not in the same way fathers in our small town had looked at me when they were giving me this kind of talk while I was dating their daughters.

I wasn't a patched member of an outlaw MC then. I was a great student, on the football team, had great manners. Still, there had been a glint in some eyes. One I learned to recognize. One that labeled me as 'other' and didn't want their daughter with a 'Chinese' boy, never mind I was Korean.

Sariah's father did not have that look.

"Something happened to her," he changed the subject, practically choking the wrench in his hand. He was reserved, an expert at keeping his emotions in check. A stern guy, I guessed. But one who loved his daughter dearly. Who loved her enough to see what was missing.

"Yeah, something happened." Lying wouldn't do much. And I respected this man. He loved his daughter. He had kept her safe the best he could.

He looked down at the wrench. "And it was bad."

My mind threw me back into that warehouse, saw Sariah chained, bloody, felt her collapse against me, saw her in that hospital bed. Fuck, even before that, I remembered the girl whose hand I held on the rooftop a lifetime ago.

"It was bad," I agreed, even though he hadn't technically structured it as a question.

Though his expression remained impassive, stoic, he went back on one heel, steadying himself against the truck.

"Saw it," he croaked. He looked to his feet, cleared his throat then looked at me. His eyes shone. "I saw it," he repeated, clearer this time. "The second I laid eyes on her, I saw it. She was different. Older in a way that every parent hopes their child will never have to age." He cleared his throat again. "Is the person responsible, are they…"

My mind surged back to the basement in the club.

Granger didn't much look like a human anymore.

He was covered in his own blood and waste.

Strips of his skin hung off in places. His eyes were swollen shut. Metal cuffs around his wrists had cut through layers of skin to hit the bone. The wet, wretched sound of his breathing was the only sign he was alive.

He was only alive because we'd made it so. Because I'd held back just when I saw he was about to leave this world.

I'd been unwilling to give him that mercy. Fuck, I'd even danced with the idea of keeping him down here forever, feeding my wrath with his pain.

It was tempting. Really fucking tempting.

But I felt myself emptying. Felt parts of me becoming hard, cruel with every piece of flesh I tore off, every new injury.

He deserved pain. He deserved to feel that fear and helplessness he'd made countless other women feel. But I deserved life. Sariah did.

And she'd gone.

The night after I'd claimed her.

Though it filled me with rage, I hadn't been surprised. Her need to escape was written all over her. Fuck, even I felt suffocated in the town that had become my home. With the reporters, the fucking podcasters, every true crime junkie in the world it seemed invading our small town.

Yeah, I'd been expecting her to run. I knew I'd be chasing her. Which meant I'd be ending Granger's life. It had to be me, though my brothers had offered. Each of them was hungry for his blood, pain and death. His violence had pierced each of us.

"You didn't take anything from her," I told him as I stared at him, looking nothing more than the pathetic coward he was. "You didn't break her."

It was a lie. A necessary one. She was broken. But she wouldn't be for long.

Then, without giving him the chance for last words, I put my knife through his temple.

"They'll never touch her again," I promised Sariah's father.

He nodded curtly. "I'm a godly man," he told me, laying the wrench down neatly beside the other tools. "I don't believe in violence, in concepts like revenge. My church believes that humans are not inherently evil, just that sin pushes them further from God, that everyone can be forgiven if they ask for it. If they repent."

I didn't disagree, figuring it wasn't exactly the time to talk about my views on God, or lack thereof.

"But I'll say, I abandoned all of those beliefs just as soon as I saw that pain in my daughter's eyes," he continued. His eyes roamed over me before landing on my cut. I'd debated wearing it, fearing this reunion was going to be tense enough as it was. I didn't need to taunt conversative people with my affiliation with what they would label as a gang.

Sariah was there as I stared at my cut in the hotel room that morning. It was resting on a chair.

She didn't hesitate to pick it up, carefully, reverently, her small hands brushing across the leather. My cock hardened. She moved to put it on me, and I complied, anything to have her near, have her touch me in a way that wasn't sexual. She still struggled with affection when she wasn't in the midst of desire.

Her hands brushed over my shoulders after she put on my cut, lifting up on her tiptoes to rest her chin on my shoulder.

I grasped her hands, pulling them around my body so her front pressed to my back.

"It's part of you," she whispered. *"We're both going there as we are, not pretending to be anything we're not, and we're sure as shit not censoring ourselves for their comfort. It's up to them whether they can deal or not."*

"You're not just a mechanic, are you?" he asked.

"No." Again, lying wouldn't have served me. And Sariah was right, if her parents wanted to be a part of her life, they were a part of club life. It was up to them whether they could deal or not.

"What happened to my daughter, is it because of the life you live?" her father's tone was colder now.

I'd racked my brain, trying to figure out whether Sariah would've been hurt if she was or wasn't involved with the club. Granger had hated the club, wanted to hurt us. He also hated women he considered to be like his mother, selling themselves.

Ultimately, there was no one to blame but that sick piece of shit.

"No," I replied. "It was because he was evil."

Her father looked at me, fist clenched. "Are you gonna take care of her?"

"With my life," I promised.

His head bobbed, abandoning the tools before clapping me on the shoulder. "Right. Now that that's done, let's go and have some breakfast."

SARIAH

By the time my father and Colby showed up for breakfast—curiously together—both Mom and I had pulled ourselves together.

We hadn't spoken more about what happened to me, or about the mistakes made in my upbringing. There was both too much and not enough to say at the same time. Much too messy. And I didn't think years of conflict and resentment would be solved in a day. Surely, we had a long road to go. But this would do for now.

Colby had come in to kiss me on the forehead, murmuring in my ear too quiet for anyone else to hear. "You're gonna pay for leavin' me to wake up alone."

And, quite inappropriately, I got turned on in my childhood kitchen with both my parents in attendance.

If Colby's smirk was anything to go by, he knew exactly what he did to me.

I repaid that by trying to ice him out the rest of the morning. That didn't work since when I purposefully moved my chair far from his, he just moved his own, grasping my thigh with one hand while eating his eggs one-handed.

My mother, the queen of compartmentalizing, seemed her upbeat self, talking about everything and nothing at the same time. Though her gaze flickered to me more often, eyes shinier than normal. My father peered at the paper, but he didn't hide behind it like he used to do during the family breakfasts I remembered.

They were going to church, as they did every Sunday. Though

my mother was Jewish, she still attended Mormon church with my father. I'd never really thought about them and their differing religions, how they changed and bent their beliefs for love. Though I'd thought they were boring, stiff people, they'd taken risks for love. And they did still love each other. My father held my mother's hand after he'd finished his breakfast.

"We don't have to go today," Mom announced at the end of breakfast.

I stared at my mother. I'd broken my arm one Sunday morning, scaling a tree before church. My mother had decided the break wasn't bad enough to warrant an immediate trip to the emergency room, so I'd had to sit through church cradling my left arm to my chest.

There was simply not an occasion serious enough to warrant deviating from their routine or angering God—more accurately, ruffling the feathers of the small but judgmental circle they ran in.

"Um, no, Mom, it's okay." I wasn't quite sure how her offer made me feel. Despite the relative success of the visit, I didn't want to push it.

"We need to get on the road," Colby said, squeezing my thigh. "We've still got a bit of a drive ahead of us to get home."

"Home?" my mother questioned.

"Yes," I replied, covering Colby's hand with my own. "Home to Garnett."

My mother's eyes widened in panic. "But you only just got here."

"Well, we can visit," I hedged, not sure if I was telling the truth or not.

"Or you can come to Garnett. We'd love to have you," Colby offered.

I stared at him with a raised brow regarding the 'we.' My apartment was one bedroom. He lived in a dorm room in the clubhouse. We were not really up to hosting my parents. And we weren't supposed to be a 'we.'

My mother looked at my father who shrugged, deferring to her as he always did. "Yes," she said, looking back at us. "That would be nice."

It was somehow decided that my parents would be coming to visit in six months. I kind of blacked out during the planning, Colby making all the arrangements.

Six months was long enough to come up with alternate plans. Or move.

We finished breakfast then packed up quickly. I put on jeans, an oversized tee and a leather jacket Colby had bought me a couple weeks ago.

"You can't be on the back of my bike without a jacket. Plus, you look sexy as fuck in it," he'd said when he presented it to me.

"You'll call?" my mother asked, holding my arms in a death grip at the front door.

"I'll call," I promised her, surprising myself by making that promise so easily. Even more so, I meant it.

Something had been healed there. Not just my relationship with my parents, but something inside of me. I was far from better, but I wasn't quite as empty anymore. Didn't feel as scooped out. Hollow.

My mother hugged me once more, kissing my hair. "You deserve this," she whispered. "A man who takes care of you. A life of beauty. Whatever that looks like."

Then she let me go.

It was my father's turn. He was a man of few words and fewer emotions. It was safe to say I was shocked to find his eyes filled with tears when he pulled me into his arms.

He smelled of the same cologne he'd worn since I could remember and vaguely of motor oil. His large arms encased me, and suddenly, I was five years old again, running into his arms when I'd woken up from a nightmare, feeling like he could fix anything, like I was as safe as I could ever be.

Before he let me go, he kissed my head.

"We're proud of you, Ri Ri," he said, using the name he hadn't in years.

He looked at Colby, holding out a hand. Colby took it, and they shook firmly. All very manly.

And then we were on the road again.

On our way home.

CHAPTER
FIFTEEN

WE'D BEEN RIDING LESS than an hour when Colby pulled off the highway and took us to some kind of underpass or storm drain. Whatever it was, it was a tunnel under the highway. It was deserted though covered in graffiti to show how far rebellious teenagers had ventured in order to have some fun. I knew what it was like... Being a teenager in my hometown, we'd been willing to go even further.

"What are we doing here?" I asked when he stopped the bike in the middle of the wide tunnel.

Colby didn't answer, he just got off the bike. I frowned, doing the same.

"Unbutton your jeans and bend over the bike," he ordered coldly.

I stared at his impassive face for a moment before noticing that his cock was rock hard in his jeans. My mouth moistened at the sight.

"Here?" I stuttered.

I could hear the cars overhead on the highway. The landscape itself was quite deserted, but the beer bottles and graffiti were a sign that people came here. That people *could* come here.

"Don't make me ask again."

Shaking, and with soaked panties, I did as he asked, laying my forearms on the warm bike seat.

Colby didn't hesitate to snatch the waistband of my jeans and haul them down, panties and all.

The cold air bit against my bare skin. I felt exposed. Excited. And I wasn't prepared for Colby's palm to come down on the skin of my ass.

I jerked in pain. And pleasure.

"Told you you'd pay for leaving me sleeping, to wake up without you." Shivers raced down my spine as he spoke against my ear. Shivers that we're not unpleasant. Not at all. I arched my back higher, presenting myself to him.

His hand came down on my ass once more, in the exact same spot, pain shooting to my feet, pleasure erupting in my pussy.

"You gonna do it again?" Colby asked, voice hoarse.

I shook my head, unable to speak. I was too choked up by the variety of sensations, the highway sounds, the crisp air, the open environment, my overwhelming need to come.

Colby shifted behind me, his belt clanking, his boots crunching on the ground underneath. He seized my hips, then his cock pressed against my drenched pussy, my breath fleeing me as the head slipped inside of me.

I clutched at the bike, trying to steady myself, trying not to topple the fucking bike over, not explode right there and then.

"Sariah," Colby grumbled, warning in his tone. "Are you going to do it again?"

A small, rational and sane part of me urged me to argue. I could get out of bed at whatever time, whenever the fuck I wanted.

"I won't do it again," I rasped, trying to move myself back, to ease more of him inside me.

Colby gripped my hips harder. "Thought you'd fight me on that," he muttered, his voice tight. I could feel his hunger, his need for me. But he was controlling it. To torture me.

That only served to turn me on further.

"I'll fight you on other things," I managed. "Many things."

His lips found my neck. "Good."

Then he slammed into me.

I cried out in ecstasy as he held me steady, bracing myself against the bike as the sounds of vehicles raced above us.

My body sang for him in that underpass full of beer bottles and graffiti, the desert air kissing our bodies.

I hadn't thought I'd be into getting taken like this. I'd thought it would make me feel like trash, make me feel used.

And maybe, in a way, it did. Maybe a dark, wrong part of me liked that.

But I also felt fucking worshipped. Powerful.

No matter what, I fucking loved it.

We took our time making the journey back to New Mexico. I wasn't sick of being on the road, wasn't sick of being on the bike. And I definitely wasn't sick of Colby. Truthfully, I could've lived like that, with him, and would've been content for the rest of my life.

Maybe, one day, I'd even be happy.

But riding around the country with Colby forever wasn't really an option. Though my bank account was ample, I couldn't live off it forever, not if I wanted to retire rich—which I did. I had fantasies about being the eccentric, rich aunt who painted, had various vaguely erotic sculptures in her yard and jetted off to Europe at a moment's notice—first class, of course.

Those fantasies would not be funded by my current bank balance. I had to figure out how I was going to spend the rest of my life, if I was going to go back to school. How I was going to get to rich aunt status if I wasn't going to be a wildly alternative and brilliant psychiatrist.

Then there were Colby's commitments. I hadn't missed his phone calls, the ones he took out of earshot from me. He told me he'd been on and off the road looking for me for the past two years, spending some time with the club in New Mexico, and the rest scattered across the country. I got the feeling that being an outlaw wasn't a part-time job.

And there was the simple fact that it was time. Living on the road wasn't real life. It was a vacation from it. Sure, I had nightmares. I still felt hollow, fractured, and I still struggled with Colby's casual affection. I was still plenty damaged. But I wasn't having to live a responsible life. I wasn't around people who cared, who would urge me—gently—to face what happened, to heal. And then there was Colby and me.

We fought, we fucked, we ate good food, saw amazing places. We were cosplaying as a couple. But back in Garnett, again with those people who cared, in an environment we were both used to … that's when shit got real. That's when we would be put to the test, see if we could survive reality. We didn't talk about it, but I got the impression he understood that too.

The morning we woke up in our last hotel—glitzy and indescribably luxurious, in the middle of the New Mexico desert —we made quiet, intense love that wasn't like the fucking we had been engaging in.

Making. Love.

I came hard and intense. I had to fight myself from *crying* afterward. From telling him that I loved him. There were half a dozen times since we left my parent's house when I'd forced those three words down. They sat in my stomach like razor blades. I preferred them to cut me on the inside than set them free.

Anyone who said love was something brilliant, beautiful, and something to be sought was a fucking idiot.

Then again, not everyone who fell in love had been tortured by a deranged serial killer. That might've skewed my view on it a little.

The second we made it to Garnett town limits, my body relaxed. I'd been tense the entire day, on the edge of a panic attack. As much as I wanted to see everyone, I didn't want to face the consequences of that. Seeing the hurt on my friend's face, the reality of how long I'd been gone, what I'd missed. Add to that, I didn't think I could handle the one place in the world I'd felt the most at home being poisoned by what had happened there.

It turned out I was giving that fuck far too much power.

Sure, there was a prickle underneath my skin as we passed the police station, but that was nothing compared to the way the air fueled me. The way I felt like I could breathe again.

Okay, it probably had a lot to do with the fact that my arms were around Colby.

I rested my head on his shoulder and watched the town fly by and the desert take its place. I hadn't had to tell him where to go first.

Violet and Elden's house was breathtaking. She'd outdone herself with what she'd created. The sprawling house seemed to blend in with the landscape around it, feeling both incredibly modern and classic at the same time. The last time I'd been here—a fleeting, rushed visit in order to make sure I didn't glimpse Colby —they were only just moving in, and the garden had not grown to encircle the house with wildflowers.

The front door opened before we were even parked, then Violet sprinted out of it, her dark hair flying behind her.

I launched myself off the bike as soon as Colby parked, tossing my helmet aside and crossing the short distance between us.

"Oh my god, I can't believe you're finally here!" Violet cried, her arms locked around me.

She smelled of the same perfume she'd worn for years, the same expensive shampoo I'd always stolen from her.

Her body was warm, her embrace full of love. My skin recoiled a little, to be sure. The dirt lodged underneath my flesh felt gritty against my clothes. I ignored that.

We hugged for a long time. Until a small voice spoke.

"Momma?"

I froze, dislodging from my best friend to see Elden, standing alongside Colby, with a small, wiggling toddler in his arms.

The last time I saw her, she was smaller. Much smaller. Her hair was longer and dark like Violet's. Her eyes were wide and gray like her father's. She was wearing cowboy boots and a pink dress. And she was the cutest fucking thing I'd ever seen.

But she also looked like a little human, taunting me with how much I'd missed of her life. How much Violet had grown as a person and as a mother.

Tears bit my eyes, but I forced them back, mindful of the inquisitive gaze of the two-year-old, peering at me with confusion and wary interest.

"Baby girl, it's your Auntie Sariah," Violet cooed, squeezing my hand.

Willow frowned at me with an expression so like her father, it was uncanny.

There was no recognition. I was just a fleeting character in her life full of people who were constant, reliable. I was just some chick who bought her expensive gifts she couldn't even comprehend and left before she could commit me to memory.

"Come say hello," Violet urged her.

She sounded different. Violet. Looked different too. She was still absolutely stunning, wearing a long, flowing dress, showing off sculpted arms and a natural glow that came from the happiness pouring out of her.

But she was a *mother* now. She was a *wife*. She lived in a picture-perfect home in the desert that she had designed. All before her twenty-fifth birthday.

What a way to make a girl feel inadequate.

Elden set Willow down on her feet, and though she had seemed hesitant with me initially, she obviously changed her mind, running over to us, beaming at me then all but launching herself into my arms.

I bent down to catch her.

Though she was small, she took my breath away.

She smelled of sweet and fruity shampoo, the leather from her father's cut.

Blood. Vomit. My own urine. His putrid breath.

I fought against the memory trying to tarnish this moment, trying to wrench me back down into a pit of despair.

"Now, how about we pop a bottle to celebrate you being back?" Violet clapped her hands.

I reluctantly let Willow go.

"Yeah, I'd be down with that." I pasted on a fake smile.

Maybe the booze would chase the worst of the memories away.

Or maybe it, combined with the desert air, would ensure that I couldn't escape them.

———

The wind was chilly, but the fire chased off the worst of the cold. The air smelled of smoke and the desert. The stars stretched out overhead and everything around us was ... still. Empty. But in a good way. There were no monsters out there in the dark, waiting to strike.

"You have to stay here tonight, and maybe forever," Violet's hopeful voice broke the silence.

I glanced over at her. Motherhood suited my best friend. Everything about her was relaxed. Content.

You could feel it in the house...love. It enveloped you the second you walked in the door. Photos covered all the surfaces, in tasteful frames. Plants were everywhere around the house. Every seating area looked comfortable, inviting. Willow's toys were scattered around the place, tidily but communicating that a kid lived there and they weren't hiding the slight chaos that brought.

It felt like a grown-up home. Which I guessed Violet was. She was married, a mother, had a great job and an outstanding home. She had roots.

It filled me with joy to see that for her.

And it highlighted just how much I'd let go of when I left. Even before the incident, I'd been so sure that I wanted a chaotic life. Wanted to travel. Be the life of the party all over the world. Be fucking fabulous, mysterious, never staying in one place for too long.

Now I ached for peace. For roots of my own.

"If I stay then he has to." I nodded to where Colby and Elden were in the living room, the floor to ceiling windows giving us a perfect view of them sitting on the sofa, Willow asleep in her father's arms. Colby looked relaxed too. Content. I hadn't seen him like that in a while. I'd been the reason for his tension, for the tight posture, ready to spring into action, to chase me when I bolted.

Violet followed my gaze. "That's fine, we have thick walls," she smirked knowingly.

I couldn't help but smile, couldn't help but lapse into a fantasy where I was simply enjoying wine with my best friend while our men relaxed inside.

"I'll stay tonight," I conceded. "But I need to go back to my apartment tomorrow, begin to figure out the giant mess I've made of my life."

"You haven't made a mess of anything," Violet snapped.

I gave her a pointed look. "Babe, I dropped out of college, disappeared for almost two years on something that could only be described as a bender, abandoned all of my friends, and refused to deal with any of my feelings. You're right, it's not a mess, it's a clusterfuck."

Violet sipped her wine. "Considering what you've been through, I think it could've been much worse."

"Ugh," I groaned. "Can someone please be mad at me for my selfish actions? Everyone is being so goddamn understanding."

Violet regarded me carefully. "Fine. I'm pissed at you for being gone so long. I'm mad at you for making me worry and missing out on time with Willow that she can never get back." She folded her arms in front of her. "How's that?"

"Okay," I shrugged. "But you can't pull off mean."

She smiled. "You don't deserve mean, babe. I think we can both agree you've had quite about enough of it."

I looked down at my hands. Technically, she was right. But I was still desperate for someone to tell me off. To take off the fucking kid gloves and tell me to get my act together.

Maybe that person needed to be me.

"I'm glad you're home," Violet straightened, a smile splitting her mouth. "Please tell me it's for good this time?"

I looked over at my bestie, at her hopeful face. "Yeah, it's for good this time."

For better or for worse.

CHAPTER
SIXTEEN

AFTER A NIGHT at Violet and Elden's, we were back at my apartment.

It was clean, didn't smell stuffy, and the fridge had more food in it than it ever had when I'd lived here.

There was a bowl of fruit on the counter. A fucking cake complete with a cake stand that I did not previously own, sitting on the island. Various vases boasted fresh flowers.

The biker babe gang had come and gone.

It was nice. And it felt weird, being in this space that hadn't changed a bit when I had become a completely different person. I was not the woman who had picked the sofa, the pillows, the fucking bedding. That was a stranger who didn't know what her own blood tasted like, who didn't understand what it felt to have a knife tearing through her flesh.

Hence me pouring myself a drink when we first arrived. One day soon, I'd probably have to face my alcohol consumption and really make some changes.

But not this day.

"We need to talk," Colby said.

I stopped topping up my drink to peer at him. "Those are four words everyone loves to hear. Are you breaking up with me?"

I was teasing, yet there was real fear underneath my words. Hadn't I planned on breaking up with him when we got back to Garnett?

He'd slept in the bed with me at Violet and Elden's last night. He'd fucked me slow and quiet, twice. Then once in the morning. We'd emerged to an impressive breakfast spread with Colby's arms around me and him kissing my goddamn temple before he poured the both of us coffee.

We were, for all intents and purposes, a couple.

If he was breaking up with me, it was a good thing. A thing that I, apparently, wasn't strong enough to do.

"We haven't been using condoms," Colby said, surprising the fuck out of me.

I studied him over my glass. "What, you think I'm going to give you something?" I was pissed, glad I wasn't fearful anymore. I didn't like that.

"I'm clean." That was a lie, but technically, I didn't have any sexually transmitted diseases. They'd tested me for everything at the hospital. "You're the only man I've been with since…" I glared at him. "Unless *I'm* not the only woman you've been with recently?" I forced myself to speak casually, to take another sip of my drink even though acid churned in my stomach, lurched at the mere thought of him with another woman.

"You'd have every right," I added, putting the glass down. "We weren't betrothed or anything, and almost two years is a long time—"

"I have not touched another woman since the second I tasted you," Colby declared fiercely.

I swallowed thickly at the intensity in which he'd spoken as well as the feeling that it gave me. Safe. Warm. Happy.

"Okay, well, that's settled," I shrugged, still going for casual but failing.

Colby reached over to snatch my glass, just one of his many casual, intimate gestures that took my breath away.

"We haven't been using condoms," he repeated after taking a long sip of my drink. "And you're not on birth control."

My heart froze. "How do you know?"

"'Cause I was on the road with you for weeks. Shared bathrooms." He shrugged. "'Cause I'm nosy."

I pursed my lips. "I could have an IUD."

"Do you have an IUD?"

"No," I rubbed the back of my neck. I would've liked to lie to him. It would've been much simpler. But I couldn't do it.

He nodded. "So, we've been fuckin' a whole lot, I'm takin' you raw, finishing inside of you."

For once, him talking about the way he had been fucking me did not turn me on. Hadn't I been expecting this? We hadn't spoken about our lack of protection, and Colby was not the kind of guy to expect the woman to 'just take care of it.' In some corner of my mind, I'd been waiting for this conversation to come. I'd just been compartmentalizing.

"I'm aware of all the times we've had sex," I scoffed. "I was there."

His lip twitched. "Well, since you were aware, and since you had a period three weeks ago, maybe we cool it on this." He motioned to the drink. "Until we know."

"Until we know," I repeated, musing to myself. Colby did not sound overly concerned about the prospect of me possibly being pregnant. He spoke casually, as if it weren't the worst thing in the world. As if it was something he almost … wanted.

And that speared my fucking insides.

"I can't have children," I blurted.

Colby stared at me blankly, not even a stitch of shock, which would've been understandable considering what I'd just sprung on him. He just stared. Measuring me.

Nor did he ask any follow-up questions. He just waited in that infuriating way of his.

He'd be a really good journalist.

"It seems to be the trend here, after the biker claims the woman, he then makes it his mission to impregnate the woman, spreading his seed or whatever," I continued, my heart pounding. I wrung my hands, looking away from him. "So, I just wanted to let you know before this continues any further, that you won't be able to do that with me. I ... can't do that."

I sucked in a painful breath and looked up at Colby, whose face was still inscrutable.

"When he ... when he had me, the knives." I squeezed my eyes shut, trying to find the strength. "He had a lot of missions, to punish women, to hurt them," I whispered. "And even though he thought he was going to kill me, he wanted me to know in my last moments that he wasn't taking the life from me, he was taking away my ability to *create* life."

My hand met my flat stomach. It felt cold, despite the balmy heat coming in from outside.

"And before you say 'we'll find a way' or expect your super sperm to create a miracle, just know that not even you can defy the laws of science," I snapped. "And science has told me that he ... ruined me. There. Too much trauma. Scar tissue."

I studied the carpet beneath my shoes. There it was. My secret. The big one. Sure, there was a whole bunch of shit from that warehouse I planned on keeping from Colby until the end of time, but this was the one that affected him directly.

Maybe that was why I didn't break up with him. Because I'd figured when he eventually found out I was barren and broken, he'd move on.

"Hey," Colby whispered.

He kneeled in front of me. One of his hands was on my thigh, the other on my waist.

It hurt to look at him.

"I won't blame you, judge you," I forced the words past my dry lips. "For leaving me. It makes sense. I can't give you—"

"Stop," he hissed, holding me tighter. "You've given me more in the past hour than I expected to get in my life." His hand moved to stroke my jaw. "If you could get pregnant, if you were right now, we'd have a life that I'm sure would be fuckin' wonderful. But the life we have without that is just as fuckin' wonderful. And if you want to be a mother, we'll make that happen, however we need to."

I fought the tears obscuring my gaze.

"I don't want to be a mother," I admitted. "I mean, maybe if it could've happened by accident, especially if we *made* something —" my voice broke at just the thought. I didn't know if it was sorrow, anger or relief clogging my throat. I sucked in a breath to steady myself.

"If we made something, by accident, yes, I would've lived that life with you. Maybe before..." I cut myself off again. "I can't do maybes, wonder about what life would've looked like if *it* hadn't happened."

The 'what if' game was a dangerous one. I'd discovered that on night one of my little journey, after too much vodka and a long contemplation over a bottle of sleeping pills.

Colby rubbed my thigh. "Whether or not it happened, I still would be right here, with you."

I rolled my eyes to hide my emotion... There was only so much a girl could take.

"Well, it *did* happen, and we are here, and I can't have children and I don't want to explore other ways of becoming a mother. It's not my path. I don't know if it ever was, but now I know it's not."

Though I'd done a good job of not thinking about this conversation, I had thought a lot about the news that I'd been given in the hospital. What I already knew when he was tearing at my womb in that warehouse. I'd never carry life inside of me.

He'd promised that, hadn't he?

And these past years I'd made sure I didn't carry life, didn't *have* a life.

"I was going to break up with you when we got back here," I told Colby.

Colby smirked. "I figured as much."

That didn't surprise me anymore. Though it still irritated me. How well Colby knew me, how easily he admitted it, and how unbothered he seemed by the information. Well, I supposed it made sense for him to be unbothered since I hadn't broken up with him.

I couldn't.

"If you want a family, you deserve one," I said, my voice small. "And you need to know now, before this gets any more ... serious," I stumbled over the word. He'd been searching for me for years, had put his life on hold to save me. It was already plenty serious. "I'm not likely to change my mind about this."

Colby smiled softly at me, tucking a hair behind my ear. "I am well aware that you're stubborn as fuck."

Again, I wanted to be irritated, I wanted to spit fire, but I was just too darn in love with this motherfucker.

"Now, I appreciate what my brothers have found with their women," he murmured, voice still tender. "Seeing them with their families, it's great. I'll be happy to babysit. But I'll be more than happy to jet off to a beach or a mountain or wherever the fuck my woman decides she wants to go."

I stared at him. Had I told Colby about my desire to see the world? Yes, I must've, at some point.

"I've just driven across the country with you pressed to my back," he continued. "Fucked you in different states, watched you marvel at new sights, enjoy good food. And though we could do that with a kid, it'd be a little more complicated." His thumb brushed my bottom lip. "You give me the gift of a whole fuckin' lifetime of that, I'm gonna count myself the luckiest son of a bitch to walk the earth."

I could barely hear him over the sound of my pulse thrashing in my ears.

I hadn't been expecting any of that. Yet there it was, all laid out. He was talking about forever. With me. I was in my early twenties. Girls in their early twenties should not settle down. If they did, more often than not, they found themselves divorced in their early thirties once they realized their husband was a douchebag ... if they were lucky. If they weren't, they stayed married to the douchebag because of the kids, then they yelled at waitresses, starring in viral videos.

Or that's what I thought.

I'd promised myself I wouldn't be naïve enough to believe the first man who promised me forever. In fact, any other man who'd done this would've sent me running for the hills.

But this was Colby. Not only did he mean it, he would chase me to the ends of the earth if I ran.

And I'd want him to chase me.

"Although that's all very sweet and likely what every woman on the planet would want to hear, forever is a little much for me right now," I admitted in a shallow breath.

Instead of getting all frowny and moody, Colby's face was relaxed, and he smiled, leaning back on the sofa, taking me with him.

"Figured." He kissed the side of my head then reached for the TV remote. "How about we binge watch some TV, drink some more, fuck on the sofa, then go to bed? That kind of plan okay with you?"

I nodded. "That kind of plan is okay with me."

"Good." he switched on the TV.

Then we did all the things on his list ... and it was more than okay. It was fucking great.

———

Violet and Kate—and no doubt the rest of the women—had wanted to throw me a coming home party.

I'd been very against such a party.

We really didn't need to celebrate me running away for almost two years after getting tortured by a serial killer.

Like ... fuck no.

We settled on a dinner at Kate's restaurant since I knew those bitches were not going to back down.

It was almost ... nice. I loved being back with people I adored, being back in Garnett. I especially enjoyed Colby being back where he belonged, with his brothers. It hadn't hit me how much the club was a part of him until I saw him around the other men, exchanging man hugs and talking while the women corralled me off to the bar for cocktails and dishing.

I'd dreaded this part of the evening, fearing the women would want to inquire into my wellbeing, give me tender but pitying looks, and otherwise treat me as the fucked-up Final Girl.

Though they were kind, concerned and generally good people, I should've known better with these bitches.

All they wanted to know about was me and Colby.

Since it was very clear that there *was* a me and Colby.

We'd walked in *holding hands*.

I hadn't wanted to hold hands. I didn't like holding hands. I thought it was gross and weird and something couples did to announce to the world that they were grossly in love when in reality they were trying to convince themselves they didn't fucking hate each other.

Turned out holding hands with the man you were kind of in love with was ... nice.

Except I didn't let on to that.

We walked from my apartment since the restaurant was just down the street. The air was crisp yet warming up. Main Street was alive with people, a lot of them nodding to Colby as we passed. The desert landscape yawned past the town itself, making it feel like we were in an oasis away from the real world. Which we kind of were. Garnett always felt isolated. There wasn't a chain store to be found within town limits. All the business façades were well-kept and matched with each other. There weren't any soul-sucking subdivisions. Each structure was completely unique.

And it was low key run by an outlaw motorcycle club.

"Doesn't holding hands damage your street cred?" I groused when trying to wrench my hand from Colby's grip hadn't worked.

Colby smirked at me. "Nothing damages street cred when you're wearin' a Sons of Templar cut, poppet."

I rolled my eyes. "Cocky."

Colby ignored this, pulling our intertwined hands up so he could kiss mine. "Plus, me walking down the street, managing to get Sariah Cardoso, of all people, to hold my hand is doing great fucking things for my street cred."

Swoon.

"I'm not *letting* you hold my hand," I protested. "You're just not letting me go. That doesn't count."

Colby chuffed. "You didn't want to hold my hand, you wouldn't be holdin' my fucking hand." Damn, the prick knew me so fucking well.

Yes, he'd held tighter when I'd tried to remove his grip from my hand, but I could've wrenched my own away. If I'd really wanted to.

Which I didn't.

I pursed my lips, tilting my head and ignoring him like a petulant child the rest of the walk to the restaurant.

But we still walked in holding hands.

Hence the women deciding that we were a couple.

And I couldn't say we weren't.

———

"I'm movin' in," Colby announced.

That had come out of nowhere. For me, at least. I was just sitting there, minding my own business, painting my nails and enjoying a glass of whisky.

He was supposed to be watching the game. But when my head snapped up and I saw his eyes on me, I got the impression he'd been watching me for a while. His expression was serious, intense, full of ownership.

I bristled. "You are not moving in."

"Babe, I sleep here every night. My shit is in the closet." He scratched his neck. "Well, I've *attempted* to put my shit in the closet."

I scowled at him. When I moved back in, I'd been faced with all of the clothes I wore pre-warehouse. They were colorful, decadent, exquisite. And they were so not me anymore.

Now, getting tortured by a serial killer hadn't rendered me completely unhinged... I kept a lot of it. Like the vintage Chanel. And the YSL.

The rest I donated to the local Goodwill. Well, after the club ladies came and got their fill. Though they were all variations of 'biker babe,' they were also women who loved clothes. Designer clothes held a certain allure to every woman.

I could've made a hefty buck if I resold what remained on resale sites—despite my wild life, I took great care of my clothes—but that seemed like a lot of effort, and I was one lazy bitch.

Anyway, I got rid of a bunch, and then I bought a bunch. A whole bunch. Shipped from Saks, Bloomingdales, Net-a-Porter. My closet was refreshed and then some. Most of it was shades of black and red. A total fucking cliché, and I hated how pathetic that was, but the bright colors, any kind of flowery print, made me want to gag a little.

"Precisely why you cannot move in. I will not sacrifice the closet space."

He didn't look like he thought my argument was sound. Actually, he looked ... amused? "Then we'll find another place with a bigger closet. I'll build you a closet."

My stomach fluttered with the memory of a promise he'd made about that.

I put down the nail polish and picked up my drink. "You are not serious."

"When have I ever given you the impression that I've been anything but serious about you?"

He had me there. I held my glass harder.

"Fight me if you want," he shrugged. "I'm used to it, and I'll enjoy fuckin' you in our bed after I've won."

Our bed.

The two words settled inside of me. The prospect of a life not unlike Violet's in the desert. Minus some significant things, of course.

A little girl with a pink dress and cowboy boots.

"You cocky prick," my cheeks heated in fury. "You can't keep making these decisions like my submission is a foregone conclusion."

Colby didn't answer, instead, he moved forward on the sofa, snatched my glass away, put it on the coffee table and had my panties off in a flash.

Which was kind of easy to do since I had been painting my nails in a camisole and panties.

I let out a gasp as he hooked my knees over his shoulders and positioned his mouth between my legs.

"Isn't your submission a forgone conclusion?" His velvet breath was warm on my pussy.

I blew my hair from my face and scowled at him. "You can't just get your way by eating my pussy." I was trying to go for pissed off and powerful, but I sounded breathy and defenseless.

Colby leaned forward and licked the seam of my pussy, finishing at my clit. My entire body fought the pleasure that urged me to submit.

He had a glint in his eye when he looked up at me. "Can't I?"

"Fuck you," I snapped, but again, I was too breathy and turned on to pull off sounding angry.

Colby leaned in to taste me again. This time he did it for longer, until my nails sank into the sofa—ruining the paint job and staining the couch—and a mewl of prurience escaped my lips.

"Let me find us a home," Colby's voice vibrated against my pussy.

My eyes almost rolled to the back of my head.

"No," I whispered.

Colby didn't continue arguing, his mouth going back down. More relentless than ever. He'd learned every inch of me, was an expert in my body, how to make it sing. So he knew exactly how to take me right to the edge of climax, denying me at the last second.

"Asshole," I groaned.

Colby didn't say anything, merely moved his mouth upward.

I held my breath, on the precipice of orgasm as he pushed my camisole up to reveal the ravaged skin of my stomach.

I wanted to tear apart the sofa with my bare hands. Wanted to fight Colby off me and jump into a scalding shower in order to try to scrub the marks from my skin.

Instead, I stayed where I was, let Colby's mouth brush over those ragged, awful marks. His lips lingered over the worst one.

"Please, stop. I'll do anything."

The knife twisted inside of me.

I screamed, my throat painfully raw.

"Of course, you'd do anything, you little whore," he spat as he *wrenched the knife out. Blood and pieces of flesh went flying. His tongue darted out, licking the blade.*

"Colby," I rasped.

His head tilted upward, and I held onto his chocolate eyes, the dark hair that brushed his forehead, the strong shoulders, arms and fingers that had never once hurt me—not without me asking.

His chin rested lightly on my stomach while his finger pushed inside me.

"Let me give you a home."

I couldn't speak, my mind pulling me in too many directions at once. All I knew was that I wasn't ready to give in, not yet at least. I shook my head.

"My stubborn little minx." He gave my scar one last kiss before repositioning, taking his finger out of me and whirling me around so I was bent over the sofa, my ass and pussy presented to him.

His belt clanged. That was the only warning I got before he plunged into me.

My scalp burned as he grabbed hold of a fistful of hair, hauling it back to expose my neck.

My body reveled in the glorious pain.

Colby reached around to find my clit.

I let out a strangled moan.

"Let me give you a fuckin' home," he repeated, sounding ragged, nearly out of control. "Make a home with me, Sariah."

My mind rattled, reaching for all the reasons I'd been holding on to. I couldn't grasp any of them. None of them made sense. The only thing that made sense was Colby. Inside of me.

"Fine," I whispered.

He stilled for one second, his lips grazing my neck. "Wasn't so hard, was it, poppet?" He sounded far too smug for my liking.

I was about to take it back when he slammed into me, hard, sending me hurtling into nirvana where there was nothing but us.

———

After more delicious but manipulative sex on the sofa—then on the floor—we made it to the bed.

Our bed, I supposed it was now.

That thought set my teeth on edge, but it also made me feel a little too hopeful.

I'd been stewing on it. The thoughts of the future. Of ... us the entire night. I knew Colby sensed my introspection, because that was his way, but he didn't push or prod. He just let me wander around, putting on a silk nightgown, commencing in an over-the-top nighttime skincare routine while he read leisurely on the bed.

Well, that was until I stood at the end of the bed and shrugged off my nightgown, standing in the dim lamp light completely naked.

Colby immediately put down his book.

I crawled over the covers, straddling him. "We're doing this my way," I announced, reaching between his legs to find him already rock hard.

I smiled, guiding him past my slick folds without ceremony.

We both hissed in pleasure. The cords in Colby's neck were pronounced. His piercing eyes were glued to me, hands gently resting on my hips.

"I want a really big closet," I demanded.

His eyebrow arched, a smirk morphing his ruggedly masculine face.

"Done," he agreed without hesitation.

"And a claw footed bathtub."

"Easy."

Fuck. No protest.

"And a pink tiled shower," I added, knowing that any self-respecting biker wasn't going to shower in a pink shower every day.

"We're just gonna cut to the chase here," he murmured, sitting up.

I gasped at the new angle and the brilliant way his cock grazed against my g-spot.

"I'm gonna give you everything you want." He cupped my face.

I was already breathing heavily, but him saying that... Shit, it almost made me come right then and there.

"But please use this method for all your future demands," he winked as I rode him slowly.

"Okay," I whispered.

I didn't make any more requests after that, but I did reserve the right to whenever I wanted to get whatever I wanted. Which was a rather lovely prospect. A prospect that had me sailing right into my third—fourth?—orgasm of the evening.

———

We were naked, in bed, neither of us sleeping. I didn't know what was keeping him awake. Surely it wasn't the same thing that was eating at me.

For me, the lovely feeling of post-orgasm bliss had worn off. It had faded quickly, as the TV timer turned off, the room bathed in darkness, illuminated only by a thin sliver of light coming from the open bedroom door and the light I'd left on above the stove.

Or rather Colby had left the stove light on from when he was cooking. I didn't even know the stove had a fucking light.

Because of that sliver of light, I could see the shape in the corner.

It was always there.

When I woke up in the middle of the night, *he* was standing there, staring.

Sometimes he was there, right in my face when I woke up, dripping blood on my cheeks. I didn't react, of course. Since he wasn't real. But fuck if he didn't look real. Smell real.

I really should've seen a therapist.

Or drank more before bed.

Maybe I should've taken up running, becoming one of those people who ran miles a day, pumping themselves full of all those endorphins. Endorphins made you happy. And happy people probably didn't see the ghost of the man in their bedroom who'd almost murdered them.

"He took my blood," I whispered, unable to stand the silence of the room a moment longer. "Covered himself in it. Drank it." I bit back the shudder my body forced upward with the memory. "In almost every manifestation of what contemporary society would call witchcraft, taking someone's blood is taking some of their soul."

Colby had been solid underneath me when I first started speaking. It was the first I'd spoken of anything to do with what he did to me. I was kind of springing it on him, but I doubted there was an ideal time to start talking about such things.

Well, ideally, I would've kept my mouth shut, never spoken of it, never pollute the air he was breathing with the poison simmering inside of me. But I couldn't not. Couldn't keep staring at *him* in the corner of the fucking room. It was selfish and weak. But I'd said it. I couldn't unsay it.

Colby didn't speak. His arms tightened around me for a split second, then he was up. The lamp beside me flickered on, illuminating the room and chasing away the murderous ghost.

Colby trudged across the room, snatching his jeans and the knife that was strapped onto them.

It glinted in the soft light of my bedroom.

The bed depressed as he entered it again, holding the knife.

My heart thundered in my chest as the knife got closer, my vision splitting between the present and the past. I could see my blood on the steel, dripping down on the pool that had accumulated around me.

"Sariah," Colby's voice was firm, ripping me out of my flashback.

He was straddling me with the knife. I couldn't breathe.

He held the knife between us, my eyes glued to the sharp point. My scars started screaming as if it were tearing into them all over again.

But it was not my flesh that was opened. Colby drew the knife along his own skin, right on his chest. The cut wasn't shallow either. He didn't even flinch.

"Take my fucking blood," he demanded. "Take my fucking soul, Sariah."

I stared at him in shock as blood trickled down his torso, dripping onto me as he leaned forward.

I didn't think twice when he came closer, my mouth against his chest before I could fully process what I was doing.

He tasted coppery, bitter. And somehow infinitely sweet. Power thrummed through my veins, taking ownership over something that had previously haunted my nightmares.

Colby was giving me something. Giving me him. And he hadn't even fucking thought about it.

His blood slid down my throat as he leaned back, eyes on me. His gaze was hungry, turned on. He'd … liked this. Giving this to me.

Neither of us spoke. I put my hand on Colby's chest, blood spilling onto my hand. I communicated what I wanted with gentle pressure. Colby let me push him down on the bed, let me straddle him.

His cock was hard against me.

And I was soaking fucking wet.

But I didn't focus on that. That wasn't my plan.

My hands fastened around the hilt of the knife, and Colby froze.

"I want to give you mine now too," I whispered, my heart slamming against my rib cage.

He didn't let go of the knife. "That isn't what this is, Sariah. I'm not asking you for anything."

"I know. Which is why I want to give it to you. My soul. Whatever's left of it."

Colby stared at me for a second more before he relinquished his grip.

It felt heavier in my hand than I'd expected. It was the first time

I'd held a knife like this. First time I'd held any kind of weapon since the warehouse.

I'd been roaming around America, drinking in seedy bars, staying in seedier motels, and I'd had no form of protection with me. Colby had chastised me about that when he'd realized. I'd shrugged and let him rage on and on without arguing. It wasn't worth it. You didn't need protection when you'd already had the worst happen.

God—if she did exist, she was a woman—could be a spiteful bitch to be sure, but even she wouldn't be so cruel as to force me to endure even more suffering. My scars protected me against new wounds.

That's what I told myself anyway. Maybe I was testing her. Inviting fate to fuck me over again so I could get proof I was really being punished.

The why of it didn't matter, especially at this moment.

I held the knife, considering where I wanted it to cut through my skin. It was tempting, mighty tempting for me to go to the places that knew the blade. Reopen myself in places *he'd* damaged. Reclaim them or some shit.

But I wasn't strong enough for that.

And logistically, it presented a problem since I was on top of Colby. My palm felt like the most sensible option. Plus, it already had scars from where I'd dug my fingernails so deep into the flesh I'd left crescent shaped marks.

Without thinking about it, lest I wuss out, I sliced the blade along my palm. It hurt. My blood was warm as it spilled onto my skin. I turned my hand, riveted as droplets stained Colby's perfect face, landing on his lips.

I battled with warring sensations. With panic, pain and an uncontrollable urge to run to the shower and scrub myself clean.

Then Colby's tongue darted out and licked the blood off his lips. Licked my blood off his lips.

Then another, a much stronger sensation, trumped all my trauma.

I tossed the knife on the nightstand with a clatter.

My mouth was on his in the next breath, tasting my blood in his mouth. Just like I had in the warehouse. Except then, it was forced on me. This was my choice. I had power over who I gave my soul to. And I gave it to Colby.

CHAPTER SEVENTEEN

"WHERE ARE WE GOING?" I demanded.

We were at the club.

I hadn't been back since we arrived home. I'd been kind of busy. There were visits from almost everyone connected to the club, and if they didn't visit, I was at some kind of event or another with the women. There was shopping with Freya—which I sorely needed since I was committed to my new, damaged yet impossibly chic girl look—there was baking with Kate at her place. There were *Lord of the Rings* marathons with Macy—she was beyond happy that I was the only person in the girl gang who went hard for Middle Earth.

There were Pilates classes with Caroline since I did need to get fit and strong again, and fuck, did they kick my ass.

And then I spent all my free time at Violet and Elden's place, either hanging out with Willow—who was now my ultimate bestie —when Violet had work to do or hanging out with the entire family plus Colby whenever the men didn't have 'club business' to attend to.

So yeah, this bitch was busy.

I had wanted to go back to the club. Wanted to attend a club party. But I was anxious about that. Not a single one of the men made me feel weird or vulnerable when they saw me. They didn't look at me like I was a victim. Yet I felt it. Oddly exposed whenever I was around them. It was like every one of them knew what I looked like naked. Except *all* of them *did* know what I looked like naked. Naked and chained and at my absolute worst.

So yeah, it was going to take a minute for me to party with them again like I didn't have a care in the world.

Although I didn't think I would *ever* be able to party, or even exist, like I didn't have a care in the world.

But after an afternoon riding through the desert with Colby and some great morning sex, I was as close as I could be to not having a care in the world.

Colby had said he needed to 'pick up a few things.' It made sense since he was technically living with me now, still living out of a duffel. I'd given him a small drawer in my dresser, but I just couldn't sacrifice closet space. Colby didn't seem to mind. Probably because he had already jumped into house-hunting for us.

I wasn't involved. I didn't know why I wasn't. It had been established that I was high maintenance, and I'd never dream of letting a man pick a fucking appetizer for me, let alone a whole ass house.

But I was discovering that I enjoyed Colby taking the reins. He knew what I wanted, knew me.

Beyond that, the prospect of making such a huge decision as part of a couple was fucking terrifying to me, and I couldn't guarantee I wouldn't run if I got too close to the process.

"This isn't the way to your room," I muttered as Colby led us outside.

"Good observation skills, poppet," he replied dryly.

I scowled at him and froze when he took us around the corner.

The shooting range.

I hadn't been here in … years.

It was where Colby had taught me how to shoot. Where we'd

toyed with each other and our sexual chemistry. Where I'd played games with him purely because I could.

I was uncomfortable standing on the concrete there, reexperiencing the person I was then.

I knew that Colby noted my change in demeanor because he was Colby. He'd been treating observing me and my moods like it was his fucking job. Like I was a job. I didn't like that. Being so fragile. So fucked-up.

"Been too long." He took his gun out of the holster under his cut.

"I don't need this," I argued, feeling panicky. "I'm a great fucking shot."

"You were. But you don't stay a great shot by shooting great a handful of times then never picking up a gun again."

There it was.

A challenge.

I fucking hated it when people told me I couldn't do shit.

So, I did the only thing I could do. I snatched the gun from him, leveled it at the target, took a deep breath and pulled the trigger on an exhale.

"You were saying?" I scoffed as we both looked at where I'd put a hole in the middle of the target.

Colby looked between me and the target, holding back a smile.

"I stand corrected," he moved to stand behind me.

His hands came up to mine, lifting the gun once more, reenacting the stance we'd stood in when he first taught me how to shoot.

And just like when he first taught me how to shoot, my body responded. Enthusiastically.

The hairs on the back of my neck stood up, my breathing shallowed, and my heartbeats quickened.

And, of course, my panties dampened.

"Deep breaths," Colby murmured in my ear.

I shivered, his hand covering mine on the gun, aiming it at the target.

"I didn't bring you here because I doubt your ability," he whispered. "I brought you here to remember who the fuck you are. How powerful you are."

I sighed as his words penetrated. The old Sariah was obsessed with doing anything the men here could do. The old Sariah liked knowing how to use a gun, liked knowing how to ride a motorcycle, loved the power of it all. When my power was taken, it seemed like it had all been for nothing.

Colby was reminding me what I still had.

"Inhale," Colby rasped in my ear.

I obeyed, my finger twitching on the trigger.

"Exhale."

I pulled.

It didn't matter where the shot went—even though it was a great fucking shot—because that wasn't what this was about anymore. The gun was out of my hands, safety on, back in Colby's holster.

Then I was against the wall, my palms catching the cold concrete. Colby's hands were at my hips, rolling up my skirt to my waist.

He had told me to wear a skirt today.

He'd planned this.

"I've been dreaming about doing this since the first fucking moment we were out here," he growled, ripping my panties off.

They were ruined anyway.

His cock was poised at my soaking entrance within seconds, the concrete wall cutting into my palms.

I could hear voices coming from the garage, of men joking as they walked into the clubhouse. The breeze caressed my tender flesh.

"Colby," I pleaded.

One of his hands wrapped around my ponytail. "You were thinking about this too, weren't you?"

"Yes," I hissed.

His cock slipped in.

I gasped.

But he stopped before he filled me up.

"You gonna let me fuck you wherever I want, whenever I want?"

"Yes," I said without a second thought.

"That's my girl."

Then he slammed all the way in.

I cried out. His hand went to my mouth, covering it, silencing me as he pounded into me relentlessly.

In all of my imaginings, I could not have dreamed up the absolute ecstasy that I would experience out here.

Colby grunted in pleasure as I came, milking his orgasm from me. I felt him releasing inside of me, causing me to explode all over again.

It was safe to say I did not avoid shooting lessons ever again.

———

"What can I get for you?" I asked the customer, my mind in a million places other than the coffee shop that had become my full-time place of employment since arriving back in Garnett.

Not that the job was bad. Actually, I loved it. Julian was a fucking hoot; I got as much coffee as my system could handle; and I was constantly so busy, there was little time for idle hands.

But even without idle hands, I still had dark thoughts. I still had the ache to destroy the nice little routine Colby and I had settled into. To burn it all to the fucking ground in order to save him from me accidently ruining his life later on by being just too damn fucked-up. I was doing really good at playing normal, but the cracks were still there. And I could feel them.

"A flat white, please," the woman in front of me said. "And an interview about what it's like to be the sole survivor of this state's and this generation's most notorious serial killer."

I looked up at her, the words taking far too long to sink in.

I hadn't really seen the woman before. Looking at her now, I saw that she was older than me, but not by a lot. She was in her late twenties, maybe early thirties. Her hair was pulled back in a sleek bun, showing off harsh cheekbones and excellent skin.

She was wearing a white tee, expensive jeans and an oversized blazer. The jewelry she wore was subtle yet expensive. She was chic. Pretty.

And I had a very strong urge to strangle her with her gold fucking necklace.

Luckily for her, that urge was deeper down, the feisty part of me screaming underneath the layers of shocked silence. "Excuse me?" I finally whispered.

"Emily Ryan," she held out her hand, her voice still pleasant, maybe even warm. "I'm a freelance journalist, but I most often work with the *New York Times*. I'm here to talk to you about your experience with Beau Granger."

The sounds of the café were drowned out by the low ringing in my ears.

"Excuse m-me?" I stuttered, repeating the two words I'd already said. For the life of me, I couldn't figure out what else to say.

"I understand that you were one of his last victims," she lowered her hand, her tone conversational, like she was talking about what pastries she was ordering instead of me being tortured by a madman. "And you were the only one to survive."

I swallowed past the knot obstructing my airway, struggling to stay upright.

"I, um, don't know what you're talking about."

She gave me a knowing smirk. "I've done a lot of research, and a lot of effort was put into keeping this quiet. But I'm a good journalist. I know that you were the reason Beau Granger was found and killed. I also know the local motorcycle club was somehow involved."

Fuck.

Fuck.

This was bad.

Not only was this bad for me, but this could be a threat to the club. To Colby.

My vision cleared, my protective instincts kicking in. The club was my family.

"You need to leave. Now," I stated firmly.

"I understand that this is a lot for you to take in right now—"

"You heard what she said. You need to fuck off right now." Julian's gruff, scary tone made me jump. I hadn't even known he was behind me, let alone that he'd heard the entire exchange.

His cheeks were red, and his normally warm eyes were cold and threatening.

I'd never seen the jovial, loveable man like this. Ever.

Emily's eyes darted from him to me, uneasily but still intent.

"We will speak again, Ms. Cardoso," she promised.

"We most certainly will fucking not," I told her sweetly.

She gave me one more determined look before turning on her Gucci loafer and leaving.

My heart was still pounding.

"I'm calling Colby," Julian muttered, immediately reaching into his pocket for his phone. Julian must've been briefed on some kind of Sariah protection/breakdown protocol. Not surprising.

"No!" I yelled.

Julian paused, considering me with a shrewd gaze. The man knew me both before and after the warehouse. I was close to him. Considered him a friend. Or a wacky uncle. I knew he cared about me too, which made this more complicated. He felt duty-bound to call Colby.

"Don't call him," I repeated at a more normal decibel. "It's …
it's not a big deal." I smoothed my apron. "I can handle it."

Julian stroked his beard, not looking convinced. "She's not
going to give up." He nodded to the door the reporter had just
walked out through.

"I know." There was a pit at the bottom of my stomach.

Julian, though concerned, didn't call Colby to come to my
rescue. I went back to making coffees, and the cracks inside of me
deepened.

————

I was drunk and dancing on the bar at the club. Not an unfamiliar
situation for me. At least it hadn't been.

It had been over two years since my last appearance, and
things had changed. There were a couple of new faces, patched
members and women. Chloe, one of the newest club girls, was kick
ass and just happened to be dancing on the bar with me.

She and I had been doing shots since I arrived.

Originally, I'd gone there on the hunt for Colby. I'd been planning on telling him about the reporter at the coffee shop. He'd do
something about it. The club would do something about it. The old
Sariah would've tit punched me for going to a club full of men—
who didn't even allow women to patch in—to solve my problems
instead of bitch-slapping the reporter and running her out of town
myself. But I wasn't strong enough for that.

It seemed I was strong enough to get drunk with my biker
friends, though. I'd lapsed into old patterns easily. It felt nice to
inhabit the person I used to be, at least for a little while.

And yeah, since it felt nice, I might've gotten carried away.

Just a little.

My shirt was no longer on my body. It was somewhere on the
floor. The bustier I was wearing underneath my shirt—the one that
was almost completely sheer but with intricate enough lace to

disguise my scars—was on full display. I'd worn it for Colby. He enjoyed lingerie. Well, for about one minute before he ripped it off me. But I enjoyed that one minute. I especially enjoyed what happened afterward.

He did not enjoy me showing that lingerie to a club full of people. He communicated that by snatching me off the bar without ceremony.

I hadn't even noticed him enter the room.

"Let me go," I shrieked against the music.

Colby did not, he just pulled me closer to him, striding away from the party, the music getting quieter with every step.

"What the fuck do you think you're doing?" he hissed as he carried me down the hallway.

"This is like Groundhog Day or something," I whined. "How many times will you fireman carry me down this very fucking hallway like you have the right?"

"It is my fuckin' right," Colby seethed, opening the door to his room before roughly setting me down on my feet.

The door slammed behind him.

He was pissed. He was showing this by using his physical strength against me. I didn't like that. Not at all. No, that wasn't right. I didn't like that I *liked* that. My life had almost been ended by a man who used strength and authority against me. It should've made my skin crawl, not make my panties wet.

Boy, was I fucked-up.

"It is not your right, Colby," I spat at him, stomping to the middle of the room before turning to face-off with him.

"You're mine," he folded his arms, staying in his spot in front of the door, as if he expected me to try to escape.

Again, that certainly should've been another trigger. But I was too pissed off, drunk and horny to let too much of my trauma sink in.

"And what does that mean to you, Colby?" I asked.

"It means that you do not get wasted, dance on tables and start takin' your clothes off."

"Oh, okay," I nodded. "So, what would you like me to do?" I put my hands on my hips. "Would you like me to cover up? Sober up? Shut up?"

"Don't fucking act like I'm controlling you."

I tilted my head at him. "Physically dragging me around and telling me what I can and can't do because I'm yours is control, baby," I replied in a sugary sweet tone. "And that's just not gonna happen. You see, I think you are under the impression that because I came back here, because I'm trying this thing out with you, that I'm gonna be magically healed. That I'm going to *come to heel*."

I leisurely crossed the distance between us. "I am still me." I trailed my finger down his chest. "Even though I'm a little more fucked-up than before, I'm doubly against some man chaining me up."

Colby recoiled.

It was impossibly cruel of me to say that, and I instantly regretted it.

"This is you," he agreed, recovering from my verbal blow. "You love to party, to piss me off and to cause trouble. But there is a reason for *this*." He waved his hand at me.

"Stop knowing me so fucking well," I pushed away from him.

He smiled sadly. "Not possible."

I sighed, suddenly tired. I couldn't do another fight. I couldn't hurt Colby because I was too much of a coward to face up to myself. That bit was tired. "I had a visitor at the café today. A reporter."

Colby's expression turned stormy. He quickly crossed the distance between us, taking me into his arms, no longer pissed at me, instantly forgiving me for my childish and mean actions.

He was the only thing holding me together.

"She knows about me," I whispered, feeling cold despite Colby's arms around me. "She's going to do a story about me."

"No, she fuckin' isn't," Colby replied right away.

I tilted my head up to him, observing the anger he was feeling on my behalf, his immediate and instinctive need to protect me.

"Yes, she is," I sighed. "Unless you're going to kill an innocent woman. Because I've got a feeling that's the only way to get rid of her."

A vein pulsed in Colby's cheek. He didn't speak for a long time. I knew he wasn't considering it. Colby had a code. The Sons of Templar had a code.

"You know the Salem Witch Trials?" I asked, capitalizing on the silence.

His forehead creased as he frowned with what I guessed was confusion. The Salem Witch Trials weren't exactly related to our current conversation.

Instead of questioning what the fuck I was talking about, he just nodded.

"Yeah, they had the best publicity, even though they'd been burning women for thousands of years," I said. "For being too outspoken. Too different. Too sexual. For being creatures that threatened men's way of life. Made them uncomfortable."

Colby was frowning as I spoke, likely understanding where I was going.

"The publicity for the murders has been about him," I spat. "About what made him what *he* was. How *he* chose his victims. And the victims were talked about in regard to the way they lived their lives, how they made themselves easy prey. How *we* made ourselves easy prey."

My mind replayed the look in that reporter's eyes. The hunger.

"No one knew I was a victim," I blew out a heavy breath. "No one knew someone survived." I fingered his cut. "Now that they do, it's going to be a feeding frenzy."

I looked up at him.

"They still burn witches, Colby," I told him. "The flames are just different now."

Colby was frowning, stewing over my words.

"No," he wrapped his hands around my upper arms. "No," he repeated. "No one is burning you. No one is fucking touching you. This is stopping." He reached into his cut, grabbing his phone and putting it to his ear.

"We need church, now," he snapped at whoever he'd called.

He put his phone back in his cut, leaning in to kiss my forehead. "We're gonna fix this. I'm gonna fix this."

I nodded because he needed me to believe him. Not because I really did. I could already feel the flames at my feet.

CHAPTER
EIGHTEEN

COLBY HAD CALLED CHURCH AND, apparently, had set events in motion to transform the entire clubhouse. When we emerged from Colby's room, the party had stopped. All of the extra people were gone. Some club girls remained, cleaning up. Some of them smiled and nodded to me. I waved back.

First, Colby took me into the kitchen to get me a coffee and a sandwich. A smart idea. I'd had *a lot* to drink and nothing to eat.

The coffee and food worked to make me more alert, not completely sober, but I'd manage.

It was probably good I had a little liquid courage in me when Colby walked me through the double doors labeled 'church.' Those doors were always closed whenever I was there. Off limits. It was where club members had meetings about criminal enterprises, cock fights, which woman had been claimed and was now in trouble … fuck if I knew.

I'd thought about it a bunch, curious about the inner workings of the club.

Now I was inside.

With a full table.

I swallowed hard when eyes landed on me as we entered the

room, a prospect quickly scrambling up to give me a seat. I took it, trying to move steady, to not let my unease show.

It was impressive that everyone had arrived so promptly, considering the hour and that a lot of them had families. I shot what I hoped was a jaunty grin at Swiss when he caught my eye, and he winked back. I averted my gaze from everyone else, who were likely wondering what the fuck I'd gotten myself into now.

Luckily, all eyes went to Colby when he recounted what I'd told him.

"What the fuck is a reporter doing here now?" Colby bit out. "It's been two goddamn years."

"Caroline used her connections to bury the story—or at least Sariah's part in it," Jagger replied, eyes bouncing toward me. "We did what we could to make sure nothing led back to her. But there was always a chance that someone determined enough would get info, despite Caroline pulling strings."

I'd figured Caroline had done something since she used to be a big shot journalist. This place had been crawling with reporters, so at least one of them must've been smart enough to figure out there was more to the story. Luckily, a lot of them were distracted by the gruesome crimes and the attractive sheriff who'd committed them. He was this generation's Ted Bundy. Whoever did figure it out must've received a visit from Caroline, likely with her scarred and scary husband next to her.

I made a mental note to send Caroline a basket of French skin-care in thanks for the respite.

"We need Wire digging up every piece of dirt he can on Emily Ryan," Hansen said, jumping right into president mode.

Jagger nodded, getting on his phone.

"Hades, want to pay her a visit, try to convince her that there's no story here?" Hansen asked, thrumming his fingers on the table.

Hades turned his gaze to me for a long moment before nodding.

Smart. They were using the club's scariest dude to try to intimidate her from the story. Though I'd only had a brief interaction with her, I'd sensed that she was made of stern stuff. Hades would be testing just how stern.

Hansen focused on me. "We'll make sure she doesn't file a single word about you, Sariah."

I nodded to the president of the Sons of Templar MC, even though I didn't quite believe him.

These men were capable of a lot of impressive things, but they had yet to come up against a woman who had made up her mind about what she wanted.

Emily Ryan was going to get her story.

One way or another.

"Let's go home," Colby said once church had finished.

I suspected few, if any, women were ever invited to church. If the circumstances were different, and I'd been a little more sober, I would've reveled in being behind the doors usually reserved for bikers with dicks. I'd loudly protested against the club's misogynist rules and regulations, so any other time, this might've been a victory.

"No," I replied, slightly sickened at the prospect of going back to the apartment. "Can we just stay here?" I looked around the room. It was tidy, still cluttered with Colby's things. It still smelled of him. It was small. Warm. Safe.

"Of course," he said, smoothing my hair.

He was eager to please me—like he always was—but especially now when he could sense how on edge I was. I was way too tired to act normal and put together.

His gaze was much too heavy, so I escaped it, walking around the room, picking up things then putting them down, trying to get my shit together.

Colby had a bunch of books, bullets, random parts that either belonged to bikes or weapons. A small amount of personal care products. He wasn't high maintenance. He was just naturally that hot. The prick.

Amongst the clutter, something caught my eye. A book. A big one. Like a journal ... or a sketchbook.

"Is this Alyssa's?" I asked, looking over at him. He was still standing in the middle of the room, watching me.

He looked down, rubbing the back of his neck. "No, that's mine."

I looked up at him in surprise. "You draw?"

He shrugged. "I doodle."

"How did I not know this about you?"

Not sure why I asked since I knew the answer to that question. Because so much room in this relationship had been taken up by my suffering, we hadn't gotten around to talking about things like hobbies.

"Can I?" I asked, fingers already poised to open the book.

Colby nodded slowly, his expression odd.

He was ... nervous. I'd never seen him nervous. This was something deeply personal to him. Something I suspected he hadn't shown anyone. We'd briefly talked about his romantic history, or lack thereof. He fucked club girls and women who attended club parties. No sleepovers. No dates.

I was, technically, his first girlfriend, if you didn't count high school sweethearts, which I didn't. They dated a whole different Colby. One who didn't exist anymore.

I hurriedly opened the sketchbook, hungry to discover this new part of him.

"These are ... wonderful," I told him, slowly flipping the pages. The first few sketches were of mountains, a mixture of bikes and men wearing Sons of Templar cuts. They were all centered around the club. His life within it.

Then there was...

Me.

My eyes.

My face.

Pages of it. Different parts of me.

Then there was me. In my entirety.

But not.

It was a phoenix, rising from the ashes. Utterly beautiful, even charred, burnt. That was what made it beautiful. Its wings spanned two pages. It looked damaged yet majestic at the same time.

I stared up at Colby through glassy eyes. "This must've taken hours."

He shrugged in response.

"Is this how you see me?" I looked back from the drawing to him.

Colby nodded.

My hands shook as I put the book back on his desk, unable to look at the breathtaking artwork for a second longer.

"I don't know what to say," I admitted.

Colby stood there, staring.

"Take off your clothes," he ordered in a cold voice that managed to set fire to my bones.

I jerked at the unexpected request. I thought he'd want to talk. Tell me things. Convince me of things.

I liked this turn of events.

I started with the tee he'd put on me. Then my leather pants, stopping when I was left in nothing but the lace bustier and tiny panties.

Colby's gaze was a maelstrom of desire. "Everything," he ordered.

My hands reached for the laces of my corset, fingers trembling as I untied it and took it off. My nipples were hard and aching, my chest moving up and down rapidly. My panties were next.

With my clothes scattered on the floor, I stood in front of him, completely naked while he remained fully clothed.

The power dynamic should've made me feel weak, vulnerable. But no woman could feel weak or vulnerable when a man looked at them the way Colby looked at me.

Like I was a majestic creature rising from the ashes.

Colby's steps were measured as he crept toward me. Even though there wasn't much distance between us and his strides were long, it seemed to take minutes for him to reach me.

My knees were trembling when he stopped in front of me, the leather of his cut brushing against my naked skin.

Colby's eyes stayed on mine as his hand ran down the length of my stomach, tenderly, slowly. Dread raced through me as his fingertips ran over the raised skin of my scars.

I was getting better at coping with his hands on them. Better, being I didn't break out in a cold sweat, and my heart didn't threaten to beat out of my chest. Colby knew this. He had been patiently coaxing me into enjoying his touch, even the places I considered forbidden, dead.

"You wear the clothes you love again." He knelt in front of me to place his lips against my scars.

I held my breath.

Colby knew that I was frozen beneath his touch, but he acted as if all was well. It helped, somehow. His hands were firm at my hips, keeping me upright, keeping me anchored to the earth.

"But I've noticed you do not show this." His tongue trailed my belly button.

I was no longer frozen, my body writhing, battling between rapture and panic.

"Is it for you, or is it for them?" he asked, looking up at me.

I gazed down through hooded eyes. "What do you mean?"

He kissed another scar. "If it is for you, covering these up because you can't handle it, that I can accept." His lips trailed from one puckered mark to another. "But if you hide these because you don't want to make other people uncomfortable, that I can't accept."

I frowned at him and tried to move, too uncomfortable, but he gripped me too hard.

His eyes bore into mine. "Who is it for, baby?"

I struggled to pull in a complete breath. "If I wore the clothes I used to, people would stare, people would ask questions."

Colby's eyes narrowed, anger taking over his expression. "Anyone stares, they deal with me. And trust me, no one will utter a fucking word about your gorgeous body when I'm around."

"What about when you're not?" I whispered, hating how fucking small and weak I sounded.

"Then, my love, they will answer to you." He spoke as if the answer were obvious. "You spit fire, poppet. You're born from it."

I studied Colby. He believed that. He really believed that.

"How about you take your clothes off, outlaw," I purred, unwilling to take this conversation further. "I think, after tonight, I need to be fucked hard and dirty."

My evasion tactic worked. Colby, though determined to help heal me, was a slave to his own need for me, just like I was to him.

We didn't talk about heavy stuff the rest of the night.

And the next day, I wore a crop top.

———

An emergency girl meeting had been called.

Apparently.

I thought I was just coming to Violet's for drinks.

Not for a summit with every Old Lady in attendance.

Worse, it seemed like Colby had known. I'd scowled at him in accusation when he'd walked into the kitchen and announced that he and Elden were leaving on 'club business.' He'd just shrugged, kissed me firmly then left.

The traitor.

Normally, I loved hanging out with all the women. They were

interesting and fucking wild. There was never a dull moment with them.

But I didn't think the plan was to have a wild night.

This was a 'check the state of Sariah's mind' summit.

"I'm fine," I announced the second we'd all settled down, thankfully with cocktails, in Violet's large family room.

There was an impressive array of snacks, a great looking cheeseboard that I really wanted to dive into, but first I had to let all these women know I wasn't about to have a breakdown.

"Honey, you don't have to be fine," Kate said softly.

"We can set her car on fire," Macy offered hopefully.

Arson, yes, that was a good idea. "I'm going to reserve the right to take you up on that offer at a later date."

Macy held up her drink. "Just let me know the time and place, I'll bring the gasoline."

"Though it's tempting, we can't set fire to her car," Caroline muttered sadly. "I've done my due diligence. She's a respected journalist. A good one too. Which means she wouldn't let a little car bomb shy her away from the story. In fact, that's a surefire way to tell her there is a story."

I pursed my lips. She was right. Unfortunately.

All the women were pouting with me. This was a group of ride or die bitches. Despite being mothers and wives, they were all down to set fires and blow things up.

I fucking loved that. And not for the first time, or even the fifth, I felt myself growing roots here.

"I could pay her a visit," Caroline offered.

"No," I shook my head. "You're right. Anything we do at this point is only going to make her more determined." I remembered the hungry look in her eyes. "There's nothing we can do," I sighed. "Not now, at least. And I'm not going to run away again or have a breakdown."

"You're allowed to have a breakdown," Kate said.

"Or five of them," Freya chimed in.

"We can blow something up," Macy suggested hopefully. "Hansen bought me a minivan. *Something* needs to happen to that." She shook her head. "What the fuck kind of biker president buys his wife a fucking minivan?"

"Yes," I pointed to Macy. "Blowing up a minivan will surely help rid me of some demons."

None of the women looked convinced. Worse, I got the impression they weren't going to let this go.

"I'm pregnant again," Caroline blurted, watching me carefully.

All eyes went to her with a chorus of congratulations.

Thank you, I mouthed at her.

She smiled and mouthed, *you're welcome,* amongst the hugs and plans of shopping trips.

The heat was off me. For now.

———

I was done.

Or I'd snapped.

It didn't happen in the middle of some big blowup, not when I was drunk or experiencing a nightmare. No, it happened in the middle of the day, while I was making coffee. Only a couple of days after the girl summit.

We had indeed blown up a minivan in the middle of the desert. It was fucking awesome. But unfortunately, it didn't work to chase away my frustration and fear.

It had been bubbling inside of me for so long, it was bound to come out.

"I need to go on break," I told Julian.

He frowned at me, concern crumpling his features. Maybe it was something about my voice, my expression. Maybe he could see the crazy in my eyes.

"All right," he nodded slowly. "But I'll call Colby."

I didn't argue with him. He'd already been through the whole employee with a biker man with protective issues with Violet and Elden. He understood the status quo.

"You do that," I replied, untying my apron and placing it on the counter before snatching my purse from the cubby and walking out.

At least Julian didn't try to stop me. He knew me better than that.

I dug for my phone as I exited the café.

"I need the location of the bitch trying to dig up my story," I said after I dialed and put the phone to my ear.

"Hello to you too, bitch," Ollie muttered, but I heard tapping in the background.

Ollie had been briefed on the reporter situation and had been planning on ruining her life … virtually, at least. Which would be pretty fucking damaging. It was kind of scary, the power Ollie had with the stroke of a few keys.

"Her credit card records have her renting a house just off Main Street," Ollie said. "And her cellphone is pinging there right now."

Not for the first time, I wondered where Ollie would end up in a couple of years. Either working for the government or running from them. She was seriously talented and seriously dangerous if she wanted to be.

It was a worry, of course. But not one I had room for in my head. Plus, Ollie was smart, tough and strong. She'd be fine.

"Text me the address."

"You're not gonna like, kill her or anything, are you?" she asked without even a hint of concern. "Because I know the Sons of Templar are well versed in disposing and hiding bodies … but those are of serial killers and their enemies. Not Ivy League educated, white girls with rich daddies and a boyfriend who really sucks at dirty talk. Plus, she's got a direct line to you. I can do what I can to erase what she has online, but if she's smart, she has hard copies too. This murder would be … difficult to get away with."

I took the phone from my ear as it buzzed with a text. Reading the location and recognizing the street, I turned left. About a three-minute walk. Colby would likely already be on his way. But he had no idea where I was going. For now. Unfortunately, he'd be quick at putting two and two together, and he had his own resident hacker.

But I still had time.

"I'm not planning on killing her," I told Ollie once I'd put my phone back to my ear.

"Really? Because you've got a real *Children of the Corn* voice going on. And, honey, if anyone deserves to have a break from reality, it's totally you. But I'm just focusing on making sure that break happens in a fashion that won't have you locked up for the rest of your life."

I sighed. "I promise, I have no intention of being locked up anywhere, ever again." My spine chilled despite the balmy August heat as I recalled the telltale jangle of metal against concrete. I had to actually look down at my ankle to make sure it wasn't attached to a wall and bleeding from the metal biting into my skin.

It was bare—a nifty little takeaway from the event being that I could no longer wear shoes with an ankle strap. Today I wore wedge mules and a long, tight, striped midi dress. I loved fashion again, but my style would always be split into two sections BA—before attack—and AA—after attack.

"Okay, well, give me a call if you need anything else," Ollie muttered, not at all sounding convinced.

Ollie would never tell me to be careful. I appreciated that.

"Will do," I replied, ending the call and shoving my phone back in my purse.

It immediately started ringing. I knew it would be Colby, so I ignored it. This had nothing to do with him.

The house was like a lot of the houses in Garnett...cute, New Mexico vibe with wild but well-tended gardens. This little town was an enigma.

It was an oasis in the desert, which was why I fell in love with it in the first place. I still felt as if I didn't fit, but my gnarled roots were embedding themselves into the soil. I had nowhere else. And this bitch was trying to chase me out.

A serial killer had tried to do that already.

I wasn't about to let some plucky reporter run me out of town.

In fact, the way I was feeling right now, I'd do just about anything to make sure she stayed the fuck away from me and got out of *my* town.

CHAPTER
NINETEEN

EMILY DIDN'T LOOK surprised when she answered the door. She looked like … she'd been expecting me. That pissed me off further.

"Sariah, I'm so glad you came," she greeted me warmly. "Come on in."

Although she stepped back to let me in, I bowled forward, purposefully bumping her shoulder as I did so.

She hadn't been expecting it, so she went back on a foot. That was satisfying.

Though she definitely got the message of the tone of this visit, she didn't say anything as she closed the door behind me. She was that hungry for a story, willing to put herself in danger for it.

Not that I was dangerous.

I didn't think.

The place was nice. A smart investor had taken the small but cute cottage and renovated it, making it clean, trendy and comfortable with velvet covered sofas, funky art on the walls and lots of rugs.

The coffee table was cluttered with paper, a laptop open on the sofa.

If Hades had paid her a visit, she didn't get scared off.

Impressive.

"Can I get you anything?" she asked. "Water or coffee?"

"Why are you doing this?" I asked, ignoring her questions. "All of this." I waved my hand at the shit covering the table. "What gives you the *right* to do all of this?"

She tilted her chin up, her veil of friendliness disappearing. "I don't owe you an explanation."

I let out a cold laugh. "You certainly fucking do owe me an explanation since it's my pain and trauma you are exploiting and capitalizing from."

She had the self-awareness to look affronted. "I'm doing what any good journalist would do."

I rolled my eyes. "So, you're not looking for a cent or for any kind of professional acclaim?"

Her lips pursed. "No."

"You're a shitty liar, honey. And I might even say a shitty person, but I can't because if I were in your position, I might be doing the exact same thing." I picked up a decorative vase and examined it before putting it back down. It was tempting to throw it at her. "In fact, I was in your position, fascinated with the morbid, sickened by how enchanted I was, how obsessed. And look where that got me."

"There is no threat now," she protested, folding her arms across her chest.

"No," I agreed. "Not now. Not to *you*. You get to investigate this safely because the monster who did this to me is gone, and you think you can pick over the bones like some vulture. Because you feel you have the right."

I held up my hand, pacing around the room. She stayed where she was, watching me intently.

"I did the same thing," I told her, peering at her laptop. It was on my social media profile. I hadn't posted shit in years.

My gaze darted back up to her. "But I'll tell you right now, what you're doing is wrong. It's sick. Selfish. But you want to know anyway, don't you? Even though you feel slightly ashamed. You want to know because I'm not a person to you. I'm a commodity."

I leaned forward to snap the laptop shut, hoping the screen cracked.

I straightened and focused on the pretty woman in front of me. "You want to know how he tore off all my clothes and stared at me?" I demanded, my voice rising. "How he took away my dignity before he even started touching me. Torturing me."

I coughed, and liquid sprayed from my mouth. Some of it hit his face. It was blood. But he was already covered in it. His hands were stained crimson. Coughing up blood meant I was dying, right? Please, God, just let me die.

"Do you want me to tell you how I was chained to the wall like a dog?" I asked, quieter now.

Emily was standing with her arms folded, staring at me. Her face was blank, used to hearing horror stories, I guessed.

I could still hear him breathing in my ear, even though birds chirped outside. I'd decided to go there, into that locked drawer in my mind. Now it was all coming out.

"Do you want to know how he told me how worthless I was? What I *whore* I was?"

"Dirty, filthy, slut. You have no respect for yourself. This is your fault," he ranted as the knife went in and out. In and out.

My fault.

My fault.

Sinner.

Whore.

The birds chirped again.

I was in the living room, the warehouse. I steeled my spine at the jarring transition.

"Do you want to know how I was sure, certain I would get out of it, how someone would come for me until he started tearing into my belly with a knife? You want to know that I felt his cold hands inside of me after he cut me open? And that even though the wounds are healed, I swear, I can still feel him, rooting through my insides."

Emily looked pale. Unsure. But I could still see that light in her eyes, that sick fascination. The need for more. Fuck, if she had the opportunity, I bet she'd be writing this down in a fucking notebook.

"You want to know every detail, and you get a thrill when you find out they're worse than you ever could've imagined. Sure, a serial killer who rapes and kills his victims is interesting, but that's rather … pedestrian, isn't it? No one's gonna get a Pulitzer writing about the garden variety psychopath." I shook my head. "Beau Granger is it for you. While everyone else was buzzing around this small town, desperate for photos, for some kind of souvenir or photoshoot, you were researching."

I picked up a pile of photos from the coffee table. Crime scene photos. They made my stomach turn. Before, when I was investigating, I was able to chomp on a bagel while inspecting the graphic images. Now my empty stomach clenched with the need to force up bile.

I dropped the photos back down.

"You are smarter than all of them, right?" I asked, tilting my head and scrutinizing her. "You realized that there had to be another victim, one they weren't talking about. Maybe you weren't sure if they were alive or dead. And it took you a long time to figure that out because the police reports were confusing, not containing all the information they should've. But when you found out not only was there another victim, but that victim was alive. Wow, you hit the jackpot."

I clapped my hands. "Now that you've found me, what would you like from me?"

She opened her mouth as if she were going to reply to me, but I didn't give her time. I was on a roll. Or I was having some kind of episode. Whatever it was, this was a long time coming, and I was at the tail end of it. Thankfully.

"You would like me to give you every single part of my suffering for your fame, for your glory. You want me as a sacrificial lamb."

She picked up a coffee cup, taking an anxious slurp, not taking her eyes off me. "No, that's not at all what this is."

I didn't even respond to that. There was no reason to try to argue with her. She'd already convinced herself that she was doing the right thing for the right reasons. It was how she was sleeping at night. But by the look of her bloodshot eyes and the maniacal sipping of coffee, I was guessing she wasn't sleeping all that much. Good. I hoped everything I told her gave her fucking nightmares.

"Aren't you curious?" Even though she was uncomfortable, maybe even scared, apparently, she couldn't help asking questions. "What he was? How he got to be like that?"

"Am I *curious* about the life of a man who destroyed mine?" I laughed. "Am I curious about what he possibly could've gone through as an innocent child that could turn him into that? Am I meant to spend more time wondering about him so I can find a reason, an excuse for his behavior?" I was ranting, unable to believe she actually thought that was a valid question to ask. "No, because there is nothing anyone can go through that could explain why they would do that to other humans. There is no sense or excuse for that. And he has stolen enough of my life as it is; I'm not giving him another millimeter of space inside me."

I narrowed my eyes on her. "And I'm not letting you tear me open to show my insides to the country."

She pulled back her shoulders. "Is that a threat? Because I already had a visit from the Sons of Templar. They don't scare me."

A smile stretched my lips. She was lying. Hades most definitely had scared her. But not enough. "That's okay, they're a lot of bark and definitely a lot of bite," I shrugged. "They wouldn't hurt you physically, though." I stepped forward toward her.

She took a measured step back.

Smart.

"They would ruin you in other ways, your credit, your reputation, all that." I waved my hand. "But you probably figured out all that." My eyes slid up and down her. She was wearing sweats but expensive ones. Same with her jewelry. "You're an Ivy League girl," I deduced. "Probably come from money but are out here trying to prove to Daddy that you didn't need to join the family business or marry one of his buddy's sons in order to matter."

Her mouth tightened, telling me I'd hit close to home.

I stepped forward again. There was a TV behind her. She had nowhere to go.

I got close enough to smell her Jo Malone perfume. "The Sons of Templar won't hurt you ... physically," I repeated, relishing in the fear in her eyes. "They have a code." I leaned forward. "But I don't," I whispered.

She was holding her breath. Trembling.

It was a high, making someone feel like that. A nasty one. One that highlighted things I didn't like about myself but a high, nonetheless.

A dark urge told me to take it further, to really hurt her. I resisted that, stepping back.

"I don't have a code," I restated. "So, if you don't back the fuck off and forget my name, I will make you swallow your teeth. *That's* a threat."

On that awesome—if I did say so myself—last remark, I left the room. Before I actually hurt her. The verbal lashing was somewhat cleansing, but my fists ached to do something. I wanted to draw blood.

It didn't surprise me to see a bike at the curb and a biker on the sidewalk when I stepped out the door. I was thankful he hadn't arrived any earlier. I didn't need him for an audience. That was something I had to do on my own.

"Don't worry, I'm done," I told Colby, closing the front door as he ascended the steps to the porch.

His expression was tight, guarded. His eyes scurried over me, taking stock before he looked behind me. "Mind if I go in?" His voice was even, but his posture was coiled like a spring.

"What?" I asked innocently. "Do you think I killed her?"

"No, poppet. I know you gave her a tongue-lashing that made her forget her own name, 'cause I see it in your eyes." His gaze softened on me but turned murderous again when it crept once more to the door. "Tempted to have a few words myself, just to ensure the message was received."

My pulse spiked. "Why? You don't think I did the job well enough? Don't think I can take care of myself?"

It was a relatively stupid question considering everything that had happened in the past.

"I trust you did the job well," he sighed. "But I also want to have some words of my own."

Of course, he did. He had to make sure he made his mark. Though he had his code, I was concerned about the anger that was radiating off him. I didn't need Emily finding any more reason to look into the Sons of Templar MC.

"Let's go," I pulled at his arm instead of continuing the conversation.

He planted his feet, looking at me as if he were scrutinizing my mental state. Little good that would do.

I didn't wait on him. Instead, I walked to his bike, getting on.

"You don't get on this bike, I'll drive myself," I warned, dead serious. Colby had been teaching me how to ride. I enjoyed it. Almost enough to get a bike of my own. But that would've meant my main mode of transportation wouldn't be pressed up against Colby. Plus, there were a whole lot of outfit and hair limitations.

Colby looked from me to the house, weighing his options. He wanted his pound of flesh. But he wanted to be near me too.

He paused for one more second before quickly striding to the bike, shooting me an annoyed yet concerned glare.

"To the club please, sir," I requested in my most hoity-toity accent.

Another glare. But his lip twitched.

Then he took me to the club.

———

Colby had no choice but to follow me when I got off the bike and marched inside. I knew he was pissed off, but that didn't matter. I had a purpose. Plans. And I couldn't pause lest I bitched out.

We walked down the hall to his bedroom which had less stuff in it now. He'd moved everything important to my apartment. Except for one thing that was definitely important.

I snatched his sketchbook off his desk, opening it up.

"This," I pointed to the phoenix. "*This* is what I want on me."

He squinted, obviously confused.

"I assume the club has a tattooist on speed dial," I said, hoping that would clue him in. "I want you to call him, tell him to drop everything, or you'll kill him and his whole family…whatever it is you do to get people to do things." I waved my hand. "And I want this," I tapped the page again, "here." I pointed to my stomach.

Colby's face went blank. "You're serious."

I nodded. "As a heart attack."

He crossed the room, snatched my chin, tipping it so our lips crashed together for a fierce kiss.

Then he got out his phone and did his thing.

An hour later, I was in a tattooist's chair.

COLBY

I figured a lifetime with Sariah would mean a lifetime of surprises. Of chaos.

Not once in a million fucking years did I think I'd be sitting beside her as she got one of my drawings inked on her skin. On her scars.

The scars that she couldn't even stand to look at, to touch only a few months ago. The scars that made it so she could never escape what that fuck did to her.

Now one of the best tattoo artists in the state was expertly inking around them, making them part of my phoenix. Her phoenix.

I'd planned on getting it somewhere on my body. Getting Sariah somewhere on my body.

She beat me to the punch.

I'd never witnessed bravery like hers. Not since she was taken from that warehouse and chose helping her best friend over having her life saved. Not since she was brave enough to let me in, let me love her.

That was probably the best moment of my life.

Up until this point.

I had a feeling that a lifetime with Sariah meant I'd have a lot of fucking great moments.

But there, in the tattoo shop, I felt it. Felt Alyssa there with me.

"You deserve this, big brother," she whispered.

And for once, I got to remember my sister without her brains all over the wall. For once, I was brave enough to think of her alive instead of dead. Because of Sariah.

CHAPTER
TWENTY
ONE MONTH LATER

SARIAH

"I NEED you to not freak out," Ollie said the second I answered the phone.

I chewed on my pen as I stared at the webpage for the space I was thinking about leasing.

"I'm already freaking out," I told her honestly.

Who the fuck did I think I was, taking on a project like this? Yes, Garnett needed this. Garnett needed a grown-up to introduce something like this. A grown-up who understood what it took to lease things, get business licenses, deal with banks.

Ick.

"Well, okay, are you sitting down? Do you have a drink in your hand?"

I picked up my glass tumbler and leaned back in my chair. "Yes, and yes."

Ollie took a deep breath. "There's a copycat."

I frowned into my drink. "What? How can someone be copying *me*? Colby and Violet are the only ones I've talked to about this, and they surely wouldn't rat."

If someone had come up with my idea before me, that was

probably a good thing, right? Someone other than me would be less likely to fuck it up. Then I wouldn't have all that scary responsibility, and I could continue to sling lattes by day and party with bikers by night.

"Okay, I have no fucking clue what you're talking about, Sariah, but I'm talking about a murder."

I perked up at that, my problems melting away. The ones that had seemed so important just seconds earlier. Silly me. I'd forgotten what real problems were. I'd been tricked into thinking monsters weren't lurking outside my door, waiting for me to let my guard down.

"A copycat," I repeated, realizing what she meant.

"Yeah." I could hear Ollie typing. "Crystal Sanders, early twenties, sex worker. Found outside town limits, naked, stabbed." She relayed the information grimly. Neither of us were quite so fired up about murders now that we'd been so close to them.

I no longer followed true crime social media channels, I didn't listen to the podcasts. I didn't watch horror movies. I was all about comedies, fantasy and reality TV. I had lived a fucking true crime episode. That was enough.

"It was sloppy," Ollie continued. "There were hesitation marks with the first half dozen wounds."

Half dozen wounds.

My hand automatically went to my stomach. My tattoo had almost entirely healed. It itched like a bitch for weeks, and I'd almost passed out while I was getting it. But the guy who did my tattoo was hot, covered in ink and seemed like a total badass... I'd had to keep up appearances.

Then there was Colby, who had sat by my side, holding my hand for hours while I got it done, his eyes glued to me. He was fucking mesmerized by it. By me.

That had changed me, me getting that ink. Me purging all my shit to that fucking reporter—who I hadn't seen neither hide nor hair of.

Things had changed.

For the better.

Or at least they had been.

Though I wanted to pound the rest of my whisky, I gagged, barely able to keep the last swallow down.

"And you're sure it's a copycat?" I stared at my living room, the boxes that I'd gotten today to start packing up my things to move into the house Colby found us.

The *home* Colby found us.

It was a dream. A Spanish style ranch, out in the desert, no neighbors. Well, except Violet and Elden who were right down the road. It didn't seem like it, though. It seemed like the house was the only residence in the world. Colby was renovating the closet and the bathroom.

That was after he'd bought it. *Bought it.* The second I'd walked through, I'd jumped into his arms, kissed the shit out of him and said, "This is the one." He'd kissed me back, of course. Squeezed my ass too. I'd hoped he'd fuck me right there in the empty house.

But he left me, making a call on his cellphone.

Then he'd fucked me in the house. The empty house. Our house.

When I found out he'd bought it with his money, I screamed at him. He yelled back. It was a long fight about 'men taking care of their women' and 'feminism being a real thing.' Eventually, we'd compromised somewhat with me paying for all of the furniture. But I was still pissed. Fucking bikers.

"Pretty sure it's a copycat considering the victim, dumping ground, method of death," Ollie's reply jerked me back into the conversation about murders. I was getting déjà vu. "Though everything was pretty sloppy, messy. There was even DNA left at the scene. He's an amateur and should be caught quickly if the cops are actually doing their jobs these days."

"They will be," I mused. "All the publicity was not kind to the local law enforcement, and they won't be eager for a repeat."

A bike roared down the street, stopping outside.

"I'm guessing the club's hacker is aware of this too," I deduced, the timing a little too ideal.

"If he's worth his salt he will be," Ollie snapped.

I couldn't help but smile. Ollie and Wire had a not so friendly rivalry. It was almost cute. It could've been the recipe for a great love story if Wire wasn't already embroiled in one with some woman in Amber. The Old Ladies loved to talk about it. Apparently, it was causing a big splash and was full of drama. What Sons of Templar courtship didn't?

"Okay, keep me updated. I've got an overprotective biker to deal with," I said, calculating how long it would take Colby to park and run up the stairs.

"Hence why I stay indoors, have a virtual relationship and a great vibrator," she snickered before ringing off.

I shook my head, still smiling. One day, Ollie would be knocked off her feet by someone who got her off the net and into the real world.

The door crashed open with about as much drama as I'd expected. Colby tore into the room as if he were expecting to face off with a knife-wielding madman.

I smiled at him when he found no madman, just me sitting at the computer.

"There's a—"

"Copycat," I finished for him. "You guys get your news slow."

His shoulders were practically hitting his earlobes. "This isn't fuckin' funny." He was breathing heavily, like he'd sprinted here.

My smile disappeared. "I know. A girl is dead."

"*He* will be dead," he paced around the room. "The fuck who did this."

"I bet," I agreed.

"You're not going anywhere alone," Colby halted, his intense eyes locking onto me. "You'll have a patched member on you, a prospect at the very least. You'll carry this everywhere." He held up a gun.

I tilted my head at him, examining him in his panicked, 'must protect my woman' mode. It was cute.

"I figured as much." I hadn't expected the gun, but it was a nice addition.

His brows furrowed. "I expected you to argue about this."

I shrugged. "Yeah, but unlike all the other arguments in our future, I know I don't have a chance in hell at winning this one, so I figured I'll just embrace it."

"Embrace it?" Colby repeated, looking at me like I'd grown a second head. "No woman in the history of the Sons of Templar has just ... *embraced it.*"

"Well, I do like to go down in history." I hopped off my barstool, crossing the distance between us. "I've already experienced the bad guy catching me," I grasped the sides of his cut. "*You've* already experienced the bad guy catching me." Colby was stock-still. "It's not gonna happen again. So, if a biker has to come bra shopping with me, so be it."

Colby scowled down at me, then he leaned closer and kissed the fuck out of me.

"No fucking one is taking you bra shopping but me."

———

Protection detail had commenced.

I did not go anywhere alone. Colby was with me almost constantly. When he wasn't, Hades was. When Hades wasn't, Jagger was. You get the picture.

I didn't so much as go for a jog alone.

I didn't jog.

That's when you either discovered a body or became one... Every true crime junkie knew that.

Watching Jagger at Pilates with me and Caroline was fucking amusing, though.

Out of an abundance of caution, all the women had light protection too. But none of them were quite the blazing target that I was. Though I didn't think this copycat was smart enough to find out I even existed. Chances were he was some unhinged asshole who hated women and wasn't even original enough to come up with his own method.

It had all been pretty anticlimactic the past few days. Unfortunately, the DNA didn't match anyone in the state system. It would take longer to go federal. Odds were, he had a record. Petty crimes. Maybe domestic violence, animal cruelty. Pedestrian shit.

Just call me Jason Gideon.

I didn't look at the crime scene photos. I didn't spend my time researching who this guy might be. Other than my first thoughts, I did not waste brain power on it. There were enough smart people spending time tracking him down.

I had better things to think about.

Like the conversation Colby and I had a few weeks ago, which had spurred the research I was doing when I got the call from Ollie about the copycat.

"So," Colby said, sitting down after he'd done the dishes.

He'd cooked *and* done the dishes. I'd sat on the sofa with a glass of wine with a reality show on. He'd forbidden me to move. Granted, I'd been on my feet at the café all day and was exhausted.

Plus, I'd just gotten off the phone with my mother. She called, sporadically. And I answered. The conversations were still awkward, neither of us really knowing what to say. But they were still coming to visit when the new house was done. And I was still unsure how I felt about that. I wanted a relationship with them, but I wasn't sure how they fit here.

I wondered about Colby's family, if we'd ever go to visit them, heal that wound. It was on my list of things to do. We'd dealt with my scars, not his.

"So?" I sat up, focusing on him.

He had perched on the side of the couch, farther away from me than usual. Regularly, we were pretty much on top of each other at all times. Just how I liked it. My space and affection issues had disappeared. With Colby, at least. Immersion therapy worked.

The distance and the strange expression on his face told me he was concerned about my reaction to the conversation he had planned.

My curiosity was piqued.

"You're not going back to school." It wasn't a question. We hadn't talked about school or my plans behind slinging coffees daily.

We'd bought a house together—well, *he'd* bought it, but I didn't want to get into *that* whole thing again—and he'd said something about forever with me. That was plan enough.

"No, I'm not going back to school," I agreed.

Though I hadn't talked to him about it, I had done a lot of thinking about it. I didn't want to be half a country away from Colby for years. Sure, there were other colleges closer I could've gone to, but I knew in my heart of hearts that that ship had sailed.

"You were born to help people," he said.

"Really?" I scoffed. "I'm a college dropout with a casual drinking problem, a belly full of scars, a head full of demons and no plans beyond moving into a house with her super-hot boyfriend."

Colby's lip twitched. "I'm your Old Man, not your boyfriend."

"That's really the part you want to focus on?" I teased.

He took a sip of his beer. "Before all of that shit, you were going to school to help people. Now that you've gone through all that shit and come out on the other side—"

"That's debatable," I muttered.

His eyes hardened. "And come out the other side," he repeated. "There are plenty of women who have been hurt, damaged by men with nowhere to go and no one who understands them." He leaned forward to grasp my feet, pulling them into his lap and massaging them.

I groaned at the magic of his fingers.

"What are you even proposing?" I asked him, mulling over his words. Though I wanted to cast them aside, he'd hit a nerve.

Before the warehouse, I'd wanted to help people. I also wanted to make good money and get a Ph.D. as a fuck you to my parents. Not exactly the most noble of intentions.

Now I had money to keep me in shoes—for a while, at least—and no longer needed to give a giant fuck you to my parents. What I *did* need was a place to channel all the shit inside of me. Or it would eat me alive.

"I'm not proposing anything," Colby continued rubbing. "I'm telling you what you already know. You have the power to help a lot of women. We've got a lot of resources here. Those are the ingredients. Do with them what you will."

He didn't push further. In fact, he didn't mention it again. He didn't need to. The seed had been sown.

I couldn't stop thinking about it, the idea born from it. A totally scary and totally unrealistic idea but one that I couldn't get out of my head as I made coffee.

Until a visit from Emily Ryan served to shift my focus.

"You really don't get a hint do you, honey?" I asked the woman who I was sure I'd scared out of town weeks ago.

Her presence didn't make my lungs seize, nor did it fill me with panic. It just pissed me off. With every pound of flesh I'd already given her, she was here, hungry for more.

Fucking reporters.

I figured the murder had drawn her back in. Even though I'd scared her, she was willing to risk her physical well-being to get the story.

She had balls.

"I'm a journalist. I don't abandon my stories."

"Keep telling yourself that," I huffed, leaning on the counter.

"You're just a woman like the many who are fucking fascinated with murderers, yet somehow, you get a paycheck out of it. You should see a therapist."

We both should.

"Have you heard about the murder just outside of town?" she asked, ignoring me.

I sighed. "Yes, I've heard about it."

"What do you think about the news that there's a potential copycat out there, targeting the same kind of young women Granger did?" She clutched her phone which I assumed was recording the conversation.

Sneaky bitch.

"I think that they're sick, and they have the same kind of fascination that you do with a monster. Their methods for exorcizing the fantasy are just a little bloodier than yours," I replied in a saccharine sweet tone.

A line formed between her eyebrows. I was pissing her off. Good.

"Are you concerned that you might be a target since you are the only surviving victim, and this current murderer might consider you a job to ... finish?"

My skin tingled, and my casual façade threatened to fail me. She was good. She'd seen my exposed nerves, and here she was, poking them, without mercy.

"You know, you might be a good journalist if you took your focus away from all of this." I waved my hand at her. "If you focused on uncovering billion-dollar companies spilling toxic chemicals into wastewater or exposing all the politicians who have paid for their mistresses' abortions while trying to strip women of their rights."

The wrinkle deepened. I'd struck a nerve. Good. I hoped her Botox bill was huge this month.

"Is that why there is a man wearing a Sons of Templar patch sitting outside the café?" she asked, quickly recovering from my barb. "I know you're affiliated with the local motorcycle club. Are they offering you protection?"

Fuck.

"If you don't get out of this café, out of this town, preferably out of this state, *you'll* be scrambling to find protection from the Sons of Templar. Though they won't give it to you." I smiled at her.

Finally, she blanched. Good.

I snatched her phone from her hand, successfully since she wasn't expecting it.

"Hey!" she protested.

I stepped back when she tried to take it back from me, then I dropped it, stepping on it with my brand-new motorcycle boots. They were Givenchy.

The phone crunched underneath my heel.

"You cannot do that! That is my personal property. I can have you arrested."

I laughed. "Go on to the police station, honey. See if they're willing to help out a nosy reporter."

She glared at me, then looked around, as if to find someone to help her. Everyone averted their gaze. Except Julian who smiled happily at her, obviously amused by our little display.

She was smart enough to understand that there wasn't a hero to be found.

It was better she learned that now. I hadn't learned that until I was covered in my own blood.

I took a deep breath, shaking off the thought, then went back to making coffees, hoping that was that.

I should be so lucky.

ONE WEEK LATER

COLBY

We found out he had the reporter before the cops did. Wire said it was ridiculously easy once they got the DNA hit from the national database.

Craig Singer.

A record as long as a CVS receipt, wanted for violating parole.

I found this out too late, though. Hades was with me. We'd been at the café, picking up an order for Sariah before we went out hunting again. Although I hated it, Hades and Sariah had some kind of ... connection. Born the day he unchained her. I had punished myself for a long time for not being the man who did that until Hades took me aside one day.

"It had to be me," he said, not bothering with any kind of pretense. Wasn't his style.

"To find her that day, to be the first one to touch her," he continued. "It had to be me." He gave me a level look. "She wouldn't have been able to survive it being you."

Then the fucker just turned and walked off.

I really hadn't wanted to believe him at the time, I'd wanted to think he was a friend who saw me beating myself up and wanted to placate me with bullshit. Except Hades didn't do bullshit.

And the more I'd thought about it, the more I understood. He was the darkest fucker in the club, bar none. There was something about him. Some things that unnerved even the most hardcore of criminals. Scared them. He'd seen shit, been to places even I hadn't.

It had taken two fucking years to get Sariah to stop running from me. Months more after that to get her to believe she was worthy of me, as fucked-up as that was. It had taken everything she had to let me in. *Because* I wasn't the one who found her in her worst moment.

I fucking hated it, but without Hades being the one, Sariah wouldn't be mine, she wouldn't have my mark tattooed over her scars.

So yeah, I didn't like their connection on principle, but fuck was I grateful for it.

Because of that connection, Hades was hell-bent on finding this copycat before he could plunge her into a place neither of us could get her out of.

It had kept me up at night. Every day we didn't find him. Every moment I wasn't with her.

What was fucking laughable was that Sariah seemed ... okay. Sure, there were more shadows behind her eyes, but she smiled. Laughed. She slept in my arms, through the night, no nightmares.

She wasn't haunted by this.

And I fucking wouldn't let her be.

Until we heard that he had the reporter. Though none of us liked the bitch, no one deserved to be fucking tortured, tossed in the desert like trash. Well, the fucker hurting women deserved that.

My phone was at my ear as I jogged out of the coffee shop toward the apartment, a two-minute walk away. I could see the prospect on his bike outside. That should've reassured me, but it didn't. I had a boulder in my chest.

"I promise, I did not condone this," Ollie spluttered as she answered.

Fuck.

"I told her to call you. The police."

I ran faster, rocks in my stomach. "You told her that," I seethed, "but you also told her where *he* was, knowing her well enough to know she wouldn't call me or the cops."

"I did," Ollie sighed, having the decency to sound ashamed. "She needed this."

"My woman does not need another moment of blood, of being near a man who cuts up women," I roared, ending the call before shoving my cell in the pocket of my cut.

I'd already known Sariah wasn't going to be there. But it hit fucking home when the place was empty, her glass still half full, computer still open to the plans for her women's center.

Her purse was gone.

As was the gun I'd given her.

Fuck.

"I swear, I was watching the whole time," the prospect said when I stormed out of the building.

I didn't verbally respond to him, just punched him in the face. Hard. Hard enough for him to fall on his ass.

"Don't get up," I snarled at him. "Not in my presence. And when you do peel yourself off the sidewalk, take off that fuckin' cut, and get the fuck outta town if you want to be breathing in the morning."

I turned to Hades who was observing like he was watching the morning news.

"We gotta get there before it's too late."

He nodded.

But somehow, I already knew it was too late.

CHAPTER
TWENTY-ONE

SARIAH

IT WAS NOT A SMART IDEA.

I'd had some pretty dumb ideas in my life.

Going on a date with a serial killer made the list. Though in my defense, I didn't know he was a serial killer at the time.

This one took the cake.

Ollie had tried to talk me out of it. Persistently. But Ollie was also the one who told me there was a DNA match for the killer in the federal database and that the police hadn't found him yet.

But she had. By pinging his cellphone. Along with Emily's. They were at the same location.

He had her. Whether it was because he'd seen her poking around or she'd accidently stumbled upon him didn't matter. This was a man who wanted to kill women. He wasn't organized or meticulous like Granger. He'd deviate from his classic victim profile if he had the opportunity. And it seemed he had the opportunity with Emily Ryan.

The smart idea would be to go to the police. For any other citizen. If you were currently dating an outlaw biker, the smartest idea would've been to call aforementioned outlaw biker boyfriend. He and the club would've ridden out there to save her, kill the murderer. As they'd done with me.

I'd gone as far as pull up my phone to call him, then I imagined that exact scenario.

Something in me clicked. Or snapped. Again.

So, I got the gun that I was now an expert with, checked that it was loaded, put on my boots and rode out to the location Ollie had given me.

I'd given the prospect 'protecting me' the slip, which momentarily made me feel guilty because he'd likely be punished later. But then I realized that he was glued to his phone and didn't even notice that I'd left.

If I could get out of there without him noticing, a deranged murderer could've gotten in without him noticing.

Then I didn't feel quite so bad.

I didn't think about much on the drive there.

Or when I got out of the car at the shitty house in the middle of nowhere. All I thought about was being chained to that wall, naked, bleeding, helpless. I thought about the men who had ridden in to rescue me. The men who had ended the life of the man who'd hurt me.

I thought about all the other people who had been involved in me surviving, me being rescued, and me being avenged.

Fury, unlike anything I'd ever felt, embedded itself beneath my skin. It clouded my vision, brushed away all thoughts of consequences, fear, common sense. I was so fucking angry. So fucking angry at myself for not being the one to escape, to punish the man who'd hurt me. Mostly, I was so fucking full of wrath at these men for taking things from us. Hurting us.

The anger was probably what had me bursting through the front door without doing any kind of recon.

For all I knew, the rundown shack could've been rigged with booby traps. I was acting on a hunch, and it paid off.

The place was filthy. It stank.

I was reminded of the smell of my own puke, urine and blood. The smell of other women's.

I didn't have to search long. He didn't have her in the basement like I'd expected from all the crime shows I've watched. She was in the living room. It was emptied of all furniture, and she was chained to a radiator. He barely turned when I entered the room, confusion distorting his bloodstained face. He was young. Had dirty brown hair. Was naked. And hard. Ew.

I didn't pause, didn't let him try to beg; I just relished in the momentary fear I saw in his eyes before I calmly pulled the trigger, sending a bullet between his eyes.

He hit the ground with a thud, twitching a couple of times before going still. I eyed him for a few seconds longer. In horror movies, they always came back to life. But this was real life, and I'd just plugged him between the eyes. He wasn't going anywhere except hell, if you believed in that sort of thing.

The reporter was screaming.

I didn't blame her.

She was chained to a radiator in her underwear. She had blood on her torso, but it wasn't gushing out. He hadn't had a chance to do any lasting damage. Physically, at least.

I stepped over the dead body to kneel down in front of her.

At least she'd stopped screaming. A good thing too, as I hated the cliché of the screaming woman. But then again, you were allowed to react however the fuck you wanted when you were chained to a radiator and just watched your would-be murderer get shot in the face. It was a lot.

Her eyes were wide, terrified, yet hollow. Gone was the brave, determined reporter willing to do anything for a story. In her place was a terrified, traumatized woman.

He'd taken that from her. Her zest for life. He'd given her something else. Darker. Dirtier. Something that would live inside of her without her permission.

"You're not going to be okay for a while," I told her honestly, mimicking Hades's words to me on the worst day of my life. "But he's dead, and you're breathing."

And to that, she burst out crying.

I didn't blame her.

———

The cops arrived only a minute before the bikers did. Which was a good omen for me because that meant Colby didn't get to drag me away and yell at me or whatever.

He did all but leap off his bike, snatch my arms, do a head-to-toe scan and then haul me into his chest. I went willingly. Though I put on a really good front, I was a smidge shaken up.

Then the sheriff had cleared his throat and informed Colby he had to get my statement. Colby had demanded to know everything that had happened. Which was why he stood by, hard-nosed while I gave my statement. His arms around me had constricted when he heard about me pulling the trigger.

The rest of the club milled around along with the paramedics tending to Emily. She wasn't being rushed to the hospital, which was a good thing. She wasn't dying. Rattled and scratched up, which was enough.

When I was done being questioned, Colby ordered me to not move a muscle. Apparently, there was some sort of conference that needed to be held between the club and the cops.

I, of course, didn't obey that command. It would've been boring, standing in one place with all of the action going on around me.

So, I walked to the ambulance where Emily was sitting, looking shell-shocked.

She watched me approach warily, her gaze empty, unbelieving, as if she were trying to convince herself this was a dream.

"Thank you," she whispered, clutching the blanket around her.

I recognized the look in her eyes. I still saw it in the mirror.

"I already told the police it was self-defense," she murmured, her voice hoarse. "That he came at you, you had no other choice."

"Thanks," I smiled, deciding not to mention that it was kind of unnecessary.

The brand-new sheriff wasn't brand-new at all. He was a lifetime resident of Garnett and a friend to the club.

No way was I getting into any trouble.

From the law, at least.

The angry biker in a huddle glaring at me on the other hand? Yeah, I was in big fucking trouble.

"The story, it's dead," Emily continued.

I returned my attention to her, my eyes widening. "What, you're not going to file it now that you have first-hand experience?" I scoffed. "That just might get you the critical acclaim you're looking for."

"I'm not going to file it *because* I now have first-hand experience." She looked ashamed. "I'm sorry. I learned my lesson."

I nodded. "I think that getting kidnapped and almost murdered wasn't the best way to learn this lesson, but thanks." I glanced back at Colby. I had about ten seconds before he came over here, hauled me away and all but tossed me on the back of his bike.

"Give me your phone," I held out my hand.

"You gonna smash this one too?" she tried to joke, handing it over with a shaking hand.

"I'm going to add my number," I said, entering my details then handing it back to her. "In case you need to talk." I looked at her, at the scene. "I don't think there are many people who've been through this kind of thing, and there definitely isn't a self-help book on it, so if you need to talk, or get drunk ... call me. I'm one of the few who can tell you I know how you feel." I looked back into the terrified eyes of a woman who had survived. "I can promise you, if you hold on long enough, it gets better." The ground crunched behind me. "And you may just get a hot outlaw out of it." I winked.

"We're going. Now," Colby growled, not giving Emily a second look as his hand locked around my upper arm and dragged me off. Safe to say, he was furious.

"Get. On. The. Bike." He spoke through gritted teeth.

I did as he asked.

He gave me one last glare before he got on the bike himself, kickstarting it. I grabbed on to him tightly. His hand covered mine for a split second, squeezing it, reassuring me that he was still in there, underneath all that fury.

Then we roared off into the growing twilight.

———

It was a good thing Colby couldn't speak to me during the ride home. I figured it would help him calm down.

I figured wrong.

He all but dragged me up the stairs to the apartment, cheeks red, chest heaving, grip tight enough to leave a mark.

"You have no idea how fuckin' furious I am at you," he slammed the door behind him so hard it literally came off the hinges.

The force of that surprised me. I knew he'd be pissed. Really pissed. But I didn't think he'd lose control completely. Which he had.

The look in his eyes was wild. Feral. His forearms were corded with veins. The air about him was electric.

Some kind of latent survival instinct told me to run. That I was in danger. That this was a predator.

I held fast.

"The door has some idea how fucking furious you are," I deadpanned even though my heart was hammering.

"For the second time, you were in the presence of a man who

enjoyed hurting women, killing them," he seethed, striding toward me.

"For the first time, *I* was the one who hurt him, killed him," I pointed out, spitting a fury of my own.

That made Colby's steps falter. Slightly. I saw it. He was worried about me. Concerned about what this had done to me. I'd killed someone, after all. But he was livid. He was trying to fight off whatever rage these men lapsed into when shit like this happened.

"You need to fuck me," I decided, my body no longer afraid.

He stopped in his tracks, hands fisted at his sides. "I can't. I won't be gentle."

All of his considerable strength was going toward holding himself back, restraining all those dark urges I'd been feeding these past months.

"I don't want you to be gentle," I told him, crossing the distance between us.

He backpedaled, but that didn't stop me.

"I need you to be rough." I grasped the sides of his cut. "I need you to show me I'm alive."

He didn't ask me if I was sure. I don't think he was capable of asking any questions in that moment. He had been hanging by a thread, and I'd just cut it.

His hands were all over me, tearing at my clothes. Mouth on mine, teeth opening up my lips, making me taste blood. Mine. His.

We didn't waste time getting completely naked. We couldn't. There would be time for that later.

"I had to entertain the thought I'd never do this again," Colby growled, pushing his finger inside of me.

I gasped in ecstasy.

"I fuckin' thought I'd never taste you again." His finger was no longer inside of me. It was in his mouth.

"You put yourself in danger." His eyes danced with ire, intensity, fear, lust ... so many fluctuating emotions. "And you fuckin' fought for yourself. Saved someone. I'm so goddamn proud of you." A glimpse of tenderness shadowed his face but that was quickly gone, replaced by a desperate need.

I was spun around, my hands automatically splaying on my kitchen counter.

My jeans and panties were pushed down. I stepped out of them, about the only thing I did other than lean against the counter, panting, desperate for him.

"Need to hurt you," Colby bit out from behind me.

"Yes," I hissed right before his hand came down on my ass.

The pain was exquisite.

I thought it would last longer. That he'd punish me thoroughly. But Colby didn't seem to be able to do that. Seconds after his palm came down on my ass, he was inside me.

I cried out at the magnificent intrusion, at him brutally pulling my hair, pumping into me without mercy.

I knew my orgasm would obliterate me. I knew it would happen quickly, what with all the adrenaline already running in my veins.

I needed to say something before I lost all sense.

"Colby," I gasped.

"Yeah, take me like a good fuckin' girl."

My body responded like it always did to that praise. In a big fucking way.

"Colby," I tried again, my vision clouding, limbs coiling. "I love you."

He couldn't stop, I knew he couldn't. I'd told him this at the best possible moment, when he was seized by the animal inside him.

"Sariah," he continued fucking me harder than he'd ever done.

I cried out, unable to comprehend sound, space, fuck, anything but the way Colby was ruthlessly fucking me.

He growled, teeth grazing my neck as I came around his cock, pulling his own climax from him, both of us reveling in the beauty of our coupling.

I was alive.

That much was very fucking clear.

———

"This is going to hit you at some point," Colby murmured.

We were in bed.

Naked.

There had been sex.

A whole lot of sex.

And a shower.

Where there was more sex.

So there hadn't been much talking.

I'd stayed relatively quiet, apart from my obligatory sexual phrases. I'd said enough. I'd said the three words that had been simmering inside of me for months. And uttering them had been more terrifying than pulling the damn trigger today.

Colby didn't say it back. I didn't need him to. I wasn't unsure about our relationship. He had made it clear how he felt about me every fucking day. He'd made it clear for *years*.

"What? The sore muscles from the acrobatic sex?" I deliberately misinterpreted him. "Yeah, I need to work out more."

He nipped my lip in warning. "You know what I mean." His arms were wrapped around me. "Pulling that trigger, it's going to hit you."

Ah, there it is. One of the subjects I'd been dreading.

I wasn't sure which I dreaded more, talking about this or my 'I love you.' No, I knew. The mushy stuff was a little scarier than speaking about the man I killed.

"It might," I hedged.

Colby must've heard the edge to my voice, tilting his head down to survey me. "You ended someone's life, poppet. Even though he was a piece of shit, he was a human being. It'll fuck with you."

He was speaking from experience. That I didn't doubt. We didn't talk about the club a whole bunch. I wasn't one of the Old Ladies who needed to know every little detail. The men broke the law in various ways, I knew that. Colby had reason to clean blood off him after coming in the front door every now and then. He had reason to be constantly armed. He knew how to kill people.

He *had* killed people.

And it fucked with him.

Because he was Colby. And although he was a really hot badass, capable of kicking ass and taking names, he also had a heart underneath that. A kind one at that.

It was scarred, to be sure, after what he'd been through, but it still remained soft. Parts of it hadn't been calcified.

Mine might've been soft, at least a tiny part of it. A much smaller part than Colby's. The soft parts of my heart belonged to him. Violet. Willow. There wasn't any more to go around, certainly wasn't more to feel guilty over ending the life of a murderer.

"It wasn't a human being," I disagreed. "He wasn't. He forfeited the right to be called that the second he plunged the knife into the flesh of an innocent woman." Of their own volition, my hands went to the scars on my stomach, though they weren't scars now. They were vibrant feathers in my phoenix.

I looked into Colby's eyes, seeing love, pain, concern, anger, fear. "I've got a little monster in me, I know that now. He ... created that."

I put my finger to Colby's lips when he opened his mouth to argue.

"Before you talk about how I'm perfect and not at all evil, that little monster inside of me was what made me survive. What made it so I'm still here, me ... more or less."

"More," Colby barked. "Most definitely fuckin' more."

I bit back my smile. "It's fucked-up. Like really fucked-up. But I think killing him … *healed* me in a way. It's not going to give me nightmares. I've had enough of those. Lived enough of those."

It was the truth. It wasn't pretty, but Colby could handle the ugly truth. I trusted him to hear it and not think differently about me. I trusted him.

"You never asked what I did with Granger," Colby murmured after contemplating my words.

Ah, there it was. I'd been waiting for him to bring it up. I wondered if it had been driving him crazy, me not mentioning Granger, me seemingly not caring about his fate. Apparently, this was a night of confessions.

"I didn't need to," I brushed a lock of his hair from his face. "I can guess what probably happened. The end result being him in a grave that no one visits."

Colby didn't say anything, so I took that as confirmation of my guess.

I cupped his jaw. "I don't need to know what you did to him. I don't need to know anything other than that he's worm food, and I'm here, in bed with my man, a whole life ahead of me."

Colby flipped us so I was on my back. "I love you so fucking much, Sariah."

My mouth went dry, and my heart stuttered.

Okay, I lied when I said I didn't need to hear that. I totally did.

"I know," I whispered, trying to play it cool.

"I'm gonna make sure we have the greatest fuckin' life," he promised.

I smiled. "I know."

EPILOGUE

SIX MONTHS LATER

COLBY

MY GUTS CHURNED as my boots hit the pavement. I hadn't been able to choke down a bite of food today.

Fuck, the only taste I needed in my mouth was my woman's pussy. I got that. Got to feel at home inside of her, feel safe, feel fucking centered.

My woman gave me life. Every day I woke up with her. She gave me strength. Every moment I looked into her eyes, watched her smile, watched her laugh.

She was the reason I was here, standing in front of the place I'd vowed never to come back to. The house where my sister had taken her last breaths. Where her blood and brains had stained the walls.

My parents hadn't moved. They'd replaced the carpet, painted the walls. But they hadn't left the place where Alyssa died.

First, I thought it was because they were trying to gloss over it all, trying to fix it, forget her, act as if nothing had happened.

Now, with the privilege of hindsight, I considered another reason. They didn't want to leave the house where my sister had taken her first steps, spoken her first words. To them, maybe it wasn't the house where she died, it was the only place she'd *lived*.

Sariah's small hand squeezed around mine. "We can still leave," she offered.

I glanced at her.

Her hair was longer now. Darker too. It was thick, wild from the ride. The dark locks covered her nipples when she was naked.

She'd painted her full lips red, had dark eyeliner on to highlight her burnt copper eyes. Her face was fuller now, healthier. There was a glow about her, a fire that burned brighter every day.

I wrestled my gaze from my woman to the house I grew up in. It hurt to look at it. To remind myself of the person I used to be. My parents had wanted me to be a doctor, a lawyer, and I was coming back to them wearing a patch and a stain of a life they'd never understand.

The chances of them slamming the door in my face were high.

And fuck if that didn't scare the shit about me.

I looked back at my woman.

The one who came out of the ashes stronger than ever, who amazed me every fucking day.

I'd stood at her side when she went home again, when terror coated her very pores and she stepped forward anyway.

"No," I said firmly. "We're goin' in. Together. Gotta do somethin' first." I pulled her to me, our lips crashing together. I kissed her hungrily, needfully.

The taste of her remained on my lips after I let her go, right up until we made it to the front door. My woman's kiss gave me strength. Courage.

SIX MONTHS LATER

SARIAH

The water in Positano, Italy, was sparkling sapphires. The colorful houses and villas perched on the cliffs looked like they were straight out of a postcard. The cobblestone streets were full of tourists and locals alike.

The curtains blew sea air into our exquisite hotel room. The one with a tub you could swim in and a balcony that looked out onto that incredible water.

We had breakfast there every morning.

"How do you like it here?" I asked Colby.

He was languidly trailing my nipple with his fingertip. Though we'd just finished some excellent sex, my body sizzled in appreciation. And hunger.

"I love the way your skin has tanned from the Italian sun." His hand moved to my shoulder, trailing over the tan that was a result of a lot of lazy sunbathing with an umbrella drink in my hand.

"I love the way that Italian food has agreed with you." His hand slid back down, past the swell of my breast to my stomach. My phoenix spanned my torso, from rib to rib.

I wore a bikini at the beach.

If people stared, I didn't notice. Maybe because Colby noticed them first and did the whole menacing badass thing.

It barely hurt when he touched them now. Which he did, often. I didn't think that pain would ever entirely go away. It was a part of me.

His hand landed on my hip which had a bit more of a curve to it now. I'd filled out plenty at home, but I'd indulged a lot in everything Italy had to offer.

You could no longer see my rib bones. My face wasn't gaunt, all angles. It was full, rounder. I looked … *nourished*.

"I'm not asking what you like about me in Italy, I'm asking what you like about Italy," I rolled my eyes at him. I was acting like I was tired of the sweet murmurings, but I was never tired of them. He still gave me fucking butterflies.

Me, Sariah Cardoso, getting *butterflies*, from her fucking boyfriend.

Or fiancé, as he wanted to be called now that I had a square cut emerald on my fourth finger.

I'd argued against the label, for whatever reason. Maybe because it was habit. Maybe because arguing with him was my favorite form of foreplay. And just maybe, I was still fighting against whatever version of happily ever after we were living.

We'd moved into an amazing home together.

Colby's parents were back in his life. There had been some hiccups. A lot. Who would've thought my parent's introduction to the life we were living would've been the one that went smoothly.

Then again, I'd somewhat prepared them my entire life for me to be shacked up with an outlaw biker, dropping out of college to pave my own way.

Colby's parents, on the other hand, had raised a son to lead a prosperous life. A safe life. And, up until the gunshot that changed everything, Colby had been on that path.

Their one remaining son was living a dangerous life that they couldn't understand. It was hard for them to swallow.

But they were trying. Because they loved him. That was plain to see.

His mother was quiet but gentle, small in stature, and stunning. She had more wrinkles and gray hair than a woman her age should have. Trauma and grief aged her. She carried around a gentle grace coupled with enormous sadness.

His father was quiet, stoic, not unlike my own father. He was the one who had taken it the hardest. There had been clipped arguments between the two, tense dinners, but it was getting better.

My shelter finally opened, though it wasn't exactly a shelter. It had a small section of bedrooms for temporary emergency housing, of course. But we were also working with local landlords—a lot of them happened to wear Sons of Templar cuts—to get women into more permanent housing. And we were working with local businesses to get them jobs and educations.

I had social workers, therapists, manicurists, yoga teachers and lawyers collaborating with my little company.

I also had a whole bunch of help from all the club women, desperate to contribute in whatever way they could. Suffice it to say, The Phoenix Center was doing amazing. I'd put my blood, sweat and tears into it over the past year. I worked seven days a week, staying there until Colby dragged me home, demanding I needed to do things like sleep, eat and fuck him in every room of our house.

Colby lived and breathed for The Phoenix Center whenever he wasn't at the club. He was there every second he could be, helping with whatever I needed. Heavy lifting, fixing things, building things.

He had painted the huge mural that greeted everyone when they walked into the building. A gorgeous phoenix on a stark white wall, an explosion of fire and color. Not unlike the one on my stomach.

"My favorite thing about Italy is that you're in it." Colby's warm breath hit my neck, bringing me back to our fabulous hotel room.

I smiled, leaning into him, reveling in the warmth of his skin, his scent.

"My favorite thing about Portugal was watching you eat pastel de nata," he twirled my hair around his finger. "My favorite thing about Prague was watching you geek out over the historical buildings."

"You don't have *any* favorite things about traveling to some of the most incredible countries in the world that don't involve me?" I asked him.

"Nope," he replied without hesitation.

I shook my head, chuckling. I did that more often now. Chuckled. Laughed. Smiled. Enjoyed life. Cherished it like I used to.

Granger watched me from the shadows of our hotel room.

He was still here. Less now. And he didn't seem as solid, as powerful. When Colby wasn't in the room, I occasionally flipped him off.

I didn't tell Colby about seeing him. He didn't need to know that.

He knew enough. I'd told him snippets, but nowhere near all of it. I wouldn't do that to him. To us.

Besides, I paid a therapist a lot of money to hear all those sordid details.

She was good. Although I thought the best benefit I got from the sessions was me purging everything I needed to without worrying about the effect it would have on those I loved.

Hades was the one exception.

We met for a drink once a month.

We didn't say much. Sometimes we didn't say barely anything at all. Other times, I shared about things. Horrible things. Whether it was something horrible that had happened to me or it was something horrible I was thinking, he listened. Without judgment.

Sometimes, enough to count on one hand, he told me things.

I listened. Without judgment. Interestingly, hearing all of his horrible things made me feel better about mine.

"Do you think everything is running okay?" I asked, my mind darting back to Garnett.

Colby sighed then moved to hover above me. "I know everything is going great because you have great people there making sure of that. And because you call every day for updates."

I grimaced. I did do that. And I had people I trusted implicitly running everything. Deep down, I had absolute faith it was running smoothly. But this was my baby. The one thing I'd created that did good things. Something born out of the worst time in my life that did good things. Granger had been wrong; I still retained the ability to create life.

"I know, but we've got that emergency case coming in." I was thinking about the woman coming with her infant child, fleeing a really bad situation with a dangerous man who'd be looking for her.

"Yeah, and the whole club is on it, protecting her. Kate is taking point on her intake," Colby stated all of the things I already knew.

This woman would be well taken care of.

"You can't enjoy our last night before we go back?" he nudged his now hard cock between my legs.

I was instantly wet for him.

"I'm enjoying myself plenty," I whispered.

He smiled, his molten eyes sparkling, the expression warming up my insides. Right before his cock set fire to them.

"Love you, Colby," I rasped as he slowly fed his cock into me.

He paused, froze, like he did every time I said those words.

"Love you, poppet."

And then it was my turn to freeze, no ... to melt, every time I heard those words.

Because I got it.

A good ending.

This might not be what happened to all the Final Girls, but it was what happened to *this* Final Girl.

ACKNOWLEDGMENTS

I know a lot of you have been waiting for this one. I was writing it before I even finished *Wilting Violets*. Sariah and Colby were READY for there story.

I was sure that this book would pour out of me.

And maybe it might've.

If life hadn't happened. As it tends to do.

But I think life HAD to happen in order for this book to be what it is now. This was not easy to write. I know it's not an easy read.

Whenever I write about people who are broken in different ways, it feels difficult, frustrating, heartbreaking. It's always so complicated.

But that's why I love it so much.

Taylor. My husband. You're there for me when I'm a mess about deadlines, storylines and full of self doubt. You've taken such good care of me throughout this season of our lives. I can't wait for our future together.

Mum. You have told me since I could remember that I could be anything I wanted to be. Whoever I wanted to be. Without your support, I wouldn't be here today. Thank you for always believing in me.

Dad. You're not here to read this but so much of who I am is thanks to you. You made sure that I could do anything a boy could do and that I could do it better. You gave me expensive taste. You made me fearless.

Jessica Gadziala. Yet another beautiful soul who gives me advice, who lets me vent, who gives me a safe space. You are supremely talented and a wonderful friend and author.

Amo Jones. My ride or die. I love you endlessly. We are soul sisters.

Cat Imb. Your light is so bright, your heart is so big and your talent is endless. Thank you for creating covers that make me want to write a book worthy of them. Thank you for being my friend. I adore you.

Annette. You handle my crazy always. I would be so fricking lost without you. I'm so grateful to have you as my friend.

Kim. Yet another badass woman who handles my crazy. Who edits these words tirelessly and is so dedicated to make this story the best it can be. Thank you for all of your hard work.

Ginny. Thank you so much for always being there. For loving my characters as much as I do. For telling me what I need to hear. You are the best.

My girls. Harriet, Polly & Emma. You're half a world away but distance means nothing. You've all gotten me through some of the hardest times of my life and I'm so so lucky to have you as friends, as sisters.

And last but not least, **you, the reader**. Without you, dear reader, I would not be here. I would not be creating stories as a job. Thank you for making my dreams come true.

ABOUT THE AUTHOR

ANNE MALCOM has been an avid reader since before she can remember, her mother responsible for her love of reading. It started with magical journeys into the world of Hogwarts and Middle Earth, then as she grew up her reading tastes grew with her. Her love of reading doesn't discriminate, she reads across many genres. She can't get enough romance, especially when some possessive alpha males throw their weight around.

One day, in a reading slump, Cade and Gwen's story came to her and started taking up space in her head until she put their story into words. Now that she has started, it doesn't look like she's going to stop anytime soon, with many more characters demanding their story be told as well.

Raised in small town New Zealand, Anne had a truly special childhood, growing up in one of the most beautiful countries in the world. She has backpacked across Europe, ridden camels in the Sahara and eaten her way through Italy, loving every moment.

Now, she's living her own happy ever after in the USA with her brilliant husband and their two dogs.

Want to get in touch with Anne? She loves to hear from her readers.
You can email her: annemalcomauthor@hotmail.com
Or join her reader group on Facebook.

ALSO BY ANNE MALCOM

THE SONS OF TEMPLAR

Making the Cut

Firestorm

Outside the Lines (Hansen & Macy)

Out of the Ashes

Beyond the Horizon

Dauntless

Battles of the Broken

Hollow Hearts

Deadline to Damnation (Jagger & Caroline)

Scars of Yesterday

Three Kinds of Trouble (Hades & Freya)

THE SONS OF TEMPLAR - NEW MEXICO

Wretched Love

Wilting Violets

UNQUIET MIND

Echoes of Silence

Skeletons of Us

Broken Shelves

Mistake's Melody

Censored Soul

GREENSTONE SECURITY

Still Waters

Shield

The Problem With Peace

Chaos Remains

Resonance of Stars

THE VEIN CHRONICLES

Fatal Harmony

Deathless

Faults in Fate

Eternity's Awakening

Buried Destiny

RETIRED SINNERS

Splinters of You

THE KLUTCH DUET

Lies That Sinners Tell

Truths That Saints Believe

JUPITER TIDES

Recipe for Love

Method for Matrimony

STANDALONES

Birds of Paradise

Doyenne

Midnight Sommelier

Hush - co-written

What Grows Dies Here

A Thousand Cuts